THE POISON AND THE PALADIN

THE BOOK OF ALL THINGS

USA TODAY BESTSELLING AUTHOR
SARAH M. CRADIT

ISBN: 978-1-958744-34-5

Cover and Interior Design by The Illustrated Author Design Services
Map by The Illustrated Author Design Services
Hardcover Art (The Whispering Wood) by Nora Adamszki
Edriss and Lorcan Portraits by Alexandra Curte
Until the World Ends by Steffani Christensen
Editing by Novel Nurse Editing

Publisher Contact:
sarah@sarahmcradit.com
www.sarahmcradit.com

SARAH M CRADIT

WEAVER of WORLDS

For everyone who has waited so patiently to find happiness.
Your time is coming.

PRAISE FOR
THE POISON AND THE PALADIN

"With Sarah M. Cradit's signature blend of dark fantasy, political intrigue, and sizzling romance, The Poison and the Paladin had me fully addicted. The forbidden love, dangerous alliances, and heart-wrenching deceptions destroyed my emotions in the best way, while the complex world building, deadly rivalries, and strong female characters gave me everything I needed to satisfy my House of the Dragon cravings."
~*Tessonja Odette, author of the Entangled with Fae series*

"A gorgeously written, powerful tale of empowerment. Sarah is a master of weaving her story's rich, layered worldbuilding and gripping political intrigue within an unfolding romance that both beautifully breaks and puts the heart back together. I was absolutely riveted."
~*Jesikah Sundin, multi-award winning author of The Ealdspell Cycle*

"Another epic adventure in the Westerlands! Full of forbidden love, betrayal, and so much angst. Moments that will make your heart melt and moments that will make you want to pull your hair out. An absolutely enchanting tale of true love conquering all."
~*Heidi, @bookish.heidi*

"Another fantastic hit to this gripping and swoony series. Keep them coming until the end of the world!"

~*Candace Robinson, Author of Vampires in Wonderland*

"This is a must read for lovers of un-put-downable forbidden romances. Returning to the warring Westerlands, The Poison & the Paladin is a story full of longing, danger, and political intrigue."

~*Rachel, @rachelsbooktea*

"The Poison and The Paladin is a stunning installment to the Book of all Things series. Get ready to fall hard for Edriss and to once again be transported to the captivating world that is the Kingdom of the White Sea. Sarah M. Cradit's books are fantasy at its finest."

~*Michelle @BookBriefs*

INTRODUCTION

There exists a kingdom set upon an isle, surrounded by a sea no one has ever traveled beyond. The Kingdom of the White Sea it is called, or simply the kingdom, for they have no other name for it.

The individual Reaches—Northerlands, Southerlands, Westerlands, and Easterlands—once ruled themselves. Two centuries past, the Rhiagains washed upon their shores, claiming to be gods. From gods, they became kings.

There were some men who had lived in the White Kingdom from time immemorial. The Blackrooks were one such family. Their inauspicious start began as clever botanists, and they rose through the ranks to become lords of their Reach, the Westerlands. Popular for their fairness and sense of noble responsibility, they and their people enjoyed many hundreds of years of unchallenged prosperity.

But a family is only as strong as its weakest member. Two generations before the start of this tale, Lord Andarian Blackrook decreed magic a threat to the sanctity of his tranquil Reach—and his authority. In the name of peace, he started a war, one that led to the horrific persecution of thousands, mainly women. His son, Aeldred, escalated his father's campaign with zealous fervor, and when he died, he left a smoldering, ruinous inheritance for his second son, Evrathedyn, who was forced to assume the mantle of leadership when Aeldred's eldest son perished days after he did.

Reluctant to lead but determined to save his people, Evrathedyn found himself in the far north of the kingdom, where he met the enigmatic Ravenwood priestess Rhosynora. She was desperate for freedom and he for purpose, and their needs—and

i

hearts—were in harmony. A war was waged and won for Rhosyn's right to be free, and from that victory, they formed a new family made of both worlds: the Blackwoods.

The Blackwoods of Longwood Rush ushered in a new era of peace, signing a truce with the realm's authority on magic, the Sepulchre. Magic was again free for practice in the Westerlands.

But not everyone was so eager for change.

The Defenders of the Righteous Dawn hold on to the fractured values of a world on fire, one where women have no place in power and weak men are unchallenged by stronger voices. They would do anything to see the Westerlands return to fear and ash.

There's nothing they won't do to achieve precisely that.

Evrathedyn doesn't see the danger sitting at his table, on his very council. He ignores those who advise him to cut ties with men he believes can and will have a change of heart. For all the peace he's brought, he is still very young. His need to believe there is good in all men is at odds with his promise of serenity.

Edriss, his vibrant younger sister, has been surrounded by dark, dangerous men her entire life. She knows a traitor when she sees one, and she's seen several. Confiding in the person she trusts most, Lorcan James, she believes together they can reach her stubborn brother before everything they've worked for goes up in flames.

Years before, Evra chose university over family, leaving his younger sister to be haphazardly tended by a madman—a void the noble Lorcan quickly filled. He became her unofficial protector, a sacred charge shielding her from the worst. Over the years, their closeness blurred, creating confusion that only grows harder to decipher as time passes.

But Lorcan is a man of honor, and though Edriss is now of age to marry, it would ignite a scandal of reputation if her guardian became her husband.

In the midst of this careful dance of hearts, a new challenge presents itself to Lorcan, one he has never been able to resist: a friend in need. Arwenna, Rhosyn's sister, is being blackmailed by the Defenders, and if Lorcan can't help her, the Blackwoods and their closest allies will be executed in a violent seizure of power.

The Westerlands, and all that made it wonderful, will be gone.

To help Arwenna, Lorcan will have to betray the one person he's sworn never to hurt.

Edriss, facing an unwanted betrothal and cold shoulders from everyone she's close to, has to rely on her own cleverness—and her unequaled skill with botanical poisons—to save her brother and the Westerlands.

The Defenders have no use for rules, playing only by their own. Mere weeks separate them from wedding one of their sons, Finnegan Derry, to Lady Edriss, legitimizing their claim to wrest power from the Blackwoods once and for all.

Once the ink is dry on the marriage contract, everyone loyal to the Blackwoods will be as good as dead.

Everyone Edriss has ever loved.

Including the one who owns her heart, broken pieces and all.

The web of lies and treason weaving through the Rush grows more snarled by the day.

By the hour.

Honor alone won't save the Westerlands.

To fight the enemy's flames, Edriss will have to become the fire.

But make no mistake…

Win or lose, all fire eventually ends in ash.

BLACKWOODS OF THE HALLS OF LONGWOOD

Capital
Longwood Rush

Reach
Westerlands

Lord & Lady of the Westerlands
Lord Evrathedyn Blackwood, 21
Lady Rhosynora Blackwood, 18

Lord's Children
Alastrynia, 1

Blackwoods
Lady Edriss Blackwood, 18
Arwenna Ravenwood, 19
Lady Alise Blackwood
Dowager Lady Meldred Blackwood

Deceased Blackwoods
Former Lord Aeldred Blackrook (Father of Evra)
Former Lady Fyana Blackrook (Mother of Evra & Edriss)
Astarian Blackrook (Brother of Evra & Edriss)
Arathedyn Blackrook (Uncle of Evra and Edriss)

Lord's Council
Lorcan James/Rohan James
Rafferty Tyndall
Lady Alise Blackwood
Lady Edriss Blackwood
Osman Derry
Cressida Wakesell
Meira Ashenhurst
First Rider Thennwyr Blackfen
Enchanter Grimoult
Leonarde Bristol

WESTERLANDERS

Greystone Abbey
Steward Rohan James
Lorcan James, 21

East Derry
Steward Osman Derry*
Fignola Derry, 24
Finnegan Derry, 21*
Farmina Derry, 18

Wildwood Falls
Steward Rafferty Tyndall, 22 (twin)
Renardy Tyndall, 22 (twin)
Ridge Tyndall, 20

Whitewood
Stewardess Cressida Wakesell, 19

Pine Bluff
Steward Oliver Richland*

Windwatch Grove
Roland Ashenhurst*
Stewardess and Rush Rider Meira Ashenhurst, 22

Whispering Wood
Steward Walter Glenlannan*

Valleybrooke
Steward Leonarde Bristol*

Greencastle
Steward Tedric Blakewell
Feldred Blakewell, 25

Others
First Rider Thennwyr Blackfen
Malcom Fox*
Minister Warrenhap
Marckus Carlisle

*denotes possible affiliation with the Defenders of the Righteous
Dawn

OTHER WESTERLANDS LOCATIONS IN THIS STORY

Foothills
Deramore
Jademarch
Rivermarch

Whispering Wood
Felgarden Rest

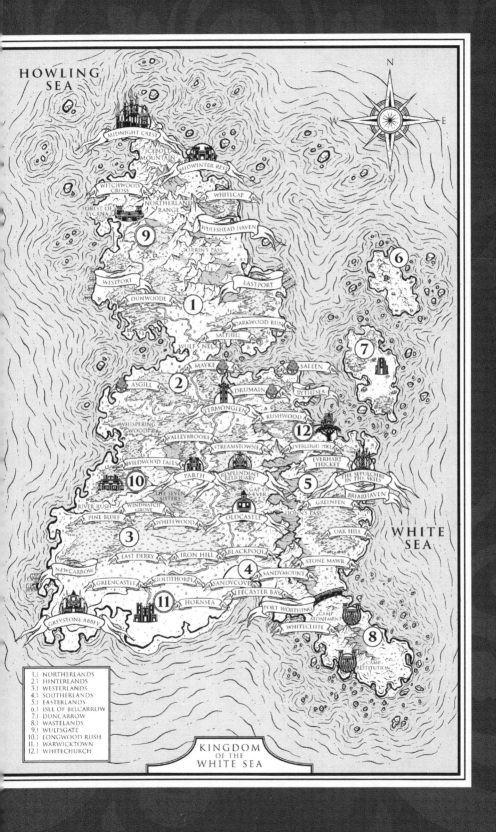

KINGDOM
OF THE
WHITE SEA

A REALM
ON FIRE

ONE

ALWAYS

One Year After The Epilogue Of The Raven And The Rush

The moment her slippered feet hit the sodden, familiar gloaming, Edriss Blackwood knew she had him beat. She inhaled a lungful of mossy air and launched into a sprint, nearly forgetting, in her excitement, the terrible reason she'd brought Lorcan James to the woods to begin with.

The Whispering Wood was *her* world, the place where her heart beat the surest. She grinned at the sound of Lorcan's low grunts behind her, set to the clanging of his scabbard skipping against his pretty paladin boots, which would need a proper cleaning after the night was through. After all these years, he should know better, but it wasn't like she'd given him a chance to change.

He called after her with a slew of indignant objections, but it only spread the joy to every corner of her face and sent her stride aflame.

She'd always chased Lorcan James, and she would not squander the gift of him chasing her for once.

"Can we not do this later, Hemlock?" His words bounced with every squishing land of his heavy boots.

Edriss laughed to herself even as the fat raindrops ran into her eyes, blurring her vision. Dusk waned, concealing the last of the day's light. It was her favorite time of day, when the purplish hues of the sky faded to the eclipsed darkness and she had to rely on her secondary senses to guide her. She'd spent so many hours happily lost in the forest that she no longer feared it. There wasn't much she feared at all anymore, save for helplessness, and she had no intention of ever being *that* again.

"Edriss!"

She pushed on, instinctively lifting her gait in the right places as she dodged fallen logs coated in slick, dangerous moss, weaving through thorns and briars she couldn't see but knew were there. They would slow Lorcan, but he'd still follow. Maybe not for the reason she wished he would, but she'd learned to temper her expectations, hanging them in the same frame of disappointment that had watched over her life—first as the daughter but now as the sister of the lord of the Westerlands.

The old watchtower stood in the middle of a bramble-filled clearing. It had been abandoned long before she was born, replaced by sturdier structures in more strategic locations. No one bothered tending the listing edifice, or trimming the weeds overgrowing the base, which threatened to return the entire thing to nature. Her family should've torn it down years ago, but if they had, she'd never have witnessed what she had.

She linked her arms above her head to catch her breath and waited for Lorcan. Moments later he appeared, bowled over—his hands on his knees and his head tilted toward her with a slow groan—and whispered, "You can't be serious."

"You can go back if you like," she said with a light, taunting click at the end, which she knew would ignite his enthusiasm for a challenge. She used the leather strap in her pocket to tie her dark hair back and off her face, coated in a blend of rain and sweat.

"And leave you out here alone?" Lorcan's sidelong glare was incredulous.

"Ah, yes, you go *weak* for a good damsel in distress." Her playful grin shifted to grim contemplation. "Or…Would you consider that a strength?"

"You're being ridiculous. And when have you ever been a damsel in distress?" His soft face flushed. He turned his eyes back on the leaning tower with a curt nod. "*That* is completely unsafe, Edriss. I forbid you to climb it."

"Forbid me?" Edriss tucked her chin. "Well, you're too late for such a meaningless threat. I've been climbing it since I was a little girl."

His laugh was full of relief. "Evra might believe the lie, but I know everything about you."

Lorcan was right, of course. For over a decade, he'd been her protector, her dearest friend, and lately…lately she didn't know what he was. At seventeen, she was too old to be his charge but too young for him to see her as anything else.

No one knew her secrets like Lorcan did. But some were just for her, and sharing one with him was a choice she was still debating the wisdom of. "I don't tell you everything, Lorry."

"That right, Hemlock?" He squinted against the steadily increasing rain.

Edriss loved his nickname for her. Maybe she shouldn't, for it was a nod to her exceptional expertise with poisons, having surpassed both her aunt's and grandmother's talents by the time her age moved into double digits. Lorcan always said it in a teasing way, but the pride in his eyes made her wish he'd say it more.

She rolled her shoulders back, weighing her response. There were few sounds as calming as the patter of drops against the overhead canopy of leaves. Maybe she should have left him behind, so she could enjoy it in peace. It might be the last peace she'd find for a long time.

But he was the calm in her storm. She'd always intended to bring him one day, and as far as reasons went, she couldn't think of a better one than what she had to show him tonight.

3

"Much as you delight in torturing me," Lorcan said blithely, "it can't be why you brought me out here."

"I think you know I'm capable of far more creative methods of torture."

"I go to sleep thinking about them every night."

Edriss laughed before lowering her eyes to the fallen leaves at her feet. "I wanted to show you something."

"This death trap? Well, great." He looped his arm through hers and started to turn them back. "Now I've seen it, and we can go back to our happy, safe, *dry* lives inside the Halls."

"It's not a death trap," Edriss insisted, tugging him back into place. The heat of his nearness hastened her heart beyond the swiftness it was already beating, felt even through the thick fabric of his emerald-and-silver armor. Her throat constricted as she tried to swallow down the hard lump that inevitably formed when she was around him lately. "And this isn't what I wanted to show you."

"It gets worse?" His brows fused together.

Edriss rolled her eyes. "You worry too much."

"About you?" He scoffed and squeezed her arm tighter beneath his. "Always."

Her heart continued its confusing, hammering beats, but they were sadly unwarranted. Lorcan was her older brother's friend, the one who had stepped into the gaping void left when Evra went to study in another part of the kingdom. Lorcan took his duty seriously, and aside from the regrettable—to him, anyway—kiss on her sixteenth birthday, he'd never dishonored himself.

You're the little sister I wish I'd had was among the vexing things he'd said that day. Throwing her into the River Rush in midwinter would have been less painful.

Edriss forced a smile and turned back toward the old guard tower. "I could tell you, but I think if you *see* it, you'll be more apt to believe it." *And so will my brother.*

Lorcan's mouth wavered between words and silence. His gaze traveled from her to the tower. His humor dissolved as she watched him. "You seriously mean for us to go up there?"

"Yes."

"And you won't just tell me?"

Edriss sighed. "I've tried. With others. But no one wants to hear what I have to say."

"You've talked to others about this but not me?"

Because I could handle the derision from anyone else but *you.*

"You didn't think I'd believe you?" His voice lowered to a tone of concern. "Edriss, I'll always believe you."

Reluctantly, she tore away from him and moved into the clearing. Dark clouds left an ominous pall over the dying underbrush, a fitting tableau for what she needed him to see. "Well, then when *you* see it, Lorry, Evra will believe you, where he dismissed me."

"I wouldn't be so sure he'll listen to me any more than you." He whistled behind her, his boots crunching as he moved to catch up. "But now you've piqued my interest, damn you."

Edriss moved into a jog and then a sprint, equally running from his questions as her feelings. She shouldn't be having them, and if Lorcan knew her heart beat only for him, after he'd told her the way of things, their friendship might never recover.

She'd lost nearly everything in her short life, and he was the one thing she couldn't live without.

But her pulse was thrumming for another reason. If she was right, and Lorcan saw what she'd seen for the past three nights, she might yet save the Westerlands. Save her family.

She didn't look back when she reached the rotting ladder. The climb was rough, but she knew all the missing rungs, the weak spots where one wrong step could spell disaster. "Follow where my feet fall, Lorry," she called when she sensed him hesitating at the bottom.

"Then maybe consider slowing down?" The ladder tugged with his added weight, and she waited for him before continuing. She heard him muttering and cursing under his breath, but his voice stayed close. When she reached the top, she stretched one hand above her head and swatted to push open the trapdoor. It slammed to the old wood with a resounding thud, and she clambered the rest of the way up, then heaved a relieved breath when she rolled onto the damp, slimy boards.

"Guardians deliver us, Edriss," he panted and flopped next to her on his back, flinging his arms wide. They hit with a wet *thwack,* followed by a garish shimmer of his scabbard bouncing. "Now that you've got me all the way up here, you can admit it. This is payback for beating you so soundly at tricks last night, isn't it?"

"Calm down. You won't be meeting the Guardians today," she said and shot to her feet. She dusted off her trousers. Wearing them was a bigger risk than climbing a dilapidated war relic. Evra didn't care, but his subjects did. They wanted to see the Reach's most eligible bride for the beacon of femininity they expected her to be. "And you always beat me at tricks, you knave."

Lorcan closed his eyes and continued gathering his breath. He moved his hands to his chest. "Are you implying what I think you are?"

"That you're a cheater? I would *never.*" Edriss pointed above her to the flagging roof of the small, boxed space. "You wanted out of the rain? I delivered."

Lorcan's mouth screwed into a tight frown when he glanced up. "There are more holes than boards."

"Stand under the boards, not the holes," Edriss muttered. She moved to the railing on the south side. In the distance, the Halls of Longwood took up the entire horizon, lit with thousands of sconces. The leveled gardens leading into the keep were lined with paint that reflected the moonlight, illuminating them as though from magic. Deep inside, Evra and Rhosyn would be finishing supper and readying newborn Alastrynia for bed.

Edriss spun away and turned her attention to the north side. It was mostly more forestland, but there also were less-traveled paths leading from the woods into Longwood Rush. Few used them, as there were better and safer routes, and most caravans couldn't navigate the deep ruts and overgrown roots.

Which made it the perfect place for treasonous snakes like the Defenders of the Righteous Dawn to plot sedition, right under their lord's noses.

But would they show up again tonight? It would be just her luck for it to be the one night they didn't.

Lorcan sidled up behind her. His chest brushed her back, igniting a dangerous fire within. A bitter taste pooled in her throat. When he rested his forearms atop her shoulders, she feared she might pass out and fall to her death.

All the things that once felt so casual and comfortable had become the same things unraveling her thread by thread.

"So, what am I looking at, Hemlock?" His breath was a whisper against her ear, a rush of delicious warmth that left her shivering.

"Nothing. Yet."

"Just wanted to get me up here alone, didn't you?"

He was teasing, but his words struck so deep, she stopped breathing. She knew he'd never have said it at all if he didn't believe she was over what he'd once called her "innocent childhood crush." The only thing accurate about that was the way those words had crushed *her*.

He started to come around and look at her, so she quickly shook her head. "Am I so transparent?"

He laughed. No one else laughed like Lorcan James. It was the ring of pure joy, like a man who had brushed close to darkness but never stepped into it. His happiness was contagious to everyone around him, even against the darkest moments. It stole her entire focus and held her in a thrall she had become so used to, she should be better about breaking.

Lorcan had too much light in him, in a world that was in a constant vise of darkness. He might not have been born with mystical talents, but his gift was its own form of magic, and it always worked on her, no matter how she fought it.

Evra will marry me off to a son of one of the Greater Families soon, and this won't be a problem anymore.

Edriss swallowed hard and was forming another jest to protect her breaking heart when she spotted her reason for dragging them into danger. One mounted man emerged from the forest path to meet two others riding from the direction of the keep.

Lorcan's arms slid off her shoulders and down her arms. He left them there and reached past her to clasp the railing, effectively pinning her. His head came to a rest beside hers. "Is that…"

"Yes," she said, but her voice cracked, and she had to say it twice more before it stuck. "Steward Bristol and Steward Derry, meeting with Steward Ashenhurst."

"I…I *knew* it." Lorcan pushed off, and Edriss released a breathy gasp. He paced from one end of the tower to the other and then returned to the railing and settled beside her. His head shook with the incredulity of the deeply wronged. "Defenders, right? Bristol and Derry are in on it with Ashenhurst now?"

Edriss felt like crying, though it wasn't sadness plaguing her but exasperation. "Everyone already knows about Ashenhurst, but the others…Evra refuses to see reason, Lorry. He knows those men have darkness in their hearts, that they were not only supportive but *enthusiastic* about burning every woman in the Reach they thought might be even remotely connected to magic."

"I know." Lorcan's hands rolled into a tight grip on the rotting wood. "I don't think he wants to see it."

"I *know* he doesn't." Edriss spun to face him. Rain battered in on a hard wind, soaking them both. "Evra is already a better lord of the Westerlands than our father ever was." Edriss choked on the word *father*. Aeldred Blackrook had never been her father, and everyone knew it. "But you know him. He's too trusting. He wants to believe Bristol and Derry can be better men, but they *aren't* better men. Do you understand why I needed a second witness?"

"Maybe they're not meeting about that." Lorcan squinted, wincing. "No. No one would meet with a banished man, at night, on a disused path if they had good intent."

"Exactly." Edriss sagged into her relieved sigh. "Exactly."

8

Lorcan leaned against the railing, lengthening his arms into a tight stretch. "I would have believed you if you'd have just told me. You didn't need to risk both our lives."

She waited for his laugh, but it didn't come. "I know you would have, but...Evra..." She twisted her mouth to press emotion back.

"He loves you, Edriss. He does trust you."

Her chin dimpled as her head shook. "He doesn't."

"He should." Lorcan moved closer. "You're probably the most competent adviser on his council, even if you are the youngest. You know his court better than anyone, except perhaps Lady Meldred and Lady Alise. He forgets you were raised in the thick of it, because he wasn't. While he got to run away to his studies, you were here, living every moment of Lord Aeldred's reign of terror."

Edriss scoffed. She angled away when tears burned her eyes. They were as much from frustration as pain. "He doesn't see it that way. I'm only there because I was his heir before Alastrynia came along. To send a message of Blackwood unity. Not because he values anything I have to offer."

"That's not true." Lorcan brushed wet, matted hair from her eyes with the back of his hand. "You're brilliant, Hemlock. Everything you touch becomes better for it. You pick up skills in an afternoon most need years to master."

"Lor—"

"I've learned so much more from you than you ever have from me. And it would be impossible for him not to see what is inescapably obvious to everyone else in the Rush."

The softness in his voice made fighting tears so much harder. She broke away and looked down before he could read the truth in her eyes. "It doesn't matter. I needed him to hear it from *you*. Not you repeating something I told you but something you saw, with your own eyes."

Lorcan turned back toward where the men were coalesced in a tight circle. "What do you think they're talking about?"

"I don't know," she said quietly. "But I worry about you going to Deramore tomorrow. Are you sure they can't send another tender?"

Lorcan shook his head. "Another tender would sentence the woman to death. I mean to save her if I can."

"This is the one claiming to be a lost Rhiagain princess?"

Lorcan nodded.

"Do you believe her?"

He shrugged and exhaled toward the north, his breath furling in a dense cloud that dissipated before he answered. "It doesn't matter whether I believe her. She's upset the people of Deramore, and they want her to pay for it. I just need to get her to renounce her claim, and no one will question my choice to release her. Sometimes people forget the authority of a tender of death is absolute. They don't have to like it, but they'll respect it."

"We shouldn't even *need* tenders, when my brother banned burnings a year ago. It's absolutely ridiculous this is necessary at all."

"We shouldn't," Lorcan agreed. "But he can't be everywhere at once. Eventually we'll get ahead of it, but for now, our old system of tending is the best way to protect the women still being accused."

"Evra should just stamp them all out." Edriss's anger flared into her cheeks. "Wipe these cursed towns off the map."

"You don't mean that," Lorcan said gently. "And remember, he gave them a year to disband their systems. A fortnight from now brings us to the year mark, and then any man still claiming magic is a crime will be branded a traitor and will lose favor, land, and more." He nodded into the dark night. "Bristol and Derry won't be able to hide in the transition period soon. They'll be outed for what they are, and they'll have to choose between their money and station, and their bloodlust for innocent women."

"That day cannot come soon enough." Edriss wrapped her arms tight around herself and moved farther away. "That's all I wanted to show you. I just didn't want..."

Lorcan pulled her against himself before she could create more needed distance. He lay his head sideways atop hers and pressed her face to his chest as she squinted away more unwanted emotion. "I'll always believe you. I'll always believe *in* you." He inched back slightly to look down at her. She couldn't meet his eyes, in the same way she couldn't look directly into the sun. "I'll try talking to him when I come back from Deramore. Maybe if I can get him away from the others, he'll be more open to hearing what we have to say."

His choice of *we* both healed and broke her heart in the same breath. "Thank you." She tipped her forehead against his chest for a moment longer and then backed away. "Be safe, Lorry. Please."

Lorcan's easy grin illuminated the darkness. "For you? Always."

TWO
A PERFECT CIRCLE OF MISERY
One Year Later

Lorcan hunched his shoulders and pulled his furs taut at his neck, but the adjustment was purely ceremonial. There was no relief to be found from the brutal wind ripping off the Seven Sisters of the West, nor the situation they were about to ride into.

Jademarch, named for one of said mythical sisters, a cozy mining hamlet in the foothills just south of Pine Bluff, sat far enough from any roads and trails to keep many visitors from passing through. The absence of foreign life was starkly evident in the scattered commerce and lack of wagons passing through.

Men gathered on the roadside, half covered in filth, ripe with distrust, and something else. Something worse.

Lorcan shivered. He leaned in to give his horse, Frog, a pat, sensing her unease that matched his own.

"Ignore it," Evra said, speaking from the side of his mouth. They didn't hide the Blackwood banners as they rode into town, which were outnumbered by the Defender flags hung in windows or snapping against the wind. The black fabric, stitched with peaceful white doves, was anathema to peace, a

13

contradiction lost on the rebels. Evra only ordered their emerald standards flown higher, wanting everyone to know the lord of the Westerlands was coming and that his loyalists were not afraid. "Some of these villages were never going to approve of our alliance with the Sepulchre, Lorcan. They were never going to honor the armistice. They would have burned every woman and girl they knew, however loose their justifications, wives and daughters alike."

"I can't ignore it," Lorcan muttered. The main road was short, but it might as well have been a thousand miles for all the rueful glares threatening to spear them from their mounts. It reminded him of his final, fateful trip to Deramore a year ago. Brutal recollections of that horrible, hard day hit him so suddenly, he nearly jolted from his saddle. "I don't trust any of this."

"I never said to trust it." Evra started to smile, but it never formed. He nodded at men who spat in return. They whispered about the boy lord who was beholden to his sorceress wife—the boy who had renamed their entire legacy, for her. For a *witch*.

But if not for Rhosyn, thousands more would be dead. Evra had inherited a Reach smoldering in the ashes of pyres used to burn their own people, reducing their history and legacy to rubble. The bigotry, the fear, the rage…Those were all part of his heritage. Love had never been part of the plan, but his heart had chosen Rhosynora Ravenwood, and that choice energized his campaign to heal the Westerlands.

Not everyone wanted the peace Evrathedyn Blackwood was offering though, and as Lorcan and his father were dangerously aware, those working most ardently against the young lord were some of those closest to him.

Lorcan thought Evra should have sent men in his stead to deal with the problem in Jademarch. Boldly strutting down a road full of people who would rather see him dead than rule as lord was reckless but not out of character. The young scholar who had once been ardently reluctant to lead had become someone else entirely in the past two years.

Women huddled with children outside patchwork tents. Babies were wrapped in Defender flags, nursing from their mothers in the fierce cold. The women wore the same scorn as their fathers, husbands, and sons, but there was fear there too.

"Over here." Finnegan Derry waved from behind a raised tent flap. He blew into his other hand, knees bouncing as he beckoned Evra and Lorcan in. Once inside, Lorcan immediately sighed in relief from the wave of warmth.

"Got him. The tender." Finnegan kicked at the chained man, who hadn't yet looked up. The prisoner was huddled in the middle of a tent that must have belonged to him. The sumptuous living quarters were decorated with gilt furnishings and an elaborate bed, made of the rare ebony wood of the Great Darkwood, which would have taken months to source and twice as long to carve. Colorful caged birds, no doubt illicitly imported from the Golden Coast of the Southerlands, trilled songs out of unison from both back corners. "The one who ordered the burnings against your command."

Evra crossed his arms in inspection while Lorcan moved closer. He knelt several feet before the bound man and tried to get a glimpse of his face. *What kind of tender were you? A man who fulfilled his duty with depraved gusto? Or one who did his best to save the ones he could?*

The man's even, hollow stare locked onto Lorcan's.

"Thank you, Finn," Evra said, one hand pulled at the stubble on his chin, his eyes pointed stoically toward nothing. "Are you a traveling tender or a local one?"

Finnegan kicked the man again, causing the heavy chains to jangle.

Lorcan flinched.

"Your lord asked you a question, pig."

The tender spat his response. It was mottled with blood, a hint of what had transpired before Evra and Lorcan had arrived.

"All he knows is filth," Finnegan muttered and spun away in disgust.

Lorcan remained squatting, still trying to get a read on the man. The tender's lip curled, as though readying to hurl the vilest of insults, but the way he diverted his eyes betrayed hesitation. *What kind of tender were you? What would you have done had you been called to Deramore that day?*

"I didn't come here to torture you, tender. Every man takes his orders from somewhere," Evra said, pacing to the side. He stared at one of the brightly plumed birds in bewilderment before shaking his head and turning back. "Tenders of Death are servants... or were, before I dismantled their order. I only want to know who you serve."

The prisoner reared back and laughed. "Certainly not *you*, Lord *Blackrook*." This earned him another kick from Finnegan, who seemed all too eager to deliver it.

"You know his name, pig."

"It's all right." Evra's calm was jarring in the middle of the troubling scene. "He has no power here anymore. There's no need to take more of what he doesn't have."

"Lord Blackwood, this man *openly* defied you."

Evra nodded. "And yet, that order came from somewhere. Somewhere much higher than he'll ever rise."

Lorcan studied the gold flecks in the tender's deep-brown irises. The quickness of his blinks, when he realized he was being studied. His was an old profession, one made obsolete. Lorcan and his father had been part of the order because sometimes one had to be in the system to make it better.

I saved more than I lost, he thought. *That's what kind of tender I was, no matter what happened a year ago.*

But that was not the kind of tender huddled before him.

The man chained and spewing vitriol would die before he surrendered his violent ideology.

Lorcan suddenly wished he were back in his own tent, lost to dreams he could tell no one about—least of all the one they were about.

16

"Tender." Lorcan didn't mean to whisper, but his throat, dry from the long ride, added a rasp to his voice. He said it again until the man looked up. "You have cherished your charge as a decider of death. We all find our joys where we can, I suppose."

Finnegan snorted and slurred something under his breath. Evra folded his arms and watched.

The tender ran his tongue along his cracked, sooty lips and shook his head. "And what would a squint like you know about it?"

"Me? I was a tender. Once."

The man balked, but he was clearly interested. "Bollocks."

"Family business." Lorcan made the symbol of the tender on his chest, fighting the shudder that threatened to follow. The last time he'd made the symbol was in Deramore, when he'd promised Cesarina he would save her, then came across her smoldering pyre the next morning.

"We were just doing our jobs," Lorcan said. Who was he trying to convince, the tender or himself? "Wasn't up to us where we went, who we were assigned. So does it matter if we liked it?"

The tender's dirty face crinkled. "You're taking the piss."

"My favorite pastime." Lorcan cracked an empty smile. "But not right now. Right *now*, I want to help our lord find the *right* person to be having this conversation with. The generals of the Defenders of the Righteous Dawn should pay for what happened here in Jademarch, not their foot soldier. Don't suffer and die for one who would not do the same for you. The one who left *you* here to answer for *his* commands."

Behind him, Finnegan made a nervous grunt. Evra started to speak, but then the captive man cleared his throat and hocked his phlegm straight at him.

Evra dodged it with a weary sigh and a hard look at Lorcan. "Can we speak outside?"

"I'll watch the pig," Finnegan declared. Lorcan thought he sounded almost too eager for it.

"It was a mistake, telling him you were a tender," Evra said once they were outside. A chill wind whistled across the

17

encampment. It cut through the din of blended conversations. "I know *why* you did it, but the thing is, Lor, you two aren't alike at all. He knows that. He saw it."

"I almost had him," Lorcan said, jumping to his own defense. He laughed and pointed a hand toward where they'd emerged from. "Finn's crass insults got nothing more than spit out of him. When I told him who I was, *that's* when he started talking."

"Well, he's not talking now, is he?" Evra scratched the back of his head, sweeping a heavy gaze around the area, where dozens had gathered to watch. "Maybe these really are just rogue cells popping up. Maybe this whole…'conspiracy at the top' rumor is just that. Steward Derry seems to think so."

Osman Derry was one of the Defenders. Lorcan had seen it with his own eyes, thanks to Edriss and her clever—albeit dangerous and worrisome—sleuthing. But Evra wouldn't hear it. He'd already carved significant rot from his council and peerage, and he didn't want to cut deeper.

Lorcan would never, ever forget the desperate way Edriss had dragged him up the old guard tower a year before. The urgency in her eyes, her need to be believed. He'd told her he would have believed her even without climbing the old death trap and seeing the Defenders conspiring, which was true, but then he *had* seen. But she'd grossly overestimated his ability to convince Evra to listen to reason.

So much had fallen apart since that night.

Lorcan moved in front of his old friend with a hopeful grimace. The tender would be put to death either way—it was the law, and they couldn't enforce it without respecting it—but he was certain he could appeal to him. Not to his honor, for he had none, but to the innate selfishness of self-preservation. "Give me just another minute with him. Just one, Evra. And then you can do as you must."

Evra pulled his groan from somewhere deep and nodded, threading a hard breath through his teeth.

Lorcan stepped back inside, but fresh horror had him reeling back. He heard Evra ask what was wrong, but Lorcan's mouth hadn't caught up to his eyes. He was slowly putting together how Finnegan was standing over the tender's lifeless, mangled corpse, blood streaming down his frozen uniform, splotching his boots and spreading across the expensive white fur at his feet. Finn's knife was suspended in midair, as though he were not quite finished.

"Finn?" Evra approached the scene with appropriate annoyance. "Care to explain this?"

Finnegan pointed the knife at the dead man. "He jumped me!"

"The man wearing heavy chains jumped you?" Lorcan cried, finding his voice. "Jumped you *how*, exactly?"

"He came at me—"

Lorcan's eyes bulged, his attention passing between Finnegan's lies and their dead chance to prove who was behind the burnings. "*Came at you?*"

Finnegan wiped his arm across his nose, painting his face in crude red. "Ah, well, you were outside, so how would you know?" His other hand pitched the knife around the air.

"Because I know a chained man can neither jump nor come at you, Finnegan." Lorcan spread his arms wide in horror. "We were so close."

"Close." Finnegan snorted. His eyes twitched. "About as close as you'll ever be to Edriss's bed. That what you mean by close?"

Lorcan braced for Evra's reaction, but he was distracted. Shame burned Lorcan's face. The jab went deeper than the ribbings they'd given each other as friends, which had clearly been Finn's intent.

"All right," Evra said, stretching his arms from one man to the other. "All right! That's enough. We'll finish this discussion later when we debrief." Evra clapped Finnegan on the back and looked at the knife. "Get cleaned up, and meet me in my tent."

Lorcan, struggling to regain his composure, shuffled toward the tent flap and looked out into the drizzly, chilly afternoon.

He suppressed the tremble tickling his voice. *He* had been *close to talking. Finnegan knew it, and he silenced him. He silenced him because he's doing his father's bidding.*

He pointed his glare at the foggy camp, instead of where it belonged, and forced the anger from his voice. "Don't stop to play with yourself either, Finn. We can still make it to Greystone Abbey by nightfall. My father has a warm meal waiting for us at the Mule, and you and I both know how I get on an empty belly."

Finnegan cracked his neck, livelier after Evra had temporarily taken him off the hook for explaining himself. "Need a nap too, James?"

Lorcan sighed and feigned a crude gesture to keep up the joke. Once he was far enough away, he turned his head toward the cloudy sky and released a shivering exhale.

It was good Finnegan thought Lorcan's sole concern was filling his belly.

Better than him knowing Lorcan no longer trusted him.

The stew was the best his father had made in a long time, but Lorcan's appetite was too spoiled to appreciate it. Their half-day ride had been a restless one. He couldn't stop thinking about the guilt in Finnegan's eyes when they'd caught him hunched over the tender's corpse.

Even harder to take had been Evra's insistence to let it go.

Drop it, he'd practically begged Lorcan, when he'd started to question Finnegan again at their first stop to water the horses. *Please. For me.*

What about the debrief?

It will happen. Later.

But, Evra, he's—

Whatever you were going to say, don't. And you're not yourself. You're usually the one telling the rest of us to smile. Lorcan the Lightbringer.

Lorcan had never taken to the childhood nickname. Some meant it as a compliment, but there were others who clearly thought his predisposition to happiness and laughter—to spread it to others who were hurting—made him weak.

He slopped meager spoonfuls of the dark broth into his mouth, his eyes stubbornly fixed on Finnegan across the table. Rohan James had closed and bolted the doors when Lord Blackwood's small company had arrived, but it wasn't exactly necessary. The Long-Trodden Mule grew quieter and less patronized by the day, as residents reluctantly left Greystone Abbey for better opportunities in towns closer to the sea, or bigger cities. Half the chairs in the old tavern lived permanently atop tables that rarely needed cleaning. The nightly sweeping produced more dust than crumbs. But Lorcan's father carried on as though the Mule were a high-priced establishment in the middle of its boom.

Evra lifted careful glances at Lorcan in between bites. Finnegan was more talkative than usual, telling ridiculous stories and using too-fast words, betraying nerves that, apparently, no one but Lorcan could see. He sounded like a man who had gotten away with murder.

He had.

Lorcan would spare no mourning for the dead man, but he'd clearly been about to finger Finnegan's father, or Bristol, and then they could have *finally* moved on from the haunting legacy of the late Aeldred Blackrook.

Who knew when another opportunity like that one would arise?

How many more would die before it happened?

"And I said, you've *got* to be kidding, Ridge. That would be like taking Meira to bed!" Finn chortled and took in a mouthful of food, flaring his ale-flushed cheeks. What he said next was completely unintelligible.

"I suspect you wouldn't be talking about Rider Ashenhurst like that if she were standing in this room with her longbow," Rohan said with a chastising tone.

Finnegan reddened in embarrassment.

"And we don't talk about any women like that here, son."

"I'd hardly call—"

"Finish that thought at your own peril," Rohan stated, pointing a chunk of bread at him. He passed a look at his son, so brief no one else took note, but it was enough to take the edge from Lorcan's agitation. After supper, they would talk, and whatever Lorcan said, his father would believe him. He would have the right wisdom for the situation. He always did.

"Meira could cut you down with a look alone, Finn," Evra said. He laughed to himself and then turned tired eyes on the steward. "Thank you for your hospitality, Rohan. We could've returned to the Rush straightaway, but then we'd have missed out on your famous stew, and there's been enough disasters in our lives lately."

"Well…" Rohan swatted the air, but Lorcan caught the pride in his father's eyes. Greystone Abbey had never been a strategic stronghold for the Reach, but the James men had been devoted to the Rush for centuries. Despite that, Evra had been the first lord to visit the Abbey in almost a generation.

Evra shared a knowing look with Rohan, which put a small crack in Lorcan's relief. "Well then. I know you and your son have something important to discuss, Steward. Finn, shall we?"

Finnegan looked at his unfinished stew and then back at Evra with disappointment. "Right. Thank you for supper, Steward."

"Of course. You're always welcome here, Finn. Always have been."

Finnegan nodded and followed Evra. Lorcan watched his father watching them—studied his polite expression darkening when the men were out of sight.

"Don't trust that one anymore," Rohan muttered. "I can see, neither do you."

Lorcan pushed his bowl away and told his father the entire story in what felt like one breath. When he was done, he sat back in his chair and closed his eyes. The warmth of the hearth made him wish he were home on better terms. It made him long for simpler times, when a hard day was helping his father pour ales and carve up fresh-caught meat. "I could've made the tender talk, Father."

Rohan breathed in through his teeth. "*We* got into tending to help people, but *most* men did it for the love of it. The tender in Jademarch wouldn't have just been betraying his master if he'd talked, he'd have been betraying himself."

"I don't understand that kind of evil." Lorcan shook his head. "That kind of depravity."

"Your heart beats differently than men like him. And a damn good thing it does." Rohan refilled their ales and sat back. "You saved more than you lost in your tenure as a tender, Lorcan. Always remember that."

Lorcan half smiled. It was the ones he'd lost who haunted his nightmares—the last one in particular. *No one stands for anything anymore,* Cesarina had said when he'd urged her to renounce her claim of being a Rhiagain princess and she'd refused to deny herself. *Death doesn't sound so bad in comparison.* "Do I wear my thoughts so openly?"

"Just know where they go if someone isn't there to reel you in."

Lorcan quirked his brows. "Nothing gets me going in the morning more than a little self-destructive penitence."

Rohan laughed heartily. "And here I thought you might carry this dourness with you onto the road tomorrow." His playfulness expired, a more serious look settling upon his face. "I know you feel you failed today. And that this failure has pushed us back a dozen steps in our efforts." He lifted his shoulders in a hard sigh. "But it was never going to be the word of a disgraced tender that outed the Defenders. They're far too careful. There would have been a dozen men in between Ashenhurst or Derry or Bristol and that tender, and none would have known the name of the former or the latter. It was never going to lead us to anything more than more frustration."

"Ah, so it's hopeless then? Perfect." Lorcan's eyes fluttered as he drew a sip of his ale.

"No." Rohan fingered his thick beard. "It's not hopeless. We've just been coming at this all wrong, thinking there are any men doing their bidding who will give us what we need." He leaned in closer. "The men we want are in the Rush already. Time we stop going around them and go *through* them."

Lorcan met his gaze with confusion. "What?"

"You heard me."

Lorcan laughed. "The stewards already know we're watching them. They're not stupid enough to implicate themselves when we're around."

"Probably not," Rohan agreed. "But there are other ways."

Lorcan started to rebut, but the look in his father's eyes stayed him. He knew that look. He'd seen it often enough when Rohan had had to be both father and mother to a son who could never sit still for long. "Whatever you're going to suggest—"

"I want you to take my place on Lord Blackwood's council. And with this appointment, I'll be actively seeking a suitable bride for you. It's time." Rohan visibly deflated after speaking, seemingly both relieved and more anxious than before he'd begun. "Hear me out. Please."

Lorcan's hands slipped off the table, dropping to his sides. The candles lining bars and nooks blurred with the hard flame of the hearth. It didn't matter whether he heard his father out or leaped from his chair and fled into the night. It wasn't a discussion. The decision had been made, and all that was left was to soften Lorcan into accepting it.

And Evra was in on it. *I know you and your son have something important to discuss, Steward.*

Lorcan wet his lips and cocked both brows. "Why would I think you've lost your mind? Sending a son with no political experience to sit on the lord's council in the middle of a coup sounds perfectly reasonable to me."

Rohan's patient expression was maddening. "No one, aside from his own kin, is closer to Evrathedyn than you."

24

Lorcan laughed. "You think he listens to me? Or his own kin, for that matter?"

Rohan folded his hands atop the table. "The transition is over, Lorcan. The men who hid behind it have nothing to hide behind now. They'll be exposed, cornered…and cornered men are capable of anything. He'll need someone he trusts."

"He trusts *you*."

"Look at the faces on his council. The men who died in the plague, the men who were removed, who were they replaced by? His family. His friends. He'll need you when this gets ugly, son. And it will. Trust me."

Lorcan shifted his gaze away with a short scoff. The right words evaded him. He would have replaced his father eventually, but Rohan James was in the prime of his life. Healthy, strong, sharp of mind. He was the most experienced counselor Evra had left. "You know I'll always do whatever you ask. But what do you really think will be accomplished by putting me in your place?"

Rohan averted his eyes in a way that had Lorcan's heart seizing in his chest.

"What? What aren't you telling me?"

His father tightened his mouth and inhaled through his nose. He turned back to look at him. "I have it on good authority that the Defenders have designs on Lady Edriss."

"What do you mean?" Lorcan's blood cooled. "What designs?"

"If you were inclined to stage a hostile takeover, what would your plan be for the only sister of a deposed lord?"

Lorcan fell back in his chair. He shook his head instead of responding. Images of her rain-and-tear-stained face as she pleaded with him to help her turned his belly to mush.

"I know how you feel about—"

"Don't." Lorcan cleared his throat. "Please."

"You should talk to Evra, Lorcan. Be *honest*. He might not punish you for falling in love with his sister. He knows you're a man of honor."

"A man of honor does not harbor untoward feelings for the young woman he was sworn to protect!"

"Perhaps. But you didn't set out to fall in love with her, did you?" Rohan slapped his hands on the table and dragged them off the edge. "Have you at least *tried* to have a conversation with him?"

Lorcan shook his head at the wall. "Evra has made himself *very* clear on the matter. If I were to…" He sucked in through his teeth. "It would put her entire life into question. Everyone would look upon the past ten years and wonder if I'd…sullied her. Those are not scandals young women recover from easily."

"But you didn't."

"Of course not!" Lorcan sighed. "Of *course* not. But her reputation would be ruined. Evra would never find her a suitable husband then."

"You," Rohan said with a short laugh. "*You* would be a suitable husband for Edriss."

Lorcan bowed his head and shook it. Every argument his father made was one he himself had made many times. It always led back to the same place, a perfect circle of misery.

"You should know…" Rohan held out his hands. "These designs they have on Edriss? They're more than ideas or dreams. Evra told me earlier this evening he may endorse a match between Edriss and Finnegan. Soon."

Lorcan's eyes popped open. He pitched forward, mouth hanging. No words emerged.

"We both know why the Derrys want this. You can imagine the effort they went through to lead Evra to believe it was his own idea." His father frowned before beginning again. "Evra senses Finnegan and his father are pulling away, and instead of letting them go, he would seek to mend their alliance."

Lorcan's skin tingled like he was sitting too close to the fire. A thousand thoughts, all disconnected, raced across his mind, but he couldn't grab hold of them. "He wouldn't do that. He'd never do that." He reached for his ale and swallowed it to clear the dry thatch spreading in his throat.

"There is comfort in the familiar, and Evra knows it. He knows his people need stability in the middle of all this change," Rohan said calmly. He went to pour Lorcan another ale, but he shook his head. He needed clear thoughts to process his father's shocking news. "Evra's promotion to lord of the Westerlands has brought nothing *but* change to the Reach. He upended two-thirds of his council, replacing most of them with his friends. *Four* of them are women, women picked over the men these houses felt were next in line. Some of these houses no longer have representation at all, their spots taken by Evra's own family."

Lorcan rolled his eyes. "They only have themselves to blame for that."

"What does blame matter when a man's pride is wounded? What else will the young lord do, swayed by his pretty young witch of a bride?"

"Hopefully more of what he's been doing," Lorcan muttered. Hearing his father speak of Rhosyn the way their enemies did ignited his defenses, even though he knew why he was doing it. "If he would just remove these men from power, we wouldn't even be having this discussion. We wouldn't be talking about...about selling Edriss off like a damned pawn!"

"But he won't remove them. You saw it today, didn't you? It isn't that Evra is a fool, Lorcan. It's that he needs to believe people can change, or none of this works," Rohan said. "Evra has made some very shrewd moves that no one expected. But he is still, at heart, a boy who wants to believe the best in the world. He's convinced himself the only way to heal the Reach is to keep some of the men responsible for its ruin close at his side, giving them the chance to make it right. We both know it will never happen, but by the time he sees it, things will be lost that can never be returned."

Lorcan pushed back from the table. "And what..." He swallowed, struggling to steady himself. The room threatened to spin, and the only way to stop it was to focus on one thing. "What would you like me to do as his counselor?"

27

"You are one of the few who have seen the treachery with your own eyes. I know he didn't believe you before, but things are different now," Rohan said. His voice softened, becoming distant. "If nothing else, you can save Edriss from the terrible fate of being bound to a traitor. She's already endured far more than she should ever have to."

"You think I don't know everything Edriss has been through?" Lorcan dragged both hands down his face and tilted his head over the back of his chair. "I was there for all of it."

"And will you stand idly by while she marries Finnegan Derry?"

Lorcan paled at hearing the words spoken so plainly. "She's too young to be matched to anyone."

"She's eighteen. Many highborn women have proper betrothals by sixteen."

"Edriss is not just *any* highborn woman."

"I know she's very special to you. That you don't like to speak about it—"

Another image, of Edriss's heartbreak after he'd told her the kiss he'd never forget had to be the last, sent a dark, twisting ache into his chest. He lowered his gaze to his hands, threaded in his lap. "It could never...be like that between us."

"This isn't just about Evrathedyn, is it?"

"What do you mean?"

"Edriss doesn't need you to save her," Rohan said slowly. "Isn't that about the sum of it?"

"What are you saying?" Lorcan narrowed his eyes.

"The only women you've ever pursued are the ones unavailable to you. The ones mired in their traumas and their darkness, offering you a tempting puzzle to solve."

"That's prepos—"

"Edriss has endured much, but she's not broken, is she? So what is there for you to put back together?"

"Is this really what you think of me?"

"I should never have made you a tender." His father looked down with a heavy sigh. "What happened with Cesarina broke

28

something inside of you, Lorcan. Something *I* cannot fix for you."

There was only one person capable of calming his thoughts, but no matter what his father said, there was no future for him and Edriss. No place for them to love one another safely, without the scrutiny that would ruin her reputation, forever. He loved her far too much to cause her the pain that would come with the stigma.

"And now I hear you're pecking at the raven?"

It didn't surprise Lorcan that his father knew he'd befriended Arwenna Ravenwood. But it was pointless explaining why. Despite all the nasty whispers and rumors, she could have a real future in Longwood Rush, and it would start with friends who cared enough to come to her aid. "She has few friends in the Rush."

Rohan sighed, holding a hard pause at the end. He tapped his thumbs on the edge of the old table. "And you think you can help her."

Lorcan scoffed to the side. He was still thinking of Edriss. Imagining her dangling from Finn's arms while he regaled her with dishonest tales of his "bravery" in the field. "Maybe I can help her. I helped Edriss, until she no longer needed me." Lorcan flung his arms to his sides, his voice echoing around the beams of the empty tavern. Even saying her name hollowed him. It was easier—safer—to shift the talk back to Arwenna, despite his father's gross misunderstanding of the situation. "Wanting to help people isn't a flaw."

"Lorcan—"

"You'll never understand..." He shook his head, unwilling to finish the thought. His father wasn't the only one who didn't understand.

Rohan didn't meet Lorcan's eyes. "If you're too stubborn to challenge Evra, to stand for what you really want...Edriss, by your side, where you could both finally be happy...I can't change your mind, and I won't engage you in a battle you're already losing with yourself. But the alternative is a Wakesell or a Tyndall.

Barring that, a girl from one of the Lesser Families will do." He stood and cast his glance at everything except his son. "I can feel your anger from here, Lorcan. But unless you can be honest with Evra…with *yourself*…then I need to move forward with what's best for your future."

"Expecting Evra to be reasonable about Edriss and me is like expecting the sun to rise at night. It won't happen." Lorcan held his words long enough to suppress an urge to cry. "But I'll be damned if I let him hand her over to the Defenders. So you want me to take your place on his council, Father?" He shoved back from the table and nodded. "I accept. But I advise you to adjust your expectations about me swaying Evra against those monsters, because the only one with that power is *himself*."

THREE
THE ONE WHO SAVED THEM

Arwenna had never trusted hallways. The echoes of her exposure rang with every conspicuous step, her only escape either a door or a corner, behind which lurked more unknown dangers or rewards.

For Arwenna Ravenwood, former and disgraced high priestess of Midnight Crest, there had *never* been rewards lurking beyond doors or around corners. Not then. Certainly not now.

It was a double corner, a Z-shaped path. Then a regular corner, followed by a tight one, like an abrupt alleyway with a nook unlit by the sconces otherwise illuminating the way in the dark. The men stopped there, lowering their voices to hushed whispers. Arwenna paused in the longer hall to listen, her heart pumping so hard, she thought for sure they could hear it.

"More skirmishes. That's your answer?" Roland Ashenhurst was saying. That he was in the Rush at all was an act of treason. He'd been banished from the capital when Evra had dismissed him from his council. "Pulling him away from the Rush does nothing about the men who cow to him and submit to his heathenry."

Osman Derry—perhaps the ugliest man Arwenna had ever seen—coughed, a phlegmy, sputtering sound, and then growled, making him seem even more feral than usual. He made the same sounds in the bedroom as well, but she'd learned to ignore his eccentricities and focus on the task at hand.

An uncomfortable pause had Arwenna preparing to retreat, but then Osman spoke. "You already know the *right* answer, Roland. The question is are you bold enough to see it through? Brave enough?"

Osman, unlike Roland, was still on Evra's council, still dealing in fake smiles and empty fealty. Evra was aware of Osman's questionable loyalty, but he'd insisted that filling his council with only allies was antithetical to growth and fairness. *If I'm only ever surrounded by people who love me, how will I ever understand those who do not?*

Arwenna wondered if Evra would still care about growth and fairness if he saw Osman conspiring with the man who had reignited the war against magic in the Westerlands—the leader of the Defenders of the Righteous Dawn, a faction determined to return the Westerlands to a burning nightmare.

"Brave enough?" Roland's voice plunged to a low hiss. "You *dare* use that word, with *me*, after all I've done?" He snorted, his boots scuffing the damp stone. "While you dine on roast pork with the heathen lord, I've been doing the real work."

"If I wasn't dining on roast pork with the heathen lord, who would be your ears on the inside?"

"Leonarde."

"I rue the day we brought that oily bastard into this." Osman cackled at whisper level. "Did you know he once bit the head off a rabbit? Or…Was it a squirrel?"

Roland groaned. "The Bristols have gold, and we need as much as we can get. My coffers are still in seizure. We won't have access to them until this is done."

"We wouldn't need so damn much gold if we dealt with the matter…properly." Osman growled again. Then belched. "Ahh. Better."

"You are utterly foul," Roland said, disgusted. "Why the boy kept *you* over me will be a mystery I'll never solve."

"Because *I* know when to keep my mouth shut." Osman lowered his voice further. Arwenna couldn't hear what was said next.

She released her breath, slowly, her mouth wide to keep from whistling or making another inadvertent sound that might give her away. Even the persistent drips of water through a crumbling crack in the wall heightened her sense that she was somewhere she was not supposed to be. She should go. *Quickly.* Before they caught her. There was no reason for her to be in the dungeon, ever, and she'd been too excited to see the men actively scheming—seeing an opportunity, at last, to be of real use to her sister's family—to think of a cover story before she'd blindly followed them farther and farther from warmth and safety.

Now, it was too late.

It was the middle of the night. No one would be around to hear her scream. Her magic—her only defense—had dimmed to near nothing so far from home.

Home.

The word no longer had any meaning.

"Osman, your problem is you think in the moment, without regard to the future. Many *like* the boy's foreign witch of a wife. They approve of him merging his name with hers. They're *enthusiastic* about the prospect of a Westerland heir with Ravenwood blood. Heathen blood." Roland made a revolted gagging sound. "No, as much as I'd love to watch the witch and her infant burn on the pyre, we're better served exiling them, unless we want to shift our focus to another war."

"So she can return one day and put her heir back into power? Think about what you're saying!"

"I know what I'm saying. And if you spent any time beyond the Rush, you'd know these actions *will* invite war. The illusion of compromise, a show of being reasonable, is the only way."

"We dispose of all three of them, or we admit we lack the fortitude to lead this Reach back to its former glory, Roland."

"Three and a half," Roland said distantly. "Lady Blackwood is due to give birth to her second child any day. We need to focus on our plan for Edriss. She takes too much after that crazy bitch Alise, and she'll require firm handling."

"I told you, I want Edriss for Finn," Osman said. "I'm the only one of us with a son who isn't already married. Once the Blackwoods are dead and this travesty is behind us, the last thing we need is to find ourselves distanced from the power."

"You speak of murder and marriage in the same breath? You really are mad, aren't you?" Roland scoffed, and his voice dipped below what Arwenna could hear.

She turned to ice. Her mouth froze open, catching up with her mind. It wasn't the first time she'd followed the Defenders, but it was the first time they'd clearly stated their intention to execute Rhosyn and her family.

"No time to waste," Osman concluded with a sour laugh. "And precisely why we must do this *now*. Before another spawn draws unholy breath and solidifies Evrathedyn's mission to make the Westerlands unrecognizable to all who loved it the way it was."

Arwenna closed her eyes. She'd left most of her magic behind when she'd been thrust off the mountain at Midnight Crest, left for dead. Reborn so far from home, she had nothing to offer. No ability to climb into their weak minds and place her own ideas. No chance of creating an illusion to strike fear in their hearts.

The only thing she could still reliably do was shift into her raven form, but she dared not try it in a windowless dungeon.

This is your home now, girl. Your second chance at life.

No. Midnight Crest will always be my home. This is only temporary.

Arwenna jammed her tongue to the roof of her mouth when her breathing hastened. This should have been the point where she would split herself in two and leave the brave half to deal with her foolish choice to follow dangerous men, but she was too anxious to even attempt it. *Breathe. They won't kill anyone. No one would dare touch Evra and Rhosyn and Alastrynia and Edriss.*

*They're beloved in the Westerlands. They restored peace and prosperity,
legalized magic, reopened trade lines with the other Reaches, and—*

"Well, *what* do we have here?"

Arwenna's eyes dilated in horror. Leonarde Bristol stood leering at her, the worst of all the men conspiring against Longwood Rush—the one who acted with the violent impulsiveness of someone with nothing to lose, including his conscience.

"Steward Bristol." She barely managed the words before he clamped his hand onto her chin and stretched it across her jaw. He would not have dared handle her that way in front of anyone else, but the traitors were down in the damp, moldy dungeon of the Halls of Longwood because there *wasn't* anyone else around.

"Lady Arwenna." He released her, and she stumbled back to the cold, mossy wall. "Curious finding you down here when the rest of the Rush is sleeping."

Arwenna straightened, drawing from an unexpected rush of courage. "I could say the same to you." She clenched, listening for the continued exchange of the other two men, but they'd gone silent.

Leonarde's face cracked into a grotesque grin, made more malevolent by the dying flickers of the sconces no one would bother tending again until morning. "I'm happy to explain, dear." He turned his head to the side. "You can come out now."

Arwenna dug herself against the wall. She turned her face to the side and willed herself to leave her tougher half behind so the weak, cowardly half could flee and pretend none of this had ever happened.

"Oh, *Guardians*. What did you say to her that has her looking like we're going to take turns with her?" Osman spat the words. "Arwenna. Look at me."

But she couldn't. She couldn't open her eyes or turn her head. She couldn't speak. All she could do was tremble like a scared child and wait for the moment to end.

"Really?" Osman slammed a fist against the stone. Dust crumbled to the floor in a shimmer. "I've never once touched you when you didn't ask for it."

"I told you she would be here," Roland said, a touch a pride in his voice. "She's been following you for weeks, Osman. If you weren't so infatuated with her, you'd have paid better attention to your shadows."

"How could you know that? You weren't even *here*."

Leonarde raised a hand. "I was. One of us had to pay attention."

"I would've known."

Arwenna watched the bizarre exchange, reminding herself no one would know to look for her down there. No one would even know she was gone at all until she didn't show up to breakfast with Rhosyn and Evra.

"Ahh, but you didn't." Leonarde swept his gaze in disgust over the other man and then turned his eyes on Arwenna. His dark gleam rooted her, carving her from the inside out. Osman had always unnerved her, but next to Leonarde, he seemed positively paternal. "Arwenna, darling. We're not here to harm you."

Arwenna scrunched her nose and mouth together to keep the words away, but they came anyway. "Just my sister, right? And my niece? And my brother-in-law?"

"They are a threat to our Westerland ways. You are not." Leonarde laughed. "You're *nothing*, really, are you?"

"I'm just as much of a witch as my sister," Arwenna spat. *Priestess,* she'd almost said, but he didn't care about the distinction. *High Priestess, once, until I failed my people and they sent me to die.*

"And when this is done, we'll allow you to leave and practice your heathenry somewhere else," Leonarde said, sounding almost reasonable. "Back to your people perhaps, or...wherever you please. It's nothing to me, as long as it isn't here."

"When this is done? You mean when you've committed high treason against the Blackwoods?"

"Blackwood. Even the name..." Leonarde spat. "Evrathedyn defiles his legacy, the legacy of the Blackrooks. How would you feel, girl, if some outsider came to your little mountain and stole your name and legacy?"

"It's not my mountain," she stated between clenched teeth. Her next words were a lie. "If you're preparing a threat against Midnight Crest, you can spare yourself the effort. I no longer care what happens there."

Roland snickered. "We have no designs on your little bird's nest of witches in the north, raven. And we already know you don't care, or you would still be *there*, wouldn't you? Not here, skulking about in shadows, lost for purpose…living off your unnatural sister's hospitality."

His words pierced her. The only thing worse than them being true was that others had noted it about her.

"She is a sight, this one, isn't she? Have you ever seen hair as dark as night, boys? I understand what you see in her, Osman. I do." Roland sighed, loading a small grunt onto the end as though imagining something she prayed he never said aloud. His thoughtfulness dimmed. "But I'd have to cut my prick off and feed it to the hogs if I ever tainted it so."

All three men laughed. Her relief was too coated in shame to calm her. "You said…You said you knew I'd be here. You didn't stop me."

"Of course not. We could never say what we needed to say in the halls above, where there are eyes and ears everywhere," Leonarde answered. He flicked a nod at the other men. "I suppose these two sewer rats were arguing about the necessity of the deed before I arrived, eh?"

Arwenna said nothing.

"Of course they were. Osman grows fat on comfort—"

"Either of you say one more word—"

"You draw steel and you'll die, Derry," Leonarde said with an eyeroll at Arwenna, as though they were conspirators. "Did they come to an agreement? That the lord and his family should die?"

Arwenna didn't know whether to nod or shake her head, so she did neither. Her teeth clacked instead.

"Ah." Leonarde looked at the others. "Well, it was already decided before anyone came down here. And *you*, raven, are going to help us."

"Me?" Arwenna couldn't keep herself from laughing. "You know if you let me leave this dungeon alive, I'll go straight to Lord Blackwood and tell him everything?"

"Lord Black*rook* is tending to a situation in Jademarch."

"Then my sister or Edriss…or—"

"*Anyone* you tell will be dead before you finish the words." Leonarde stepped closer, and she shrank further against the dank wall. "But we're offering you a way to save their lives."

Arwenna's eyes closed. "What?"

"They cannot rule the Westerlands. Our ways will die with them if this goes on any longer. But we could be persuaded to consider exile instead. It's what our late Lord Aeldred would have wanted for his son and grandchildren." Leonarde inhaled a sharp breath through his nose. "Problem is none of us have the trust of the boy's allies. They know we're against him. They know we'll never share his heathen values. So how are we supposed to get close enough to Evrathedyn to depose him *and* save his little family?"

Arwenna shook her head, eyes still squeezed shut. "I don't know what you're saying."

Leonarde backed off. "Edriss."

Arwenna finally knew what they wanted with Edriss, but she had no idea what part they intended for *her* to play.

"If you think hard enough, raven, you already know what we want from you."

Arwenna curled her toes in her boots, tightening her muscles all over in an effort to regain even a modicum of control in the utterly bizarre situation. "I don't know."

"You do."

A sudden image came to her, of Lorcan James grinning at Edriss as he practiced his swordplay with her in the training arena.

She closed her mouth to keep from gasping.

"Not entirely dim then," Roland grunted.

"Lorcan will soon take his father's place on the council," Leonarde said. "Which means he'll be in the Rush for extended periods. If he's in the Rush, he'll be spending every moment of his free time with Edriss."

"I hardly know Lorcan." It was mostly true. Lorcan was a kind man, and he was her friend, though that was an overly generous way of saying he occasionally looked in on her to see if she needed anything.

"Lorcan is a man. And you, despite your heathenry, are a lovely creature."

"He doesn't see me like that," Arwenna stated. "He only has eyes for—"

"Do witches know naught but trickery?" Osman groused with a snort. "You and I both know how *persuasive* you can be, raven."

"You don't know the power you wield," Roland said. "The power to do the one thing we cannot, and keep him away from Lady Edriss. *Distract* him, so he forgets his inappropriate love for his lord's sister."

Arwenna furrowed her brows. "Why do you care about Lorcan and Edriss?" She knew the answer. She needed to hear them say it again.

"She's ours. More specifically, though saying so vexes me, she's Finnegan's, for my own sons are already married, and Roland has none," Leonarde said with a rueful roll of his eyes. "Painful though it is, it will be a Derry on the top seat in the Rush, but that will be far better than the alternative."

"What did I say?" Osman muttered to Roland.

"Get close to him, Arwenna," Leonarde said, hands at his sides like a peace offering. "Drive a wedge between him and Edriss by showing a genuine interest in him, before he does something foolish like angle for a betrothal with her. And if you can keep them apart until the wedding, we will do our best to keep Evrathedyn, Rhosyn, and the children safe during this necessary transition of power."

"And Edriss? What becomes of her?" Arwenna already knew Edriss would never willingly agree to what they had planned for her.

"She'll rule the Reach. Second to her husband, of course."

"You mean you'll force her into subjugation?"

Leonarde shrugged one shoulder. "I won't quibble over details."

Arwenna slinked to the side and backed down the hall several steps. *I'll go straight to Evra and Rhosyn. They'll know what to do.*

"Of course, we all know where your loyalties lie, so let's test them." Leonarde turned toward Osman. "You have your woman tending the infant in her nursery tonight?"

Osman grinned. "If I don't send word by two, she has her orders. Did you know, over half of the wee folk in the Westerlands never make it to their first year at all?"

Arwenna gaped at the men, horror spreading from her face down into her arms and feet. She had no reason to doubt their threats. They were the masterminds behind the burnings in the Westerlands—the ones who had ordered women and children ripped from their beds to be scorched on pyres, for no reason other than to satisfy the cruel bloodlust of evil, fearful men.

"Say a word to anyone, raven, and you'll find out in a most unfortunate way how serious we are about discretion," Leonarde said.

"Even if I was willing to help you…" Arwenna swallowed her treason. She couldn't be seriously entertaining any of it. The men standing before her were monsters, and a victory for a monster was a loss for everyone good and kind. "What makes you think it will work? That he'll be interested in me? He loves Edriss. Would do anything for her. He…As far as I know, he's never looked at anyone the way he looks at her."

Leonarde's grin was brief but full of knowing victory. "I don't know what the men were like at Midnight Crest, raven, but the men of the realm are easily persuaded by the right…chasm. Isn't that right, Osman?"

Roland and Osman laughed.

"Lorcan is too young yet to understand his feelings are a weakness. He's smitten and foolish, and those things will serve us well. *You* will serve us well."

"No," Arwenna whispered, wondering who the word was for. Whether saying it even mattered.

"You once meant something to your people, until they no longer wanted you," Leonarde said. "You could mean something again. Here. Now. To your sister and her new family." He closed the gap between them and whispered his last words. "You could be the one who saved them."

Edriss was keeping a watchful eye on Arwenna's nerves. The raven's temples dripped with sweat as she tried to get ahold of the tremble in her hands, preparing to apply the gritty, dangerous paste to Lady Meldred's swollen ankle. Edriss was astounded her grandmother allowed anyone other than her daughter or Edriss to touch her, but Arwenna was ready for her first test in healing balms, even if she didn't believe she was.

She nodded to urge Arwenna on. Alise clucked in annoyance from where she sat perched in her colorful chair, but she'd never enjoyed teaching others, and Arwenna was only just learning the balance between improving life and giving death.

"Oh, do get on with it!" Meldred declared, lifting her cane from the bed and waving it in the air. "I watched you crush the henbane and willow bark myself, raven. You think I'd let you kill me?"

"It's all right, Grandmother. Let her take her time if she needs to." Edriss expected another barb from the old woman about the meaning of time at her old age, but her only response was a hard sniff.

"It's not as though you're in any great rush, Mother," Alise said, in an uncharacteristically soothing tone that left Edriss wondering what she'd really wanted to say.

Arwenna was plainly terrified of the poison mistresses of Longwood Rush, but Edriss was determined to make her friend one of them, so she'd finally calm her restless soul and realize she had a place in the Rush. Two years Edriss had been mentoring the raven though, and it was yet unclear whether she had either the skill or the desire.

"The Guardian of the Unpromised Future beckons me home soon, and I'd like to walk to him and not crawl, thank you oh so much." Meldred rolled her eyes with a flourish, dropping a wrinkled arm atop her forehead as she tumbled back on the plush pillow.

"As though you were moving beyond a snail's pace *before* you broke it," Alise muttered with a conspiratorial smile at Edriss.

Edriss ignored them both. She'd counseled Arwenna to do the same when mixing, to block out the world and its distractions, but the young woman's eyes were drawn more to the Blackwood matriarchs than the salve in her hands. "The hard part is over, Arwenna. As Grandmother said, we watched you mix and crush the herbs in the right measure. Ahead is only relief."

"If I don't perish from the boredom first," Meldred declared, shaking her graying hair against the pillow. "Edriss, darling, can you not just heal me yourself? Lay hands on me? It would be so much quicker."

"I could," Edriss said, biting back her growing annoyance. "But then Arwenna wouldn't learn anything, would she?"

"Patience, Mother," Alise chided.

"Alise, you've indulged the raven because you have a soft spot, but we both know what she really needs is a husband."

"No woman *needs* a husband, Mother." She followed the pronouncement with a slow, sly grin.

"Hmm. Does Arwenna know what happened to both of yours?"

Of course Arwenna knew, because few people ever mentioned Edriss's aunt without also whispering about how both of Alise

Blackwood's unruly husbands had met their demise at the hands of the skilled poison mistress.

"Oh, she clearly does. She's just been groomed to mind her tongue." Meldred waved a bony hand in the air. "Something else you'll need to break in her if she's to survive in the Rush."

Arwenna cradled the healing poison in her shaking hands, her gaze darting around at the dowager ladies.

Edriss swung her attention back to Arwenna. "As I was—"

"Alise, she's eighteen, practically an old—"

"Do you or do you not want your ankle mended, Mother?" Alise sprayed the words through comfortable exasperation.

"Ignore them," Edriss said in a whisper, turning her face to catch Arwenna's attention. She smiled when she got it. The urge to hug her was powerful, but she wouldn't do it in front of her aunt and grandmother, for it would only make matters worse. "You'll have to learn to block out everything else when mixing."

Arwenna's tensely locked brows softened. "How? How do you do it?"

"Practice," Edriss said with a brief smile. She flicked her eyes to the side and rolled them. "And lots of patience."

"But this comes so easily to you, Edriss," Arwenna said with a troubled scowl. "You're the princess of poison are you not?"

Edriss choked down a laugh. No one actually called her that, except Lorcan. "Don't believe everything you hear. I wasn't born knowing any of this. I've been practicing since I was old enough to hold the pestle."

Arwenna's frown lessened. "That's not what Lorcan says."

A sudden flush jumped into Edriss's cheeks. Lorcan would be returning to the Rush soon, and she couldn't wait to see him.

But first, she needed to do as she'd instructed Arwenna and focus on the task at hand.

"Lose the frown, Arwenna. No one is marrying you off unless you want it. Women of the Rush have choices," Alise said.

Edriss reached for the bowl and used it to guide Arwenna closer. "*Ignore* them. Tell me what you need to do next."

Alise and Meldred were both staring at them, waiting. Arwenna fumbled her words twice before managing to say, "Two…acorn-sized scoops. Rub them together in my hands with several drops of water and then—"

"Rub your hands together for how long?" Edriss asked, coaxing.

"Until my hands are too warm to rub anymore."

"Yes. We must heat and emulsify the salve, or it will sit on the surface of her flesh and do nothing. We can warm it over a fire, but it takes too long, and using your hands will mean you also get the benefit of the salve, which you'll need for the inevitable aches when you've finished the vigorous massaging. And then?"

"And then I work it into her ankle until my hands are sore."

"Or numb from the salve," Alise said. She turned a side-eye on her mother, who made exasperated sounds.

Edriss shot her aunt a glare. "And then…"

"I take the warmed kava leaves and wrap them carefully in layers over anywhere the salve has been laid." Edriss gave her an expectant look and Arwenna quickly said, "Overlapping so there's no gap in the bandaging."

"You know what to do," Edriss said with a nod. "All that's left is to do it."

Maybe Edriss should have laid hands on her grandmother. She was a healer of magic in addition to her skill with plants, and it would've spared Meldred hours of discomfort if she'd healed her. But the raven needed practice on real injuries and maladies, and after two years, it was time for her to use what she'd learned.

Arwenna steadied her fearful breathing. "Sorry."

"Stop apologizing for everything, raven," Meldred snapped.

"Perhaps you didn't sprain your ankle *that* badly, Mother. It certainly hasn't affected your mood."

"Arwenna," Edriss whispered, but she could see what was coming in the raven's eyes before it happened.

44

The bowl slipped from Arwenna's hands and shattered on the stones.

She turned and ran.

Arwenna almost hadn't come. After the scene she'd made with the poison mistresses—particularly Edriss, who had always been so patient with her—all she wanted was to retreat to her favorite spot in the forest, curl into a ball, and allow her mind to escape.

Rhosyn's entire face brightened when Arwenna walked past the guards into the Lady's Chambers. Although she was the highest-ranking woman in the room—in all of the Westerlands—Rhosyn had never cared much for protocol. She pushed away from her chair, cradling a very pregnant belly, and waddled toward her older sister.

Edriss's troubled gaze followed both women.

Arwenna frowned over Rhosyn's shoulder as she regarded the meager table. She was relieved not to see Meldred or Alise, though their absence was unusual. "Where are the others?" she asked, after she smoothed Rhosyn's silver hair off her forehead with a kiss. Her second child would arrive any day, and the physicians wanted Rhosyn in full confinement, but Arwenna would have been more surprised if her stubborn sister had obeyed the order.

"Lady Alise is tending her mother's ankle," Rhosyn said, and Arwenna knew no one had told her about her earlier failure.

"She's fine," Edriss said quickly. "I already healed it. It wasn't so serious to start with, no matter how she carried on."

"I thought you were going to see Baron Lawrence tonight?" Arwenna asked. She started to look up, to meet Edriss's eyes as she usually did, but guilt turned the act impossible.

Edriss picked at her cloth napkin. "I don't know that I'm much help to him anymore." She laughed wryly. "If I ever was."

"Nonsense," Rhosyn said. "If anyone can help a willful, grieving man, it's you."

"He needs a new wife," Edriss said. "Someone he's duty bound to listen to. Whatever I suggest he does, he gleefully does the opposite."

Rhosyn ambled back to the table. "You volunteering to wed him?"

Edriss's nose scrunched in horror. "Absolutely not."

Rhosyn dropped onto her chair with a quick grimace. "A man who puts so much energy into being cross with you is likely hiding deeper feelings."

"How unfortunate that would be," Edriss muttered, stabbing at the sliced carrots on her plate.

"For him or you?" Rhosyn said, teasing her.

Edriss mimed throwing a carrot at her, and they both giggled.

Arwenna never ceased to be amazed at how easily her sister fit into the world of men, when Arwenna had never fit into *any* world.

Rhosyn pointed at the spread on the table. "All your favorites, Wen." Then she ignored everything green and pulled two cuts of venison onto her plate.

Even the scent of cooked meat turned Arwenna's belly. She'd never get used to it, not the way Rhosyn had. But she smiled graciously and gathered two spoonfuls of cooked vegetables.

Edriss played with the choker at her neck, a poison vial strung between two heavy straps of leather. She wore it always, and everyone whispered about what was inside as though it couldn't really be poison. But it was. "Alastrynia feeling better?"

Arwenna stopped chewing. "What's wrong with Alastrynia?"

Rhosyn swatted the air, but she couldn't hide the worry in her eyes. "Her belly was a touch sour. Edriss came by earlier to help."

"What do you mean, sour? What was the cause?" Arwenna's blood iced over.

"With little ones, could be anything." Rhosyn's explanation was nonchalant, but her glistening eyes gave away her distress.

"But she's better now?" Arwenna felt Edriss's gaze burning her and eased off. Her friend had an uncanny gift for reading people, and the last thing Arwenna wanted was to be read.

Friend. Arwenna no longer deserved the designation, not with the illicit thoughts streaming through her mind.

"She's resting." Rhosyn forced a smile. "She'll be fine. Edriss tells me you're getting better at your healing salves. Perhaps you'll be onto serums and tinctures soon. I only wish I had more time to learn the trade."

Arwenna felt herself sink deep into the chair, weighted by her shame and regret. She'd once been a powerful healer. So had Rhosyn, but both of their magics had dulled when they left Midnight Crest. Some of their powers still worked, but with less efficacy. Others had gone away altogether.

At least she could still shift, though she'd intentionally kept that a secret from everyone except Rhosyn. She didn't know why she felt compelled to hide it, but she'd learned to trust her instincts.

Rhosyn stretched a hand across the table and clamped it atop Arwenna's wrists. "I know what you're thinking. Don't. We gained more than we lost in leaving that cursed place. If I had to make this choice a thousand times, I would never make it any differently. We're safe here, and we have all we need. We're *home*."

Arwenna nodded, lowering her eyes to her lap. Guilt turned her veins to stone, clogged her throat. Rhosyn and her family *weren't* safe. They'd never be safe in the Rush, and if Arwenna couldn't rise to meet the traitors' sick demands, they wouldn't be safe anywhere.

She felt Edriss staring at her again. Fear kept her from even glancing her way. If Edriss *did* know…

No. She couldn't. She would have said something.

Or she's waiting for the right time to mention it. The poison mistresses hoard knowledge the way a poor man hoards food.

"Evra will be home soon," Rhosyn said breathlessly. She nibbled on a carrot and dropped it back to her plate. "I wish he was comfortable delegating. He doesn't need to be putting himself in danger every time some new menace appears."

"My brother understands the importance of being seen as a leader, not a faceless figurehead," Edriss said. She wrapped one arm around her torso and sipped her wine with her free hand. Her eyes glazed as though her words and thoughts were disconnected. "Our father never traveled the Reach. He never shook hands with his citizens or visited their farms. Cowards hide in their keeps. Men go where they're needed."

Rhosyn cast her hollow stare toward the fire. "He's needed here too."

"You're a lady of the Westerlands now, Rhosyn. We're made of the toughest bark and the sturdiest stems." Edriss's smile was filled with warmth. "*You* are made of these things."

Arwenna wasn't though. Even sitting next to her sister, when she was embroiled in a sordid game of treachery behind the scenes, was a betrayal bigger than she could bear.

Rhosyn wiped at both eyes and smiled again. "Of course, Edriss. You're right. But I cannot help worrying about all these skirmishes requiring his attention. There seem to be more and more reports coming to the Rush every day. It isn't only Evra I worry about but all those still losing their lives to something that should already be over. When does it end?"

Edriss tossed her napkin onto the table. "Look, we have three-quarters of the Westerlands with us. Even if there *was* a full-blown war—"

"War!" Rhosyn's face crumpled in horror at the possibility.

"It won't come to that." Edriss briefly glanced at Arwenna before she spoke again. "But perhaps you can use your influence to help guide him toward culling the remaining traitors from his council..."

Rhosyn gripped the edge of the table with a dark laugh. "You don't think I've tried? Everyone can see Derry and Bristol are passionate Defenders. And now there are rumors that Ashenhurst has been seen conspiring with them, right here in the Rush..."

"They're not rumors, Rhosyn," Edriss said swiftly. "If enough of us speak up, my brother will have no choice but to listen."

"Would he listen any more than he does now? When he's ignored your counsel, Lorcan's counsel, mine? I'm not so confident. Your brother has...He has his own ideas. I must trust he knows what he's doing." Rhosyn shook her head. "I hear Lorcan is coming back to the Rush with Evra. Did he tell you?"

Edriss brightened. "He sent a raven. Said he had something to give me for my birthday."

"Eighteen. A proper woman." Rhosyn's smile lingered a moment before she switched it to Arwenna with a knowing glance. Edriss caught it and lowered her eyes back to her food. Her mouth clamped closed.

"Rumor is Rohan is stepping back and Lorcan will take his place on the council," Arwenna said, reaching for her wine.

"It's no rumor." Rhosyn picked at her napkin. "There are matters in the Abbey requiring the steward's attention. It's temporary for now, but if Lorcan does well, Evra will likely seek to make the appointment permanent."

Edriss would never forgive her. Everyone else in Edriss's life had taken more than they'd given, but not Lorcan. Lorcan loved her, even if he denied himself over some misguided sense of honor. Arwenna couldn't come between what was meant to be.

She had to find another way before the Defenders killed everyone she loved, and she had to do it without asking for help. If anything happened to Alastrynia…

"I know he's dying to see you, Edriss," Rhosyn said. Arwenna looked up and saw her sister's mischievous grin. "And there's no reason to pretend you're not excited to see him."

Edriss watched them both with a haunted look. "That's not… He's not… We're not…"

"Talking about Lorcan is the only sure way to leave you speechless." Rhosyn laughed. She coiled her silver hair into a rope and tossed it over her shoulder. "Evra chose from his heart. Perhaps Lorcan will as well."

Edriss's spoon clanged against her plate. Rhosyn looked up in alarm, but Edriss shook her head and muttered an apology. "Evra has already made himself clear on the matter. He won't allow it."

Arwenna's racing heart slowed. If that were true, that Evra had already denied the match, then no matter how much Lorcan and Edriss loved one another, there was no future for them. She loathed the way this relieved her, the way the shackles of guilt snapped and dropped away. Edriss would be upset, yes, but Lorcan would never be her husband. And if that were so...

"Hmm." Rhosyn took a moment to consider what Arwenna had said, but didn't take the matter any further. "I'd like you to consider it may be time to begin courting. Springtide will be here in a month, and the Halls will be open for balls and banquets."

Arwenna nearly choked on her wine. "Marriage? No, Rhosyn. Never, *ever* again."

"Marriage isn't for everyone," Edriss quipped. "Just ask Alise."

Rhosyn studied her a moment before turning back toward Arwenna. "Your melancholy is a choice, Wen. You can be happy here, but you have to want it."

That Rhosyn even knew the meaning of the word *happy* meant she was leaps ahead of Arwenna. Arwenna hadn't been happy in Midnight Crest, but she'd been someone who mattered. Now, she was stuck in a never-ending spiral of despair, trapped between two worlds yet belonging in neither.

If happiness were a *choice*? Ahh, then she was even more powerless than she thought.

She started to drift, to detach herself and float away from the room, the conversation, which had veered into uncomfortable territory. She could leave them all behind, and they'd never know. She'd been leaving difficult moments behind her entire life.

"Do you ever think about what our life would be like if we'd stayed in..." Arwenna's mouth clapped shut. She hadn't meant to say anything aloud. It was always a risk when she split her thoughts.

Rhosyn's hands slipped to her sides as horror crept into her eyes. "Wen."

"Forgive me, I shouldn't have said—" Arwenna returned her full mind to the conversation before she could share more of her forbidden thoughts...before Rhosyn knew how Arwenna pined for Midnight Crest after all this time, still.

"Arwenna, you'd be *dead*," Edriss whispered in horror. "They ordered your execution, did they not?"

"Yes, but..." Arwenna didn't expect Edriss to understand. None of them could. "They had every right to. I didn't...That is, I couldn't...There was no heir..." Arwenna was too flustered to finish.

"Our brother tortured you for two full years and then rejoiced in your fate," Rhosyn replied, each word more heated than the last. "They *all* did—"

"Except Mother—"

"Especially Mother!" Rhosyn slammed her palms onto the table, causing Edriss to jump. "You think better of her because she helped you evade death after they hurled you off the mountainside? A real mother would have used her voice in protest against such madness. A *real* mother would have changed the system that destroyed every woman who ever wore the mantle of high priestess."

"It's not her fault I failed." Arwenna felt herself growing smaller. "It's not her fault—"

"You didn't fail anyone, Arwenna. She failed *you*. In allowing her son to torture you for years without punishment or recourse. In doing *nothing* except smiling and putting on a good show for the rest of the Rookery, to maintain and lift a culture that pretends to revere women while slowly killing them."

"Rhosyn." Edriss shook her head with a concerned nod at her belly.

Rhosyn sank back in her chair and threw up her hands. "I can't talk about this, Wen. Not with you. Not ever. You want to pine for a world that saw us as objects and treated us accordingly? You want to ignore the second chance fate has given you, to dream about a world that happily *watched you die* to satisfy their sick need for order? To forsake happiness?" She shook her head with a scoff. "Well, I can't stop you. But I won't indulge it, and I want *no* part in it."

Rhosyn nearly tripped when she pushed back from the table, lifted her skirts, and rushed away, toward her bedchamber.

Arwenna sat back in stunned silence. Her vegetables had grown cold on her plate, matching the frost in her heart.

"Some secrets are gifts," Edriss said after an empty, painful silence. "But some rot us from the inside out. They curse us." She stood. "Rhosyn is too distracted to see you're hiding something, and I prefer she stay that way until she's safely delivered."

"I don't—"

"Whatever it is, I can *help* you, Arwenna. You're not alone here, no matter how it must feel to you after all you endured to get here. Are we not friends?"

Arwenna could neither nod nor shake her head.

Edriss lifted her cloak from the rack and fastened it. "And if it has something to do with those turncoats, I need to know. Because I intend to do something about it, even if Evra won't. I'm going to save this Reach before there's nothing left of it."

"What are you going to do?"

"I'm already doing it." Edriss shook her head. "If Evra knew what I've been doing, he'd have me confined to my apartments, but he doesn't know. No one does." She fingered the emerald fastener on her cloak. "You see, I have secrets too. Perhaps we'll find a time and place where we could share them with each other. Share the burden on our hearts, so it becomes less for us both."

The urge to say the words was so inviting, Arwenna had to turn her hands into fists to stay the compulsion. Edriss *could* help her, but what if involving her put her in even more danger than what the Defenders already had planned for her? What if Edriss learned of their intent and confronted them? What if they hurt her and then followed through on their threats against the rest of the family?

Arwenna would never be able to live with it.

She had one choice, and one choice alone. Unless another presented itself soon, she would move forward with exactly what the Defenders had asked her to do.

Edriss nodded with a light sigh. "You know where to find me."

FOUR

A POET, A PIRATE,
AND A PLAYWRIGHT

Edriss watched Arwenna disappear behind the corner. She was tempted to follow, to see if she could decipher what Arwenna was too afraid to tell her, but the raven was intensely private.

Finnegan Derry and his father, Osman, shared a knowing glance when they passed in the hall. Finnegan's gaze lingered a second longer than it should have, his eyes sweeping her with such overt intent that Edriss felt the need for a bath.

She'd once liked Finnegan, even fancied him for a time when they were younger, but that seemed an entire lifetime ago. How Evra still trusted him—

"Oh!" Edriss cried out with a start, leaping forward when two hands encircled her waist from behind. She'd started for the dagger strapped to the inside of her wrist when her favorite sound in the world removed all evidence of danger.

"Miss me?" The words were whispered against her ear, a rush of warmth and familiarity.

She turned to see Lorcan's lopsided grin stretching between his soft round cheeks, dirt-caked from a week on the road. He released her, withdrawing his hands. In them was something poorly wrapped, which he regarded with an unsure glance before trying to hide it. She was faster.

Edriss bit down on her lip as she snatched the gift from his hands. Her heart raced hard enough to make her eyes feel like they were throbbing in time. The way he watched her, in anxious anticipation, made it so much worse, and she had to move to a nearby bench to sit.

Maybe this is it.

"You gonna open it?"

"What is it?" She shook the box. It was heavier than jewelry would be, but Lorcan was fond of japes, and it wouldn't be the first birthday he'd given her a small gift in a big, clunky package.

"You know, there is *one* surefire way to find out." He sat next to her and draped an arm across the back of the bench. His fingertips brushed her shoulder. "You seem restless, Hemlock. Everything all right?"

"Everything's fine," she whispered, weighing the box in her hand. "Been an odd day is all."

"Want me to make it odder?" He waggled his brows.

Edriss looked at his comically serious face and erupted in laughter. "No one does it better than you." She looked back at the gift. With a deep breath, she pulled at the stays of the loose wrapping and reached in.

She pulled out a heavy wooden box. Along the top, carved into the ivory bark, were a series of plant-shaped swirls and an inscription: *For My Princess of Poison.*

Lorcan leaned in and kissed the side of her head in a chaste peck. "Happy Birthday, Hemlock."

"I..." Edriss's breath choked as she turned the beautiful box in her hands. Strapped to the bottom was a key, and she tilted the wood up to see the sturdy lock.

"You said you needed a place to securely store your private formulas. Now that you're a woman..." He rattled the words off as though she would think the gift silly. "I know you can get a box

54

anywhere, but you hadn't *done* it yet, not that you weren't going to—that's not what I mean, but more that…Anyway, so I had this one made in Pine Bluff while we were dealing with the matter in Jademarch. I know it's…" He scratched his head and scowled. "It's a terrible gift, isn't it?"

"What?" Edriss asked breathlessly. It wasn't an intention ring nor a binding necklace or anything that might give her the impression he'd had a change of heart about their future. It was more. It was the manifestation of desires no one else cared to hear. It was the sum of their entire relationship, the spellbound attention he'd never failed to offer her…the way he made her feel like the only person in the entire world who mattered. "How could you think…" Tears burned her eyes. She sucked in through her teeth to gather herself. "It's a beautiful gift, Lorry." She turned to smile at him. *I love you. I've always loved you. I don't know how to face a world in which you don't love me back.* "My favorite."

Lorcan's cheeks flushed in relief. "That's…Well, that's good, because I didn't have a backup. If, uh…it doesn't quite meet your needs for your botany, I'm sure there's another use for it. Could always put your undergarments in there, if nothing else."

Edriss pretended to be scandalized and nudged herself into him. He shifted his arm from the bench to her shoulders and tugged her close, pulling a giggle from her. She closed her eyes and let him hold her, oblivious to the people passing in the hall.

"I missed you," she whispered.

"Of course. How could you not?" Lorcan quipped. He ran his fingertips along her shoulder again. "I hope you didn't spend too many hours crying into your pillow."

"Only all of them."

He laughed. "How awful for you." Then he whispered, "I missed you too, Hemlock."

Edriss's heart flooded with warmth, both wonderful and terrifying. She shifted topics to keep him from reading it all on her blushing face. "Was everything all right in Jademarch?"

"No," he said, dropping his voice lower, his humor swiftly vanishing. "I'll tell you about it later."

"That bad?"

His head shook. "Not here." He kissed the top of her head again and released her. "Go for a walk with me tomorrow? Around noontide?"

Edriss swallowed and nodded.

"Great." He pushed to a stand with a long stretch. "Have you seen Arwenna?"

Edriss felt herself deflate. "Arwenna?"

"Sorceress, dark hair like yours, might shift into a raven at any moment."

Edriss grinned in spite of the ache in her chest. "I had supper with her. I think she's retired for the evening."

"Evra asked me to check in on her, but if she's gone to rest for the night, I'll happily do the same. Your brother is allergic to taking breaks on the road. I think I'm only still standing by sheer luck." He offered her a hand and pulled her to her feet. "I'm so sorry I missed your birthday."

Edriss held the box up and smiled. "You didn't miss it, Lorry. You got it exactly right."

Lorcan looked down the hall and then back at her, stifling a yawn. "Tomorrow then?"

"Tomorrow," she replied and watched him walk away.

Arwenna slinked down the hall, keeping to the shadows. Though it was late, there were men milling and buzzing about, following the early return of Lord Blackwood and his company. They hadn't been expected until morning, but she'd heard enough whispers to piece together what was going on: Evra wanted to surprise Rhosyn by coming home early. They'd ridden hard for two days to make it back to the Rush a half day ahead of schedule.

She'd also heard whispers he had business in the Rush that couldn't wait, but Arwenna knew the truth. Evra was hopelessly in love with Rhosyn, and something had been off in their relationship for several months.

Something had been off with *Evra* for several months.

Sweat beaded at her brow and between her breasts as she struggled between hurrying and staying invisible. The only gazes ever afforded her were the hungered type. In Midnight Crest, she'd happily been the center of everything, but in the Rush, her greatest desire was to be unseen.

Arwenna waited for a group of men to rush past before she continued. She kept her head low, her cloak wrapped tight and high. She passed the gardens without so much as a second look and moved on, entering the apartments the Blackwoods reserved for guests.

As she rounded the corner, an arm snaked out and grabbed her, whipping her the rest of the way. Startled, she stumbled back to stability and met Osman Derry's singeing gaze.

She ripped free and looked around, but they were alone. "What do you want?" she hissed.

"You've made yourself scarce these past two days." Osman towered over her, casting a broad shadow. "I needed to know you were ready for the James boy's return."

"Stalking me?" Her accusation fell flat. Osman had nothing to fear from her, and she had everything to fear from him. "He only returned this evening. I haven't seen him yet, and even if I had…You overestimate my ability to make him forget how he feels about her."

Osman sighed in aggravation. "You better hope you're wrong, girl. The only thing I need from you is to keep him away from Lady Edriss. If you can't do that, you're useless to me."

"Impossible. You *under*estimate how close they are."

"He's been too familiar with her." He tweaked his nose and checked their surroundings. "Finn and Edriss will be betrothed within the week. You need to make sure Lorcan does nothing to prevent it." He coughed. "How is your little niece, raven?"

Arwenna balked. Cold sweat coated her neck.

He made a face and rubbed his belly. "All better now, is she?"

She backed away, reaching for the wall, but it was too far away.

He stepped toward the corner and peered around it. "Next time I come to you, either you have something I want or I take something you love."

Osman thundered away with such quickness, Arwenna felt the air depart with him.

Lorcan kept walking when he reached his apartments, continuing down the hall until he approached another hall and then another before exiting into the night. He kept going, down the fifteen flights of steps bisecting the maze-like tiers of gardens, stalked through the quiet courtyard, and passed beneath the raised portcullis without pausing.

All of it was second nature, a staple of his youth, of springtides spent in the care of the cold and cutting Lord Aeldred, who had never been happy to see children underfoot. Lorcan and Evra had spent hours in the outdoor gardens, playing with Edriss, Finnegan, Cressida, Rafferty, Renardy, Ridge, Meira, and others whose names and relationships had dwindled with the passage of time. They were all phantoms of their former selves, still straddling the narrow precipice between childhood and the interminable responsibility of adulthood.

Nothing underscored that more than the way being close to Edriss had him questioning everything he knew to be right. The way her private smile made him almost forget he was her *protector*, not her lover. Crossing the line would put the past decade of both of their lives into sharp scrutiny.

But Edriss Blackwood no longer needed protecting, if she ever had. She no longer needed anything. What she *wanted*...

No. He couldn't. Evra had made himself abundantly clear: Edriss deserved better than the reputation that would follow her if she married the man who had sworn to keep her safe.

And his father seriously wanted to open discussions of marriage for him?

Lorcan struggled to imagine *any* woman by his side, save the one he could never have.

When he reached ground level, he turned toward the forest. The Whispering Wood had been the backdrop for everything his childhood imagination had ever conjured. He'd been a pirate, a poet, and a playwright there—had saved damsels and kidnapped them. He'd been the last of his friends to grow out of the place, but Edriss had stayed. She'd never stopped pretending to need his rescue…never stopped swooning at his silly poems.

Passing the large bowing trees and stepping through the gloaming sent the fire in his chest aflame. He was once more Entwin the Bard and Regan One-Eye the Brigand.

The moon disappeared behind a cloud, taking the dark illusions with it. He was again a man of one and twenty, fighting feelings for the same damsel he'd saved over and over, bearing the too-heavy burden of knowing how close the Westerlands was to total chaos once more.

Lorcan pushed on until he heard the light roar of the stream. It ran fast, joining with the River Rush at its most turbulent point. He'd sailed and sunk ships in the tempestuous waters. When Evra's elder brother, Astarian, had still been alive, he'd taken the boys fishing in the same stream, and they'd caught enough whitefish to serve the entire keep that night.

He slowed and turned his head toward the sky to exhale. As his breath left him, he disconnected from the world, from himself. He never wanted anyone to see him this way, vulnerable and in desperate need of the same light he was known for giving others.

The light he'd seen in Edriss's eyes when he gave her the damnable box he had been so anxious about presenting to her.

I'm so sorry I missed your birthday.

You didn't miss it, Lorry. You got it exactly right.

59

He'd witnessed this truth written in a thousand languages across a face he'd seen so many times, it was as familiar as his own reflection.

Walking away from her had felt different this time.

Anything having to do with her lately came with a hazy veil obscuring right from wrong, love from duty.

One thing was certain; he would not stand back and watch Evra marry her to a traitor. It was clear Edriss hadn't yet been told, and if Lorcan could figure out a way to stop it before she was, she'd never have to know her brother had ever entertained such a betrayal.

A short, strangled cry had him whipping his head back down, pulled from his haze of reflection. He searched around for the source, but darkness made the task difficult. Then he heard it again, swallowed by the rush of the stream, and he slowly followed it down the small hill to the water.

He found her stretched out on the bank, one hand above her head, her feet pointed at the toes.

"Arwenna?" Lorcan squinted at the darkness as he stepped sideways on his approach. He moved his sword hand to the hilt, his overactive imagination taking him down another path, but when she raised her head, he sighed in relief. It quickly turned to confusion. "What are you doing out here? Are you all right?"

She pulled her limbs back in and coiled her arms around herself before he reached her. Her pale face was angled away, but in the tickle of moonlight dotting the forest opening, he saw tears staining her cheeks.

Arwenna drew her self-protection tighter. "What are *you* doing here?"

"Me?" Lorcan scratched his head with a laugh. "Don't all men enjoy a midnight forest frolic?"

Arwenna turned toward him, her jaw parted in shock. "Frolic?"

"You know...playing...I don't know a better word for it."

"Playing," she said. The distrust in her eyes faded. "Frolic means something else where I come from."

60

Lorcan's eyes widened in embarrassment. "Oh! Oh, no, Arwenna, that's not what I meant at all. Not that, you know, there's anything *wrong* with you—" He slammed his mouth shut and shook his head. "Ignore *everything* I just said. Please. For both our sakes."

Arwenna's cheeks rose, forming little red apples. "I forgot how you speak the things other people only think."

Lorcan shifted his gaze to the ground and kicked at some leaves. "I'm sure someone, somewhere, must think it's charming."

"Edriss does."

Lorcan's heart flipped in his chest.

"Where I come from, no one speaks their mind. If they did…" Arwenna's mirth faded. "I suspect things could be very different. Then again, maybe not."

Lorcan came closer, stopping several feet from her along the bank. He descended to a crouch. "I came for some fresh air. Needed to clear my head after the trip. You?"

"Clear your head? Why?"

"Are you asking from curiosity or an attempt to divert me from helping you?"

"Helping me?" Arwenna's chin tucked in. "And just what help do you suppose I need?"

He held out his hands. "That's what I'm trying to find out."

"Not all women are looking for men to come save them, you know." Arwenna diverted her violet eyes back toward the stream. "Some women prefer to save themselves."

"I knew it!" Lorcan slapped his knees. "I knew Evra had nothing to do with Rhosyn's escape. Making up all that nonsense about climbing a mountain, taking a dagger to the gut… The filthy liar."

Arwenna struggled against a smile. "You have an answer for everything, don't you?"

"If not, you can be sure I'll make one up."

"And how would one know, when your truths are so colorful?"

Lorcan grinned. "It's all part of the fun."

"Fun." Arwenna's mouth twisted in a grimace. She looked off to the side, and he sensed a lie coming. "I came out for the same reason as you."

"Ah, so you were also reflecting on the impending doom facing the Reach?" He said it so fast, he had no time to decide whether such a revelation was prudent.

Her brows furrowed, and she again looked away. "And what would be the source of this doom?"

He shouldn't speak so openly with anyone but Edriss. But Evra had asked Lorcan to check in on his sister-in-law, and he had no reason to believe she was untrustworthy. "Just a sense."

Arwenna nodded but didn't look surprised at all. "You find your meaning in challenges," she said with a flippant shrug.

The crease between Lorcan's eyes deepened. He read the underlying implication. If Edriss were there, she'd laugh and point out he was doing it again. *You sense vulnerability, and it's like quicksand. You can't resist the opportunity to solve someone's problem, whether they want your help or not.* "You say that like it's a character flaw."

Arwenna folded her hands in her lap and dropped her gaze there. "You'll figure it out. You're clever. Clever people never struggle for long."

"You think you're not clever?"

"Forget I said—"

"I may not know much about what your life was like before you came here, but I know enough to know a less clever woman would not be sitting here having this conversation with me."

Arwenna laughed in scorn. "Because I'd be dead against the mountain, right?"

"That...or you'd still be there. Bearing children for your own kin. Living under their restrictive, choking—"

"You don't know what you're talking about." Venom streamed through the center of her words.

He recoiled in surprise at her ardent defense of a world that had used her, tortured her, and ordered her death.

"I'm so tired of men thinking they understand the world I come from when they don't. They really have no idea."

He thought of the way Cesarina had described her life as the king's daughter: cloying, repressive, unbearable. She'd disliked Lorcan's easy handling of serious matters, and so he'd simply listened and acknowledged her words.

Perhaps that was all Arwenna wanted too. "You're right. I'm sorry."

Arwenna's eyes narrowed, her mouth twisting. "Do you always give in so easily?"

"Pardon?"

"Nothing." Arwenna's dark hair shimmered when her head shook. "Nothing. Am I understanding right that you'll be staying in the Rush for a while?"

Lorcan puffed his cheeks with a whistling outbreath. "For a spell, yeah."

"Edriss will be happy." She grinned to the side. "And so should you be, if you weren't so determined toward martyrdom."

His chest tightened. "It's far more complicated than that."

"Is it? Seems rather simple to me. You adore her. She adores you. You know each other best in the world. Your trust in one another is implicit, unshakable. What is happiness, if not what I've just described?"

Lorcan swallowed a hard, dry lump. "Edriss is…She's like a sister to me."

"Do all men of the realm look upon their *sisters* the way you look at Edriss? Or is it strictly a Ravenwood tradition?"

He felt himself growing redder. Sinking into the ground sounded better and better each moment.

"I suppose it doesn't matter. Evra intends to move fast with her betrothal to Finn."

The words left him lightheaded. Numbness spread from his face, settling in between his shoulders. "So it's true."

Arwenna wore a trapped look. She glanced away and said, "Why would your father give up his place on the council when he's in good health?"

"He has his reasons." Lorcan reached for his cloak and unpinned it. Before Arwenna could argue, he moved close and draped it around her.

"And they are?"

Lorcan didn't answer.

Arwenna lifted her shoulders. The movement was barely discernible with the way his cloak swallowed her slight frame. "You don't have to tell me."

"I'm not being vague for sport." Lorcan twisted his mouth to the side. "But it's really between my father and me."

Arwenna's eyes slowly widened. Her mouth parted slightly. "Is it that serious?"

"I never said…" He stopped talking before he said too much.

Her shoulders lifted in a sigh. "I've had enough air. Walk me back?"

Lorcan said a silent prayer that he hadn't made a mistake. "Of course."

Once Edriss was certain she was no longer being watched, she slipped out of her apartments, clothed in the disguise that had served its purpose unfailingly for the past year, and dashed for the stables.

FIVE
SWORD OF INDICTMENT

Evra hadn't said a word. The uncomfortable tension stringing together the men and women of his council knotted tighter with each passing minute of silence, the only sounds the clearing of throats and shuffling of dresses. The council room looked different at night, shrouded in darkness that wasn't helped by the dim illumination from the thin smattering of candles.

Lorcan's gaze darted around at all gathered, but it settled on the men huddled at the far end of the deep table, stewards Bristol and Derry.

Evra tented his hands under his chin and inhaled a deep sigh through his nose that drew everyone's attention to him. He spread his palms atop the wood as he exhaled, drawing it out. Sometimes he looked younger than his twenty-one years. Today, he could have been an old man.

Lorcan had no idea what he was building toward. He glanced at Edriss, who seemed equally uneasy.

"I know I've called you here on little notice, and so late in the evening. Some of you have delayed travel plans, and some

65

have only just returned, as I have," Evra said, spacing his words in a slow, even cadence. "But it has come to my understanding, Counselors of the Rush, that Roland Ashenhurst has been seen stalking our shadows here at the Halls. And that some of you are not surprised at what I've just said."

"Traitors, if so," Cressida Wakesell muttered. She'd replaced her father after he'd passed from the plague that had run rampant across the Westerlands. Half the deaths in the Westerlands had been from the sickness, the other half unjust burnings. Evra's peace with the Sepulchre—and the resulting return of magic to the Reach—eased both. "Anyone who would say nothing has no place at this table."

Edriss nodded approvingly as she fingered the delicate lace on her cuffs, a gentle contrast to the fire raging behind her eyes. With each passing year, she reminded Lorcan more and more of her formidable aunt, Alise. But Alise was cold and calculating, while Edriss was so bursting with compassion, the only way to contain it would be to snuff it out altogether.

"And what of it, if we have seen him, my lord?" Osman Derry's chin dimpled as he shrugged hard enough to rattle his chair. "Last I checked, his mother doesn't sit on this council."

Laugher followed, most of it polite. The dark twinkle in Edriss's eyes set Lorcan's nerves on edge.

But Evra remained as placid as a lake. "What I expect is for the men and women loyal to this Reach, especially those sitting in this room, adorning my table, to have the decency to let me know that a man banished for his disloyalty is walking our halls."

"I haven't seen him," Rafferty Tyndall said with a panicked, shifting gaze. "Derry, you're not seriously suggesting you *have*?"

"Don't have to answer a little squint like yourself."

Rafferty sneered. Like Cressida, he'd only recently stepped into his role, but he took the honor seriously. "Aye, but you do have to answer your lord."

Osman snickered, but Evra turned his sight on him, and his laughter cooled. "Yeah, all right, I've seen him. But I thought you knew, sir."

"You thought I knew? That a traitor whom I had banished from these halls indefinitely has casually returned?"

"Well, it's not as if he was hiding—"

"Wasn't he though?" Meira, the banished man's daughter, asked. She'd been the first of Evra's friends to be elevated to the council—and also the one given the most trouble for it. She was the only female Rider of the Rush, and the harassment following her hard-earned title was unsurprising, for those most vocal about it were the same ones burning women simply for speaking their minds. "If my father had been traipsing these halls as he pleased, most of this room wouldn't look so shocked. Interesting, Derry, that among us, only you and Bristol seem unruffled."

"Unnatural bitch," Osman hissed.

"Mind your tongue if you intend to keep it," Edriss retorted, at the same time Lorcan lunged forward and said, "Watch it."

Meira rolled her eyes. "Thank you, but I can handle Steward Derry with both eyes closed."

Thennwyr Blackfen, First Rider of the Rush, twitched. He was naturally protective of his Riders, particularly Meira, but also of Edriss. The reason was the worst-kept secret in the Westerlands: Thennwyr was her real father, a product of a love affair between him and Fyana, Edriss's late mother. Aeldred had known from the beginning and had punished Edriss through contempt and neglect, while Edriss and Thennwyr had met quietly and fostered a relationship. Ever since Evra had taken over as lord, though, Thennwyr had been away more, and it was beginning to seem intentional.

Evra leaned forward across the table, though he'd clearly heard. They all had. "I thought I heard you disrespecting Rider Ashenhurst. But that cannot be right, as I've already told you and others this is unacceptable. Furthermore, you and I have other business, don't we?" His eyes flashed, narrowing. "Would be a shame for it all to fall apart over something so unnecessary."

Lorcan looked around to see if anyone else knew what *other business* Evra meant, but other than Bristol, everyone looked confused.

The betrothal was still a secret then.

"Of course. Sir." Osman shifted, tweaking his nose, his eyes on the table. "But a man's own daughter should be the one he can count on, no matter what he's done."

"I'm loyal to this Reach, to Lord Blackwood, and to all those who embrace his bid for peace," Meira stated, head high. "My father was loyal to none of those things."

"Was? He's still alive, squint."

"And walking our halls like a cherished visitor, apparently," Alise quipped. Beside her, Enchanter Grimoult tapped his pointed fingernails against his glass in support.

"You know who's *not* walking our halls? Any man who crossed words with Alise Blackrook!" Osman declared.

Alise sat back with a prideful grin. Edriss twisted her mouth to the side to stifle a laugh.

Lorcan wanted to grin too, but those words, *other business,* were still piercing the back of his mind.

Evra held up both hands, silencing the squabbling. "I don't know what my father's council meetings were like, but there's been far too many insults slung around in mine over the past two years, and it stops now. We don't have to agree about everything, but we *will* preserve the respect and dignity of the council tradition."

"My lord, we'd hoped to discuss a tax increase—"

"And we will, Rafferty," Evra said. "But not tonight."

"All due respect sir, but we can hardly afford the upkeep of the roads, and our grain stores are nearly empty."

"The boy is right," Leonarde said. "Costs have risen, but our taxes have remained flat. We're digging into our own coffers to cover the difference."

"I understand. And we'll...*I'll* figure it out. In time," Evra said. The corner of his mouth lifted in a twitch of impatience.

Lorcan exchanged a tense look with Edriss. The tax matter was only one example of trouble in the Westerlands that Evra had struggled to handle. His reluctance to consider the needs of everyone, barons and citizens alike, had driven more and more supporters to the side of the Defenders, who used those inadequacies as fuel for their raging fires.

Evra sighed and continued. "Tonight, I need to know the ten people sitting before me would protect my back when standing behind it, not stab it. I've just returned from Jademarch, to what I wish I could say was a rare occurrence. But these burnings are cropping up in small villages all over the Reach. This would not happen without the sponsorship of someone in power." He sat straighter. "Any man who confesses here, today, their role in these transgressions, will be pardoned."

Stunned murmurs rippled across the table.

"I'm not finished. Pardoned, so long as they identify the others involved and the burnings cease." Evra chewed his lip thoughtfully. "Before any of you decide me weak for this move, understand this: We're on the brink of civil war. I would spare one man's life if it meant saving thousands more."

"Should line them all up for what they've done to our Reach's women," Cressida muttered with a sideways, conspiratorial glance at Edriss, before returning her glare to Leonarde Bristol.

Lorcan observed Edriss carefully but couldn't read her with all the cross talk and tension filling the room.

"And we will," Leonarde said, his chest puffing. "My lord, we will find every one of the men who have sullied our Reach and hold them to account."

Lorcan crossed his arms and watched Bristol. The man's choice in words had been specific, intentional.

"Thank you, Leonarde. We've had our differences, but…" Evra shook his head. "I've put aside the past, and I hope you all can too. Roland Ashenhurst has not. He is at the very top of the ranks of the Defenders of the Righteous Dawn, and his followers grow by the day. If any of you know anything, my offer stands. I will pardon anyone who helps me end this."

"And when they don't?" Lorcan asked. He hadn't intended to say much in his first council meeting, but he couldn't hold it in anymore. "When you discover Ashenhurst isn't acting alone and there are others…others in power who are behind this?"

Evra shot to his feet. "I'm choosing to lead with trust." He bounced his gaze across all ten, one by one. "Don't make me regret it."

Evra asked Edriss to remain behind as the council left. When Lorcan hovered nearby in a protective stance, Evra waved him in, indicating he could stay as well.

"I'm due at the baron's soon," Edriss said with a glance at Lorcan. "He'll be wanting his sleep tinctures." She snorted. "He'll assure me he finds them perfectly useless, but if I forget to bring them, I'll never hear the end of it."

"This won't take long," Evra said and gestured for them to sit.

Edriss did, but Lorcan remained standing. She wondered if he knew something she didn't.

"There's something I need to talk to you about."

"Good. I was hoping we would. Are you really, truly going to pardon those who would see you and your wife burn? Your child burn?" Edriss fought the crack in her voice.

"Edriss." Evra's voice was tinged with exhaustion. He dropped his hands onto the table and hung his head. "I didn't ask you to stay so we could argue."

"This is not a mere difference in opinion, brother—"

"Edriss!" Evra sighed. He pulled back and dragged both hands down his face. "I'm tired of hearing you accuse the same men, over and over, with no proof. That is not the way the world works."

"Respectfully, Edriss isn't wrong," Lorcan said. He was close at her side. She felt stronger and taller with him there, backing her claim. "You already know I share her suspicions—and have for some time."

Evra tilted his head upward and flicked out his hands. "Suspicions are all they are, Lorcan. Over a year now you've both been at my ear, but in that time neither of you has ever shown me anything but more *fear*. Are you not tired of it?"

"Of course I'm tired of it." Edriss's laugh was strained. She was tired of *this*...tired of the pointless repetition, of all of it. Evra had changed in the past few months, desperate for approval from his adversaries. He would never hear reason, and she'd accepted it, hard as it was. She'd found another way. A better way. Quarreling with him was a waste of precious energy. "I love you, and I love Rhosyn, and I would give my life for Alastrynia, but how can I ever protect you against what's coming if you yourself will not see it?"

Lorcan rested a hand on her shoulder, curling his fingers in with a gentle squeeze. A light shudder rippled through her, one riddled with so many confusing feelings, she didn't know which one was safe to feel.

Evra's eyes traveled to Lorcan's hand with a quick frown. "It's my job to protect *you*. And that's what I wanted to speak to you about."

Lorcan's grip on her tightened. "She has a protector."

The room went uncomfortably silent.

Evra cleared his throat before speaking. "And I thank you, Lor, for all you've done for her over the years. But she's no longer a child, and it's time for another man to take over."

"Another man to take *over*?" Edriss's head shifted forward. "As though the men in my life have ever offered me anything greater than disappointment?" She flicked her eyes upward in apology, but Lorcan would know she didn't mean him.

Evra blanched. "I know I haven't always been here for you—"

"We don't need to rehash it," she snapped. "But I'll thank you for not giving credit to those who are not deserving of it. I was largely ignored when you went away to university, Evra. Lord

Aeldred hated me. Astarian rarely had time for me. Have you already forgotten I nearly died because healers weren't allowed anywhere in the Westerlands? That the man everyone believed to be my father would have rather watched me *die* than make peace with magic? Alise and Grandmother did what they could, but…" She reached up and clasped a hand atop Lorcan's. "Only one person was always there, no matter what."

Evra folded his hands under his chin. "Can I speak with my sister alone?"

"No," Edriss stated. "*I* want him here."

She felt Lorcan stiffen behind her, torn between her wishes and Evra's authority, but Evra nodded with an exasperated sigh. "You know I've been entertaining betrothal offers for you."

The only person she wanted to marry was standing right behind her. But if Evra had Lorcan in mind, he wouldn't have asked him to leave. "Yes."

"I've narrowed it down," Evra said. He lowered his hands and lifted his shoulders with a deep breath. "It will be a man you grew up with. Played with."

"Can this not wait?" Lorcan's hand slipped away. He stuttered a disbelieving breath. "She's not ready."

"Most women are betrothed at sixteen. Wed by nineteen."

"Your sister is not *most* women, Evra." Lorcan stepped back, scoffing through his next words. "What man could ever be deserving of her? Could ever know her, accept her exactly as she is? Give her space to grow and not stifle the very things that make her so special?"

Edriss wanted to take his hand and wish them both away to another world.

Evra stood, understanding dawning on his face. "Have *you two* been…"

"No," Lorcan said. He stepped farther away, as though using distance to strengthen his rebuttal.

"We've spoken about this. You know why a betrothal between you two is imposs—"

72

"It's never been like that between your sister and me. You know that."

But Evra was looking at Edriss. He'd no doubt noted the tears stinging her eyes, the flush rising in her cheeks.

"For your sake, Lorcan James, I hope to the Guardians that's true. My father trusted you…I trust you. And if it comes out she's been compromised—"

"I'm sitting right here!" Edriss cried. She stood to move farther away from Lorcan. His words had wounded her more when said in front of Evra than they ever had when said in private. She didn't want either of them to see it. "Is this how you think of me? Like a pawn to be kept clean, unsullied?"

"No." Evra closed his eyes briefly. "*No*," he said again. "It's not, Edriss. But you have to understand my confusion. You knew this day was coming. You were always going to be married to someone, but I'm trying to find a man you'll be happy with. And the one I've decided on—"

"Do we not have more important matters to deal with in this Reach right now, Evra? Do we not have treason afoot, right here in the Rush?"

"Edriss, you need to stop—"

"I *saw* them." She thrust a hand toward Lorcan. "*We* saw them!"

"Talking." Evra crossed his arms. His nose flared in anger. "You saw them *talking*, which is not treason in this kingdom."

Edriss shook her head as the first of her tears fell. Her skin burned with shame…with heartbreak and frustration. "You never listen to me. You never have."

Lorcan cleared his throat. His voice broke. "Are you still… narrowing it down?"

"There've been plenty of suitors," Evra said with a short laugh. "Too many, in fact. Even the baron put his name into consideration."

"He what?" Edriss asked, perplexed. "Baron Lawrence? The man who can scarcely tolerate me?"

"Most of the men who throw their name into consideration know they've no chance, but they show their loyalty with their interest." Evra stretched his hands to his sides. He rolled his neck with a low groan. "I'm sorry, Edriss. I'm sorry I can never seem to get it right with you. But a wedding *is* happening. Soon." He started toward her, but she stepped back. He sighed. "One day, you'll feel differently. When you have children, you'll know sometimes you have to make choices they won't like until they're ready to see reason."

"I am *not* your child, Evrathedyn. I'm your sister. And only three years younger, so let's not pretend there's an ocean of time and wisdom between us. Not all of us could run from the real world and our responsibilities. Some of us grew up long before we should have." Edriss ground her teeth to keep from breaking down. "But I won't wed *anyone* until this rebellion is quashed, and the men responsible held to account. *Anyone,* Evra. I don't care who they are."

Evra looked to Lorcan for help, but he was silent. Edriss wondered what he was thinking, feeling.

Concern?

Pity?

Certainly not jealousy. *It's never been like that with your sister and me.*

Hasn't it though? Haven't we known all along how our hearts beat stronger together? How our worlds find color when we're together and mute to gray when we're apart?

She's like a sister to me.

Edriss bowed her head and forced her weaknesses down, for that was what her love for Lorcan was: weakness. Maybe he didn't love her. Maybe he did and wouldn't admit it. But the entire Reach hinged on her ability to stop the rot spreading across their lands, because Evra wasn't going to see that the men sitting at his table, eating his food and drinking his wines, couldn't be won over. If he ever did, it would be too late.

Her own heart meant nothing if the pulse of the Westerlands ceased to beat.

Evra glanced toward the windows and the settling dusk beyond. "We'll speak more tomorrow, once you've had time to let this conversation settle."

Edriss burst out laughing. "I won't magically forget the very real problems we're dealing with. I won't decide the matter of my marriage is somehow as or more important than people *dying*." She swiped the back of her sleeve across both of her eyes. "Nor should you ever want me to. I'm one of the few people who will speak true to their lord, who will say what others will not. Do you know who else silenced voices of wisdom, Evra?" She almost didn't say the word, but he needed to hear it. "*Father.*"

She didn't wait for his reaction. She didn't want to see it. It had been a low cut, an unfair comparison that she knew would wound him, but what did he expect? He was handling her like goods to be bartered, not a valued sister and counselor who had proven her contributions in more meaningful ways.

Lorcan caught her when she reached the hall. "Edriss. Wait. Please."

"Why?" She spun on him with a bitter laugh. "You said so little in my defense when it mattered. What could you possibly have to say now?"

He grabbed her arm and drew near, lowering his voice to a whisper. "You think I'd let him wed you off to anyone you didn't approve of? Didn't want? Really?"

Edriss wrenched her arm back. "What does it matter to you, anyway?"

"*What?*"

She dropped her hands to her sides with a heavy sigh. "Why do you even care, Lorcan?"

His expression crumpled. "How could you ask me that?"

Edriss rolled her eyes and turned away, running her tongue along her lips. She wished she could pretend she lived in a world where she was free. Free to live. Free to love.

"Edriss, what's going on?"

"Nothing," she lied, flashing an unconvincing smile. "I have to go."

Lorcan scoffed. "I'll escort you to Felgarden. You're not traveling alone at this hour."

"You're not my protector anymore. Didn't you hear Evra?"

"I will…" Lorcan's throat jumped. "I will *always* protect you. Always, Edriss. There's no one else in this world…You mean everything to me." He shook his head. "Your age has nothing to do with it."

"Do I? Mean everything to you?"

"Of course. Where is this *coming* from?"

Edriss crossed her arms over her chest and sighed. "Please just go. I need to be alone right now. I need to think, before that, too, is taken from me."

"Edriss—"

"*Please*, Lorry." *Before my heart breaks altogether, and I can't hide it anymore.*

He backed up in surrender, but the wounded confusion never left his eyes. "All right. I'll go. For now. But I'll be calling on you for breakfast tomorrow."

Edriss groaned. "I—"

"I wasn't asking." An intense, dark look passed over his eyes. "I meant what I said in there. There's nothing I wouldn't do for you. And there's nothing I won't do to keep Evra from making a careless mistake with you." He inhaled deeply and trapped it for a moment. "Good night, Hemlock."

"Good night," she whispered and left, headed not for Felgarden Rest but for the one place she still had the power to set things right.

Lorcan watched her walk away. He waited until her footsteps were no longer echoes. But before he could head the other direction, toward the visitor apartments, Evra stepped out and joined him. Together they looked down the empty hall in tense silence.

"I know you don't approve," Evra said slowly. "I know you think I'm rushing her into something she isn't ready for. But Finn, he'll be good to her. Good *for* her. And if I can make a match that helps the Westerlands too, then I see no downside in that."

"So...It is Finn then." The words burned in his chest.

Evra nodded. "Of all the choices I entertained for her, he was the best. And if it comes with an alliance to a man who thinks more like our enemies, then we all benefit."

"Why didn't you tell her tonight?" Lorcan's hands had turned to fists at some point. He unraveled them before they pushed his anger higher. "Why pretend you were still deliberating, that you hadn't already decided?"

Evra cocked his brows with a short laugh. "As you could see, she was in no mood for the conversation. You heard this from your father then?"

"Yes. Yes, he told me when we stopped for the night, and I think you're making a terrible—"

"Better you don't finish that thought, Lorcan."

Amid Evra's cool confidence as lord, it was easy to forget he'd once been so reluctant to lead the Westerlands that he'd tried to run away. He didn't have the heart for politics. That hadn't changed. But his resolve had hardened him, and for every ten good decisions Evrathedyn Blackwood made, there was a misguided one to throw it all back into chaos.

Lorcan braced himself for more of Evra's annoyance, unable to keep the words back. Edriss's hurt-filled charge, *You said so little in my defense when it mattered, what could you possibly have to say now*, was a sword of indictment, hanging over his head and heart. "Edriss is the most noble-born woman in the Westerlands now. Any man you wed her to could and likely will use her to usurp you and take your place. And yes, Evra, this includes Finnegan."

"It's as though you've forgotten he's our friend."

"*Friends* don't plot against friends. They don't conspire to—" Lorcan stopped when a couple of men passed. He waited for his gust of anger to subside. Evra seemed to be harnessing his own. "We were different people as children. Everyone is. But the man he's become is *not* right for Edriss. He does not belong at her side, doesn't *deserve* to be at her side. He doesn't even…even love her."

"He cares for her, and she's fond of him. It's better than most women of her station are allowed. Most marriages don't begin with love," Evra said through a plastered smile, nodding as more people passed.

Lorcan crossed his arms. "Yours did."

"I'm grateful for the gift of choosing Rhosyn. I would never choose differently." He pressed his mouth tight. "But you see what my choice has done to this Reach."

Lorcan couldn't help but laugh. "Marrying Rhosyn didn't tear this Reach apart. It brought it together, for the first time in almost three generations! Those responsible for this madness were perpetrators of chaos *long* before she came into the picture. Before you returned. They're using her as an accelerant for the fires they would have built no matter what. And now, we can see them for exactly who they are. And yes, it includes dear friends like Finn."

"When did you become so cynical?"

When I found your little sister sobbing by the river after you left, all those years ago. When I watched your father berate her, exclude her, and threaten to sell her to a house for midnight women. When I held her, night after night, until she no longer had a reason to cry. "You left the Rush because of men like your father," Lorcan said, careful to leave the emotion swelling in his chest safely stored. "You came back to keep men like him from ever holding power again." He shrugged and exhaled. "And maybe you're right, and Edriss and I are overreacting about the things we've seen. But if we're not, every day that passes is a day closer to our destruction. Can this truly not wait until a time of peace?"

Evra didn't respond right away. "If I find out you're lying to me about you and Edriss, there will be a trust broken between us beyond repair. If you're asking me to stall because you…you, yourself, are in love with her…"

Lorcan again felt Edriss's soft lips on his. The tiny little sigh she swallowed after the kiss had ended and her eyes had opened, full of hope for something he could never give her no matter how right it'd felt, how *perfect* it'd felt. "I won't deny we're close—closer than is probably appropriate for a young woman and a young man past their childhood." Lorcan glanced again down the hall. "But I love her far too much to do anything that would cause a scandal for her. More than anything in the world, I wish for her happiness. And that's the reason I will always stand up for her, even when no one else does."

Evra scowled from the side. "You don't think I stand for my own sister?"

"I think…" Lorcan paused. Evra didn't want that truth. Not yet. "I think few in your family have suffered the way Edriss has. And no one is more loyal to you. She deserves better than what life has given her. She deserves to be heard."

Evra wore an indecipherable look as he listened. Finally he nodded. "I'll give it some thought."

"That's all I ask," Lorcan said. He wondered if Evra heard the lie in it. The last thing he wanted to do was betray his oldest friend, but Evra was wrong about the trouble in the Westerlands, and he was wrong about the timing of Edriss's betrothal. He was *especially* wrong about his choice in groom.

The only thing powerful enough to test Lorcan's loyalty to Evra was his loyalty to Edriss.

Lorcan prayed he never had to make the choice.

SIX

OUR LITTLE SECRET

Lorcan watched the Halls of Longwood come to life in stunned disbelief.

Men and women sprinted both ways down the hall in haphazard dashes, smashing into each other, their cursing and screaming blending into more nonsensical chaos. Evra gaped at Lorcan with dawning horror, whose expression was a mirror of his lord's. Evra whipped around to face the Blackwood apartments, where his family would already be sleeping. His fears didn't need to be voiced.

Lorcan said, "Go."

Evra left without responding, and Lorcan went the opposite way, headed the direction everyone was running *from*. He unclipped his scabbard, in case he needed to quickly draw his sword, and pushed on faster, ignoring the fear bidding him to turn around and return to safety.

Screams echoed from the guest wing, some following those fleeing, some rooted at the source. It was impossible to focus on any of it, but he knew, he *knew* there must be a reasonable explanation for the pandemonium.

He caught bits and pieces of harried whispers as he passed, declarations of blood and death that killed his hopes of a misunderstanding. With every slam of his boots on stone, he conjured some new hypothesis, each one worse than the last.

Please, please let Edriss be far away from here.

Lorcan spotted a huddle of servants congregating outside a door he recognized. His heart beat faster as he neared, praying to the Guardians that whatever had happened, whatever horrors had unfolded, could be mended.

When they saw him, they dispersed, leaving the door untended. There was no one else, no guards nor help of any kind. Lorcan yelled at the women to call for aid, but they were already halfway down the hall, hopefully doing exactly that.

Lorcan held the air tight in his lungs and entered. He choked out the same breath when he saw the lifeless body of Renardy Tyndall lying in a growing pool of blood.

Hovered over him was Arwenna, shaking, both of her bloodied hands pressed to her face. In her hands, smashed against her mouth, was a crumpled piece of vellum.

Lorcan didn't waste time with questions. He gathered her in his arms, hustled her out of the room, and guided her into the empty one on the other side of the hall.

He closed the door behind them both and flattened himself against it with a failed attempt to catch his breath. "Arwenna, what…What *happened?*"

Arwenna's shoulders shook with her sobs. She gripped a nearby table, the vellum still wadded in her hand, gasping for breath.

"Arwenna." Lorcan approached, but she held up a hand to hold him back.

"You need to go," she said in breathy spurts. "You need to go now."

"Go?" Lorcan took a single step forward but stopped himself. "A man is dead, and you are clearly in shock."

Not just a man. A *friend*. Someone Lorcan had played with as a child and had respected as they grew into men. Rafferty and

Ridge would be devastated. The people of Wildwood Falls would be devastated.

But Lorcan couldn't allow any of it into his thoughts until everyone was safe.

Edriss.

"Arwenna, why was Renardy in your room?"

"I didn't do it!" she screamed, thrusting her free hand out at her side.

"I know, I know. I only want to understand—"

"We had dinner together," she said in a rush. "We...It was nice...It was...and then...I left for only a moment, and...Oh, Renardy. Gods help us."

"All right," he said, as calmly as he could manage. "All right. It's okay. We'll get help, and—"

"He's dead because of *me!*" she cried and shoved the table, knocking it on its side with a series of bouncing thuds. She stormed away.

"That can't be true," Lorcan said, his mind whirring in a thousand different directions. Nothing about what he'd walked into made sense to him, but Arwenna seemed to know more than she wanted to tell him.

"I said *go*, Lorcan! Before someone sees you with me, and thinks you had something to do with it."

"I was with Evrathedyn," he said distantly. He couldn't read the situation; he couldn't read *her*. Her fear was palpable, but there was more there, something she was guarding with her life.

Arwenna rocked against the mantle, her eyes closed. Her mouth moved in wordless conversation, her tears spilling down her cheeks and over her lips. "When you wouldn't tell me what you and your father were planning...Did it have to do with the men committing treason against the Westerlands?"

He nodded, still trying to catch up to all that had happened—and was still happening—right in front of him. "He hoped... hoped I'd have more luck where he'd failed. But Edriss and I have known for some time...We've tried to talk to him. But without physical proof, Evra won't hear any of it."

"Edriss." Arwenna swallowed. She chuckled to herself, a short, bitter sound. "If his own sister cannot get through to him, there's no hope for any of it, is there?"

"For what?" He took another step. He locked his mouth tight to internalize a sigh and then said, "Whatever it is, we can help you."

"Ah, yes, you can never resist the call to distress, can you? Is it the only thing that gets you excited?"

He'd never seen her cruelty before. "Let us help you, Arwenna. Edriss and I have been fighting this battle for over a year, and *we* can help you."

Arwenna moved toward him so fast, he stepped sideways. Her eyes narrowed, and he knew she'd read his fear, was disgusted with him for it. She thrust the vellum at his chest with a punch and went back to the hearth.

Lorcan watched her before smoothing out the note. The ink had run from mishandling, but the words were clear enough: *Next time it will be someone who really matters to you. Time is not on your side.*

"Time is not on your side," he muttered and held up the note. "Who sent this to you?"

Arwenna snorted. "Could be Bristol...Derry...or even Ashenhurst. I hear he's roaming the halls freely now."

He glanced back down at the note in befuddlement. "Was this note for you?"

"Who else would it be for?" she hissed. Her eyes rolled before she turned them back toward the fire. "Of course it's for me. They own me now."

"Own you..." He stifled the rest of his words, cognizant of her annoyance growing worse with each passing moment. She expected him to put the puzzle together on his own, but how could he when she was keeping many of the pieces to herself?

Understanding slowly dawned. He shoved the note in his pocket. "They want something from you. They've made threats against your sister, haven't they?"

Arwenna nodded, still looking away.

"What have they asked of you?"

She half turned, regarding him over her shoulder. Her glossy violet eyes blinked and then closed. "They..." For a moment, it seemed she wouldn't finish, but then she did. "They want to know what Evra's allies are up to."

"Evra's allies? How would you..."

She spun all the way around and sucked in her bottom lip. "You. They want me to get close to you and persuade you to tell me what you know." There was more she wanted to say but wouldn't. He saw it in the way her mouth didn't quite close at the end, as though waging a battle.

Lorcan crossed his arms and paced away. His head was splitting. Everything else ached like he'd just swum the length of the River Rush. Beyond, the sounds of boots finally filled the halls, people flocking to the scene of the crime. "What do they think my father is up to?"

"How should I know?"

"But there *is* no plan beyond exposing the Defenders and their cohorts."

Arwenna scoffed. "So my sister and her family will die for nothing."

Lorcan shook his head. "No one is dying, Arwenna. Just give me a moment...a moment to think."

"What exactly are you going to do about it, Lorcan? Obviously, you're not going to tell me about any grand schemes the loyalists have cooking."

His thoughts pulled him away from the room. They drifted back to the state he'd found her in at the creek, the sudden sense it made. There was nothing he could give her that would appease the Defenders. Nothing that would fix this for her.

"They sent you a message," he said. "They aren't seeing you taking them seriously, and they want you to know they are."

"Oh, you think so?" she asked with enough sarcasm that it felt like she'd gashed him with a sword.

"They don't think you're taking them seriously," he said again. "So we just need to come up with a way to change the perception."

"And?"

"And…" Lorcan's mind was at last working for him, rather than against. "We just have to make something up. Send them on a diversion of sorts."

Arwenna lifted one side of her mouth in a confused frown.

"I don't know *what*, exactly. Not yet. But I will. I'll…I'll think of something."

"And when they disprove it? What then?" Arwenna laughed. "They'll know."

She was right.

"Then I just need…I need to think. I need more time to come up with a better idea."

Arwenna glanced away. She tapped the mantle, grimaced, and looked back at him. "You and I both know there's nothing between us."

Lorcan laughed at her blunt assessment. "All right."

"But *they* don't know that, do they?" Arwenna's eyes darted to the side in thought, but there was something odd about the way she did it…as though the motion had been rehearsed. "No, they thought I'd have no trouble seducing you."

Lorcan choked on another laugh. "You're beautiful, Arwenna, but we're just friends."

"What if we weren't?"

"Pardon?"

"What if…" The thoughtful look returned to Arwenna's face. "What if we were seen together more? Enough to lead others to think we fancied one another. That we were…I don't know… courting?"

Lorcan hadn't been expecting that and didn't know the right response for what she was suggesting. "You want us to pretend we like each other?"

"Will it be so hard to pretend? We're friends, as you said."

"You can't feign this sort of thing," Lorcan said weakly. "They'll know."

"Why? Because you're in love with Edriss?" Arwenna seemed to stifle a wry smile.

Lorcan glanced toward the door and the melee beyond. "I want to help you, but I don't think this is any better of an idea than mine." He squinted the exhaustion from his eyes. "Even if they thought we were a couple, what would it gain?"

"Time," she said, so fast it was clear she'd had the answer ready. "Time, Lorcan. Time to find a better way to best them. If they see us together, they'll think I'm taking them seriously."

"And when you…" Lorcan's mind spun wildly out of control. Her suggestion was half-baked and mad, but he didn't have a better idea. "When you don't provide them with anything useful, what then?"

"I never said it would work forever, Lorcan." She seemed angry with him. "Just long enough."

"Can we not just spend time together as friends?"

"We could," she replied. Her tears had dried up, and she had become all business. "But would it not be more convincing if they thought I'd managed to seduce you? Weakened you?"

"I…" He didn't know what to say. He began to understand she'd been planning these words, that the idea wasn't spontaneous.

"I'm not betrothed to anyone, and neither are you. We won't be breaking any vows or rules or laws. It would just be…our little secret, until we take them down."

Lorcan turned away. He searched for a chair, a table…something to hold onto, but there wasn't anything close enough. "And when they come looking for information you don't have?"

"We make things up. We keep our false conspiracies close enough to the truth to seem credible." Arwenna laughed, with a

87

quick shrug. "As you suggested. But if we're smart enough, we'll find a better way before they're wise to our plot."

Lorcan shook his head. "I'm not as creative as Edriss. She has a far more useful imagination than me and will come up with some kind of misdirection to buy us time." He couldn't fathom trying to explain any of this to her. "I don't think she'll *love* this plan, but she adores you and will want to help. She'll have ideas I could never dream—"

"No." Arwenna left the hearth and came toward him. "No. No, Lorcan. Edriss can't be involved in this. She can't know."

"Can't know?" Lorcan recoiled. "She was the one who first came to me when she learned what they were up to. She'll *want* to help. She wouldn't have it any other way. *I* wouldn't have it any other way." He sighed. "And Edriss and I don't have secrets, Arwenna."

"Lorcan, she *cannot* know. You will *not* tell her!"

"Do I—"

"*She cannot know!*" Arwenna cupped her cheeks and tugged. "If you tell her, Rhosyn and Evra and Alastrynia will be as good as dead. *None of them can know.*"

Lorcan was more confused than ever. "Why would telling Edriss put them in more danger?"

"If my explaining this to you is the cost for helping me, then you can leave."

"But…" Lorcan pressed his mouth tight. What Arwenna was asking of him made no sense. Edriss was the smartest person he knew.

And how could he *not* tell the one person he told everything? She'd never forgive him. She'd think—

"If you tell her…and *any* of them die…" Arwenna's face erupted in emotion. She sobbed into her hands. Lorcan went to her this time and pulled her into his arms, unsure of what else to do.

Whatever she needed, he had to do it.

Not just for Arwenna but for Evra and Rhosyn and Alastrynia.

For *Edriss,* who would not survive the loss of what remained of her family.

When it was over, he'd tell her everything. She'd know he was only trying to keep her loved ones safe—that none of it was real. She'd be angry, but she'd understand.

Maybe he was doomed to repeat his mistakes.

But there was no one else with the power to help Arwenna in her present predicament.

What happened with Cesarina could never happen again.

Arwenna pulled back and looked up at him. She slid her soft palm up the side of his face and wound it in his hair to pull him in for a kiss. He was too startled to do anything but freeze.

She dropped back onto her heels and wiped her mouth. "If we're going to pretend to be enamored with each other, we need people to believe it."

Lorcan chuckled to cover his discomfort. "I don't think we need to go so far to convince people. A bit of hand holding in the garden should do."

With a resigned sigh, Arwenna said, "We don't have to like it. Let's try again."

Edriss was almost to the stables when she was stopped by one of the last people she wanted to see.

Finnegan Derry grabbed her arm, but she was faster, ripping away from him with an affronted grunt. She hadn't meant to look so disgusted, but she didn't need to explain herself either. If anyone owed anyone explanations, it was Finnegan and the way he'd slid so easily into a life of treachery.

Until Lorcan had told her about what had happened in Jademarch, she'd still hoped Finnegan might have distanced himself from his father's evildoing. Watching the hurt creep onto his face, as he looked down at his hand and back at her, reminded her of the sweet boy who had gone with her into the Hidden Cave at high tide so they could watch the sunset. Finn had always been willing to do what Lorcan was afraid to. That recklessness no doubt served him even better in his current dealings.

"You can't leave right now, Edriss," he said, flexing his gloved hand before clasping it with the other. His eyes darted around before fixing on the keep. Mouth parted, he started to say something else but stopped short.

"Lady Edriss," she stated, correcting him with a glare. She swept her eyes over him in judgment. She'd once believed him handsome, but he was utterly repellant now that she saw him for who he truly was. "And you have no authority over me."

Finnegan seemed more confused than shocked as he shifted from one foot to the other, clearly struggling for words. He reached up to run a hand through his white-blond hair and then grunted. "*Lady* Edriss, I don't know what I've done to offend you—"

She scrunched her nose and scoffed. "Don't you?"

"But you really can't leave right now. There's been—"

"When I say you have no authority over me, Finnegan Derry—"

"Will you let me *finish?*" He hurled the words, and she stumbled back. "I didn't mean to raise my voice at you, but there's been an incident in the Halls, and I need to get you somewhere safe." He looked again at the Halls, and she followed his gaze this time and saw a tumult of blurred sconces, matched by indistinct yelling that seemed far more sinister in light of Finn's own panic, which seemed real.

Her eyes narrowed. She calculated her odds of getting past him and into the stables, but Nightshade wasn't yet saddled. "What kind of incident?"

Commotion in the distance drew their attention. Edriss stepped forward on the path until she had a clear view through the trees. The Rush Riders were swiftly riding *back* to the Halls of Longwood. She'd watched her father leave, knowing it would be months before she saw him again.

So why was he back?

"The Riders have returned," Finn said with a breathy sigh. "What the Guardians is going *on*?"

"If there's trouble at the halls, I've no doubt you're fully aware," Edriss stated and brushed past him quickly, before he could see the worry in her eyes. Something *had* happened—bad enough to bring the force of the Riders back to the Halls, and to stir the keep into a frenzy.

"What does that mean?" Finnegan asked distantly. His focus was trained almost solely on the disorder.

Edriss didn't stay to answer. She darted away from him and back down the path, toward the north entrance, which was always less busy. He called to her but couldn't match her pace, and she used the disadvantage to gain a greater lead. She dipped under the arches of a servants' entrance on the first level before he could see where she'd gone.

She hustled down the dark, windowless hall. The air was thinner and the stone walls closer than they were on the other floors, but she only saw one other person before she made it to a stairwell at the end of the passage.

Edriss stopped to catch her breath. Heavy bootfalls echoed in the distance, ahead and behind. She cursed and continued, slipping onto the balls of her feet to keep Finnegan from hearing which direction she took.

"Edriss, wait!"

"Guardians deliver us," Edriss muttered and tiptoed up the stairwell until she rounded the first corner, where she waited for him to pass.

"Edriss, I don't know what you meant back there, about me, but…I'm genuinely worried about you." He came to a stop at the base of the stairwell. She held her breath tight and squeezed her eyes shut in annoyance. "I hate to even say this, but what's happening could involve your family, and I won't let you go on alone until we confirm the situation is under control."

"As if you don't know." Edriss clapped both hands over her mouth as soon as she realized what she'd done.

91

Finnegan started up the steps, but he moved slowly. "I don't know why you're upset with me or what you think I've done or—" He stopped, and she saw his palm flatten on the stone wall. His grandfather's ruby ring caught the dim light of the sconce. "Is this still about Jademarch? Lorcan tell you I murdered that bastard tender?"

Edriss lifted one foot and backed up another step. She gently tapped her boots to find the solid footing to climb another. She wasn't sure what she wanted less, to face whatever horrors were transpiring upstairs or to discuss Finnegan's treason with him. "Hoping to convince me you didn't wait for my brother and Lorcan to leave so you could stab a defenseless man?"

"Defenseless…" Finnegan scoffed. "That man murdered hundreds of women, Edriss."

Another step. "Surprised you didn't pin a medal on him then."

"Why would I…" His leather boots scuffed the stone steps. "Why are you saying these things?"

"Why are you pretending to be my brother's friend?"

"Pretending?" He started moving again. "I would lay down my life for Lord Blackwood. And for you."

Edriss's acerbic laughter echoed off the stones. She hastened up more steps but missed one. She spun toward the wall to save herself from falling. "I suppose you would want to keep me safe, wouldn't you? If your father has half the wit he should, he's no doubt positioning you as a potential groom for me. What a prize I must seem." She turned to see how close the next level was. The door to the main hall was just ahead. "But know this, Finnegan. If so much as a hair is out of place on my brother, his wife, or their child, you'll have more to fear from me than a hundred men in chains."

Then she bolted, and he was fast behind her, right on her heels as she tugged on the heavy door and stumbled into the main floor hall, entering at the end of the guest wing. Immediately she was assaulted by the bewildering sight of dozens of men rushing about, their efforts focused on what seemed to be Arwenna's room.

"No," she whispered and pushed through, making her own opening in the crowd. Finnegan still called for her, from close behind, but his betrayal was far from her mind as she neared her friend's room, her heart thumping so hard, she had to stop and breathe before continuing.

But there was no way into Arwenna's room. A throng of men was gathered outside, filtering in and out with solemn purpose. Even stretching atop her toes couldn't get her a view of anything except...

Blood.

Edriss inhaled a gasp and staggered straight into Finnegan. "What is it? What did you see?"

Edriss flung him off and ran the opposite direction, slipping into the room across the hall to gather herself.

A fresh seam of pain hit her before she'd fully entered. Wrapped in an embrace at the hearth were Lorcan and Arwenna, engaged in a kiss so unexpected, she felt the only appropriate thing to do was apologize for intruding.

Finnegan entered right behind her and abruptly stopped. "Oh," he said, sounding almost embarrassed.

Lorcan broke the kiss and moved away from Arwenna. His eyes dilated in horror when they met Edriss's, his cheeks reddening through a slow, dazed shake of his head. "Hemlock."

Arwenna looked almost pleased, like she'd secured a victory in a battle Edriss didn't know she'd needed to prepare for.

Edriss shook her head in strong, bold passes. Her throat felt like she'd stuffed a blanket inside it, and her heart felt ten times worse, bloated and breaking from the force of a love over a decade in the making.

It exploded like a million tiny stars in a single instant.

Lorcan paled. He couldn't seem to find his voice.

"I was so worried about you when I saw the blood," Edriss said to Arwenna. She heard her own voice as though in a daze, like she were watching herself fall apart but was not present for it. "I thought something had happened to you, and..." She looked back at Lorcan, then returned her attention to Arwenna. "But you're fine, aren't you? You both are. Wouldn't even know something terrible had happened right across the hall, would you?"

"Edriss," Lorcan pleaded, a word coated in everything he didn't say—and wouldn't. He started after Edriss, but she shook her head harder and mouthed the word *don't.*

Finnegan's hands fell upon her shoulders. She wanted to shrug him off, but he steadied her, kept her tethered to the earth before she floated away and detonated with her heart.

"Let's go," he said, guiding her back toward the door.

"Edriss," Lorcan called. He sounded weak and pitiful, and in that moment, she hated him.

Though certain she'd regret it later, she let Finnegan take control. She accepted the hand he offered and forced herself to meet Lorcan's eyes one last time. What she saw confounded her all the more.

Jealousy.

But Lorcan didn't want her.

He never had.

She'd just been too stubborn—too blindly in love—to listen.

It no longer mattered. *Nothing* mattered but protecting her family, and she couldn't do that when half of her longed for something that had never been hers.

After seeing the secret he'd kept from her, she was ever more certain he could never learn hers.

It belonged to someone she trusted, but now, she could trust no one except herself.

"I'm going to find my family," she said. She glanced up at Finnegan. "Come with me or don't, but I intend to roll up my sleeves and help however I can."

"I'm coming with—"

"No, Lorry." Edriss said the rest as she left. "Not this time."

Our Little Secret

DANGEROUSLY, WICKEDLY ALIVE

SEVEN
NO MERE GIRL

Edriss drew the dense, musty curtains as wide as the space allowed. She sputtered a cough and backed away, burying her face in her sleeve to escape the billowing dust catching the noonday sun in swirls.

One look down the long row of monstrous windows reminded her she was only getting started.

She could already hear Baron Lawrence's booming objections. He had one for every occasion. The glum widower was more than content to live the rest of his days in darkness, succumbing to a heart so broken, people whispered that only guilt could cause such a decline in a man.

But Edriss wasn't spending several days each week at Felgarden Rest to watch the once-formidable soldier mope himself to death. It had been Aunt Alise's idea for Edriss to come help the fractured man, who had been Evra's top financial patron when he'd started his campaign of peace. The baron continued to give gold at the same pace, but his enthusiasm for anything but seclusion had died with his wife.

If he could ever return to his former self, he could do more than heal his heart.

He could help her excise the unchecked rot encroaching upon every inch of her homeland.

Edriss paused and uncorked the wine carafe, checking to see who was watching before taking an unladylike swig straight from it. With a satisfied groan, she replaced the cork and regarded the work remaining with mixed emotions.

He'd close the curtains again when she left, just as he'd closed the ones on the second floor, and the third, last week. His enjoyment in life seemed to be watching her run herself ragged to help restore his good humor, only to undo it all.

Maxim Lawrence was even more stubborn than she was.

I very much doubt that, she heard Lorcan saying in her head, and she missed him all over again. She still dreamed of his pliant lips crushed to hers on her sixteenth birthday...the way he'd wound his hand through her hair at the base of her skull. The deep flush in his cheeks when he'd pulled back, mumbling an apology he hadn't meant and she hadn't wanted.

He'd called on her every day since the terrible night they'd found Renardy Tyndall murdered in Arwenna's apartments. His failed attempts were always chased by a bittersweet ache in her chest, not unlike the sickness she sometimes felt when recalling the loved ones she'd lost in the plague years.

"What did I tell you the last time you were here? And the time before?"

Edriss turned to see Maxim, slouched sideways against the doorframe. His dark hair was predictably mussed, matching his well-tailored-but-not-well-kept suit. He looked more like a man pushing sixty than thirty.

"You do so love the darkness," she quipped and snapped open the next set of curtains.

"You should go."

Edriss crossed her arms. "And yet, unlike those actually *paid* to come help you be less miserable, I will not."

Maxim ground his jaw. His neglected beard shifted when he swished his mouth, clearly searching for a better way to kick her out. "You're wearing a dress."

Edriss gaped down at herself in mock horror. "So I am!"

"You prefer pants." His words came out in a grumble.

"Well, you prefer darkness and squalor, but we don't always get what we want, do we?" She eyed the decanter of wine with guilt and reached for a glass. "Wine?"

"Offering me a glass when you don't bother with one yourself?" Maxim shook his head and glanced toward the bright windows with a disapproving furrow in his brows. "No reason for you to stay. I'll be retiring to my office until nightfall."

"Doing what, exactly?"

Maxim's dark facade cracked in shock.

"Not working," she answered for him. She took a beat to decide whether to continue, but maybe a kick of shame was what he needed. The baron had once been a powerful force for good against the tide of evil. He wasn't just responsible for funding a good portion of Evra's cleanup efforts. He'd also been behind the rebuilding of the Westerland Guard. If he could find even a glimmer of his vigor again, she might finally have someone to partner with in taking the Defenders down. "You haven't done *that* in over a year. Praise the Guardians you were born wealthy, Baron."

"If you're trying to—"

"Get you worked up about something other than your misery?" Edriss unwound her arms and held them out with a sheepish grin. "I shan't deny it."

"I've never been more relieved to not have children, for this is what happens when they are raised without a mother," he muttered to himself.

"Or in my case, without either parent," Edriss said with a flippant shrug she hoped hid the precise nature of the wound. Her mother had died bringing her into the world. Her real father, Thennwyr Blackfen, had been there for practical needs she couldn't have had satisfied anywhere else. Teaching her archery and self-defense. It was from him, the First Rider of the Rush, that she'd learned to cultivate her bond with Nightshade to become more than just a passenger.

But in the past few years, he'd distanced himself from her, and she was too hurt to ask why.

Lorcan filled the other holes that had been formed growing up motherless and, ultimately, fatherless.

Or had.

"You're an odd girl," Lawrence said with a glower.

"I don't believe that's the slur you intend it to be." Edriss pinched her shoulders back. "I rather like being different. And if I were a man, no one would say a word about it."

"When is your brother going to wed you off?" He snorted. "Woe betide whoever assumes that burden."

"Is that why you put your own name into consideration?"

"Along with every other single man of means in the Reach. Mere formality, I assure you."

Edriss stifled a recoil. "I believe he's already chosen some-one. He hasn't told me who yet, but he will. Soon." Some of her mischief faded. Evra had definitely already decided. She felt it every time he cast his eyes away from hers when he used to meet them. How bad was it that he'd taken to avoiding her rather than telling her?

She'd meant what she'd said to him. She wouldn't even enter-tain a wedding, with anyone, until the Defenders were squashed. And if he forced her anyway…Well, she'd been making contra-ceptive teas for women since she was a girl. Perhaps it was time to make some for herself.

"Not soon enough." Maxim groaned. He scratched his beard. His blue eyes regarded her with an equal mix of curiosity and hostility. "Stay. Go. It's nothing to me." He pointed at the win-dows. "But leave *those* alone. You think you're helping, but you're making it worse. You know who else loved the sunlight, Lady Edriss? My wife."

With that, he stomped back the way he'd come, taking Edriss's enthusiasm with him.

An hour later, Edriss crept up two flights of dusty stairs and headed for the baron's office. She'd only seen it once, so it was hard to navigate in the baron's preference for darkness, but all she had to do was follow the pattern of footsteps in the carpet, which hadn't been beaten in years, to find it again.

Despite the teasing she'd given him, she approached the room expecting to find him engrossed in something important. But when she found the door and stepped sideways to quietly announce herself, the only thing she saw was a tired man, aged beyond his years, slumped in his chair. He stared her way, but his eyes were so glossed over, she wondered if he was even awake.

She lightly cleared her throat, and the baron jumped. In his surprise he knocked over a pot of ink, but Edriss leaped forward and caught it before it could spray its contents all over the beautiful wooden boards.

"Good thing you corked this," she said, stretching her arm to place it back on his desk. She held back and waited for him to gather himself.

"You shouldn't be up here." Lawrence dusted his hands down his half-open vest with a sour look. He blinked hard through narrowing eyes. "What *are* you doing here?"

"So." Edriss folded her hands behind her and began, following the path she'd rehearsed in her head for over an hour. "Fair to say you don't want me here. Yes?"

The baron gave her a quizzical stare, almost humorous. "You didn't come all the way up here to state the obvious, I should hope."

"It's called conversation, Baron. You don't just jump right into the point."

"Would you mind?"

Edriss grimaced as she rifled through her thoughts, mind-stepping past the small talk she'd hoped to engage him in to soften him. Standing before the miserable man, she had no idea why she had thought any of it would work. "I don't have a choice either. My aunt asked me to come here, to help an old friend. She's fond of you, and I don't have to tell you how rare that is."

The baron smirked. His eyes danced off to the side, the barest hint of reminiscing caught in their dark twinkle.

"But..." Edriss tensed. She was losing her nerve. The idea had sounded so much better in her head. What if he sent word to Alise, repeating everything she said? Or worse, to Evra?

"But?" Lawrence rolled his hand in the air with an impatient twitch.

She hung her head but snapped it right back up. He was grieving, but he wasn't a fool. He had once been a fine general, reputed to be one of the best in the Westerlands. Shrewd and relentless, but fair. If she wanted his help, she had to ask for it with her shoulders back and her eyes on his. "I have somewhere I'm needed more. But it's becoming harder and harder for me to get there after Renardy's murder and the increase in security."

"If you're asking—"

"I'm not asking you for anything, Baron. I'm proposing an exchange. Of desires, if you will."

The baron's brows fused together.

Say it. Speak true, or he will eat you alive, mourning or no. "I've been secretly traveling to Rivermarch in disguise, to aid the wounded. While I'm there, I've been...listening. Trying to draw out information about the ones responsible...the Defenders."

Lawrence launched forward, slamming both of his hands onto the unused desk. "Are you a fool, girl?"

"I've been called many things, Baron, but fool is not—"

He shot to his feet so fast, she stumbled backward. "Lady Edriss, you are playing a man's game with the tools of a child. How do you think it will end for you when you're recognized?"

"I wear my disguise every time."

"Look at you!" He thrust his arm at her. "No disguise could hide those eyes. Anyone who has ever seen you before would know." He closed his eyes and lowered his arm. "Edriss. Don't be daft. What you're doing is *reckless*. You're going to get yourself killed, and for nothing."

Edriss laughed. "You call what I'm doing the business of men, but what man dares do what I'm doing? What man is doing *anything* about these monsters? My own brother, the lord of this land, refuses to acknowledge there's an issue at all!" She shook her head with a steep inhale. "No, Baron. It's the women who have always done what is needed to be done in the world I live in. Alise wants me here. You do not. The compromise is simple enough, as I see it."

His upper lip lifted at the corner. "You want me to lie for you."

"I want you, if asked, to not deny I was here. And in return, I won't burden you with my presence a moment longer."

Baron Lawrence shook his head at the ground, mulling her request with a sharp frown. "The Defenders are too big to be defeated by a mere girl."

"I'm no mere girl," Edriss said with a quick, hard smile. "And the Defenders wouldn't be so damned big if men with power were doing anything about it."

"What does your brother say?"

Edriss rolled her eyes toward the ceiling. "He refuses to see the traitors sitting right at his table with him. He thinks he can *change* them." Her tone was mocking. "He's too trusting. Too naïve. His world was isolated, insular...*easy* at university, and he thinks he can reason his way out of hatred. The rest of us...The ones who stayed..."

"We know better," Lawrence mumbled. He lifted his palms off the table and lowered them in jittery motions. "He'd murder me himself if something happened to his foolish sister."

"*Nothing* is going to happen," Edriss stated. She chanced a step closer. "I've been successfully subtle so far. No reason it won't continue to work." She laughed under her breath. "No one looks at a stable boy expecting to see a lady. As long as I keep on as I have been, they'll keep seeing what they should."

"And? Have you found anything?" The way he said it suggested he already knew the answer.

"If I had, this whole mess would already be over, Baron."

Lawrence stood and pulled his hands down his face, tugging his features. The groan that followed felt long in the making, like a bear awaking from winter slumber. "And you won't keep fussing with my windows and being a general annoyance?"

"Promise." Edriss crossed her arms over her heart. "I'll even close your curtains before I leave."

"If you get yourself killed, girl…"

Edriss brightened. She curled her toes to mask her glee. "I won't."

He crossed his arms and turned away, toward the window. "Go on then."

An hour later, after she'd closed every curtain she'd reopened, Edriss stepped onto the stones of the baron's courtyard and into the cool evening. Multi-hued, fallen leaves swirled through a breeze that had taken on an untenably brisk chill. The last of springtide had faded to midwinter's call, and the first storm was already brewing in the mountains. Baron Lawrence's manor sat atop a hill, and from there she could spot all but two of the peaks of the Seven Sisters of the West looming in the distance, the terrestrial guardians of the Westerlands.

"It's going to rain," Finnegan said.

Edriss jumped at the intrusion. "What are you doing here?" she asked on the end of an exhausted exhale. She already knew the answer. He'd been following her ever since that terrible night. He had an answer for every argument she made to get rid of him. *Whoever killed Renardy is still out there. Someone wanted to send a message. You're not safe. Your family isn't safe. I care about you. You're my friend.*

And on and on, each reason more pitiful and disingenuous than the last.

"Lord Blackwood has asked for your presence at supper tonight in his private chambers."

"My brother doesn't need to send his lackey to ask me to dine with him," Edriss said and flicked her hand at the air as if he'd offended her. He *had*, by his very presence, but it burned her up more that Finnegan Derry was the one delivering messages to her from Evra. It wasn't like her brother to rub seasoning in an already-festering wound.

"With Lady Rhosyn and Miss Arwenna," Finnegan replied. He rolled his shoulders back and stood taller, as though trying on different stances. A comically serious look brewed in his eyes. She might laugh at how ridiculous he looked if she didn't think he'd take it as encouragement. "Lord Blackwood has made this request."

"I can sup with my brother whenever I wish." She removed her dusty apron and balled it in her hands. "And I can find my own way back." *After another more important stop.*

Finnegan started after her, but she could read his hesitation without looking back. "I've been asked to personally escort you back to the Halls. Before you take my head off and turn it into a trophy—"

"Don't give me ideas!" Edriss said and then she did laugh, because the thought of dipping Finnegan's head in gold and planting it on her mantle was unexpectedly amusing.

Finnegan grumbled behind her. "If it had been anyone other than Lord Blackwood, I would defer to you instead. My lady."

"My lady! How it must pain you to use titles you think my family is no longer deserving of."

"Why would I—"

Edriss nodded at the young groom, Sidney, approaching with her horse, saddled and ready. He glanced from Edriss to Finnegan with the panicked look of one expecting a firm upbraiding. But it wasn't the boy's fault Finnegan was overstepping. She smiled graciously, accepted Nightshade's reins, and mounted without waiting for her unwelcome shadow to right himself.

She heard clanking behind her, as he no doubt tried to settle atop his own saddle without stabbing his poor horse. Finnegan was tall, even for a Derry man. When they were children, the stable hands had to make special accommodations for him to ride. His father ended up purchasing him a horse from the family of a fallen Rush Rider, a beast several hands taller than the ones most nobles rode, but the horse had been old when they got him, and the one Finnegan was riding was not adequately tall enough.

Edriss hoped his feet dragged the ground and gave him blisters.

She grinned to herself and shifted to a gallop. He matched her pace but held enough space to save himself from more of the fire burning her tongue. She was full of it lately, her only defense in a time when she'd never been more alone. She couldn't turn to Lorcan anymore, even if she could swallow her pride and look past her heartache, for he spent his days with his new girlfriend. Her once-delightful friendship with Arwenna had unsurprisingly cooled, and though Aunt Alise would patiently listen to her lament about her broken heart, the price for it would be Edriss never mentioning the topic again.

Cressida Wakesell was still in the Rush for another few days, but Edriss didn't want to burden her old friend with her whining. Besides, Cress had enough to contend with, freshly orphaned and installed as the new stewardess of Whitewood.

Finnegan left her to her stewing thoughts until they reached the stables of the Halls. Once they'd dismounted and gathered their things, he made a dramatic show of clearing his throat.

"Choking on your treason, Finn?"

He threaded his hands behind himself and looked not toward her but past her. A wince traveled from the left to the right of his face in a series of awkward tics. "I'd hoped to adequately warn you about something."

"Warn me?" Edriss crossed her arms and reared back. "To what do I owe this unusual honor?"

"Edriss, I don't know what I've done to upset you, but what happened in Jademarch, you only have half that story. The half you have came from a man whose best interest involves making himself look as gallant as he can for you."

Edriss scoffed and shrugged. "Lorcan? He hardly cares what I think."

"He wouldn't want you to ever see him as anything other than the hero in every story."

Edriss gestured upward, toward the Halls of Longwood. Only half the garden levels were visible, the rest disappearing behind a dense blanket of fog that made it seem like the dark sky was swallowing the keep whole. "We talking about the same Lorcan? The one who can't even remember his duties as a junior steward for all the time he spends chasing a raven?"

"Is it easier for you to forget he's always been like that? Always finding the ones who need saving?" He scoffed. "They don't call him Lorcan the Lightbringer for nothing."

"You solved your own equation then." Edriss wrapped her cloak tight and stepped out of the stables. "I've never needed Lorcan James, or anyone else, to save me." She turned a sneer on him as she looked up. "And I certainly don't need *you* convincing yourself my life isn't complete without your false show of chivalry."

Finnegan sucked in through his teeth and kicked the ground. "Well, about that very thing, Edriss. You're not going to like what Evra has to say. Just remember, this isn't my fault. I had nothing to do with it." He glanced up at the sky. "If we don't go now, we'll be late."

He held his arm out to gesture for her to go ahead. With her heart racing in curious fear, she turned one last glare on him before marching ahead.

Lorcan focused on his latest kiss with Arwenna outside her apartments. He gave her the best he had, for a man who was only acting, chasing a sense she was perpetually disappointed in his performance. As soon as those watching turned the corner, she pulled back and wiped her mouth with a tight grin. Her gaze was on the floor, the wall…anywhere but on him.

"I believe that's enough for now." She entered her apartments without parting words, leaving him unable to decide what he was feeling.

Relief. That was what it was.

Lorcan quirked his mouth and stared at the door as it closed on him. He didn't know what she wanted. The whole thing had been her idea, but there were times he thought she was repulsed by him.

For the past week, he'd let her lead. Better for her to decide her comfort with their deception. They still hadn't come up with anything to tell Leonarde and the others, and Roland had been spotted returning to Longwood Rush the night before. Fear kept his mind from conjuring anything useful. He wasn't like Edriss, who did her best thinking under pressure.

He still didn't understand why Arwenna was so insistent on keeping it from her. Every day the deception continued—and he couldn't tell Edriss the truth—drove an even deeper wedge between him and the one person he'd sworn never to hurt.

She wanted nothing to do with him. Nothing he'd said or done had warmed the ice that had formed around her heart the night everything fell apart, because he wasn't allowed to say the words she needed to hear. He deserved her cold shoulders, her calculated barbs projecting her pain back onto him. Trying to put himself in her place by imagining her kissing someone else only deepened his wounds.

You don't have a choice. She'll understand your imperfect ruse when you can explain everything. When you can tell her you did it to save her family.

"What part of 'I don't require an escort' is unclear to you, Finnegan?"

Lorcan spun and saw Edriss marching toward him, Finn several paces behind her. Finn must have been purposely hanging back, because he was a full foot taller and a much faster walker.

"I'm not intentionally invoking your ire, you know," Finn said with an eyeroll.

Lorcan almost laughed because Finn would never have done it if Edriss were looking.

But his amusement faded when he saw her splotched face and wide, worried eyes. She sharply averted his when he tried to catch her gaze, storming past him and into the lord's apartments. Finn's shoulders rose in a deep, steadying breath as he paused before following her in.

"Did something happen?" Lorcan asked. Finnegan was the last person he wanted to ask about Edriss. It burned him up that he might know more than Lorcan did, but she'd shut him out entirely. Until he had permission to explain himself, the chasm between them would only grow wider.

Finn sighed. "She hates me, for one." He flicked Lorcan a sidelong glance. "Thanks to you."

Lorcan suppressed a twitch of joy. "And two?"

"Ah, well…She doesn't know to be mad about that yet." Finn frowned at the closed door. "But I imagine you'll hear her rage from the other side of the keep once she learns we're betrothed."

Lorcan's arms tightened at his side. He'd sent seven letters to Evra requesting a private audience, to follow up on their conversation about the betrothal, and none had received a response. He'd hoped it meant Evra was still considering things. "He's telling her *tonight*?"

Finn nodded dismally. "I'd always hoped, but never thought…" He shook his head. "I always thought it would be you, mate. But Evrathedyn is full of surprises, isn't he?"

"Evra would never allow a match between us," Lorcan replied. His mouth dried up. He tried to swallow but coughed instead. It was impossible to believe Evra's rebuffs had been anything but intentional. "Besides, she's…She's like my own sister."

"Say it enough and you might believe it, aye?" Finn's laugh was humorless. "Doesn't matter now. Lord Blackwood's decided, and I doubt he'll waste much time before the wedding." He clapped

Lorcan on the shoulder and started for the door. "Beseech the Guardian of Trial and Tribulation on my behalf, would you? I'll need their intercession if I'm to survive this dinner."

Lorcan watched his once friend disappear into the lord's chambers in numb disbelief.

Edriss was already stiff by the time Evra rose to kiss her cheeks. She met Rhosyn's eyes over his shoulder, but her sister-in-law quickly averted her own with an apprehensive frown. Beside her, Arwenna was thoroughly enraptured by her cloth napkin.

Finnegan snuck up behind Edriss, causing her to jump forward. He turned a reverent nod on Evra before taking a seat at her right, the move earning him a repulsed glare that was born of disgust as much as surprise that he was staying for dinner. His brows flicked up, his eyes flitting to the side.

"Is this a dinner or a coup?" Edriss leveled the words in clear accusation, for it was evident everyone else knew why she was there. "You really should have invited Alise, Evra, for no one has quite her gift for hostile takeovers."

Finnegan chuckled. The urge to backhand him was strong enough to make her wish he'd do it again so she could.

"I told you this would have been better addressed just the two of you," Rhosyn said. Her mouth pursed. She shook her head at her empty plate. "Something you can still remedy, you know."

"*Someone* better explain what this is before—"

"Will you please sit down?" Evra asked. He seemed to recoil a bit, as though expecting to be struck. Her suspicion mounted higher. "Please, Edriss?"

"No," Edriss said and crossed her arms. She backed up a step. Rhosyn and Arwenna exchanged a look, which amplified her sense of vulnerable isolation. "I don't think I will."

"Just tell her already," Arwenna muttered.

"Tell me *what?*" Heat flamed into Edriss's cheeks. She felt herself retreat, judging the distance to the door. The eyes of

112

everyone in the room singed her like an unholy conspiracy. That even *Arwenna* knew her fate was a direct hit to a festering wound.

"I wasn't trying to..." Evra folded his hands atop the table and bowed his head, making her feel worse, as though she'd been the one to wrong *him*. "In hindsight, I see now that...Guardians..."

Edriss caught Finnegan staring at her, and he whipped his gaze down so fast, she wondered if he was dizzy. "You're in on this?"

"That's not exactly how I'd describe it. I did *try* to tell you, but—"

"Tell me *what?*" Edriss screamed the words. She was miserable enough without their adding to it. What she wanted was to rewind time, refuse the supper invitation, and ride for Rivermarch instead.

She reached for a wine carafe and raised it in the air, took a swig, and turned to leave, but Finnegan leaped up and looped a hand through her arm. She gaped at it in abhorrence, then gave him the same look, and he fell away.

But then she knew.

She *knew.*

"No." Edriss shoved the wine carafe in the air toward her brother. She trained her focus forward, refusing Finnegan's attempt to lock eyes. "*No,* absolutely not, Evrathedyn. Of all the options available, you would really do *this,* to *me?*"

"You understand politics, better than I do," Evra said, and Rhosyn made a disappointed face.

"Yes. I do. Better than you. And thus you should have consulted me before *ambushing* me in front of the family and the traitor you expect me to marry!"

Arwenna puffed out a breath and fixed her attention on her lap.

The rest of the room went excruciatingly silent.

"Finn was once a good friend to you," Evra said slowly. He watched the two of them with careful intensity. "And I've heard your concerns. But I would not have brought you both here to discuss this together if I believed any of what's been said."

"Discuss together? He *knew*." Edriss thrust the carafe at Finnegan without looking his way. "He knew before I did, Evra. How can that be?"

Evra sighed. He looked to Rhosyn for help, but she was busy fuming in silence. Her fingers gripped the stem of her glass with nearly enough force to snap it. "I discussed it first with Steward Derry, because that had to happen before anything else, and he evidently shared the news with Finn before I could speak with you. But you must understand, Derry is offering the protection of his men at arms—and his full support in hunting down the ones responsible for what happened to Renardy."

"Not much of a hunt. Just needs to find a mirror."

"We *need* the help, Edriss. We're no closer than we were a year ago to rooting out the evil in our land."

Edriss couldn't believe what she was hearing. "And why is that, brother? Why is that? Could it be that your most trusted counselors are telling you precisely *where* to find this evil, and you refuse to listen?" She sliced her tongue along the back of her teeth. "Why am I even bothering? I'm tired of wasting my words when you'll never listen. But you could have told me sooner, Evra. You *should* have told me sooner."

"There simply wasn't time," Evra said with a long exhale. "I'm sorry."

"I've known for weeks," Arwenna muttered. She looked up when everyone turned their attention her way.

"Wen," Rhosyn said with a warning look.

"Weeks?" Edriss blindly handed the carafe to Finnegan and approached the table again. "You mean to tell me *Arwenna* has known for weeks, but you couldn't find a single opportunity to discuss this with me any sooner than tonight?"

"I don't know how Arwenna knew, Edriss. I didn't tell her," Evra said, shaking his head in rebut.

"So even more people knew before you told me!"

"I already said I was sorry—"

"No. No, you haven't said you're sorry." Edriss's eyes fell on Rhosyn. She wished her sister-in-law weren't present for the debacle. She was the only person in the room Edriss didn't have a problem with, and she should have been resting. "You said...It doesn't matter. None of this matters, does it? Because I won't do it." Edriss threw her arms out with a short laugh. "I refuse. You'll have to truss me and drag me to the wedding, and how will that look to your subjects?"

"You were right," Evra said amenably. His cheeks were flushed dark red. "Why don't you and I go for a walk, and we'll discuss this privately."

"I'll pass on that generous offer, which you should have made weeks ago," Edriss said. Hot tears burned her eyes, but she couldn't dare let them spill, not there. "And whatever appetite I had no longer exists, so if you'll excuse me, I have somewhere more useful to be."

Edriss fled before she could read the pity in Rhosyn's eyes— the gloating in Arwenna's. Evra would think her unreasonable, but he was more concerned with being equitable and diplomatic. As for Finnegan—

"Edriss, wait."

Of course he'd followed. He'd won a contest he shouldn't have even been allowed to enter, and she was the prize. But she had no intention of being handed over to the son of a traitor...a man following in his father's footsteps with enthusiastic aplomb.

"Please."

"Don't bother with niceties, Finnegan. They disguise intent, and I much prefer to know who people are," Edriss said, half under her breath but loud enough for him and those passing to hear.

He caught up to her at the end of the hall and gently tugged her back. Her eyes flared in rage, causing him to release her, but he didn't retreat.

"There was a time when you used to enjoy my company, Edriss. You almost always picked me as your husband when we played our games. I know I'm not Lorcan—"

115

"Lorcan isn't a traitor to the Reach," Edriss retorted. She swept her gaze over him. "Being handsome doesn't dull the stench."

"You keep using that word!" Finnegan ran his hands down his face with a groan. "I am *not* a traitor."

"Your father is."

Finnegan's chin twitched in his silence.

Edriss shook her head with a hard laugh. "You aren't denying it."

"What am I supposed to say? You don't believe anything I tell you."

"Well, we agree on something." She crossed her arms. "Is that all?"

"Edriss?"

Lorcan's voice cut through her. It wrapped her in a warm hug and split her in two.

Edriss turned around and forced a thin smile. "Arwenna is in with Evra and the others."

Lorcan shook his head. "I was on my way to the dining hall. I saw you, and I…" He trailed off and looked at Finnegan.

"Wait…*You* knew as well?" Edriss's jaw dropped.

"I've been trying to get some time alone with Evra to discuss the matter. I didn't want to upset you needlessly—"

"Upset me? Like I'm a delicate rose, unable to withstand the slightest wind?" Edriss fingered the poison vial at her neck. It was a reminder, always, how close she was to death and how easily she could offer it to others.

Marriage to Finnegan would be a death of sorts.

Standing between the man who had broken her heart and the one who would crush it into dust was another kind of death.

"You *know* I don't think that," Lorcan said softly. He kept his glare on Finnegan. "I—"

"Are no longer my protector, and thus, I am no longer your burden."

The color drained from his face. He wore a stricken look as he glanced at Finnegan and then back at her. "That's unfair."

116

"You don't get to talk to me about unfair, Lorcan James. In fact, I prefer you not talk to me at all." Edriss lifted her skirt and dashed off before either of them could see her tears falling.

EIGHT

MISERY WITH NO END

Finnegan followed Edriss everywhere.

In the beginning, his stalking had been the result of mischance.

He'd originally planned to go to Rivermarch to collect quarterly rents on his father's behalf. But then, days before he was set to arrive, tragedy hit the small village when a fire razed half of its structures to the ground. Arson, it was said, a lesson for any community who would protect witches. Finnegan had instead used his trip to assess the damage and prepare a report for his father, suggesting some relief for the quarter.

But it hadn't just taken homes and businesses. Two hundred townspeople had lost their lives. Twice as many toiled on cots in the old monastery, where they'd piled the injured, having nowhere else for them to go. Those well enough to travel were sent to Longwood Rush for their convalescence. The rest suffered with the lack of adequate medicines and a shortage of physicians willing to put themselves in danger.

119

It shouldn't have surprised Finnegan to see Edriss had come to offer her aid.

Even when magic had been illegal, he'd known about hers. He'd kept her secret, even from his father. *Especially* from his father.

But she hadn't been using magic that day in Rivermarch. She'd dragged a satchel full of salves and elixirs from cot to cot in the makeshift infirmary, treating every patient with the same compassion.

Finnegan hadn't been sure it was her, not at first. She'd been dressed as a hedge-born boy, face smeared with soot, hair tucked under a scruffy hat. But as the day wore on and exhaustion set in, she was less careful with her disguise. He saw her dark hair peek out from the sides of a cap so bedraggled, it eventually fell off altogether. Her violet eyes had flashed in defeated fatigue when she looked out upon the sea of people and realized she'd never be able to help them all.

Finnegan had been careful she hadn't seen him. He'd never told her about the day—or the subsequent ones—when he'd hung back to let her think she'd escaped notice.

Her hatred for him was dispiriting, but it encouraged him to continue. He was so used to the stony scowl always etched on her face that he'd forgotten what her smile looked like.

She'd mostly visited Rivermarch in the daytime, using Baron Lawrence as a cover story for her long absences, but on the days she had gone to Felgarden, she'd reserved her clandestine nursing for the evening, slipping out after supper when no one was watching. But something had shifted recently; she was no longer going to Felgarden at all, though that was precisely where her brother and others thought she was.

He still waited outside her apartments sometimes, enough to let her believe he was following but not enough for her to realize he was always watching, whether or not she could see him.

When she knew he was on her tail, her destinations were benign. A ride in the forest. The herbarium to practice her recipes.

To dine with Rhosyn—though never Evra, whom she wasn't speaking to, nor Arwenna, who deserved Edriss's anger, as far as Finn was concerned.

And definitely not Lorcan, who she'd iced out with astonishing determination.

"Again?" Edriss asked as she locked her door. She strode away, cape flapping, and as usual, he moved into formation behind her. He saw what her billowing cape tried to hide: a satchel.

"If Ashenhurst is truly in the Rush again, as they say, you're not safe." His objections had become so rote, he didn't even have to think about them.

"Well you'd know, wouldn't you?" Edriss turned a corner, probably wondering how she was going to get rid of him.

She wouldn't have to wait for long.

He sighed, the reaction she was after.

She turned back with a cool grin.

"Fine," he said, hands up, burying his smile lest she pick up on his thoughts. He'd heard she could read minds, and it wasn't the time to discover whether that was true. "See you tonight?"

Edriss flounced off without responding.

Now he did grin.

She'd be watching her back until she was clear of the Rush. He had at least that amount of time to grab some bread and fill his wineskin.

After all, he knew where she was going.

She didn't scream. Many of the worst days of his life had been full of sound, but not this one. Cesarina's silence reflected onto the gathered. Lorcan watched the laughter and comments fade, becoming worry, becoming fear. Could the witch curse them, even bound to the pyre, her feet already consumed by flames?

His pulse pounded in his ears, vibrated his eyes. He tried to get closer, but the crowd was too thick. All of Deramore had come out to see the woman claiming to be a Rhiagain princess, but not one had the courage to petition the king and verify her story. Their prejudices ran too deep. Senselessness gathered meaning, dark became light, and not one seemed to understand the irony of murdering others to save themselves from damnation.

Lorcan had known he was damned the moment he'd risen to the pungent stench of smoke. The baron had overruled his decision as tender. Had declared there hadn't been nearly enough burnings to deter witches from misbehaving, thanks to the campaign of peace Lord Blackwood was trying to push on everyone.

Lorcan had used every tactic in his arsenal to wear Cesarina down. She'd finally relented, and he'd never been more relieved in his life.

You and I will know the truth, he'd said, though he didn't believe she was the king's daughter any more than the wicked townspeople believed it.

Cesarina lifted her head toward the sky and grinned. Worry rippled among the crowd at the silent witch, the one who had not even cried when her sentence was read, they'd said.

Lorcan had enough tears for them both.

He was still crying.

He could hardly see through tears and smoke and shame.

Gasps rippled when Cesarina's dark-red tresses caught fire. They burned fast, the destruction done before she could lower her head.

She belonged to the fire now. Perhaps she always had. Perhaps it was why she seemed so unafraid as it came for her.

Her head came down, face swallowed by flame, leaving the crowd stunned back into silence.

But it wasn't Cesarina grinning anymore.

It was Edriss.

Lorcan's own screams woke him. A startled attendant dropped Lorcan's laundry and screamed with him.

He pitched forward, flinging the blankets away from his flesh, still scorched by the memory of burning flesh.

"Sorry," he whispered, panting. Then again, louder. "Sorry. Forgive me. Sorry."

"Are you all right, sir?" The attendant knelt to gather the spilled clothing but didn't collect it yet. "Another nightmare?"

Did they know about his bad dreams? "I'm fine." He rolled his head down and ran his hands through his sweaty hair and down across the back of his clammy neck. He saw Edriss, flames tickling her teeth and rolling off her tongue, and had to clench down another scream.

"Can I get you anything?"

"Actually, yes." Lorcan scrambled from the bed and picked his clothes from the day before off the floor. "Can you send word to Lady Edriss to join me for breakfast this morning?" He shimmied into his pants, flashing the attendant more than he'd intended in his rush to dress. "She'll give you some choice words about it, but tell her…Tell her it's important, please. Say whatever you need to in order to convince her."

"What should I…How should I do that, sir?"

Lorcan shook his head. He blinked the sleep from his eyes. "Be as creative as you like." He had to see her. He had to make things right. "As long as you bring her here."

He was dressed and emptying a goblet of wine from the night before when the attendant returned. "I'm sorry, sir, but she wasn't in her apartments."

"Not in her apartments?" He stumbled back to peer out the window. The sun was still rising from behind the Seven Sisters. "But it's hardly dawn. Where else could she be?"

She looked at her feet. "Another attendant informed me she left nigh an hour ago."

"Left?" Lorcan started forward. "Left her room?"

"Left…the Halls."

That couldn't be right. Edriss never visited the baron before noontide. A pleasure ride so early in the morning seemed just as unlikely. "Did they…" He cupped his chin stubble and squinted to bring himself further into the land of the wakeful. "See where she went off to?"

123

"No. But they said if we wanted to know, we might ask Sir Finnegan Derry."

"Finn?" Lorcan braced against the wall. "Why would Finn..." He shook his head with a grumbling sigh. "Thank you."

He made his way to the Derry guest apartments. Finn was in the hall, checking his cloth armor and sword belt.

"Lorcan." He started to smile, but it never materialized.

Lorcan flexed his hands behind himself and stepped forward. "I'm looking for Edriss."

"Oh?" Finn turned back toward his apartments. "Well she's not in there. Not yet anyway."

He's trying to get you to rise in anger. Don't give it to him. "Do you know where she is?"

"I might." Finn shrugged. He crossed his legs and propped himself sideways against the wall. "But I'm not saying anything until we clear the air between us."

Lorcan clenched his jaw through a forced smile. "You're the only one who can do that."

Finn shook his head at the wall with a snort. "We can't clear anything if you refuse to believe anything I say."

"You're right," Lorcan said. "So tell me where Edriss is."

"You really don't know. She hasn't told you?" Finn moved toward him. The buckles from his boots clanged, making shrill echoes. "I find that curious. But then, you had a secret of your own, didn't you?" He whistled. "Top marks for bagging the raven, though I don't think you're the first in the Rush to crash the nest."

Lorcan pursed his mouth. Finnegan was undoubtedly saying similar things to Edriss to stir her anger even more.

"I want you to agree to hear me out." Finn squared up. "I want you to listen and keep an open mind."

Lorcan swatted the air in annoyance. "Do you or do you not know where Edriss is?"

"Why are you in such a hurry?"

"I just am!"

124

"All right." Finn flinched his jaw. "Fine. But you and I, we're having an ale later. And you're going to listen to me and reserve your opinion until I'm done saying what I need to say."

Lorcan held out his hands in surrender. "Where is she?"

Finn's brows ticked upward. "I could tell you, but you'd never believe me. You need to see it yourself." He swept his gaze over him. "You good for a ride? Need to change out of your pretty boots first?"

Lorcan's eyes narrowed. "Where?"

"Rivermarch."

Edriss's hand shook as she wrapped the salve-coated cloth around a man's ankle. The flesh bubbled up, black and angry, leaving her once more with the urge to put aside her herbs and heal him properly.

But they were all just as hopeless. A sea of red and black and misery with no end.

She wasn't the only helper. Women from nearby villages had left families behind to nurse strangers. Physicians came up from places like Whitewood and Windwatch Grove to remove gangrenous limbs and stitch open wounds, while ministers read the dead-given rites over the ones who couldn't be saved.

"This one is more dire, boy," a faceless man said as he passed her. That was what they all called her, *boy*, and each time came with the fluttery sensation of victory. Lady Edriss Blackwood could do little for these men, women, and children, but *boy* could proffer relief to many. *Boy* could slip near to conversations that would have ended the moment Edriss walked up. *Boy* would be the one who finally heard something that could turn the tide of the war on magic.

"Aye," Edriss acknowledged, voice low in pitch and volume to buoy the facade. She finished wrapping the man's ankle and moved on to the other man.

She wrung her hands through the filthy rag sitting atop her satchel. It was coated in a blend of green and brown and yellow, like a bruise. She'd helped over twenty today, but as she gazed into the sea of injured through bleary eyes, it felt like she'd done nothing at all.

"Thank you, kid. I've been waiting for hours…"

Edriss wiped her brow on her filthy sleeve and looked at the man speaking to her. He was young, perhaps the baron's age. He'd lost an arm, and no one had yet bothered to bandage it. A makeshift tourniquet was still tight above the exposed meat and flesh. The rest of his body was a battlefield of burns and gashes.

She used her boots to push her bag along the stone floor and went to him. Though she'd started the day on her feet, she had too many hours behind her, and the man needed more than a quick salve. She searched around for something to sit on and found a discarded bedroll to slide under herself.

When he looked up, she nudged her cap lower and dipped her head, assessing the work ahead.

"You're not from here, are you?"

Edriss shook her head. She reserved speaking for when it was inescapable. The less she said, the better.

"Nah," the man said, rolling his gaze upward. "You couldn't be, could you? There are no boys in Rivermarch walking around without so much as a scratch." He winced when he shifted to allow her better access to his bloody stump. A tear popped into his eye. "Why did you come then?"

Open-ended questions were harder to avoid. "Wanted to help," she grumbled.

"Help." The man laughed. It was full of thick congestion…full of death. "One of the good ones then. Not many of them."

In silence, Edriss cleaned the open wound where his arm had been.

"Would have been one thing had it just been the witches, but look around us…innocent children. Guardian-fearing men."

Her hands stilled, but she used the lull to reach for a clean strip, burying her excited expression in the satchel. *Defender.* The

126

man was a Defender. Hundreds she'd cleaned and nursed and helped die, and not one had been in league with the rebels.

Until now.

She recovered herself and nodded, which she knew he'd either take as encouragement or acknowledgment.

"How do you know who to help?"

Edriss tilted her head to indicate he should explain.

"We're all mixed together here. Heathens and blessed-folk. How do you know who is who? How do you know you're not saving one of *them*?"

Edriss shrugged and wrapped the more troublesome part of his exposed flesh. The man buried his knuckle in his mouth and bit down on a scream. Her hands started to shake, her heart pumping so fast, her breathing accelerated. How badly she wanted to grind her fist up into the wound, to give more pain than she took. But that would not make her a better person, only another flavor of the same evil.

"Don't care? Or don't know?"

"I came to help," Edriss said again. Her voice had nearly cracked. She needed to finish with this one and move on, but how could she do that when he might, finally, be the one who could tell her something useful?

"But there's only some of us who deserve your help." When Edriss didn't respond, the man grimaced in pain and closed his eyes. "Where'd you learn this trade anyway?"

Edriss's answer didn't come right away. She obviously couldn't tell him the poison trade had been passed to her through a lineage of powerful women. But a lie felt no better. No safer. None had questioned her aid before, and she sensed what path this man was leading her down—one where she'd out herself as one of the heathens he still, despite his mangled state, righteously believed in punishing. He wouldn't care that she'd almost died of a terrible illness, that her own magical healing had been stifled by this sickness and no mix of herbs had been enough. That the magic from another was why she was there at all, mending his arm, giving him comfort he'd only squander.

"My family can never afford proper medicine." She forced herself to slow her words down, so her own voice didn't crack through.

"Farmers," the man concluded aloud. "Times are tough under the boy lord. We all do what we must." He fell into a restless silence as she worked on the tenderest parts of his arms.

Edriss continued cleaning and dressing his wounds, happy for a reprieve to address her racing thoughts. The man was at best a sympathizer and at worst actively working with the Defenders. If she could get him talking...but then she'd have to speak. Every word she uttered was a slow unraveling of her disguise. Every word brought her closer to discovery...and if he discovered who she was, there was no telling what he might do.

But she'd been coming to Rivermarch for *weeks*, and it was the first time anyone had said anything that might be of use.

An old weakness crept up. *I wish Lorry were here. He'd know what to do. We'd make a plan together.* But Lorcan wasn't there. He had different priorities. She wasn't one of them anymore, and apparently, neither was saving the Westerlands.

She was entirely on her own, and it was time to accept it.

To act like it.

"Where could..." She cleared her throat when her voice started too high. "Where could a boy get involved in such blessed work?"

The man perked. His head came up off the cot. "Lower your voice, lad. Place is crawling with Blackwood sycophants." He smiled. "What did you say your name was?"

She hadn't been asked for a name in all the time she'd been coming, but she'd prepared one just in case. "Uh...Henry."

"I won't ask for your family name. You'd be smarter to lie. You can call me John."

"John. How does one—"

128

"Aye, I heard your question. Don't need to repeat it for the rest of the realm." John glanced briefly at his arm before he winced and looked away. "You keep me from dying in this bed, Henry, and I'll answer." He coughed again, this time bringing up blood. It wasn't the amputation or the cuts that would kill John. It was the death in his lungs. No salve or elixir would cure it. "I'll do you one even better than that, farmer. I'll take you along with me to our next meeting. Introduce you to the right people. People you *want* to know. The ones who are going to save this Reach from damnation."

Edriss checked the excitement skipping in her chest. It clogged her throat, rendering words impossible. Not only was John involved, but he had access to people who made decisions. Taking her *to* them? Well, that went beyond her wildest dreams.

"Think you can save me then, Henry? Save a fellow brother?"

Edriss adjusted the mask higher on her face so it covered the bottom of her eyes. She could conceal her hair, but her violet eyes were harder to hide. John was consumed by sickness and injury, but what would he notice if he weren't? What might he remember later, when the fog cleared?

There won't be a later. He'll die here. Nothing I can do.

But there is *something.*

She'd sworn magic had no place in her trips to Rivermarch. It was risky under the best of circumstances, but the town had been attacked for protecting magic practicers, which made it positively hazardous.

No matter how she might wish to save them all, she could not proffer miracles without drawing eyes, and no salve or elixir could save a man whom death intended to take.

But magic could.

"The prospect so daunting, it stole your words?"

"Sorry," Edriss muttered. She coughed to expel the tremble in her voice, the ragged draw of her quick breaths. "I'll do my best."

"That's what physicians say to men on their deathbeds, Henry. What say you, to me, right now? Speak true. If I'm to die, I want to know."

129

You will die. You should *die. I could never kill you myself, but watch death take you? Yes, that I could do.*

"That's it then?"

I'll take you along with me to our next meeting. Introduce you to the right people.

"I…" Edriss was suspended between right and wrong. The line was oft blurred, but she'd never experienced such conflict about what even *was* right, what was wrong. Whether a wrong could lead to more rights, or if a right could lead to more wrongs.

But what else did she have? A naïve brother too sure of himself to listen? A best friend who no longer cared? She could go to Alise, but Alise would poison every man she suspected was complicit before they could reveal the full extent of their treachery, and then where would the Westerlands be?

"I can save you." She came to the resolution as she said the words.

Time would decide whether she could live with making it.

Lorcan spent the day tearing cloths into bandages. He hid behind a cluster of pillars while he worked, watching Edriss move from one wounded person to the next. She offered the same beaming smile to everyone, even when exhaustion crept into her eyes around midday, making her forget to adjust her mask as often as she should. Had she taken off the disguise, her smile would have lit the entire infirmary. The constant sparkle in her violet eyes would have given them all hope, as it had always done for him, even in his darkest moments. Those eyes had saved his life after Cesarina and Jademarch. They'd brought him back to life and reminded him his purpose was not limited to one terrible failure.

Some might have said he was the lightbringer, but for him, it had always been Edriss.

Edriss was largely ignored. Those who paid her mind bossed her about, directing her where to go, who to help. She kept her head low and obeyed, keeping anything but shallow attention at bay. She looked like the dozen or so other boys who'd been sent to assist physicians and nurses. She might be the only "boy" using salves and elixirs, but no one questioned what was clearly a gift in the midst of so much death.

She spent a roughly equal amount of time with each patient, until she reached a man who looked steps from death. Someone had directed her to the man specifically, and so she went, but within minutes of meeting him, her entire demeanor changed.

Did the patient see the fleeting moments of hesitation—the careful, steadying way she reached into her satchel to buy time? Would anyone else *but* Lorcan have read those things as fear?

Lorcan looked for Finn, but he'd gone outside to wait. It was a relief to be free of him. Lorcan hated that Finn knew something about Edriss that he didn't, especially something so significant.

Why *hadn't* she told him?

She was understandably upset about the Arwenna situation, but according to Finn, her jaunts to Rivermarch had been going on longer.

You are no longer my protector, and thus, I am no longer your burden.

Edriss had been building to those words for longer than he realized, and they'd hurt even more than he'd expected. Maybe she *had* outgrown needing a protector, but Edriss was his singular constant. He was hers. Some truths were bigger than age and time.

And until her farce of a betrothal was called off, Lorcan was still the only one standing tall for Edriss—even if she'd never see it that way.

She sat with the man for nearly an hour before helping him to his feet and guiding him to a corner behind two screens, where Lorcan lost sight of her. He set aside the cloth, determined to get closer, but Finn clamped a hand on his arm.

"She sees you, we can't keep her safe anymore."

There is no "we" where Edriss is concerned was Lorcan's instinctual response, but if Finn knew one of Edriss's secrets, how many more were there? Would Lorcan ever uncover them without Finn's help? Even the day's trip to Rivermarch set his and

Arwenna's plan behind. Every day he was away from her was a day the Defenders might assail her for something she didn't have. "What's she doing?"

"Something she doesn't want others to see." Finn flicked his eyes sideways. "You see that man over there? The one with the scar?"

"Yeah."

"One of Baron Lawrence's men. We aren't the only ones following our Edriss. What does that tell you? How I see it, he's just as worried as I am about the danger she's in." Finn nodded at where she'd disappeared. "Did you see who she went back there with?"

Lorcan was still pondering the baron's role. "Ah…same man she's been tending for the past hour. He's in bad shape. I'd be surprised if he lasts the night."

"Curious," Finn said. "Keep an eye on the screens. I'm going to casually ask around about the patient."

"Why?"

Finn left without responding. He disappeared into the thick of nurses and helpers.

Lorcan handed a full basket of cloth strips to a helper without taking his gaze off the corner. He tore more bandages in mindless rips, counting the seconds and measuring them against his growing worries. Finn knew Edriss was in danger. Even the *baron* knew. But neither had put a stop to her recklessness.

When Edriss finally emerged, her cheeks were flushed so red, he wondered if she'd slipped out the back and gone for a brisk run. She glanced around the busy space with a furtive, darting gaze and then waved her hands.

Lorcan's breath caught.

He almost didn't recognize the man who followed her. He'd gone into the corner missing an arm, but now he had both. The blood crusted around his mouth was clean, the battlefield of wounds healed.

Oh, Edriss. No.

Why?

Why him?

132

Edriss whispered something to the man, then pointed, indicating he should go to the left. When she broke off in the opposite direction, Lorcan caught the wild look in her eyes, the dangerous smile spreading between the tops of her grimy cheeks.

He'd never been more scared for her than he was in that moment.

"Where is she?" Finn asked in a breathless, hasty whisper.

Lorcan shook his head. He didn't want to answer, nor did he have one.

"Lor. Is she still with that man?"

"No."

"Thank the Guardians." Finn dropped back against the table and dragged his hands down his face. "He's dangerous."

"What?" Lorcan snapped from his daze and spun around. "Do you know who he is?"

Finn lowered his voice and leaned in close. "Defender."

Lorcan balked. "How…Do you know him?"

"Are we back on this?"

"Why is he here?"

Finn shrugged and sighed. "I don't know. But you can bet Edriss knows where his loyalty lies, and it's why she spent so much time with him."

"She's in *way* over her head." Heat pricked Lorcan's face, turning to numbness as it traveled from his neck to his shoulders and down into his tense hands. "I don't care if she sees me, I need to warn her—"

"Absolutely *not*. Gonna warn her about what she already knows? Lose our ability to protect her?"

"It's not your—"

"I'm going to be her husband." Aggression tinged the edge of Finn's pronouncement. "And it *is* my job to protect her. It will always be my job, for the rest of her life. I brought you today as a show of faith, to help you see I'm not your enemy. But do not make the mistake of thinking I'm asking for, or would welcome, you sticking your nose where it doesn't belong. You're here because I made a place for you."

Lorcan stepped back as though he'd been struck. It felt like he had. The sensation of a thousand punctures prickling his flesh was replaced just as swiftly with anger. "And you shouldn't make the mistake of thinking you know her. It was I who was there when Evra left. When Aeldred hurled his abusive threats. When she was scared and alone and when she was dying. Where were you?"

Finnegan threw his head back with a laugh. "Oh, Lorcan, it's almost like you don't realize how all these things you did to 'help' her only isolated her from people who also cared! She was my friend too. Cressida's. The Tyndalls'. But you edged us out, until it was just you and Edriss against the world. And now look at her. She's been escaping so damn long, she doesn't know how to keep *herself* safe."

But that wasn't true. The real secret of their relationship was that Edriss had never needed him the way she thought she did. They'd needed one another equally, and though Edriss liked to say Lorcan had saved her life, she'd done the same for him more times than he could count.

"You don't know her," Lorcan said again. The din of shouted orders mixed with coughs and crying crept under his skin. Heat built behind his eyes. His jaw locked. "You have it all wrong."

"She's leaving," Finn said. He pulled out his flask, took a swig, and replaced it. "Ease off. We give her a head start. She always stops at the stables to change her clothing. That's when she quits looking over her shoulder."

"How long have you been following her here?"

"Long enough." Finn grimaced and peered around Lorcan. His eyes narrowed. Lorcan turned to see what he was looking at and spotted the fully healed man. "I'll be back in a few. Refill your wineskin. We leave in half a tick."

Edriss locked her door the second it closed. She slammed both bolts at the same time she shimmied out of her cloak. The rest of her clothes she left in slapdash piles across the floor on her way

134

to the chair, where she unlaced her boots so fast, one of the straps slapped her in the mouth. She flung them both across the room. One slammed into the hearth and landed dangerously close to the fire her attendants must have started hours ago.

They'd be wondering why Edriss had fastened not only her bolt but the servant lock. If her heart hadn't been racing louder than her thoughts, she might have had the foresight to let them know she wanted a night without disruption, so they didn't make a fuss, but her attendants were the last thing on her mind as she slumped low in the leather chair, wearing only the thin blouse of her undergarments.

She'd either acted brilliantly or foolishly, but it couldn't have been both. There could be no gray area when consorting with traitors. Edriss was positively certain he would have killed her had he looked a bit closer and uncovered her truth.

But he hadn't.

She was alive.

Dangerously, wickedly alive.

She tapped her bare feet against the stone in frenetic rhythm, her smile growing wider as she considered how bravely she'd dealt with the Defender, how well she'd played him. The day came back to her in flashes, memories of her cool handling...of the way she'd found just the right words in the right measure.

The healing had been a bold risk, but her suspicion had proved true; the Defenders only cared about magic when they couldn't benefit from it. Giving the man his arm back hadn't changed his righteous cause, but he hadn't refused the offer either.

I'm gonna overlook this one, Henry, because of what you did for me. Because I can see into your heart and witness for myself you're no heathen, despite what you may have been born with. But don't let others see it...Not all will appreciate the benefit of having one of them *on our side.*

She'd had no choice. She told herself so a thousand times on the cold ride back to the Rush. He would have died. If he'd died, she'd be right back where she'd started.

135

But to save him, she'd exposed the most dangerous part of herself. What if the clarity of dawn offered John a new perspective? What if, his mortality no longer a concern, he instead lured her into a trap?

We meet on the last turn of autumnwhile. Return here to the old abbey, and I'll escort you to the meeting place. But come alone, Henry, because our leader is wary of unfamiliar faces, and I can only vouch for yours.

Alone.

Into a den of snakes.

Edriss leaned over to the table and uncorked the wine carafe. After she drew a sip, she shook her head and laughed, a mix of terror and delight. The sense she'd come so close to death and yet had never been more *alive* caused her to take another sip, then another, until she finally sat back and cradled the carafe to her chest.

Best of all, she'd proved to herself she was perfectly competent on her own.

Lorcan had been…

Her heart swelled with a sudden rush of pain. Hot tears stung her eyes.

A temporary reprieve, a balm for her lowest moment.

If the Guardians had intended him for her future, he would have been there on the biggest, boldest night of her life.

But he wasn't.

He'd been with Arwenna, doing…whatever it was they did together.

The spirits settled. A soft, welcome blur stole over her vision, and she let her eyes close with slow blinks, holding fast to the wine.

Alone.

She'd always been alone.

And she realized it was precisely as the Guardians intended it.

NINE

A THIN VEIN OF ANXIETY

Lorcan managed to wait until morning to approach Edriss, but when he reached her apartments, her door was locked. An attendant sat on a chair outside, wearing a bewildered look, as though she'd been banished there after a sound scolding.

"Where's Lady Blackwood?"

The attendant sighed with a longing glance at the door. "She's locked us out, sir."

"Why?" Lorcan frowned. "When?"

"Since her return last night. We heard she'd come home, but by the time we made it here, she'd already locked the door."

"But you have a key."

The attendant shook her head in dismay. "She slid the servant bolt as well."

Lorcan stared at the door as though it would offer an explanation the servant couldn't give. "But it's past breakfast already. She hasn't eaten?"

"No, sir. The kitchen brought her a tray, but the food went cold, so they removed it."

"Did she say she wasn't hungry?" He reframed the question. "Has she said anything at all?"

Flustered, the attendant looked down at her joined hands. "She did say this morning she would like to be left alone to rest."

"To rest."

"Yes."

"But it's…" Lorcan shook his head. There was no point in explaining what they both already knew, that Edriss never slept in, never missed breakfast. "I'd like you to send someone to tell me as soon as she wakes. Not a moment later. It's…important. In fact, better you not tell her I'm coming at all."

"Sir?"

"Thank you," he said and left before the attendant could probe him further. He'd tried to respect Edriss's need for space, but circumstances had changed. She was playing games with her life, and if she thought his days as her protector were behind them, she was sorely mistaken.

Arwenna waited for him in the second-tier garden. Roses of many colors, hundreds of thousands, spanned the perimeter. Some varieties grew nowhere else in the kingdom. Blackwood detractors claimed it was the poison mistresses' dark magic at work, but their botanical magic had always been more about beauty than death.

She greeted him with a chaste kiss, but when they spotted a group of men heading down the long staircase, she pulled him in for a deeper one. When she suddenly released him, Lorcan muttered an awkward series of incomplete thoughts, but she was too busy frowning at the backs of the men.

"I hope more avail themselves of the unusually warm day. Otherwise this will be quite the waste of time," Arwenna said. She smoothed her deep-blue gown with her hands. "Where were you yesterday?"

Lorcan started to tell her the truth, but something stayed him. "I was unavoidably detained. Did something happen?"

"No," Arwenna said, still looking off into the distance. "But I saw him. Ashenhurst."

"He *is* back then?"

She nodded and started walking, passing her hands across the air above the roses. Carnation-yellow buds turned to butter yellow and then to sunset pink before she spoke again. "I think...That is, I get the sense...Something is about to happen."

Lorcan matched her pace. "What gave you this sense?"

Arwenna didn't answer directly. She squinted toward the sun, dimmed by a patch of clouds. "Did you know Evra has gone on another trip?"

"No." Lorcan felt the failure of not knowing. He added it to the steadily growing list. The bigger problem was that Evra being gone meant further attempts to kill the betrothal were on hold. "Where? Who did he take with him?"

Arwenna shrugged and shook her head. Her dark waves caught the crisp wind. There were times she reminded him so much of Edriss, it stole his breath. But the illusion went no further than a glance. There was no one else in the world like Edriss. "It's all very hush-hush. Not even Rhosyn knows. I thought, perhaps, it was where you'd gone yesterday, but I suppose not."

"Unrelated," he murmured. He caught sight of Finnegan and his father, Osman, slipping down the back path from the forest edge, toward the north entrance. He tensed in suspicion. A father and son walking together shouldn't spur distrust, and whether he agreed with Osman or not, Finnegan had the right to spend time with his own father. But if they were both in the Rush, then neither had accompanied Evra.

Right on time, Arwenna hooked a hand behind his head and kissed him for their new audience. She opened her eyes and darted her gaze sideways before pulling away. "I can't tell if they saw us."

"I'm sure they did." Lorcan's mouth buzzed from the whirlwind of Arwenna's performance. "Is Rhosyn all right with Evra gone again so soon? I know she's due any day now."

"She's worried, naturally, but she has me. She has Alise and Meldred, who have both brought babies before." With an odd look, she said, "And Edriss. Though she isn't speaking to me these days."

"Me either," he said. "I don't understand why we can't tell her, Arwenna. She wouldn't do anything to put her family in danger. And I'm confident she would have a better idea for how to handle this problem."

"Because..." Arwenna thinned her mouth into a tight line. He witnessed the precise moment she changed her mind about whatever she was about to say. "There's a rumor she's been spending considerable time away from the Rush. Do you know about this?"

He said nothing. The fewer people who knew Edriss's secret, the better.

"Someone should warn her to be careful. She should assume the wrong eyes are on her, always."

"What do you mean? What have you heard?"

"Enough." She shrugged.

Her words prompted an idea—the first useful one he'd had.

Lorcan braced and turned toward her, waiting for her to stop as well. "Arwenna, I realize my offer to help came across with more confidence than I've shown you so far. That you must be wondering if I actually *can* help you."

Arwenna raised her brows with a scoff. "In fairness, Lorcan, I had no other options. You're far too honorable to ever sell your own father out, and even if you weren't, it's as you said...There is no secret defense lurking in the shadows waiting to strike at the heart of the Defenders. There's only...us."

Not just us.

"Can I be honest with you?"

Arwenna shrugged. "I'd prefer if you were."

Lorcan shuffled in the packed dirt. "I panicked when I saw you that night. I shouldn't have committed to anything without having had time to think."

She laughed and trailed her gaze after Osman and Finnegan. "I know."

"Right." Lorcan directed his laugh at the ground. "Well, what if I said I *did* have something we could tell the men harassing you?" It was risky. Maybe too risky. But what other option was there? Wait for someone else to die? Wait for Edriss to get herself killed because she had something to prove?

If it worked…He could help Edriss and Arwenna both.

"I'm listening."

"Rivermarch. Have the men mentioned this, even in an off-handed way, in their dealings with you?"

Arwenna cast her gaze aside with a dark look. "Our conversations consist of threats and promises."

"Of course, but…Sometimes men reveal things by accident."

She rolled her shoulders back in annoyance. "I really don't know where you're going with this, but I don't *know* anything. If I did, I'd have already gone to Evra with it, and we wouldn't have to parade around the Halls of Longwood, pretending to be in love with each other for lack of a stronger defense."

"It has been awkward," Lorcan said quickly. Everything about the conversation made him uneasy. *Arwenna* made him uneasy, but that reason was harder to pinpoint. She'd slowly become a different person, one he hardly knew at all. "So nothing about Rivermarch?"

"Where the recent attack was, right?"

He nodded. "I believe Defenders are still *in* the village. Perhaps even among the wounded."

Arwenna tossed her head in confusion. "How does that help us?"

"I'm not supposed to know about it. No one is. But if you tell Derry and Bristol and Ashenhurst you've come upon this information, they'll, at the very least, know you have information about their whereabouts that didn't come from them."

"And why should they believe me? I can't prove it."

"It would be hard to prove but even harder to disprove. They'll know you know something you shouldn't, and it will buy more time for us to figure this out."

141

"It's mad," Arwenna said. She flung out her arms, the sleeves draping near to the ground. "And makes little sense."

Edriss was the cunning one, but she wasn't there to give him needed wisdom. He'd have to make his own. "Do you have a better idea?"

She tilted her head back. "Me not having a better idea doesn't mean yours is good." With a sigh, she lowered her head. "Fine. I'll let you know what they say." She ran her hands down her arms with a shiver. "It's grown cold. I think we've been seen enough."

"More than enough," Lorcan muttered and followed her back inside, wondering if Edriss had emerged from her apartments.

Edriss's nightmares were relentless, full of death and destruction, each dream more explicit and horrifying than the last. The Westerlands burned to ash. Tattered shreds of emerald and silver dangled from splintered poles and littered the bloody road. People she knew, loved, lined along the main road, hung on crucifixes. Her family's heads stuck on pikes, greeting visitors.

"Are you sure this is a good idea?"

The voice startled her alert. She was almost certain it wasn't part of her dream.

Edriss blinked. She tried to push forward onto her elbows, but her body felt drawn and heavy, like a glob of molasses. Her soft bed offered no help, nor did the hard glare from the candelabra that had been lit sometime in the night.

Which was...impossible. The door was locked. Bolted.

It wasn't candlelight at all, she realized. Midday sun beams spilled into the room, cutting across her bed. The light bounced off the mirrors to create a blinding prism, as it often did in the hours between teatime and supper.

Edriss lunged forward in bed. Murmurs and skitters followed, and it was then she saw Alise and Rhosyn standing several feet away, watching her with expectant looks.

"How did you get in here?" Edriss pulled her hands down her face and then slapped both of her cheeks. Judging by the sun, she'd been sleeping fifteen, sixteen hours. More. Healing John had taken even more out of her than she'd expected.

"Not easily," Alise snapped. "Do you know how long it will take to repair a door that's been sawed in two?"

Edriss squinted past the women and saw her door had, in fact, been sawed in two. One half lay propped against the wall, the other still holding valiantly to its hinge. "Bit of an overreaction, don't you think? Do normal people do this?"

"Oh, I don't know. Is sleeping from one night into the next normal?"

"Alise." Rhosyn sighed. She stepped forward. "Edriss, you know I'm always forthright with you. Your aunt and I are worried. Your grandmother is too. We know you've been leaving the Rush most days, and we know you're not going to Felgarden. At least not every time."

Edriss whipped an indignant smirk from one to the other, praying it kept the rest of her scattered emotions from surfacing. "And am I not allowed to do so? Am I not a woman grown? A person of my own?"

"For the love of henbane, girl, your flair for the dramatic serves *no one*."

"Yes, thank you, Aunt Alise. As you've always been more than eager to point out, you preferred me better when I was unwell and thus pliant to the mold you've built for me."

Alise rolled her hand through the air in exasperation. "Twisting words is sport to you. I never desired children, Edriss, but you may as well be my daughter. Your mother never had the chance." She turned toward Rhosyn. "You have the draught?"

Edriss cocked her head. "What draught?"

Rhosyn nodded with a sigh. "I do. Are you sure it's necessary?"

"*What draught?*" Edriss scrambled sideways out of bed. "If you even dare put carrion oil under my nose—"

"You'll what?" Alise cradled the small vial with a grin. "Get out of bed so we don't have to use it on you?"

"I would've been sick for days if you gave me that!" Edriss cried. With a glance down, she remembered she'd slept in only a thin shirt, then reached for her robe. She turned away from the women and shrugged it on. As she belted it, she became aware of the pounding force of her heartbeat. It was from more than being abruptly ripped out of her restless sleep. It was everything accumulating at once, the mess of her whole life crammed into a thin vein of anxiety that needed so little to sever and leave her defenseless.

If Alise knew she'd been riding to Rivermarch and why, the intervention would have been far more aggressive. If Rhosyn knew, it would only bring her stress at a time when peace was needed.

"I've been struggling with my thoughts, if you must know. Long rides clear my head." She stretched her jaw to release the tension and turned to face them. "Being betrothed may suit most women, but it's been a shock for me. Even knowing the day would eventually come, I wasn't ready. I'm...dealing with it, in my own way."

"I always thought you had a thing for the boy," Alise said.

"Once...perhaps..." Edriss said distantly. "It's hard to explain what I'm feeling, and I'd venture you don't particularly want me to."

"She isn't one for feelings," Rhosyn agreed with a quick laugh. Her face was paler than usual. She gripped her belly with an extra bit of protectiveness.

Edriss would need to be judicious about how much time she was spending away. Rhosyn would soon need her.

Alise shook her head. "Fortunately for you, Finnegan doesn't take after his toad of a father. His mother was taller than most men, Guardians help her, though it certainly works for her son. Did you know Osman came to Aeldred the day his wife died, to ask for my hand?" Alise twitched her nose. "Aeldred didn't hate me *that* much, thankfully. Or perhaps he preferred I not deal with the matter in my usual way."

"Yes, we know how you deal with unruly husbands," Edriss quipped.

Rhosyn grinned.

Alise rapped her nails along the hearth. "This isn't about Lorcan and the raven, is it?"

Edriss stiffened. She tightened her belt. "Lorcan is free to consort with whomever he wishes."

"Someone ought to remind him it isn't proper to go around kissing in front of the Guardians and everyone. However will we find a groom for Arwenna if all the prospective husbands have watched her shove her tongue down poor Lorcan's throat?"

"I hardly think Lorcan is suffering, Alise," Rhosyn said. She shot Edriss a look. "We came to invite you to supper. Just the three of us. Arwenna will not be joining us, and your brother is, as you may know, once more away."

"And that's another thing we need to talk about," Alise said, oblivious to the shift in topic. "It's really no longer proper for you to visit the baron without a chaperone, not so close to your wedding."

"I didn't need a chaperone before. I certainly don't need one now," Edriss stated. "And if you knew the baron as the man he's become, you'd be convinced of how unnecessary it is. He's fully embraced his curmudgeonry. He prefers being broken. I daresay joy is anathema to him, let alone pleasure."

"Is that a word?" Rhosyn asked. "Curmudgeonry?"

"Edriss, if anyone even heard you referring to pleasure in the same breath as you speak of that man, your reputation would be in tatters," Alise said with a disapproving eyebrow raise. "Not that I hold any love for tradition, but *you* are not *me*. And just the same, I'd like you to begin bringing Arwenna along with you, so she's ready to assume the baron's care when you're married."

"No!" Edriss exclaimed. "Absolutely not. He's my responsibility."

"I didn't realize you were so fond of him."

Edriss snapped her spine straight and scrambled for an excuse. "I'm not *fond* of him, but he tolerates me. I've made some progress, even if not much. Evra made it clear he values the baron's full recovery, and *you* chose me for a reason."

"Your mind salves," Alise agreed. "And how are those working out with your beloved curmudgeon?"

"They'll work decidedly less if I have to stop using them. I could teach Arwenna to mix them, but only I can apply them." Edriss wrapped her arms around herself and spun away. She needed to get ahold of herself, or they'd worry more. "I'm fine, as you can see. I drank a little too much wine last night. That's all."

"Alise." Rhosyn made a bracing sound. "I don't suppose you'd allow me to speak with Edriss alone?"

"You don't require my permission, Rhosynora," Alise said evenly. "But don't believe for a moment this is only about the wine." She stepped close and said the next in Edriss's ear. "If I have to follow you, Edriss, I will. Whatever it is, ask yourself if you want the kind of subtlety I bring to troubling matters. And if the answer is no, then you'll appreciate that it means your secret is a dangerous one—to you and perhaps others."

"You're making more out of it than there is," Edriss said. She couldn't look at her aunt. Alise would read her lies so easily. "But if it pleases you, I'll shorten my rides."

"It does please me. But I'll still have an eye on you."

Alise strode out without saying good-bye. Edriss waited for the sound of the half-sawed door flapping closed before turning around. She exhaled in relief and slumped onto a chair with a soft thud.

"She means well." Rhosyn used her arms to steady herself as she slowly took her own chair. "I don't have to tell you that."

Edriss bowed over her knees and sighed at the floor. "I appreciate your kindness, Rhosyn, but you should be resting."

"Nonsense," Rhosyn said with a dismissive wave. "It's been easier the second time. You remember how it was with Alastrynia."

"I know it's hard when Evra leaves—"

"He does what he feels is right. His methods are not always the ones I would choose, but he leads with his conscience and what it will allow. It's why I love your brother as much as I do. It's why I married him. Because I *know* his heart is always in the right place. If he feels he can better serve all of us by riding into danger, he has his reasons."

Edriss looked up. "You know where he went?"

"No, but he said he'd return in time for your betrothal dinner."

"Betrothal dinner?"

"He didn't tell you?" Rhosyn shook her head. "He's scheduled a formal dinner here in the Halls, a couple nights hence. After, he wants to revive some old tradition that I didn't quite understand. He thinks the fetes will help lighten your spirits and…perhaps melt the ice you have for Finnegan."

"If only you knew…" Edriss tugged on her braid, loosening it the rest of the way. Her dark hair tumbled around her shoulders.

"Is it Lorcan?" Rhosyn watched her with a soulful look. "I see how you look at him, Edriss. How he looks at you. I don't know why Evra has been so determined the two of you should not be matched, but perhaps if I talked to him, he might come around. It isn't too late. The betrothal has not been announced across the Reach yet."

Edriss shook her head. She drew her knees to her chest and wrapped her arms around them. "It's not just Evra. Lorcan and I…There *is* no Lorcan and I. He's made his fondness of Arwenna known, and I expect he'll make his intentions known next."

"Let me at least try."

"Rhosyn—"

"He may yet listen to me—"

"I don't want a man who does not want me back!" Edriss closed her eyes and winced in apology. "I didn't mean to yell. Forgive me." She brought her knees down and pushed out of the chair. "I *am* actually quite starved. Shall we have supper brought here or to yours?"

147

Rhosyn watched her with something close enough to pity to sink Edriss's heart. "I already asked them to bring it to mine."

Finnegan had been standing outside of his father's apartments for over an hour. An *hour*. Osman only needed five minutes with the raven, or any woman these days. So either Arwenna was enjoying the affections of the bloated, arrogant steward, or Osman was really putting her through the paces.

A little of both, Finnegan presumed. Arwenna didn't sound like someone who was just playing along. She sounded like she couldn't get enough.

Finnegan, though, had heard *more* than enough. But Osman didn't trust anyone else to play sentry while he plowed the raven. No one could know. Not his friends, not Evrathedyn, and certainly not Lorcan. It was obvious why *Arwenna* wouldn't want Lorcan to know she'd been spending time in the steward's bed, but why would Osman give a fig what Lorcan thought?

It wasn't his place to question. Osman had made that clear.

He groaned and leaned back against the stone, wondering what Edriss was doing. His footman had said she hadn't left her room since returning from Rivermarch. If she'd done what it *looked* like she'd done, it wasn't surprising. Edriss being a healer of magic was one of the worst-kept secrets in the Rush, but it was still shocking she'd risk her disguise. The man she'd healed might overlook a nameless boy who'd saved his life, but if he'd realized he'd had Edriss Blackwood in his grasp, he'd have turned his sights on her. Malcom Fox was not a man she wanted to know her face or name, unless she were there to further his cause.

He shouldn't have brought Lorcan. He'd just been so euphoric to know something Lorcan hadn't, and the delight had clouded his judgment. Now Lorcan would be like a dog with a meaty bone, and he'd never let it go.

That, more than his father's command, was why Finnegan Derry was standing outside his father's apartments, listening to his disgusting throes of pleasure. As long as Lorcan was smitten with the raven—as long as he didn't know what she'd been up to when she wasn't glued to his face in the gardens—he'd be too busy to interfere with Edriss.

Finnegan jumped when the door opened. He glanced over in time to see Arwenna stealing a kiss with Osman before she flitted away, rushing down the hall before she was seen.

"You can go," Osman said, his pants open wide and half around his thighs, and slammed the door.

"Arwenna!" Edriss appeared from nowhere, racing after where the raven had gone.

Finnegan hooked an arm around her waist and caught her mid-run.

"Let me go! Did you not see—"

"Hush," Finnegan hissed in her ear. "Lower your voice. Please. Yes, I saw."

Edriss wriggled, and he tightened his hold with a sharp tug.

"If I let you go, you can't go after her."

"I need to know if she's all right! She just came from—"

"I *know* where she came from. I've been here for over an hour, waiting for them to finish," Finnegan said through a clenched jaw. "Arwenna is fine. She's not being held against her will. She comes here every day, on her own, for the same reason."

"No." Edriss squirmed harder. "I don't believe you."

"Edriss." Finnegan grimaced, fighting to hold her in place. "*Listen* to me. She's been coming for weeks. You think if I thought my father had coerced her, I'd have done nothing to help?"

"Yes, yes, I *do* think that, Finnegan, because he's your *father*, and you and I both know—"

Finnegan clamped a hand over her mouth. "Don't. Say. It. Not here." He guided her around the corner. "You can say whatever you want to me. But do *not* let my father know you suspect him of treason."

Edriss tore his hand from her mouth and spat at the wall behind him. "Why? Will he be mad you couldn't keep your new prize in line?"

"Edriss Blackwood, for the love of the Guardians, and for the last time, I am not your damned enemy!" Finnegan released her.

She went sputtering back but didn't bolt.

"You want to ask Arwenna about it? Go ahead. But if she wanted others to know, she wouldn't be sneaking about in the shadows, would she?"

Edriss pressed herself against the wall like she was trying to melt into it. "But Arwenna is with Lorcan."

Finnegan fingered his chin and tried not to laugh. "Arwenna has been visiting my father's bed longer than she's been kissing on Lorcan. Bristol's, too, or so I've heard. I don't know what she's playing at, but I know she's not in an exclusive relationship with *anyone*."

Edriss's mouth opened and closed without her speaking. She pressed her lips tight and stared, expressionless, at the empty hall. "Why would she do that?"

Finnegan sighed. "It's a mystery to me too. My father has been trying to lure women even uglier than he is into his bed for years, with little success. How he managed—"

"That's not what I meant." Edriss lifted her shoulders with a controlled breath. "I *know* Arwenna. This is completely out of character. Don't you know the life she escaped coming here? The horrors she faced in Midnight Crest, inflicted by those with more power than she?"

Finnegan nodded. "Aye. But I'd have thought messing about with a man she knows you're in love with would have been out of character as well."

"I know." Edriss shook her head at the floor. "I know. None of it makes any sense."

He stepped closer and dropped his voice as low as he could to still be heard. "Maybe you don't know as much about your 'friend' Arwenna as you think you do."

TEN
THE FIVE TENETS OF BETROTHAL

Edriss turned away from the door when it opened. Even if she hadn't memorized the cadence of his steps, the tentative pause in his breathing when he prepared to speak, she would've known it was Lorcan.

Her man-at-arms.

Betrothal season had officially begun. Evra was determined to revive the archaic marriage traditions last used by their great-grandfather to appeal to men who hated him—to show them that, for all his progressiveness, he was still a traditionalist at heart.

No thought had been given, Edriss fumed, how parading his sister around and celebrating a marriage she'd rather die than see through would make said sister feel.

The Five Tenets of Betrothal were the Westerlands' way of honoring the Guardians, who were said to either bless or curse every marriage. Each tenet was an homage to a specific Guardian, and there was even a sixth one, for the Betrayer, who no one with any sense ever beseeched unless they were asking for trouble.

The Call of the Ushers, the first event, honored the Guardian of the Treasured Past. The prospective bride and groom would enter the banquet flanked by two loyal loved ones from their past, there to usher the unhappy couple into their unwanted future.

Finn's man-at-arms would be his father, following tradition. His lady-in-waiting was his sister, Fignola, in place of the mother they'd lost as children.

Edriss didn't have a mother, and her father was hardly acknowledging her. It should have been Evra and Rhosyn in their place, but it had been decided they would pass these honors to others so they could perform their duties as hosts. Rhosyn chose Edriss's lady-in-waiting for her, picking Cressida, and Evra chose her man-at-arms.

Lorcan.

It was almost as though Evra was *trying* to punish her.

Lorcan didn't speak when he stepped into her room. He stood with his hands folded over his torso and waited to be addressed.

Edriss picked at the satin along the hem of her neckline, trying to tug her dress higher, to no joy. The bodice of her sapphire gown was shaped like a heart, plunging deeper than she was comfortable with. She had always been slight of build, not well endowed, but all she could see when she looked in the mirror were the pale arcs of breasts that had been lifted and separated for everyone in the Rush to enjoy.

The dress had been their mother's, Evra had said. Edriss could only trust it was true.

Lorcan cleared his throat and shuffled in place. "I know you don't want to speak to me—"

"And you said you can't read minds," Edriss muttered. She adjusted her matching sapphire necklace to the center of her chest, just to the right of her heart. The absence of her poison vial left her feeling disarmed. If she hadn't promised to wear her mother's jewels, she'd never have agreed to take it off. "I don't know why Evra chose you, but there's no requirement in this silly tradition for us to speak, so let us embrace what little silence is left to this night." She spun around and inadvertently met Lorcan's eyes.

He lowered his gaze and swept it over her, leaving her feeling even more exposed.

"I didn't pick the dress," she grumbled and brushed past him.

She waited for some wisecrack to follow, some judgment to dig a deeper hole for her shame.

"It's stunning." Lorcan's voice had a high, cracking pitch. "*You're* stunning." He made another clearing sound with his throat and stepped in behind her. She felt the warmth of his hands, hovering just above her shoulders. "If you're embarrassed—"

"I'm not embarrassed," she snapped. "Nor can you read me as well as you think you can."

"Nothing has changed. Nothing has changed for me." His tone had a pleading edge. "I miss the way things were between us, Hemlock. I miss...I miss *you*."

You mean when you treated me like a little sister? Where I slowly fell in love with you, but all you saw was who I was before, never who I was becoming? Who I would become?

"What you miss no longer exists, Lorcan." Edriss opened the door and flounced out.

The entire banquet hall turned her way when she entered with Lorcan and Cressida. The crush of too much light blurred everything, blinding her, which was almost a blessing. She'd never enjoyed being the center of attention. Blending into the shadows was more than a preference; it had been essential to her survival growing up under the harsh eye of Aeldred Blackrook. Instead of sending his dead wife's love child away, he'd paraded her in front of visiting highborns, dangling the prospect of a betrothal to secure alliances.

The one thing Aeldred would have seen eye to eye with Edriss on was the matter of her marriage, even if their reasons were different. He'd never have attached her to a Derry. It was a waste of a match when there were stronger political allies.

Edriss wished she'd pushed back on the dress and chosen something she was more comfortable in. Women scrutinized her. Men ogled her. She was conscious of every exposed inch of flesh. Her arms were occupied by her escorts, so she twisted to shift the plunge in her dress higher, but it was no use.

"You look gorgeous." Cressida said the words without moving her mouth. She smiled when Edriss couldn't, nodding at the people when Edriss didn't. "That's why they're staring."

"You're used to men watching you."

"You mean I enjoy it?" Cressida grinned, continuing her campaign of greeting.

"I didn't say that."

"Wouldn't be a lie if you had." Cressida squeezed her arm. "Anytime anyone spends more than a passing glance on you, they've given up a piece of their power. It belongs to you now. And from the way everyone is looking at you tonight, Edriss, you've become a very powerful woman."

Cressida's confidence had always been alluring to Edriss. The tall blonde was one of the most beautiful, eligible women in the Reach, but she had famously turned down every offer of betrothal that had been sent to her mother. With Steward Wakesell dead, there was no one to force his three daughters into any life they didn't want.

"This isn't the kind of power I desire," Edriss said. She tried to keep her focus on the path ahead as they made their way to the table at the head of the banquet hall. Women whispered to each other without averting their eyes, while men were either reverent or vulgar—there seemed to be no in-between. Worst among them was Osman Derry, who looked at Edriss and then nodded at his son, waiting for her at the long table, and made a crude gesture.

"Ignore it," Lorcan muttered.

"Power," Cressida said again. She tossed her head subtly from side to side. "You're Lady Edriss Blackwood. Nothing they say, nothing they believe—nothing they do can take that from you."

They're already trying.

Finnegan watched her approach with his hands linked behind his back. His grin widened when she neared, sending a shiver tearing down her spine.

Of course he's smiling. He's about to inherit everything, through me. And Evra is going to just watch and let it happen.

Edriss noted her brother at the left end of the table, with Rhosyn. It felt strange seeing him sitting off to the side instead of the middle where he belonged, but those two seats had been reserved for her and Finnegan. At the opposite end sat Osman and his second daughter, Farmina, both of whom stared at Edriss with an intensity akin to a predator sizing up prey.

Arwenna was there too, next to Rhosyn. Edriss felt a thrill of guilt when she realized the raven wouldn't be seated next to Lorcan.

Lorcan and Cressida escorted Edriss to her seat next to Finnegan. Lorcan took the seat directly to her left, and Cressida sat on the other side of him.

"You look beautiful." Finnegan's hot breath, already ripe with spirits, swept along her neck with his whisper. "In full transparency, Edriss, I'm rather relieved I can say it in a place where you can't yell at me or call me terrible names."

"You mean like traitor?" She pinched her bare shoulders in a cringe, and he settled back onto his chair.

"You'll be my wife soon."

"Are you suggesting that makes me a traitor as well?"

Finnegan sucked in an exhausted breath. Edriss hid a grin. "*No,* I'm merely suggesting how tiring it will be for you to constantly suspect me of wrongdoing when the law has forced us to share a bed and food."

"You force Edriss to do anything she doesn't want to do, the law will be the least of your worries," Lorcan muttered. Finnegan leaned over, waiting for him to repeat it louder, but Lorcan returned to sipping his wine.

Edriss smiled at the woman who filled her glass. As soon as the attendant passed, her feigned joy disappeared. "You'll find your bed to be colder than ever, unless you intend to continue the steady stream of midnight women you're so known for."

"No midnight woman could ever compare to you, Lady Blackwood." He practically spat his response.

"A theory you'll neither prove nor disprove."

"You certain about that?" Finnegan leaned close again. He nodded and grinned at people kneeling their respects before filtering off to their own tables. "I seem to recall a young woman who *always* chose me as her husband when we played happy families as children."

She glanced to her right and saw Lorcan running his fingers along the seam of his napkin with rapt interest.

"I daresay you weren't committing treason as a child." She cocked her head. "Or were you?"

"Keep your voice *down*," he said in warning. "You want to say terrible things to me in private? Fine. I might even like it..."

"Revolting," Edriss said with a snort. "I have no interest in your unnatural proclivities."

"You can even call me Lor—"

Lorcan slammed his palms flat on the table. When everyone turned to look, he grinned sheepishly and mumbled something nonsensical.

A hard clink of metal on glass slowed the conversations to a din. Evra stood and raised his glass, waiting for everyone to take their seats.

"I thank all of you for coming to my dear sister's betrothal dinner," he said. Edriss felt him throw a smile her way, but she pretended not to notice. He still hadn't explained his latest absence from the Rush. None of his recent behavior was indicative of the brother she'd so fiercely loved. "As you might suspect, finding a man suitable for a woman who is not only my sister but also the formidable Edriss Blackwood, Princess of Poison, was no easy feat."

"Aye, good luck with that one, Finn!" someone cried out from the crowd.

"Hope you've secured a proper food tester!" said another.

Laughter followed.

Edriss clenched her toes in her boots.

Lorcan moved his tense fidgeting to his lap.

"Our Reach has seen so much strife," Evra said. "And while we in this room were not always on the same side, we are now aligned on a way forward." He turned toward the other end of the table. "Steward Derry, we reinforce our friendship and alliance by joining our houses—by offering my sister and your son into a union that will prove to one and all that we are one Westerlands. We are one people. And we will prevail."

Thunderous cheers and applause drowned his last few words. Osman's dark eyes gleamed with hatred as he clapped along.

This is all going to prove to be a bad dream. Evra is playing some long game he hasn't clued me into. He can surely see the loathing dripping from that awful man. Everyone else can.

Everyone turned toward Osman, awaiting his own speech, but Finnegan stood instead. Edriss jammed her tongue against the roof of her mouth to keep her acerbic temper from reaching her face. She didn't care what *he* thought, but she wouldn't have all of Longwood Rush knowing how he'd gotten under her skin.

"Instead of a speech, I wanted to share a story," Finnegan said. His grin seared her. She'd never wanted so badly to sink into a floor and become one with the dirt. "A story about Lady Edriss and me."

Scattered ribald jokes and jests from the celebrants made their way to Edriss in disjointed pieces. For all she blocked, some still filtered through.

"If it's anything like the meandering stories you told as a boy, I'll come back in a week!" Cressida exclaimed. She tossed a wink at Edriss when she looked.

Finnegan shook his head with laughter. "Of course, you never did have the attention for more than flirting and cakes, did you, Cress?"

Cressida took the joke in stride. "What more could a girl ever want?"

Edriss stole a moment to review the faces of the celebrants, spread into every inch and corner of the banquet hall. They were people she knew, but they felt like strangers who had come to watch her execution. The one face she wanted to see, her father's, was missing. He'd never have been allowed to take his rightful place at the table, but it still hurt not to see him in the back of the room, supporting her from the perimeter.

"Three years ago…" Finnegan tapped a hand on Edriss's shoulder before continuing. "My father and I were visiting the Rush. It was a nice day, and I thought I'd go for a walk in the forest. So I do, and it's where I find Edriss, alone at the riverbank. Not unusual, if you know our Edriss. She's as familiar with these forests as the beasts and birds."

Nods and laughter followed.

Edriss's limbs froze, one by one.

He was going to tell *that* story, and there was nothing she could do.

"What *was*, however, unusual was that she was *entirely* in the nude."

Lorcan pivoted sideways in his chair with a sharp breath, something only Edriss could have heard over the roar of laughter.

Edriss ignored them both and gritted her expression into ambivalence.

"Yes, nude." Finnegan chuckled. "Not for nothing either. Apparently she'd been climbing a tree, the branch she'd been standing on broke, and she went tumbling down into a thatch of raspberries. Whilst, of course, wearing a *white* dress."

Edriss's shame deepened. She felt Lorcan staring, but she refused to look up. She'd never told him about that day because she was afraid he might have done something stupid, like challenge Finnegan to a duel.

"You can't reliably sneak into the Halls of Longwood, at least not *naked*, and she was afraid of the sound scolding Lord Aeldred would have given her when word reached him, so she did what any reasonable person would. She stripped off the dress and tried

158

to wash it in the river." Finnegan shifted with another laugh. "Only to discover her privy garments were also...red. So, off they went as well."

"He's lost his mind," Lorcan muttered. He tossed his napkin onto the table. "This is out of order."

"Can we skip to the part where you acted chivalrous?" Cressida quipped. "Or is this yet again a tale of what a scamp you are?"

"You would know, Cress!" someone called.

Cressida shrugged with an impertinent grin.

Heat coursed into Edriss's face. She should say something— channel Cressida's wittiness to show others how unbothered she was by the entirely inappropriate story Finn had no business repeating in public.

All she could do was stare forward.

"Would I tell a story that made me look bad?" Finnegan asked with a lopsided grin. "As soon as she spotted me, Edriss was horrified, of course. *All* her clothing hung on a nearby tree, drying. She eyed the dead leaves as though they might help, but there was nothing she could do to hide her nudity, nor my...witnessing of it. And I would love to tell you all that chivalry prevented this... witnessing...but alas...this is how I know my future wife has an absolutely delectable ass."

Everyone roared with laughter at Edriss's expense. She desperately wanted to say *something*, but her mouth was as frozen as the rest of her.

"And, Cressida, I'm not a *total* scamp. After lingering several seconds longer in my perusal than I probably should have, I surrendered my own cloak, despite the chill air of the day, and ushered her in through the servants' entrance without so much as a second glance. I'd told no one until today." He grinned down at Edriss. "Nor, I'd guess, had Edriss, judging from the scowl poor Lorcan is wearing."

Her nose flared in response. All eyes were trained on her, from the left and right, from the front...from above, where he towered over her, surely no accident.

"Finn," Evra cautioned, too late. "Skip to the toast?"

Finnegan raised his glass. "To my soon-to-be wife. May she never lose her many sparks. May her beautiful ass stay just as high and tight long after she's borne my children." He drew a sip. "And may the Guardians smile upon our bed and shower us with sparks of another kind."

"I swear on those same Guardians…" Lorcan started to stand, but Edriss snatched a hand out and clamped it atop his knee in warning.

She finally exhaled when the applause came, hazarding a glance at Lorcan, who looked positively murderous.

Edriss reached for her wine when a surge of cool liquid sent her gasping. She looked at her gown and saw garnet liquid splashed all over the bodice. She quickly blotted the wine dripping into her cleavage when she realized someone was helping her.

Lorcan.

Edriss leveled him with a look so freezing, he backed off, palms up in surrender.

"Only one man has the authority to touch her like that." Finnegan handed Edriss another napkin.

"Guardians," Edriss murmured. She finished cleaning herself up as everyone she knew watched her clumsily recover from the past few minutes. The bodice of her mother's beautiful dress was ruined, stained to look almost purple, but it was still less horrifying than Finnegan's uncouth story.

He's playing for power, and he won this round.
I will not let him win the next.
I'll be ready for it.

Lorcan hated dancing, but he was relieved when the music shifted to something more lively, encouraging revelers to move from their tables to the dance floor.

He had just enough time to look at Edriss before Finnegan tugged her out of her seat and led her away.

Arwenna appeared in front of the table. "We should probably..."

"Yeah." Lorcan's gaze followed Edriss. He watched her practically trip over herself trying to match Finnegan's long-legged pace, her hand secured in his like a tether.

Finnegan, oblivious, marched on without a look back.

"I was hoping to speak with Evra first."

"You're too late." Arwenna tossed her head to the side. He followed the direction and saw Evra and a very pregnant Rhosyn in the center of a group of men and women dancing the carole.

"He's ignored all my requests for an audience," Lorcan remarked. He let Arwenna lead him to a quieter edge of the ballroom, where couples engaged in minuets. She jerked them into place, and he lost sight of Edriss and Finnegan.

"An audience about what?" She draped both arms over his shoulder, her gaze fixed on some distant point.

"About Edriss. About this foolish idea to wed her to someone we both..." Lorcan lowered his voice. "Someone we both know is complicit in everything we're trying to fight."

Arwenna shook her head. "I wouldn't do that."

"And why not?"

"Because it's none of your business what Evra decides is best for his sister."

Lorcan reared back to look at her. "I thought Edriss was your friend."

Arwenna laughed. "Kissing the man she loves rather put an end to that, wouldn't you say?"

Lorcan winced inwardly. "You seem...different today."

"Realistic," she corrected. "Evra has no interest in disagreements, not after his mind has been made. You want to help Edriss? You're doing it now."

Edriss certainly didn't see it that way. She might, if Arwenna would let her into their plot, but she'd stood stubbornly firm on the matter.

"What does it matter anyway, Lorcan? You've made it clear *you're* not interested. Edriss has to marry someone, doesn't she? Finn at least cares about her."

"He's a *traitor*." Lorcan hissed the words loud enough to draw eyes from a nearby couple. "As for me…It's not that simple."

"Because Evra won't allow a match between you?"

Lorcan searched again for Edriss and found her in the middle of the floor. Her face was cradled between Finnegan's hands. Whatever he was saying had her cheeks flushed cherry red.

A growl rumbled deep in his belly. If Evra was intent on ignoring his request for an audience, he'd have to demand one. "It's more complicated than that."

"Your feelings for her aren't reciprocated?"

He sighed. "Can we talk about something else?"

"Happily." Arwenna closed her eyes. "Everywhere I go, I sense their eyes on me. Right now, they're watching us. Can you feel it?"

Lorcan took his focus off Edriss long enough to search for the source of Arwenna's worry. He locked eyes with Bristol and quickly averted them. "Have they said anything more to you?"

Arwenna's hand slid along the center of his spine. There was no warmth in the gesture, though anyone watching would see a woman gently caressing her lover on the dance floor. Lorcan himself almost believed her affection.

If nothing else, Arwenna was one hell of an actress.

But she was clearly trying to distract him.

Lorcan caught Osman Derry's stare when they made a sweeping turn. What he saw behind it surprised him enough to miss a step: jealousy. It wouldn't be surprising if the men had chosen Arwenna as their foil because they desired her, but the look in Derry's eyes was more possessive than the arrangement called for.

"The sooner we plant the seed about Rivermarch—"

"I *know*, Lorcan, all right?" Arwenna groaned in his ear. "But your idea lacks substance. It has more probability of failure than success." Her hand tightened at his back. "Edriss hasn't spoken directly to me in weeks. My own sister looks at me like I'm a

162

monster. And what of everyone else here? What must they think of the former high priestess of Midnight Crest who was passed around at the Rookery, only to come here and—"

"No," Lorcan stated firmly. "You won't speak of yourself this way."

Arwenna snorted. "Telling me what to do now?"

"What we're doing here…We do for the greater good. We haven't done anything more scandalous than kiss. You've hardly spoken to other men in the two years you've been here."

"What would you know about it?"

"I—"

"Renardy? The night he died, we were…" She made a derisive sound. "He wasn't only there for supper, Lorcan. And he's not the only one I've sought companionship from."

Lorcan was caught so off guard by her confession, he didn't have a proper response. "Even so. Your life before…That isn't your life now, Arwenna."

"Do you always speak with such authority on topics you know little about?"

Heat flooded his cheeks. "Forgive me. I only wanted you to know you have nothing to feel shame for."

"I'm not ashamed of my life at the Rookery. That's where many of you get it wrong about me." Arwenna's fingers dug against his back. He felt her heart race through the hand he held. "I *loved* being high priestess. I may have loathed my brother, but for all his faults, it was mine that we never brought a child together. It was *mine* that my people had to do the unspeakable and sentence me to death for failing to perpetuate our legacy and protect our race from extinction." She straightened with a humorless laugh. "If they invited me back today, I wouldn't hesitate to accept, though I've done nothing at all to deserve such an honor."

Lorcan understood indoctrination. He'd seen it in village after village as he'd tried to save women from nothing more than a cult of false beliefs. But Arwenna had been in the Westerlands for long enough to see her old life with the clarity it deserved. The

163

Ravenwoods were not bad people, but the way they groomed and used their women, subjugating them under the guise of revering them, was beyond the pale.

"I won't mention it again," he said. When they made another turn, he saw Edriss pinned against Finn, practically swept off her feet—except this time, she was laughing...and so was Finn. Lorcan scowled. "You said Edriss hasn't spoken to you? At all?"

"Not since you and I started our kissing campaign."

"Has she said anything to you?"

"About?"

"I don't know...Has she explained the reason for her silence?"

Arwenna laughed. "Are you being serious?"

Lorcan slowed their dancing to get a better look at Edriss. Her head was tilted back, her eyes locked with Finn's. She laughed again and shook her head.

Arwenna swung her head to grab his attention. "You are..."

Her intensity caused Lorcan to lower his eyes. "I know why Edriss is angry with me. I'm sorry this has affected your friendship as well."

"She's in love with you, Lorcan." She was no longer smiling. "Absolutely, unequivocally, irreversibly in love with you. Surely this can't be a surprise to you."

"I..." Lorcan swallowed his words. He didn't know *what* he knew anymore. After the stolen kiss, he'd been clear with Edriss it could go no further. He'd done his part in hiding his feelings away, though stifling them altogether had been an exercise in pure futility. He learned he couldn't simply turn off love. All he could do was stand strong and hold fast to his honor.

But with the cool way she'd shut him out, he could only assume she'd been far more successful than he had at smothering any lingering hope of a future together.

"Oh," Arwenna said with a long sigh. "That explains your own denial."

"My own denial?"

"The way you love her is so obvious to everyone."

164

"I do love Edriss," he said, flustered, "but it's as I've told you and everyone else who brings it up. She's kin to me."

Arwenna slid her hand up to his neck and pulled him in for a kiss. Lorcan reared back and swiftly glanced toward Edriss.

"See? Your very first instinct is to check on her, make sure she's all right."

Lorcan scoffed. "I'm her protector."

"No," Arwenna said. "You're not. Not anymore. She's a woman, Lorcan, nary a fortnight away from becoming another man's wife and, soon after, a mother to his children. There's no room for you in that future, is there?" Her response clipped the life from his. "So either you're in such vehement denial that you'd let the woman you love marry the wrong man, or Edriss was right about you."

Lorcan loosened his hold on her hand. "Right about what?" He made a conscious effort not to look Edriss's way. It was instinct, nothing more, but he wouldn't give Arwenna the satisfaction of being right.

"That you're more enamored with women you think need saving than women who are your true equal."

Lorcan released her altogether and took a startled step back. "That's an awful crass way of saying I enjoy helping people."

"And where in all this is there room for your happiness?"

He balked. "I *am* happy."

"Are you?"

"Yes!"

Arwenna shrugged and laid her head on his shoulder as the music slowed again.

Laughter drew Lorcan's focus. He looked and saw a cluster of men huddled at the edge of the floor. They were staring at Edriss. Between what little he filtered of their words and some focused lipreading, he discerned enough.

Wait 'til he breaks her in.

Imagine how she'd look bent over my knee.

Been waiting for her to become a woman for years.

Hot with rage, Lorcan untangled himself from Arwenna, but before he could say something to the disgusting cowards, Edriss had already torn away from Finn and fled the room. Many stopped dancing to watch, whispering suppositions that would soon become rumors.

"Go on then," Arwenna said. "You know you can't help yourself."

Edriss slipped through the archway of one of the dozens of gazebos lining the second level gardens and slumped onto the far bench. She pressed both hands to her face and focused on breathing.

The structures were open on the far side but closed off on the keep's side, effectively hiding her from view of anyone exiting the Halls. But she'd heard people following her as soon as she stepped outside, so it was only a matter of time before her refuge became another oppressive cage.

Nothing said should have gotten under her skin like that. Finnegan defending her only made it worse, making it seem like she needed him to fight her battles.

And then Lorcan…the horror on his face when he'd heard what everyone else had. Then he'd left Arwenna's arms and stormed toward her like a protective lover, and Edriss knew she couldn't stay.

How she wished she were in Rivermarch, doing something *useful*. Maybe she hadn't stopped the evil from spreading—yet— but she'd saved dozens of lives. Every victim who went on to be a survivor was a toll in the column for good.

Voices argued just beyond the arched entrance. Lorcan and Finnegan. Cressida. Edriss held her breath tight, drew her feet up off the floor, pressing herself tight to the wall to be as invisible as she could, and waited for them to pass.

The voices faded as someone passed under the archway. Edriss braced for the barrage of questions, but it was only Lorcan.

She stood and peered around him. "Where are the others?"

"I asked them to give us a moment." Lorcan latched the gate and stepped into the center. He crossed his arms and glanced at his feet. "Edriss…"

Edriss pivoted away, facing the open side of the gazebo. She wrapped her hand around the ledge and squeezed her eyes shut.

She'd never felt more humiliated—never felt so *small*—as she had when listening to men snickering about what she'd be like in bed, how it was Finnegan's job to tame her.

For all the freedoms she'd enjoyed since Aeldred had died, she'd never felt so caged in.

Lorcan tentatively stepped closer. He sighed and folded his arms around her from behind, without words, and held her.

Edriss wanted nothing more than to push him away, return him to the background of her life where he had no power over her heart or her happiness. But she fell into old comforts, leaning back against him like placing the last piece of a puzzle, letting him wrap his arms tighter until she was transported back to a place where she was safe, and he was her safety. Where there was no Arwenna, no Finnegan, no Defenders, and no real-world problems ripping them from the comfort of their private sanctuary. Where they could just be Hemlock and Lorry, and nothing else mattered.

Lorcan kissed the top of her head. She felt a tremble in his firm hands, and she started to turn, but he held her tighter. "I won't let it happen, Hemlock. I'll find a way to stop this."

"You can't." Her voice cracked. "You can't stop it. He won't listen…He won't even *talk* to me about it…" She drew her mouth together before she said too much.

"I've tried talking to Evra as well, but he's avoiding me. If he won't make time for me, I'll demand—"

"Lorry. There isn't time." Edriss turned in his arms and looked up at him. "Can I be honest with you?"

He swallowed hard and nodded. "Always."

"*This* doesn't help." She passed her eyes over the firm hold he still had her in. "Acting like my protector, like…more. But you're not more. You'll never be more. Arwenna has your heart, and I…" She pressed her hands to his chest and gently pushed back. "I don't need you to fight my battles for me anymore. I can fight my own."

Lorcan raised his arms like he was going to put them around her again, but he dropped them. "The truth is, I don't know how to act around you anymore, Edriss."

"And that's the problem." Edriss backed farther away. "You're holding on to the way things were when everything has changed. *We* have changed."

He tapped his chest, shaking his head. "But I *haven't* changed."

Edriss closed her eyes and inhaled. "Then it's me who has changed. *Me* who's grown up and sees the world differently." She steeled herself to meet his eyes. "You can blame me for the end of our friendship, if it makes it easier. It is my fault, after all, for falling in love with you, isn't it? For breaking the unspoken rules of our relationship?"

She lowered her eyes and moved past him, headed for the gate.

"Edriss, *wait*. Please. Can we…" He groaned into a hard exhale. "Can we *talk* about this? It doesn't have to be this way."

"For me it does," she said and left.

ELEVEN
THE WICKED CURRENT

The Call of the Ushers was behind them, but there were still four sacred tenets ahead. Edriss could think of nothing more ridiculous than reviving inane traditions when there were terrible men out there burning the Westerlands to the ground. When there were people *suffering* under cruel, sweeping pronouncements.

In less than a month, her meeting with "John" might bring all the treachery to a crashing halt. But by then, she'd be married. She was racing two clocks—one for herself, one for her people—and her heart was weary of battles.

Edriss checked the sky. Noontide was close. If she left soon, she could still be of some use in Rivermarch before the day was wasted.

She plotted her escape as she stood in the whipping wind of the large open field, listening to her brother explain the pointless events of the day to the other miserable people gathered. Finnegan gave her the respectful distance that her cool demeanor demanded, stealing glances from the side. Lorcan…

169

Well, Lorcan was with Arwenna, of course. They stood with their hands linked at the edge of a large crowd of townspeople who had come to bear witness to the farce.

"The Guardian of the Warrior's Aim receives our first honor of the day. While the Call of the Ushers represents the loyalty our bride and groom bring from their old lives, our ancestors created the Bowman's Sacrifice to demonstrate the loyalty they have to each other." Evra squinted against the howling wind. The vellum he read from folded over with each gust, causing him to stumble. Rhosyn's hair blew into his face, and she stepped away. "Edriss and Finnegan will both take three shots with their bow. Whoever is closest to a bullseye wins, and the loser's family must pay for the remaining festivities. Sounds simple enough, doesn't it?"

The crowd tittered. Edriss rolled her eyes. Evra would never allow anyone else to pay for anything. Her dowry was already being called the biggest wedding coffer ever assembled in the Westerlands, which was almost more disgusting than the wedding itself. It wasn't enough for Evra to sell her to the Defenders; he had to unwittingly fund their malicious endeavors too.

"But there's a twist!" He laughed and raised the flapping vellum. "On either side of the target will stand the man-at-arms and lady-in-waiting of the *opposite* side. So Edriss will have to make her shot with Steward Derry and his daughter, Fignola, standing perilously close to where she must aim, while Lorcan and Cressida will do the same when it's Finnegan's turn."

Edriss perked up. A grin jumped into her bitter expression.

Osman Derry would be standing next to the target…a target she could so easily miss.

But she wasn't a terrible shot. She'd always been fair with a bow, trained by the First Rider of the Rush himself, her father. She could always chalk it up to nerves…

"Edriss?"

An attendant was holding her bow. She'd carved it herself, with her father's help, over a long afternoon on the riverside. That day had been one of the best of her life, an opportunity to speak openly with a man she had been desperate to know. When Evra had become lord, she'd hoped she and her father could have a more meaningful relationship, but the opposite had happened.

Edriss accepted the bow with a gracious nod. She flexed her string hand and stepped into place, readying her bowman's stance like Thennwyr taught her: spine straight and aligning her collarbone to the arrow she nocked.

Fignola was as pale as a ghost, angling herself slightly sideways. But Osman…Osman's tight grin, the dearth of life in his eyes as he issued an unspoken challenge…

He was goading her.

He *wanted* her to slip up.

To shoot him.

Why?

"Let's not pretend you're not going to nail the bullseye on the first shot," Finnegan joked, lightening the mood. "I may as well just concede now."

My bullseye and your bullseye aren't the same, she thought as she pulled the bowstring taut. Osman licked his lips and made an *almost* imperceptible nod, which pushed her anger back to the surface.

He wants you to shoot him because everyone will know it wasn't *an accident.*

Edriss took a deep breath and loosed the arrow. It hit the direct center of the bullseye. She lowered her arm and handed her bow back to the attendant. With a haughty glance at Finnegan, she said, "I forfeit my other two shots. Your turn."

Finnegan whistled through his teeth and stepped in to take his place. Lorcan and Cressida took their places on either side of the target.

Edriss locked eyes with Lorcan. He rooted her with a silent plea.

She turned away.

The sound of an arrow tearing through the air was followed by awkward laughter. She hadn't heard it land, and there were no screams, which must have meant—

"You missed it by a mile, son! What do you think, we're made of money?" Derry said.

"Better quit running your mouth and go make some more," Bristol replied. "These are the hazards of wedding your son to a known bowwoman."

"Right into the forest it went," Rhosyn said with a soft laugh. She moved toward Edriss. "How are you holding up?"

Edriss shrugged as they watched Finnegan nock another arrow. He twitched his shoulders in circles before pulling the string back. "Not looking forward to the next event."

Rhosyn laughed. "Have that many secrets to send into the flames, do you?"

"Enough," Edriss muttered. She nodded at Finnegan. "Look at his posture. Slumped. Soft at the knees. Angled too much to the side. He's aimed right at Lorcan."

"I can hear you," Finnegan said and fixed his angle. "This better?"

"Decidedly."

"You sure? You've been awful cross with him lately." Finnegan shrugged. "Can fix it for you right here, right now."

"No, I'm not sure," Edriss said, crossing her arms. "But I'll thank you not to murder anyone *today*."

"As though I make a sport of it on other days?"

"Finnegan!" Osman boomed.

Finnegan groaned and made one more taut pull before loosing the arrow. It landed at the edge of the target, on the side Lorcan stood. Lorcan glanced down at the stuck arrow in consternation. Before he could right himself, Finnegan had released the third arrow, which bounced off the target and landed on the grass.

"Damn. So close to knocking out my competition," Finnegan said, turning to wink at Edriss before handing the bow to the attendant.

"It's not a competition if you were never in the running."
Edriss cut him down with a glare and followed Evra and Rhosyn
down the hill, where the next excruciating event awaited them.

Many thought the Unburdening was the easiest of the marriage
tenets, but to Lorcan, it was the most distressing. The Guardian
of Anguish and Tribulation demanded the sins and secrets of
both bride and groom, and while some claimed the couple would
simply lie, anyone who truly believed in the Guardians knew that
would be a truly terrible idea. Anguish and Tribulation was the
Guardian everyone was desperate to keep mollified, for to do
otherwise was to invite exactly what the name suggested.

Lorcan held too many failures in his heart. Putting words to
them would make them so much worse. If the Guardians could
look into his heart, they'd see how far he'd gone astray from the
man he wanted to be…how far he'd fallen.

Evra stood nearby, but he wasn't alone. Lorcan had been waiting for his moment, but there'd been no opportunity for private
conversation.

Even if he could get Evra alone, he still had no idea what to
say that he hadn't already said.

*You could tell him the truth. If Evra knew how you really felt, it
might soften his heart on the matter.*

But the truth was twisted and complex, much like love itself.

Lorcan stood in front of the raging fire, letting his eyes glaze
and forcing his thoughts elsewhere.

Arwenna leaned close and whispered, "So they write their
secrets on the vellum, put the vellum in the fire, and…That's it?"

Lorcan watched Edriss on the other side of the bonfire. She
sat at the small table they'd set out for her and Finn. Her quill
was suspended above the page as she stared into the fire with a
blank look. Behind her and Finn stood the minister overseeing
the ceremony.

She had at least one secret she'd kept from him. What else would she write?

"Lorcan?"

"Ah, yes. Yes. That's it. Then we return to the banquet hall for the Unbinding."

"A bit ridiculous, no? How does anyone know what they're writing is a true and accurate accounting?"

"*We* don't know," Lorcan answered. He watched Edriss put the quill back to the page with a tentative roll of her shoulders. She began writing. "But the Guardians do. And they are the authority in this realm. It isn't kings or magi." He tilted his head upward. "It's them."

Arwenna released his hand and crossed her arms over her chest with a tight laugh. "You really do believe, don't you?"

"Don't you?"

"In the Guardians? No." She ran her hands along her thin sleeves. "Those are your gods. We have our own."

"But you believe in your own gods?" Lorcan was still watching Edriss when he noticed Finn look up and narrow his eyes into the distance. He followed Finn's gaze toward his cause for alarm.

It was the man Edriss had healed.

He stood alone, covered by a thick hood, but it was his eyes that gave him away—ashy gray and deep, like the sea, and trained on Edriss with steely intensity.

Arwenna's voice blended with the others as Lorcan's thoughts tunneled on the man who had no reason to be at the event. No reason to be watching Edriss the way he was. Did she know he was there? Had she seen him as well?

Edriss went to the fire and held her fist over the flames. Tears rolled down her cheeks as she closed her eyes, releasing her secrets into the fire. Finn appeared at her side, smiled at her, and did the same. When it was done, he looped an arm around her shoulder with a tight squeeze and backed away.

Lorcan searched for the man again, but he'd disappeared.

"What's wrong?" Arwenna asked. "You've gone pale."

"Nothing," he lied. A familiar ache made his chest constrict. His breaths drew short. Cesarina's face, swallowed by flames, jumped to the front of his mind and refused to leave. "Let's go."

Finnegan had been looking forward to the Unbinding all day.

When Evra had decided to revive old traditions, Finnegan had thought the idea was ridiculous.

Until he got a look at the schedule of events.

Anything honoring the Guardian of Rebirth and Renewal—the "god of sex," Finnegan and his friends always called it—had potential for greatness.

Edriss sat alone on the chair at the head of the room. In front of her was a solid block of wood that ran waist high, to protect her modesty during what would undoubtedly be an afternoon everyone talked about for a long time.

He tried to restrain his grin while everyone filtered into the banquet hall.

"I know what you're thinking," his father grumbled as he settled in beside him. "You'd be a fool to do it."

"A fool? Like the man sleeping with Evrathedyn's sister-in-law?"

He made a sound like steam escaping a vent. "You may be a man now, Finn, but you dare speak to me like that again, and I'll backhand you in front of all of the Rush and every last fucking Guardian."

Not even Osman's anger could dull Finnegan's excitement.

And when he was married to Edriss Blackwood, he'd never have to listen to anything his father said ever again. Osman would answer to *him*. No one from East Derry had ever risen half as high. None had ever been expected to.

Lorcan cut Finnegan down with a pointed look when he passed. He shook his head, even though his friend was already on the other side of the room.

Until now, he'd been nice enough. He'd endured Edriss's anger, her accusations. He'd even tolerated it in front of others because she'd been through so much, and he wanted her to see him as an anchor, not a boulder.

But today…Today he'd send her a message of sorts. A reminder that, though he would never *actually* force her hand, he was well within his right to take what he wanted when he wanted, and it was time for her to show him some respect.

All while standing in a room full of people gathered to watch him demonstrate how he could handle his future bride.

A fluster of attendants flocked around Edriss and pulled her to her feet. They lowered into kneels on all sides of her, disappearing behind the block of wood. Edriss's eyes upturned in annoyance, but it was the freckled dots of red blotting her cheeks that Finnegan fixed his gaze on. The attendants were no doubt handling their role with care, but he would not be as dainty when it was his turn to reach up under the skirt of his bride.

"You try anything imprudent, and Evrathedyn will have no choice but to end this betrothal, which is already on thin ice, thanks to the irksome mate of yours who can't keep his mouth shut," Osman said. "Tell me you know better than to risk it further."

Finnegan ignored his father and followed the beckoning call of Evra, who stood next to his mortified sister while everyone waited for the salacious event to begin.

"I must confess," Evra said, once the crowd had quieted. "It was this event that had me second-guessing the Five Tenets altogether. My grandmother insisted the whole thing was archaic and should be buried with the past."

Meldred tapped her cane against her chair and shook her head. "When have you ever listened to me, boy?"

Finnegan chuckled to himself. Meldred Blackwood and her daughter were the only women in the Reach no man would ever speak back to.

Edriss was becoming a similar woman. If she could just see he *wanted* her to push him around...but only if it meant, when the squabbling was done, that it was his arms she longed for.

"Only when it mattered, right, Grandmother?"

Everyone laughed.

"Naturally, Aunt Alise shared her displeasure as well."

Everyone turned to Alise for her reaction, but all she did was roll her eyes.

Finnegan frowned and returned his attention to Evra's speech.

"But for all the change we bring to the Westerlands, we are, at our very core, a traditional society. Our histories are the blood running through our veins. Our legacy courses through the River Rush. It roots the mountains that both protect us and expose us. Our values are our deep, personal love for the land we stand on and the people who live in it. And so, I ask my dear sister to indulge us in an admittedly bawdy tradition, one we cannot skip if we intend to pay true homage to the Guardians on the verge of the most sacred vows you'll ever take." He grinned sheepishly at Edriss. "And let's agree I owe you one."

"You'll owe me for the rest of your life for this one," she muttered, loud enough for most of the room to hear.

Finnegan grinned when he felt eyes on him, knowing even before he looked who it was. He turned toward Lorcan's glare, and Finn responded with an impish nod before starting up the stairs toward Edriss.

"For those who are unfamiliar with the Unbinding," Evra said, "Lady Edriss has been bound with rope under her dress. I hesitate to say specifically *where* she's been bound, as she is my sister—"

"Thighs and ass!" someone yelled amid the awkward laughter.

Evra, in his discomfort, tried not to laugh. "Finnegan will need to unbind her...but *without* looking." He glanced at Finnegan. "He will go in blindly, hands up her...dress, and free her as quickly as possible. If he has not freed her by the time the hourglass runs out—approximately five minutes—the Guardians curse

177

this union to barrenness." He held up his hands. "The Guardians make the rules, not I."

"Use your teeth!" Cressida called, grinning.

"His head stays *outside* the dress," Evra asserted. "He may use only his hands and his quick mind to race the timer set by the Guardian of Rebirth and Renewal. If he oversteps the boundaries of what is appropriate, it's *me* he'll answer to. Finnegan, do you understand?"

Finnegan nodded. He warmed his cold hands by rubbing them together, so he didn't shock Edriss when he reached up her dress—though that would have been fun too. But he had no intention of squandering even one second.

"Edriss?" Evra asked.

"I understand I must have done something atrocious for you to punish me so," Edriss said. She turned her eyes upward and inhaled a shuddering breath, waiting. "For my sins."

"Are you ready?" Evra asked Lorcan.

Lorcan nodded miserably and lifted the timekeeping device to show him.

Evra lifted and dropped his arms. "And begin!"

Finnegan dropped to his knees with a thud and shoved his hands into Edriss's thick layers of skirts. She usually wore simpler, modest dresses, and she'd no doubt chosen this one specifically to fluster him.

"Having a difficult time, Finnegan?"

"Not in the slightest." Finnegan grimaced and ripped at the fabric until part of it actually tore away by accident. The crowd loved it, but Edriss kicked him. "Sorry."

"You're not remotely sorry."

"No," he agreed with a chuckle. His hands connected with her ankles, and he looked up to see her reaction. Her scowl held precisely the level of hatred he'd expected.

She was entirely at his mercy now. Her disgusted, loathing-filled looks would do nothing but encourage him.

His hands slid up her bare skin. She shivered and looked up again, away from him. When he reached her thighs, he traced the soft flesh with the pads of his thumbs before brushing them along the length of her undergarment. She made a tight whimpering sound.

How he wished he could see Lorcan's face.

Finnegan grabbed hold of the rope and traced the knots, memorizing them. Evra had said no knives—too dangerous— or other implements, so Finn would need to undo them the old-fashioned way.

Finnegan went to work on the knots, tugging and shifting them against her with more force than was needed. She jumped and lurched under his alternating soft and rough ministrations, and he could guess at her reactions by the scandalized jubilation of the crowd.

When the knots had loosened, he slid his hands up between the rope and her flesh and left them there for a moment. He looked up at Edriss. *I can't wait to taste you*, he thought, praying she was reading his mind, so he could watch her fight the flush that would take over her at the very idea of it.

All he had left to do was pull the rope out.

"Time?" he called.

"About, uh, two minutes," Lorcan said, unable to hide the disgust in his voice.

"Two minutes," Finnegan said under his breath. He passed his hands higher, sliding them around the back and under the thin fabric covering her ass. He palmed her bare skin there and held her gaze.

"The knots are finished," she hissed.

"Aye, but I'm not," he said. He slid his palms inward, causing her to tense and then jump. "I would never hurt you, Edriss."

"No? You'd just take advantage of me when I cannot fight back?"

"Have I done anything other than what the tradition demands?"

179

"You're doing it now!"

Finnegan squeezed her ass. "This?"

"*Yes.*"

"But don't you understand? I could have my hand all the way up your—"

"You vile, filthy man—"

"I *could* but it would only prove I'm exactly what you think I am," he stated. "I do want you, Edriss. I want you so badly, my mouth is watering and my..." He turned his head down and shook it with a short laugh. "But I can wait for our wedding night."

"I will *never* marry you. I don't care what Evra thinks, what tradition demands. And if you ever attempt to force yourself on me, you'll be wasting your effort because I have many, *many* ways to avoid ever bearing one of your cursed children." She wiggled to dislodge his hands. "You're not helping your case by fondling me when the rope is already loose either."

Finnegan slowly slid his hands back down her thighs and her calves, then twisted them once around her ankles with a tug before reaching back up for the rope and pulling it down.

He stood and raised it in the air. Everyone cheered.

"From the looks of it, she's already with child," someone said, and the comment took off, gaining life as others added to the supposition.

"Come to my apartments tonight," he whispered to Edriss, as her attendants covered her torn dress with a cloak. "Let's *talk.*"

Lorcan disappeared after the Unbinding. Edriss had purposely avoided acknowledging him during the embarrassing event, though his strained voice, calling the time, had made it clear he was close by and privy to the entire mortifying ordeal. When she finally gathered her courage to look his way, he wasn't there.

Alise stepped to her side as everyone transitioned down to the river for the final event. "I know that was difficult for you. Evra is right that I don't approve, but none of that matters, Edriss. What

I saw on the stage was a man taking what will never be truly offered to him, and a strong woman holding her ground. And you can be sure it's what everyone else saw as well, no matter what ill-bred commentary they may have made."

Alise squeezed her hand and disappeared into the thick throngs of swiftly moving people.

Edriss took a deep breath and followed, but she caught the eyes of a man staring right at her.

John.

Her body went cold. Finnegan whispered something nonsensical in her ear, and she nearly jumped out of her skin.

"Don't get too excited," he murmured and nudged her. "Come on."

"In a hurry to lose the final contest?" Edriss tried not to make it obvious she was watching John, but she needed to know why he was there—why he was watching her with such concentration. Did he know she was Henry? Or was he there supporting his Defender friends?

"Yes, actually," Finnegan said, scratching his head. "My pride can only take so many hits."

"I'll bear that in mind." She spotted Cressida and jumped in beside her.

"That was unexpectedly sexy," Cressida said with a conspiratorial giggle. "Did he…"

"Guardians, no." Edriss scoffed in disgust. "I'd have punted him into the crowd had he gone an inch more."

"What I wouldn't have given to see that."

"Don't you and he have some history?"

"We've fooled around a few times, if that's what you mean, but I wasn't interested in what he had to offer." Cressida's laughter faded. "You really *don't* want to marry him, do you? This isn't an act?"

Edriss frowned in confusion. "Why would I say I didn't want to marry him unless it were true?"

Cressida shrugged. "I don't know. You've always been contrary."

"Not for the sport of it, I assure you."

"That's not what Lorcan says."

The mention of his name had Edriss searching for him again, but she didn't see him in the crowd. She'd lost sight of John as well.

"I can't find him either," Cressida said, sighing. "Some usher he makes, eh?"

"Probably with Arwenna." Edriss repressed a sour look.

"Arwenna is with Lady Rhosyn." Cressida glanced at her from the side. "Lorcan's not himself today. Have you noticed?"

Edriss shook her head. She listened to the rest of Cressida's ramblings without interjecting a word on the long walk to the banks of the River Rush. Every few steps, she glanced over her shoulder to see if John was there, but he didn't appear again.

Maybe she'd imagined him...conjured him from her fears on a day that was as much disgusting as it was distracting. She *should* be in Rivermarch, helping and learning. Instead, she was being subjected to the carnival her brother thought would win the Defenders over to his side.

The only thing he'd done is give the Defenders an excuse to grope her in public.

Evra was talking with some of his council by the riverbank when she and Cressida stepped off the path. Edriss felt a gentle tug and saw Rhosyn, who was pulling her out of the crowd.

"Are you all right?" Rhosyn asked. She fluttered her hands around Edriss's face but landed them on her shoulders instead. "Be honest, Edriss. I'm asking because I care about you, and I can see this day hasn't been easy."

Edriss lowered her eyes and nodded.

She was.

She had to be.

So many lives depended on her ability to shrug off indignities and push forward toward what mattered most.

"Evra is..." Rhosyn sighed with a whimsical look toward the river. "He's struggling. He really is. He desperately wants to

182

believe in the good in all men, even ones you and I know have no desire to be good. He thinks this day—this union—will give those men reason to love him and follow his lead, but I'm not so sure."

Edriss cocked her head. "Why aren't you saying this to him, Rhosyn?"

"I have." Rhosyn stopped speaking and smiled broadly when Arwenna passed with Alastrynia in her arms. She beamed and waved until they passed and then her expression was somber again. "And he does listen, even if it doesn't seem like it."

Edriss snorted. "It doesn't."

"He's doing his best. He's finding his way."

"And is listening not to those who can help him but those who would destroy him." Edriss lowered her voice. "He completely disregards *any* warnings others give him, and just gives into everything his enemies ask for."

"That's only half the truth. He's prioritizing based on risk."

"He's *prioritized* Osman Derry's happiness over my own, Rhosyn. His *sister*. You know, the one he supposedly went north to save? The reason he met you?" Edriss crossed her arms and angled away with a long, bloated exhale. "Forget *me* for a moment. Think of what happens if he empowers men like Derry. Bristol. If he overlooks Ashenhurst skulking his halls. If you have *any* sway over him, Rhosyn, you'll help him see it, before more of us die because he refuses to." She flicked her gaze toward Rhosyn's belly. "I'll be by later to check on you."

Edriss stalked away. She saw Arwenna pass Alastrynia to the nanny and then turn and fold herself into Lorcan's arms. Edriss braced and continued until she reached the river, where she waited for the attendants to remove the lacing from her dress. She wasn't allowed to swim in her shorts, like Finnegan was, despite that she'd swum in her underwear her whole life. The shift dress would slow her, but she'd still beat him. She'd won every swim contest she'd ever entered, and she had been swimming in the volatile River Rush her entire life.

"This final event honors the Guardian who has long been seen as the unofficial Guardian of the west: the Guardian of the Unpromised Future. This is our god of life, our god of death. The one who decides how long or short our promise is, and we are never closer to them than when we are facing death and choosing life. The Sacred Swim, across a river that has taken far too many lives, is not a test of our mettle but of theirs. Let the Guardians decide who will reach the other bank. Who will not." Evra's voice faltered. "Thankfully, both Edriss and Finn have been swimming in this river for years." He turned toward the river. "This is one of the widest points—and the most dangerous. Logs, branches, and other detritus sweep down the current fast enough to knock a man senseless or send a ship off course. This represents the many obstacles life gives all of us, and serves as a reminder that, no matter what the Guardians lay at our feet, we are asked to fight. To persevere. To earn our right to life until our promises are spent." He stepped away and approached Edriss. "Be careful. Please."

"Forgive me if I have trouble believing your concern for my safety is anything more than theater," Edriss responded. She couldn't look at him. Her gaze was fixed on the river. On the west bank. "You could have at least let me swim the way I'm accustomed."

Evra frowned. "I won't have the entire Rush ogling my sister's half-nude body."

"But it's all right for them to watch me get groped by Finnegan?"

Her brother balked. "Was he untoward?"

"Would you care if he had been?" Tears burned her eyes. She grunted in annoyance and stormed off.

Edriss ignored the questions he called after her. She ignored the voices wishing her luck. A smirking Finnegan made some challenge, but she didn't hear that either, instead moving to his side without acknowledgment.

The last thing she saw as she launched herself into the river was Arwenna leaning up to kiss Lorcan.

With the image burned into her mind, Edriss plunged into the ice-cold river and swam for her life.

The initial shock was familiar, welcoming, like returning to a place of comfort after an extended absence. Swimming had become impossible after she'd fallen ill, then the Westerlands had been thrust into chaos, shifting her priorities from happy indulgences to more immediate, practical concerns.

She heard Finnegan gasp and scream curses so vile, she almost started liking him again. Evra was right. Finn had been swimming in the river his whole life as well, but not like Edriss had. Swimming had always been her favorite escape. The one place she could be truly alone with herself.

Memories of splashing around in the river with Lorcan, Finnegan, Cressida, Evra, and Meira flooded her thoughts, but they were unwelcome. The worst lesson from growing up had been realizing children became different people as adults. Some for the better, others for worse, most products of the environment they had been raised in. Edriss prided herself on being stronger than the world she had been born into, but it didn't dull the sting of all she'd lost.

A burning seam parted her shoulders, evidence of the strength still there. She pumped her arms in perfect fluidity, metering her breaths at the right cadence before plunging beneath the surface, where it was safer.

The silence was her favorite part. The blurred muting of the world beyond, however temporary, was its own form of magic. There was nothing under the water except blissful solitude.

Edriss closed her eyes and disappeared into her rhythmic strokes. So far removed from the world, she had no sense of Finnegan's progress, the crowd...any of it, and she forgot it was a contest at all. Flashes of her childhood rose in her mind, of Lorcan gleefully cheering her on from the opposite bank. He'd always bet on her. Never anyone else. No one had ever believed in her the way Lorcan James had.

Before she could lose herself to painful reminiscing, she came up for a gulp of air and forced herself back down, pushing harder against the wicked current. Her eyes opened briefly, and she saw shadows of logs and branches overhead, moving downstream. If even one of them hit her, she'd be knocked off course, or worse. But she knew this river. Knew how low to swim to avoid—

Darkness splattered her vision, followed by a dull shock of pain reverberating through her head, creating a deafening sound that blurred understanding. She flailed her arms and breached the surface, but the sky winked away and then it was night.

Lorcan leaped into a boat and paddled furiously against the unremitting current. He screamed through the burn, plunging the oars into the water with such vehemence, he snapped one. Cursing, he hurled it into the river and dove in instead.

By the time he reached the far bank, Finnegan had already pulled Edriss out of the water. He crawled over the top of her, trying to pump water from her chest using compressions.

I'm coming, Hemlock.

A half dozen small boats launched from the other bank. Evra screamed an order to lower the drawbridge downriver, but that was a fifteen-minute ride, and whatever had happened to Edriss would be decided long before anyone crossed and made it to her side.

She was the strongest swimmer he knew. He'd never even considered she might struggle in the event.

Lorcan's hand tapped wet earth, and he used a tangle of roots to hoist himself out of the water. He gave himself only a second to catch his breath before rolling over and clambering to his feet.

He dropped onto the grass, where Edriss lay unmoving, her face pale and her lips blue. He smoothed matted hair from her face. "What *happened?*"

"I don't know." Finnegan panted, hands laced and jerking through the compressions. His head whipped back and forth.

"I just saw...One moment she was under and then she was floating."

Lorcan needed to remove her dress before she caught a deeper chill, but they had nothing to replace it with. He glanced at his own wet clothes in helpless despair.

He said a silent prayer, leaned his head against her chest, and listened for her breathing. Shallow but there. He remembered what Edriss had done when Meira had nearly drowned years ago. "We need to roll her over. Onto her side."

"No, what we need is Alise or Meldred. *Now*," Finnegan said.

"By the time they get here, her fate will already be decided. Roll her the fuck over or get out of my way, Finn."

Finn stared for a moment and then crawled off of Edriss. Lorcan already had her in his arms before Finn could get situated. He gently adjusted her until she was on her side and held her there, one hand tracing her back in soothing passes.

Lorcan saw Edriss's face consumed by flames, as a town full of Defenders cheered her demise.

He winced the vision away.

She's not Cesarina. She'll never be Cesarina. I would never let that happen.

Edriss jerked, sputtering and coughing up river water. Lorcan angled her face to keep her from choking, tracing his hand down her back in even more zealous caresses. The desperate wheezing sounds she made sent his fear hurtling back to the surface, but her breathing evened out, and she was able to draw a full breath again.

Lorcan bowed his head and whispered his relieved gratitude to the Guardian of the Unpromised Future. He wiped his eyes and breathed deep.

Edriss peeled out of his arms and scooted herself away from them both. She drew her knees to her chest and practiced breathing with her eyes closed. It was then Lorcan spotted blood matted in her hair. He'd missed it at first because of how dark everything was, soaked by the river water.

"Stupid," she muttered, shivering. "Utterly idiotic and avoidable."

"Edriss, you scared me to *death*." Lorcan crawled toward where she'd isolated herself, but her eyes issued a warning to stay away.

Lorcan reluctantly retreated, assessing the situation, and breathed out. "Finn, go help at the drawbridge. We'll need blankets, fresh clothes, something warm—"

"I'm not going anywhere, mate," Finn stated. He wiped a wet arm across his face and coughed. "Edriss and I appreciate what you did—"

"You don't speak for me," Edriss blurted. She reached a shaky hand toward her head and withdrew a palmful of blood. Her eyes rolled back, and Lorcan surged forward again, but she swatted him away. "Nor do you."

"He needs to learn to accept his place," Finnegan said. He pushed to his feet and towered over them both. "To respect *my* place and stop acting like he's the one you're marrying."

Lorcan shook his head with a scorned laugh. "It is entirely possible to love someone and not have ulterior intentions. Or is that kind of love foreign to you?"

Finnegan gesticulated wildly. "Do you really think we're all blind? That none of us can see what you're doing? The denial you live in? Does Arwenna know, or does she even care, seeing as she can't decide which bed she enjoys visiting the most?"

"Finn—" A cough kept Edriss from finishing. She shoved a hand outward when Lorcan tried again to go to her. Each denial was more painful than the last. Watching her shiver, alone, gutted him. He fought his urge to go and wrap her in his arms no matter how she resisted.

"Only a scamp would bring up Arwenna's past to make a point." Lorcan shifted to his feet to get a better view of the progress on the other side of the river.

"Her *past*?" Finnegan grunted. He tapped his bare chest with a disdainful laugh and jumped to his feet, charging toward Lorcan. "What must it be like to live in such delusions?"

"If I ever wanted to know, I'd just ask *you*." Lorcan stood his ground. He shouldn't let Finn get under his skin. Why he did—why it kept working, over and over—was a problem he lacked the heart to solve. He owed no explanation to anyone, aside from Edriss.

It wasn't irrational to not want to see someone he cared about wed to a traitor.

And yet, what have you done to stop it? Why haven't you forced your way in front of Evra? Is it because he'll only accept your deepest truth? A truth you refuse to acknowledge yourself?

Lorcan cleared his mind of all but the necessities of the moment and backed away from Finn. They needed to get Edriss back over the bridge and into a warm bath and make sure she had no lingering trauma. Everything else could wait.

"All right, let's—" His mouth slammed shut. The spot where Edriss had been sitting was empty. He swung around, searching for her. She wasn't in the water, nor did he see her on the bank path.

"She just disappeared. How did she disappear?" Finnegan spun around with a blank look.

No one knows this forest better than Edriss, Lorcan thought, glancing into the dark woods. "You head that way..." He pointed in the direction of the bridge. "I'll go this way."

Finn nodded and took off.

Lorcan squinted after him, watching his pale form shift into a jog. He'd need something warm too, before the chill took him, but there were plenty of others around who could help.

When Finn rounded the bend, Lorcan turned and entered the forest.

190

TWELVE
STAY

Her bag was exactly where she'd left it. There was no reason it shouldn't have been, but little else had gone to plan, so she'd half expected it to not be in the stable's fourth stall when she'd slipped inside to check.

It had taken her over an hour to lose Lorcan's forest trail before she felt safe making a run for the stables. A quick check confirmed she was alone, so she spent a few moments to catch her breath, change into the dry clothes of a make-believe boy named Henry, and grab a few bites from her dried meat rations.

By now, Evra would have declared her missing.

He wasn't wrong.

Edriss eyed her meager satchel. Some part of her must have seen the day coming, for the purse full of gold had never been needed for her day trips to Rivermarch. The other helpers had always provided any nourishment she needed while there, and aside from her botany supplies, nothing else she carried with her was strictly necessary.

There was enough gold to live modestly for a year. If she went without, perhaps two. She wouldn't need half as much if she succeeded in bringing the traitors to light. If she didn't...

She couldn't even fathom the thought of never coming home again. But until the Derrys and their cohorts were exposed, Longwood Rush was no longer her home.

Drowning would have been a preferable outcome to marrying into that vile, wretched family.

Edriss hoisted the satchel and started to bridle and saddle her horse when hard, thundering rain started outside. She paused and listened. Storms swept in quickly and outstayed their welcome this part of the year. Only diviners could predict their length with any accuracy, but she didn't have a diviner to consult, nor did she have time.

She glanced at Nightshade with a weary exhale. Staying would be risky. They'd eventually find her. But she couldn't go back either.

There was one place though—one place she could go to ride out the storm.

"I'll be back when the rain clears, Shade. Don't tell anyone I was here, all right?"

Edriss secured her satchel and reached into the cubby to grab the second cloak she'd left behind the last time she had been caught in a storm. She tossed it over her head and moved to the doors of the stable. Before she could change her mind, she ran.

Her boots sloshed in the already-flooding ground. She adjusted her pace just enough to keep herself from sprawling into the gloaming. The wind whistled past her face, rain hammering from all sides as it gusted through the forest unabated. If anyone saw her, it would be over, but no one would. She'd perfected the path over the years, memorizing every fallen log, every broad trunk.

When the forest opened to a clearing, Edriss paused long enough to check her surroundings. Still alone. She drew a deep breath, said a silent prayer, and bolted across the open field. She didn't stop until she reached the rickety ladder of the guard tower.

She clambered up the slick rungs. Her boots lost purchase, so she used her arm strength to power through. Rain whipped her face and stole her outer cloak, which went flapping away into the wind, lost forever.

When she reached the top, she flopped forward with a relieved crash. She kicked closed the trapdoor and rolled over onto her back to collect her breath.

She bolted upright with a startled gasp when a face stared down at her.

Lorcan.

Soaking wet, like he'd been standing under the gaps instead of the boards.

"What are you..." The question hung unasked.

"You know, I waited here," he said, rushed as though running through a speech long rehearsed. "Everyone else thought you'd disappeared on the west bank, but I knew...I know you." He tapped his head and paced away, breathing deep. "And I know you're unhappy. I know that unhappiness...that I've..." He reached for the railing and wrapped his hands around it.

Edriss shifted to her feet. "What are you doing here, Lorry?" she asked cautiously. She moved to the edges to see if she'd missed anyone in the clearing, but it seemed they were alone.

"I could ask you the same, but I already know the answer." He stared into the stormy night without turning. "But I'm asking you, Edriss, *not* to do this."

"Do what?" She left purposeful space between them. Any closer and he might hear the damning race of her heart.

"I *know*, all right." He loosened his hands and looked over his shoulder. "I know where you've been going...what you've been... doing."

Edriss stilled. She backed up to the opposite railing. "You'll have to be more specific."

"*Rivermarch*, Hemlock." Lorcan pushed back and turned. His eyes were closed, his brows knit together. "Why didn't you tell me?"

Edriss shifted from denial to defense in a blink. "Tell you? Really? Why would I?" Cruelty slipped into her tone, and she embraced the security of it. The lie came just as easily. "You keep holding on to something, and it doesn't exist! You say you miss me and nothing has changed for you, but you're deceiving yourself, Lorry. You're living mired in lies that are easier than the truth, which is…which is that you've outgrown your care of me. Your concern for me. And I've…" Edriss fought the rising lump choking her. "I've moved on."

"You don't—" Lorcan tented his hands under his chin with a hard squint. "You don't get to tell me how I feel. How I don't feel."

Edriss tossed her head back with a laugh. "You've *told* me how you feel, Lorcan. You looked me in the eye and told me that kissing me was a *mistake*. That you could…could never see me as anything other than a sister." She raked her tongue along her teeth. "I've told you before. I don't need another brother."

Lorcan snaked a hand out and slapped the far wall. "You wound me by assuming that's all I have to offer you now that you're grown. Assuming my friendship isn't enough."

"When have you time for a friendship, when you spend most of your waking hours locking tongues with Arwenna?"

"I'm here now, aren't I?" His boots slapped the wet boards when he stepped forward. "I'm *here* with you now, and not her."

Edriss looked away and shook her head. "No woman wants to be a man's obligation. You being here makes me feel worse, not better. Like I've put *yet another* challenge into your life, something you didn't ask for and have no choice but to stand by."

Lorcan was quiet for several grueling moments. "Is that what you think, Edriss? That I felt *obligated* to be your protector?"

Edriss said nothing. She didn't use to believe that, but her heart had been pulverized beyond recognition. Her truths were taking on the same shape as her lies.

He tugged at his wet hair as he moved closer. "You don't think…" He grimaced and rolled his jaw. "You don't know what I…"

Edriss gasped when he charged toward her. She went stiff at the crush of his arms, despite how badly her body wanted to melt against his. Limp and furious, she searched for the words damning enough to hurt him the way he'd hurt her, but the rough press of his lips against hers made her forget every horrible thing she'd ever thought, ever said. The slide of his hand up her back, fisting her hair at the nape of her neck, sent her heart into an even more dangerous spiral.

Lorcan moaned, a sound filled with lust as much as loathing. He closed his fist around her hair and held her tighter, his warm mouth even more perfect than her heart had remembered.

Edriss wound her hands up his back and deepened the kiss. She heard him whisper her name between hungered kisses, each utterance more desperate and lost than the last.

He sighed when he pulled back. Forehead pressed to hers, he rolled his head back and forth. "Don't go."

"Tell me why I should stay." Edriss didn't recognize the woman speaking. She couldn't decipher the change sweeping over her. She was still buzzing from the cause.

"Even if…" Lorcan shook his head and put a step between them. He slid his hands up and down her arms. "You should stay because I would be lost without you."

Edriss trained her eyes on her feet. "That's not fair. Nor is it an answer."

He angled his head down to plead with her. "What answer would make you stay?"

Edriss swallowed a roll of emotion flooding forward. "You're in love with someone else, and you're here, kissing me. Arwenna might not care who she hurts, but I do."

"You're wrong. It's all I can say, Hemlock. Just…you're wrong."

"You leave me so confused." Edriss squeezed her eyes closed in frustrated agony. "You can't imagine what it's like to be standing where I am."

Lorcan lifted her chin with his thumb. "I know. I'm sorry. I shouldn't have kissed you. Not then…not now."

She held his gaze. "Not if you don't mean it. Not if you're kissing someone else as well."

"I..." He tilted his head back and closed his eyes again. "Guardians, Edriss. What is wrong with us?"

He'd never address his feelings directly. She'd already known it, and yet, once more, she had walked into the same frustrating refrain, chipping away at her vulnerabilities until she was defenseless.

She could tell him about Arwenna and Osman, but what would it solve? It would break his heart, which would break hers.

Edriss didn't want to be any man's second choice.

"I can't stay." A crackled edge coated her words. "If you know about Rivermarch, then you must know how bad things are there. They *need* me." She glanced toward the keep, blinking in the darkness. "And no one else is going to put an end to this plague taking over our home. Don't you see that? Even you've given up."

Lorcan's head practically swiveled he shook it so hard. "That's *not* true. I've never—" He snapped his mouth closed, like he was about to say something he shouldn't. "I haven't given up, Hemlock. I will *never* give up."

"Thousands of our own citizens are still being burned, with no answer, Lorry. Renardy, our *friend*, is *dead*. The men responsible sit on my brother's council. How can I stay here, where I can do nothing? Why should I not go somewhere I can make a difference?"

"Because it's dangerous, Edriss!" He dropped his hands to his sides in frustration, turning them into fists. "The man you healed? Yes, I saw. I saw you act with utter carelessness toward a monster who would burn you with his own hands even after you saved his life. Did you know he was at the events today? Did you see him?"

Edriss lowered her eyes. Few things stung worse than Lorcan scolding her.

"So you did." His laugh was humorless. "And yet, you'd walk right back into this same fire, wouldn't you?"

Edriss lifted her gaze and held her head high. "Yes, Lorcan, I *would*. I *will*. All that's here for me is more agony—and a husband who would drag me into the depths with him. And the absolute only thing you could ever do to stop me would be to tell Evra what I've been up to, and if you did? If you *dared* betray me like that?" She didn't finish.

He shook his head at the ground, mouth pursed in a tight frown. "That's not the only thing I could do to stop you."

"Oh?" She crossed her arms, waiting.

Lorcan looked back up. He swallowed and took a deep breath. "I…" His head shook, his thoughts engaged in a battle she both wished she could see and was grateful not to. "Edriss, I—"

The trapdoor slammed open, and Finnegan grunted as he hoisted himself up. "*There* you are." He sprung to his feet, dusted himself off, and joined Edriss at her side, ignoring her stunned offense. "I was so worried, Edriss. Are you all right?" He shot an odd look at Lorcan.

Edriss nodded. She didn't have the heart for words. Both men had thwarted her escape, but they couldn't watch her at all hours. Rivermarch was out of the question, with her secret out, but there were other towns in need. Other people she could help.

"And…Am I…interrupting—"

"No," she said quickly, flicking her eyes up at Lorcan, a warning. "I was just waiting for the rain to pass, and *Lorcan* was just leaving."

Lorcan watched her, his jaw clenched like it was the only thing keeping his words from spilling out.

"Mm." Finnegan passed a frown between them. "I rode here. I have an extra cloak in my saddlebag."

"I don't need—"

"Not everything has to be a fight," he said with a long sigh. "Let me take you back. Please?"

Edriss glanced once more at Lorcan. He wore a miserable look that once would have made her heart ache but just left her hollowed. Maybe he did love her, deep down, but it meant nothing if honor kept him from acknowledging it. Every rejection ground her further into dust.

Finnegan, for all her terrible suspicions of him, had been undeniably consistent. He'd remained stubbornly resilient against her constant barrage of accusations and, aside from his cheeky showing at the Unbinding, had respected her boundaries. Her once-powerful crush on him had pushed its way back to the surface, and however unwelcome, it left her feeling far more whole than the eternal game of push-and-pull she and Lorcan had been playing for years.

In that moment, she needed Finnegan more than she needed Lorcan.

Soon enough, she'd need neither of them.

She forced a smile and looped her arm through Finnegan's. The dark cloud passing over Lorcan's eyes seemed like jealousy, but she was bone tired of trying to read him. "Yes. I think that would be best."

Stay

UNTIL THE WORLD ENDS

THIRTEEN

DERAMORE

One Year Earlier

Lorcan waited for the sun to set before spurring Frog and riding out of the forest. He passed beneath the untended gates of the quaint village of Deramore with his hood pulled low over his face as he maneuvered the sparse main road, dusk doing its part to obscure locals and travelers alike. He was neither, but if anyone recognized a tender of death moving through the town square, the night would erupt into chaos. The task ahead would be exponentially difficult with a rabid audience.

It was a job that could only be done in darkness. There was no room for light in justice.

Lorcan was in his second year traveling the circuit. At twenty, he'd been old enough for years to own property, take a wife, and be held to account for his crimes, so his father felt him also ready to take on the family trade and mete "justice" to the "heathens" practicing magic illegally in the Westerlands. His tenure should have ended when Lord Aeldred had died, but Evra's quest to heal the Reach still had far to go, which meant the James men still had lives to save.

He thought of Edriss, as he often did in the spaces between his usual deliberations. *I worry about you going to Deramore tomorrow.* He couldn't tell her it worried him too. Admitting it would be a strain on his courage, but there was also the crippling fear she'd follow him and inadvertently reveal her magic. It scared him enough already that she'd revealed it in front of trusted friends.

Refocusing on the task at hand, Lorcan brought first one fist and then the other to his mouth to warm them, shifting the reins as he traded them out. The air was heady with the musky aroma of a coming storm, nearly masking the rich perfume of gamy meat wafting from the row of taverns. They were the only establishments still open, but then, they never closed. Men could find cause to drink and fornicate at all hours, and there was money to be found in both.

Witches though… They practiced their illicit deeds under the spell of moonlight.

Or so said the dark whispers. Whispers had begun the war on magic. They'd prevented it from ending when it should have. They were the reason that the work Lorcan and his father were doing still mattered.

The urge to pick a shingle at random and dip into the promise of warmth and sustenance was almost more powerful than his fear of failing.

He rode through town with the even pace his father had taught him. Both fast and slow enough not to rouse suspicions, Rohan James liked to say, as if the precise speed was intuitive and not a constant, careful battle.

Most in Deramore, and other towns, were still glad to see a tender roll in, ever eager to be rid of vile witches—less eager to see the practice of burning put to bed, with Lord Blackwood's bid for peace. But few things divided people more than determining what a witch even *was*, and by the time anyone could agree on anything, wives and daughters were lost, businesses leveled, and lives ruined.

Lorcan and his father had always saved many more than they'd condemned. It was the only thing making the task bearable, knowing they were protecting lives that would have otherwise been lost under the proclamations of more bloodthirsty tenders. Arriving early enough to do so, while still negotiating the cover of darkness, was critical to their success.

Bone tired, he pushed on.

He couldn't wait to get back to the Rush and give Edriss her birthday gift. The rare book was poorly wrapped, stuffed deep in his satchel, but despite his excitement, he was still vacillating between actually giving it to her and throwing it into the river, alongside his nerves about the whole thing.

Lorcan reached the dark, rectangular building hulking at the base of a moderate hill. He tethered his horse in front of Deramore's town jail, wondering when they were going to rename the place for what it was: a persecution chamber. Guardians help them if they had any real crime, for the jail was full of nothing but women locked away on the thinnest justifications. The ban on burning had changed nothing in many of the smaller villages, where they continued on as though there were no armistice at all. And until Evra was willing to take sterner action against offenders, the burning—and thus his tending—would continue.

His arrival was for a special case, according to the raven sent to his father. No one knew who this woman *actually* was or where she'd come from. It had been her absurd claim—that she was one of the king's daughters—that had drawn authority's eyes. Only a witch would have the audacity to defame the Rhiagains with such a ludicrous charge.

He secured his satchel, swallowed one last lungful of clean night air, and ducked under the low, splintered arch of the Deramore jail for what he hoped was the last time.

Lorcan sat for nearly an hour before a hulking giant of a man grunted for him to follow. His boots squished on the damp stone, the smell growing danker and moldier the deeper they went. Halfway through the journey, he remembered the Deramore jail was burrowed into the hill itself—and remembered his old fear that the whole thing might cave in.

Water pooled near the end of the hall, running down the dirt like waterfalls. He squinted to make out the light at the end, a flickering orange glow caught on an invisible breeze. His hand fell to his sword, but he felt immediately foolish. The women locked away were no criminals. It was the jailers he should fear.

The cells were jammed into the walls, tiny and forgotten. A row of twelve there were, all of them full. Full of witches…of *women* whose crimes were arbitrary, decided by men who sought to eliminate what they couldn't understand.

Lorcan swallowed a wave of guilt. He wished he could save them all. It wouldn't end until Evrathedyn punished the men leading the Defenders from the shadows.

Lorcan looked into each of the prisoners' eyes as he passed. He refused to cast his gaze aside in fear and shame, like the men who had locked them away would.

These exchanged looks lived in his heart.

"Here." The man jammed a rusted key into the lock of the last cell. He ripped the door open and beckoned Lorcan in.

Lorcan shivered and stepped forward after a pause the guard noted with a grunt. It wasn't the first time Lorcan had been afraid entering a cell, but he'd been particularly unsettled by the young woman's situation since the raven had come in. *No visible magic. Just a stubborn refusal to renege her claim of being a princess. We fear it's some new foul witchcraft that will sweep across the rest of our women if not dealt with swiftly.*

He muttered his thanks, jumping when the guard's response was to slam and lock the cell door.

Lorcan breathed deep, raised his gaze, and found one of the most beautiful women he'd ever seen. Condemnation lived in her dark-brown eyes. Her strawberry-colored hair was poorly plaited, her golden gown filthy and torn, but in that moment, he believed with his whole heart that the woman huddled on the bench was royalty.

"Miss?"

The young woman held his gaze. Her arms were wrapped around her knees, drawn to her chest. Her bare feet were so caked in mud, there were cracks running through the layers of coating. He couldn't make out her toes.

"Here to kill me or listen to me?" Her voice was startlingly deep for someone her age, which was admittedly tough to determine, given her current state. Lorcan guessed she wasn't much older than him.

"Listen," Lorcan said. The word came out croaked.

She snorted and squeezed her knees with her thin, bare arms. The gown had once had sleeves, but they'd been torn off, judging from the uneven seams left. "You'd be the first then."

Lorcan leaned against the crumbling wall. A rat skittered somewhere in the shadows. "They aren't listening because they don't like what you're saying."

"They don't like the truth? That I'm Cesarina Rhiagain and I'm trying to get home?"

Lorcan twisted his mouth. "If you *were* the princess—"

"I thought you came to listen." The girl rolled her eyes. "It would be so easy to prove, but no one wants to write my father and verify my claim."

Lorcan lowered to a crouch. "Or...You could retract the claim and be done with this."

A dark smile spread across her face. "They think I'm a witch, Tender. There's only one way out of this for me."

"Lorcan," he said. "Lorcan James. You can call me Lorcan or just Lor." He almost said *Lorry*, but only one person called him that.

"Tender," she replied with an upturn of her lip. "You might think you're on the right side of this now...the one who can walk away when the tending is done...but when my father finds out you've executed his daughter..." She laughed, a hiss rolling off her tongue like smoke. "You'll wish for the easier death you're about to sentence me to now."

"I didn't come to sentence you to death," Lorcan said, though he shouldn't have. The tender might make the final pronouncement, but he had to choose his mercies carefully. Usually the "witch" in question had to first renounce her witchcraft, feigning both guilt and remorse believably. The ones who stayed firm and proud to the end were beyond his aid, unless he wanted everyone to know he was working under the direction of Lord Blackwood, not the Defenders...and then he'd not be saving half. He'd be saving none.

"Right." The girl stared through the bars.

"Miss, all you have to do—"

"Can't even call me by my real name?"

There was no way she could be Cesarina Rhiagain, the king's second daughter. If she'd truly been missing, the crown would have been in a panic, searching the entire kingdom for her. She'd never have been allowed to be locked away in a filthy cell at the edge of civilization.

"Cesarina," he said anyway, because whatever her actual truth, she'd embraced a new one, and he would get nowhere if he didn't address it. "Just say it was all a lie. It doesn't matter *what* the truth is—"

"It matters to me." She pushed her words through a clench. Strands of her red hair hung like curtains around her eyes. "It matters to me, Lorcan James. If someone said you were not who you know yourself to be, would you retract your claim to yourself? Your very identity?"

"I—"

"You wouldn't," she answered for him. "Because without that truth, does it matter whether you live or die? If you are told by those in authority you cannot be who you are and must pretend to be someone else you don't even know, then what is left?"

Lorcan searched the tiny cell for evidence of her treatment. A piss pot was overturned in the corner. Tin bowls full of inedible mush were stacked, untouched.

He reached into his satchel and withdrew an apple and a half loaf of bread. He preemptively flinched when he stretched to hand them over, expecting her to spit at him or hurl them back in his face, but to his surprise, she snatched them both. She hid her face as she tore into the bread with soft, desperate grunts.

"There's more, if you want it," he said gently. The look he earned in return was feral. He held up his hands and tried to grin. "Then again, I made the bread, so maybe you're better off passing."

Cesarina stopped chewing and stared at him.

Well, I have her attention at least. "I can't tell if you're looking at me like that because the bread has turned your belly sour or if you're just stunned to hear a man knows his way around the kitchens."

She shook her head, rolled her eyes, and went back to her solitude.

"Learned from my mother," he said, watching her carefully for any physical response. "Before she died, she spent as much time baking as the staff. They had a nickname for her: Tartiana. Instead of, you know, Tatiana." Lorcan frowned against the woman's hard glare. "You know, because she baked…tarts…eh…never mind."

"James. Greystone Abbey. You're highborn," Cesarina said through a full mouth.

"You sound surprised."

"Don't look it," she muttered and tore off another bite. "Or sound it."

"Well, neither do you, princess, but here we both are."

Cesarina whipped her head upward with another heated glower, but a slow smile carved through her grime-covered face. "You want me to like you, don't you, Tender?"

"What?"

"Do you always use humor to ease tension? To get people on your side?"

Lorcan balked at her frank assessment. "I…suppose I do."

"Hmm." She nodded off to the side. "And does it usually work?"

Lorcan almost smiled, but the conversation wasn't a victory, and he'd be remiss to treat it like one. Not yet. "Not as much as I'd like."

"Time to try something new," Cesarina said. She brushed the crumbs from her dress as though it weren't covered in mud and dust. The move seemed instinctual rather than calculated, and Lorcan wondered how others had discarded her claim of royalty so easily.

He pulled himself back to a standing position but didn't start toward the bench. "Any suggestions?"

Cesarina squinted at him. "Is having a conversation part of your charge, Tender, or can we get this over with?"

Lorcan pointed at the empty end of her rotting bench. "Can I?"

"No. You cannot."

He jumped when a rat passed across his boots. Cesarina didn't even flinch at its high-pitched squeals. She only stared blandly at him from behind her curtains of red curls, her dark-chocolate eyes blinking through sooty cheeks. His father had relentlessly drilled into him the importance of never developing opinions beyond professional on his visits to the jails. A level head could save a woman; anything less would be her damnation.

"Very well," he said, gathering his wits. "I want to help you, Cesarina."

Her eyes narrowed. The modicum of camaraderie they'd built disappeared in an instant. "Do you?"

"I don't expect you to believe me."

"Then we understand one another." Cesarina dug into the apple, but before she could break off a piece, she pulled it away from her mouth and chucked it at the bars. It clanged and fell to the dirt, then rolled through muck. "If you will not send word to my father, then there's nothing you can do to help me."

Lorcan sighed. He'd come to the hard part, the point at which he began to see the path the woman would take. "Let's say I believe you."

"Your lies are as transparent as your jokes."

He laughed. "Fair. But if I did…Would it be enough? Enough for you to tell everyone else you made it up?"

Cesarina's face pulled into a deep frown. "Why would I?"

"Because it would save your—"

"Tell me, Tender, how many witches—*real* witches, not the poor women you drag from their beds for knowing their way around a garden—actually renounce their ways in the end? Think before you answer."

Lorcan didn't need to think. "Less than those who don't."

"Less than those who don't," she replied with disgust. "Because that would be to deny who they are. And we are *nothing* except who we are. You say you believe me? Well, how lovely. That makes one of you. But I will not stand in the town square and say I'm not who I am."

His breath hitched as the entire situation caught up to him in a blinding rush. He suddenly understood what made her special; it was the striking sense he *knew* her. And once he grasped that, the rest came tumbling forward. He didn't know this woman, but he knew someone just like her. Someone just as stubborn—just as proud and strong and bold.

It was Edriss's face he saw then, filthy and awaiting condemnation, and he knew it would be an image he'd never shake.

His darkest, deepest fear, realized.

"They'll burn you," Lorcan said, moving forward a step. He couldn't fight his shudder. "Don't you understand?"

"Don't you mean *you'll* burn me?" Her eyes glowed with simmering rage. "Or have you decided it's easier to pretend you're not who you really are?"

Lorcan knew he was going to say something he shouldn't before the words reached his tongue. He said it with Edriss's face clear in his mind and her compassion flowing through his veins. "I don't come to jails to hang women, Cesarina. I come to save as many as I can. And if the late Lord Aeldred had known this, he'd have hung my father and me years ago. Now, with his son in

211

charge and trying to mend things, it's the Defenders who would have my neck."

Cesarina didn't look impressed. "So you do deny your truth."

"I save as many as are condemned—"

"Well, come get your medal, Tender!"

Lorcan sputtered, flustered by her twisting of words. "My father and I…Two men alone cannot stand against the Defenders of the Righteous Dawn, but we try to slow the madness, as much as we can." What was he doing, spilling his truth to someone who already loathed him? All it would take is one word to the guard. He wouldn't believe a doomed witch, but he might repeat the story, and the rumor would spin until it matched Lorcan's truth.

He'd traveled to Deramore alone. No one was coming to his aid if he fell upon trouble.

"And so nothing will change. The end." Cesarina's fire dimmed. She wrapped her arms around her knees again and laid her head sideways across them, facing away. "It's why I left Duncarrow. I knew…I knew nothing I said or did would ever change my father's ways."

Lorcan braced himself on the wall. Dirt crumbled away under the tremble of his hand. "What ways?"

"Doesn't matter." Cesarina tossed her head, and he realized she was clearing tears. "I see now the king has common ground with his subjects more than I thought. The right man leads the Westerlands now, but yet women still burn, day and night. Your lord is weak to allow men to break his laws, so where does this leave his people? No one stands for anything anymore." She sniffled, laughing. "Death doesn't sound so terrible in comparison."

"I don't want you to die." Lorcan dug his hands into the loose dirt and grimaced. Why had he said it? Perhaps she was a witch after all. "I can help you, Cesarina. Let me *help you.*"

Silence fell over the cell like a shroud. Elsewhere in the jail, women banged on bars, yelling through walls. The distant sound of water dripping onto the dirt in soft pats was almost calming compared to the tempest swirling behind Cesarina's deep stare.

Whatever she said next, Lorcan knew it would be her final answer. That nothing he said or did after would sway her.

"All right, Tender." Cesarina unfurled herself and lowered her bare feet to the dirt floor. "I'm listening."

Lorcan quickly fumbled through his satchel before she changed her mind, conscious of the intensity of her eyes boring through him the whole time. When he found the pouch with the vellum, quill, and blot, he heaved the satchel at the bars behind him and rushed toward her.

"Sign this. It's all you have to do and then you'll be free to return to Duncarrow."

"Free?" She pulled the vellum from him, dividing her scrutiny between the renouncement and him. "You may succeed in springing me from this jail, but it won't make me free, and I'll never return to Duncarrow."

"You're not going back to Duncarrow?"

"No." She kept reading.

"But you said you were trying to get home."

"Did I say Duncarrow?"

Lorcan, frazzled, struggled to make sense of her riddling way with words. She'd been doing it the whole time, he realized, and it put their entire conversation into a different light. "I don't understand."

"I left Duncarrow for a reason." She snapped her fingers.

He gave them a dumbfounded look before he realized she wanted the quill. He uncapped the ink blot, dipped the quill, and handed it over.

"It's no longer home to me."

"Where is home then?" He held his breath as her hand hovered over the signature line.

"I don't know." Cesarina scribbled her name on the line. "It's what I was trying to discover when these whoresons jailed me." She thrust the vellum at his chest. "We're good then?"

"I'll need to run it by the baron, but…Yes, I believe so." Lorcan shook his head, still caught on her words about home. "You really don't have anywhere to go?"

Cesarina smiled icily. "Tempted to solve another one of my problems?"

Lorcan stuffed the vellum into his vest and backed away. The longer he was near her, the greater the bizarre sense she was melting him from the inside out—that she wasn't Cesarina at all but someone he deeply, desperately cared about. "I'll take this to the baron and return when I have his answer."

He pounded on the bars for the guard, unable to look into her dark, steely eyes even a moment longer.

Lorcan woke to the horrifying, unmistakable scent of burning flesh.

He hadn't wanted to stay the night in Deramore. The village was a ghost of the past, a constant reminder that laws only reached so far in the Westerlands. But the baron had refused to see him until daybreak. The man only did business during the sunlight hours.

Which meant there shouldn't *be* any burnings yet. Cesarina would be pardoned, and the other women hadn't yet been tended. There had to be a reasonable explanation.

Swine doesn't smell so different. It's a local butcher, smoking his meats.

He scrambled out of bed and shimmied into his pants, strapping his suspenders hard enough to sting his skin when he released them. He ripped his shirt from the chair, his eyes watering from the smoke pouring through the poorly kept windows of the old inn. *It's not what you think it is. There's an explanation, and the only way to get one is to leave this room.*

Lorcan fastened his sword belt and bolted from the room without locking the door. He raced down the creaking steps, then ran past the empty bar and out into the haze-filled morning.

He swatted at his eyes, stung from smoke, and chased the crowd streaming toward the square. His view was obscured by the dense sea of people standing shoulder to shoulder, pushing forward in fruitless but frenzied urgency. He blurred their voices into one, refusing to let rumors or whispers tell a story he needed to see with his own eyes. *Witch, witch, witch,* they cried, but it meant nothing—nothing without confirmation.

The throngs thickened the closer he came to his answer. He had to elbow his way through the tightly packed onlookers, ignoring their angry grunts about being there first, pushing blindly—*Tender coming through! Officer of the law! Make way!*—until he stumbled into the dirt at the base of a pyre.

A witch's pyre.

Lorcan's face crumpled. He closed his eyes and forced himself to bravely raise his head, to confront what his heart already knew to be true.

Cesarina was consumed by flames. Her face, angled toward the sky, showed no sign of the unthinkable pain she must have been in. Her inexplicable smile cut through the smoke and singe. Her hair, which had so fascinated him only hours ago in the cell, was gone, replaced by searing red blisters breaking out along her scalp.

"Where is the baron?" he cried out, finding his voice and his balance at the same time. He screamed the question again, but his words were drowned by the hot crackles of the fire, mixed with the fervent cries of *witch, witch, witch.* "I am the tender responsible for this woman, and I need to see the baron!"

"Tender."

Lorcan whipped right and saw the baron standing, arms crossed, wearing a pleased look.

"What have you done?" Lorcan charged toward him. He held her signed confession up, snapping it against the air. "She recanted!"

The baron lifted his brows and nodded at the pyre. "Does it matter, when the people need someone to burn?" He rolled his eyes at the signed confession. "Your lord *stole* our tradition from us. We've been forced to mete our justice in the late hours, when no one can stop us. They're *hungry*, Tender. So what does it matter if she recanted, when they've waited so long to see another witch on the pyre?"

"You cannot be…You cannot be serious! There are *laws*. This was not your condemnation to make!"

The baron ripped the confession from Lorcan's hand, balled it, and chucked it at the fire. "Tell Lord Blackrook the next tender he sends us, under the thin guise of meeting us halfway, will be sent back to him in a box of ashes." He spat in the dirt. "Be gone before noon, or I'll do it anyway."

Lorcan stumbled back and crashed into a woman, who shoved him forward again. He nearly pitched into the fire himself but instead sank to his knees at the edge and sobbed.

The crowd's malevolent zeal waned, and he knew they were nearing the end. He'd failed Cesarina. Miserably. How it had come to this was a question that would haunt him for the rest of his days. He should have known…He should have foreseen the bloodlust of a people whose twisted way of life had been yanked out from under them. How had he not seen it?

Lorcan opened his watery eyes. Cesarina had finally succumbed to the pain. Her blackened face hung downward and to the left. He watched her through soundless weeping, each breath more strained than his last.

He kept his eyes locked on her until something on her face changed. It was subtle, starting with her eyes, which were no longer brown but violet. Her lips became fuller, almost a pout. Even through the char, he could see a familiar flush rise high in her cheeks.

All his dreams, his loves, his failures swirled into one horrifying image, throbbing across his brain like a fractured heartbeat.

Edriss.

Lorcan finally loosed the scream he'd been holding in.

FOURTEEN
PERILOUS DISCARDS

Edriss trained Arwenna mostly in silence. She spoke when words were absolutely necessary but otherwise nodded or gestured through the steps. They were only days away from the wedding, and both Alise *and* Evra had been pressuring her to turn Baron Lawrence's care over to Arwenna before it happened.

Her anger stewed inside of her, unaddressed. It had nowhere to go. No place to project, nor person to hear it. She didn't even know what she was most angry about anymore, only that her other emotions had slipped into the background to make room for the flames of rage growing taller and wider with each passing day.

It wasn't about Rivermarch or Lawrence. Though he'd promised to keep her secret in exchange for his precious solitude, she'd known the arrangement wouldn't hold up forever, especially with the increased security following Renardy's death.

It wasn't that she hated Arwenna for stealing Lorcan away either, for was it really the raven's fault she'd won his heart? Arwenna couldn't steal what had never belonged to Edriss, and

217

she had been hurt enough herself to ever be the cause of quashing someone else's happiness.

What was most maddening was her protectiveness of Lorcan. Edriss *was* furious with Arwenna for leading him on when she was clearly spending time in the bed of another man—a terrible man. At least one that she knew of, but according to Finn, there were others too. She couldn't trust Finn, but nor could she trust a woman jumping into bed with Defenders.

Arwenna was distracted, was worse than normal. She'd measured the wrong amounts twice and forgotten a critical ingredient. Teaching her was pointless anyway. Anyone could learn to mix a mind salve, but it took Edriss to apply one—a perfect mix of herbs and magic.

With a weighty sigh, Arwenna finally pushed the bowl away and looked directly at Edriss. "You're angry with me about Lorcan. And until we address it, we'll get nowhere."

Edriss rolled her eyes, trying to decide whether to salvage the mix or start over.

"Edriss?"

"We'll start over." Edriss wrapped the bowl in a cloth, then wrapped another around that. She put it in what her grandmother liked to call the "perilous discards" barrel, which the attendants knew to handle with care when cleaning.

"If you want to yell at me, yell. I suppose I deserve it. I've known all along how you feel about him. You have every right to hate me." Arwenna's tone was filled with so much placating restraint that Edriss *did* want to yell. "Maybe this distance between the two of you is good, for the time being, so you can focus on the new life awaiting you. But one day, when all this is over, I hope you remember how much he cares about you."

"Don't speak to me about what Lorcan does or does not feel for me," Edriss replied. She gripped the edges of the bin and forced a deep breath. "As for how *I* feel..." She shook her head, unable to finish.

"He does love you, more than you know." Arwenna stepped forward, but Edriss lifted her shoulders in a tight cringe, and Arwenna stopped moving. "I realize how empty it sounds coming from me, and it does you little good at present, when he's...in a relationship with me. But I suppose the point I'm after is that one day, your heart will soften, and I hope you'll allow him back into your life when it happens."

Edriss pushed off from the bin and nodded at the table. "We ride for Felgarden Rest soon. Try again."

"I regret the hurt I've caused you—"

"Arwenna, I do *not* want to talk about this!" Edriss squeezed her eyes shut and exhaled slowly through her nose. "I'm trying so hard to hold my head up and not be cruel or rude or unhelpful. I don't...I don't hate you. But if you understand this is hard for me, then respect that talking about it makes it much harder."

"It's not forever. He and I...It's not as though we're going to marry." Arwenna watched her with the same pity Edriss had felt from others her whole life. But she'd never asked to be pitied. Never asked for anything.

"That doesn't make me feel better," Edriss said. She moved back to the long table to clean up anything they no longer needed. "Maybe if you really loved him, I could understand, but if he's just an amusement to you..."

"I may not *love* him, but I do care about him."

Edriss laughed. "What, exactly, are you hoping to accomplish with this conversation, Arwenna? You tell me you understand how I feel and then assure me you're just playing around, nothing serious. So either you never cared at all about our friendship, or you thought I'd sit idly by why you carelessly break the heart of the person closest to me because he's no more than an amusement to you. I can't decide which is worse."

"He knows what this is," Arwenna stated. "What it isn't."

"That a guess, or did he actually tell you this?"

Arwenna bowed her head. She plucked at the lace on her sleeves and searched for words. "I never set out to hurt anyone."

Edriss tossed her cleaning rag to the side. "Then why are you sharing a bed with Osman Derry? And others?"

Arwenna stilled. She seemed to grapple with her response before she gave it. "That has nothing to do with Lorcan."

"Derry is a *Defender*. A traitor. Surely you know this?"

"I do." Arwenna's pale face was unreadable.

"Then...Why..." Edriss thrust her hands out to her sides. "What could you possibly be thinking? Or is he...Are you in trouble?"

"No one is forcing me to do anything," Arwenna answered. It seemed to Edriss she was almost proud. "I do what I do willingly."

"You're *attracted* to the man?" Edriss gaped at her.

"I don't know what you want me to say, Edriss."

"Does Lorcan know?" She already had her answer. There was no way Lorcan knew. He'd never be content to share Arwenna with anyone, least of all Osman Derry.

Arwenna lowered her gaze. Her mouth hung open as her head shook. "It's not his business to know."

"You'll break his heart. Does that not...not stir anything inside of you? Hurting someone so kind? So willing to stand for you when no one else will?"

Tears spilled down Arwenna's cheeks. She let them run without wiping them. "You don't think I've been hurt, Edriss? That I haven't known heartbreak and pain?"

"That does not give you an excuse to cause it for others!" Edriss marched toward her, cheeks swollen with heat. "You came here to find a life different from the one you left behind. To start anew. You have so many who love you and are cheering your success, and yet you choose a path of pain and disappointment. For yourself. For the ones who love you."

"You say it as though *any* of this has been simple for me."

"I never said your life was simple. But you are not the sole claimant on suffering. And here's a secret, Arwenna. The only real cure for suffering is peace. Hurting others is a spiral you'll never return from once you've gone too far down its path."

Edriss handed Arwenna a clean rag to wipe her face. "Lorcan and I have nothing more to offer one another. And when he finally realizes what you've done to him and his heart breaks in a million pieces, *neither* of you better come to me looking for succor and comfort, for I have none left to give. I hardly have enough for myself." Edriss shook her head and went to the door. "We don't have time for another try. Pack your satchel and meet me at the stables."

Arwenna rode several paces behind Edriss. The lies permeating her life had swelled into something monstrous, beyond her control. She hardly knew up from down, right from wrong. Who was allowed to know what.

Edriss was wrong about Lorcan. He wouldn't be hurt if he knew about Arwenna's dalliances with Derry and Bristol, but he *would* be devastated if he knew she was actively conspiring with them to keep him away from Edriss. That pushing her closer to Finn was the reason Arwenna had pushed back on Lorcan's continued insistence to bring Edriss in to help. It was too bad really, because Arwenna agreed with Lorcan; Edriss would know better than either of them how to navigate her predicament.

If the wedding actually took place, Arwenna would be partly responsible. More and more, it seemed Edriss *would* become Finnegan's wife and that the only way out of the predicament would be for Evra to dissolve the union once the terrible details about the Derrys were finally provable.

By then, it would be far too late.

Arwenna would have betrayed not one but two friends. Everyone would come to know her as the woman who'd made herself the whore of terrible men—which wasn't so very different from the life she'd left behind in Midnight Crest, except she'd *chosen* this one. No one had forced her into Osman Derry's bed. Into Leonarde Bristol's. The men, for all their other terrible faults, had not abused her, had not harmed her. Even when she'd been with both men together, they'd simply taken their pleasures and sent her on her way.

Reminding herself she was doing it to save her sister's family was becoming a hollow consolation.

Finnegan rode up beside her. He'd been hanging back on Edriss's wishes. "Lovely day, isn't it?"

Arwenna looked up at the dark, cloud-filled sky and scoffed. "One thing I miss about home is that we never felt it necessary to remark upon the weather."

"Isn't it because all it does is snow up there?"

"That's not untrue. But Ravenwoods are not particularly keen on casual conversation. We prefer to speak with intent or not at all."

Finnegan nodded and looked ahead at Edriss. She was swallowed by her bulky cloak, shifting with the force of the ride. "Does she know?"

"Does she know what?"

He smirked. "I thought you liked to speak with intent?"

"Perhaps if I understood yours?"

Finnegan craned sideways in his saddle. "Many things made more sense once my father told me he'd asked you to distract Lorcan."

Arwenna kept her gaze forward. "I hear the moral authority in your tone, but if you know, why haven't you told her?"

"I have no intention of telling her. My father would tan my hide if I spoiled the wedding when we're only days away, and frankly, he'd be right. He's not the only Derry determined to see this through." He laughed. "But I'll admit, I was surprised you went along with it. I thought Edriss was your friend."

"She is," Arwenna said. "Was. And you're deluding yourself if you don't think she'll be just as disgusted with you when she knows you were part of deceiving her into the marriage."

"By the time she realizes, it won't matter. She'll be my wife." Thunder crackled above, and he raised his hood.

Despite the time she'd spent with Osman, Arwenna still had no clear sight into Finnegan's role in what the Defenders were up to. He knew about at least some of his father's intrigues, but she had a sense he hadn't been pulled into all their misconduct. She'd justified keeping Lorcan distracted by telling herself Finnegan was not his father...that he was Edriss's childhood friend and someone she used to be close to—could be close to again.

But what if she was wrong?

What if he was in just as deep?

"I've also held my tongue about your liaisons with my father and his mate, Bristol," Finnegan said. "Lorcan can keep his blissful ignorance, at least until I know he's not going to whisk her away to the other end of the kingdom and elope."

"Edriss knows." Arwenna nodded forward. "She should tell him. But she won't."

"Edriss's heart is bigger than both of ours put together," he muttered with an unreadable frown. "She doesn't want to hurt him, even though he's broken her heart a dozen times over. It grates me, how she protects him when he is so careless with her."

"His love for her confuses his sense of honor. The only one standing in his way is himself."

"And Evra. He can't have everyone thinking his sister's protector was also her bedchamber partner. Can't have any *scandals*." Finnegan scoffed. "Anyone who knows Lorcan knows he'd rather martyr himself than do something that makes him happy."

"And you?" Arwenna eyed him from the side, wondering whether Finn would be foolish enough to reveal the extent of his involvement in overthrowing the Blackwoods. "Will you be happy when Edriss is your wife?"

"Blissfully," he said wryly.

"I can't tell if you're serious."

"I've always wanted Edriss. I just never dreamed Evra would pair her with me when there are better matches." He shrugged. "I suppose he sees the value in allying with a man like my father."

"And why's that?" Arwenna asked, her heart fluttering at the prospect of his answer and what it might reveal.

Edriss came to a sudden halt. Nightshade reared up, nearly bucking her off. Finnegan pushed up to see what had happened right as an unfamiliar man rode up from the opposite direction. The man struggled to slow his harried pace and came to a messy stop.

"*Baron Lawrence?*" Edriss exclaimed. She steadied her horse. "What are you doing outside Felgarden?" Sweeping her eyes over him in confusion, she asked, "Why are you on the road at all?"

"Lady Edriss."

The baron had a solemn expression, fixed in such a way Arwenna had trouble imagining what a smile might look like on it. But he was, otherwise, the opposite of what she'd envisioned from Edriss's stories. She'd been imagining a gnarled recluse, grizzled and unkempt and pale from a lack of sun. But before her was one of the most handsome men she'd ever laid eyes on. His armor was perfectly pressed, and his face bore a gentle ruddiness, as though he frequently enjoyed an afternoon stroll.

"I was just on my way to you…I brought Arwenna…" Edriss's words trailed into more confusion. "What's going on?"

"How fortunate I caught you first." The baron fixed her with a deeply serious look. "You need to come with me. We're going back to Longwood Rush."

"The Rush…" Edriss's head shook in befuddlement. She glanced at Finnegan, who shook his head as well. "But why?"

"Something…" He cleared his throat. "Terrible has happened. It's not safe for you out here until we get to the bottom of it."

Edriss again glanced at Finnegan and then Arwenna, but they were just as perplexed. "What is it then? What happened?"

The baron responded by grabbing hold of her reins and spurring both horses on. "I'll leave the explanations to your brother. We've squandered enough time."

Finnegan acted on instinct when he pulled Edriss into his arms after Evra had delivered the news.

Seven hundred and sixty men, women, and children had been murdered in Greencastle.

The attack this time had been not on a small village but on one of the Great Cities, a key stronghold for the Blackwoods in the borderlands west of the Southerlands. The steward, Tedric Blakewell, had resigned from his place on Evra's council, neither willing to support the Defenders nor condemn them. Those were the worst kind of men, according to Finnegan's father—the type who refused to stand for anything. *I'll break bread with my enemy before I'll break bread with a man beholden to neutrality. At least I know when to watch my back.*

Edriss sobbed against his chest. Lorcan slouched in a chair with his face buried in his hands after trying—and failing miserably, to Finn's delight—to comfort Edriss himself.

The stress of the news had thrown Rhosyn into early labor, and Alise had already whisked her away to the birthing chamber. Edriss had insisted on going, but Evra had commanded she stay, because he had other plans for her.

"Blakewell lost his wife and one of his sons," said Enchanter Grimoult. Finnegan didn't even know why the old magus was there at all. His inclusion on the council was suspect enough, but he had no place in Evra's inner circle. "The local reliquary was razed." He hung his head with a haunted sound, almost a moan. "That's where most of the dead were found. The minister was raising funds to rebuild, and many had gathered..." Grimoult couldn't finish.

Finnegan wondered where his father was. Osman wouldn't ordinarily miss an opportunity to exploit tragedy into gain.

At some point, Arwenna had gone missing as well.

"Which son?" Edriss asked in a small, broken voice.

"Tedric II," Grimoult said somberly, and Edriss erupted into fresh sobs.

Finnegan bowed his head in brief reverence for the loss of an old friend.

"It's time, Lord Blackwood." Baron Lawrence tapped his cane on the stone. Edriss had once told Finnegan the formidable man didn't need it yet brandished it like a child would hold fast to a cherished blanket.

Evra bowed over the hearth. His shoulders lifted and fell in long breaths. "I know, Maxim. I *know* what you're going to say. But right now, all I can think about is extending these poor families as much relief as the Rush can offer. They're suffering, and we can help."

"You seek to ease the suffering of one man when you could prevent the suffering of twenty." Maxim's heavy steps rang across the room. Finnegan held Edriss tighter. "You're a good man. Better than your father. But there can be no middle ground with men who murder *children* without a second thought. They see your neutrality not as the quality of a man worth allying with but for the weakness it is."

Finnegan felt the air change in the room.

Edriss sniffled and pulled back. Her sobs dwindled as she watched the baron spill his bold words.

A creaking sound drew everyone's notice to where Lady Meldred emerged from a shadowed nook in the room. She held fast to her own cane—for her, an obvious necessity—as she hobbled over. "You're both children yourselves." She made a tsking, hissing sound that reminded Finnegan of being scolded by his father when he'd been younger. "And, as it is, you're both right." She held out her hand, still staring straight ahead. A flustered attendant poured a glass of wine and rushed it over. "We must help these people. And then we must strike back with unmatchable swiftness."

"Strike *who*?" Finnegan couldn't help but ask. "No one has claimed responsibility, have they?"

Edriss backed up several steps. The hatred in her eyes erased any progress made between them. Finnegan's heart sank. "You are either part of this madness or you are complicit, but you do *not* get to play the fool at such a time as this."

Lorcan looked up from his chair. He watched them both with red-ringed eyes, but mostly Edriss. He seemed to be weighing another attempt to console her.

"Edriss." Evra's warning was weak, bloated with exhaustion. "Not now."

"Not now?" Edriss wiped both her eyes and flung her hands to the sides. "Not *now*? You have just told us of the single biggest tragedy to hit our Reach in over a hundred years, and it's not enough for you to ground yourself in reality? To realize that your failure to address this evil is what allows it to spread?" She shook her head slowly. "What are you going to do when they come for Rhosyn? For Alastrynia?"

"Your sister is insufferable, but she's right," the baron said. "I have not left Felgarden Rest in many months, Lord Blackwood, but if this tragedy is enough to stir me to action, when you have been trying to lure me to the Rush since my wife spent her promise, then I should think that alone should magnify the enormity of this terrible situation."

Evra returned his focus to the fire. His hands, holding tight to the hearth, were stretched above his head as he leaned toward the flames. "You know I've appreciated your support these past two years, Baron Lawrence. You are a true man of the Westerlands."

"Do not think you can assuage my concerns with platitudes. My loyalty is to the peace and prosperity of our land and people. I offered my support to you because it seemed we shared these values. I will only offer it so long as I still believe that."

Evra nodded and shoved back from the hearth but didn't turn around. "We'll discuss our response after I've spoken with my sister. Alone."

Finnegan waited for the others to leave first, but no one moved. After a bout of awkward glances, Meldred finally waved her cane and ushered people out. The baron, Grimoult, and Meldred all left, but Finnegan stayed. He stayed because Lorcan stayed, and he was tired of Lorcan acting like he still had a claim upon Edriss.

"I suppose you both can stay," Evra said to himself and walked to the table. He gestured for Finnegan and Edriss to join Lorcan and sit, but Edriss planted her feet. Finnegan stayed where he was, waiting. "There's nothing we can do for the dead beyond making reparations to their loved ones. Which we will do. I've already given instructions to the treasury to release the funds from our coffers."

"You're wrong," Edriss said with a defiant lift of her chin. She flicked her accusing gaze toward Finnegan. "What those families want more than gold is vengeance. Justice."

Evra nodded at his lap. "I'm not ignoring what happened, sister. But I need your help with something else." He looked up. "The attackers pulled many of the children from the reliquary before they torched it. Those children...They stood and watched as their mothers and fathers were burned alive. Fifty-seven children, specifically."

"Guardians deliver us." Edriss dropped onto a chair with an astonished look.

Lorcan watched her with a heated, intense stare, locked in some sort of debate with himself. Finnegan was ready if he tried anything foolish.

"They have ahead of them many hard days, Edriss, but we can make those days a little easier. *You* can make those days a little easier."

Lorcan finally stirred from his trance. "You want Edriss to use mind salves on *fifty-seven* children?"

Evra nodded. "If there were anyone else, I'd send them. But Edriss is the only one who has..." He squinted briefly at Finnegan before continuing. "There is no one else."

"But you know...You know what it takes from her." Lorcan pressed his palms to the table and leaned in. "Her ability isn't without limits. She cannot carry the burden of all those poor children."

Finnegan snorted and rolled his eyes. He'd been waiting for the Lorcan he knew to show up.

"I don't need you to defend me," Edriss said, but her words lacked her usual fire. "And I don't...I don't care what it does to me. Of course I'll go."

Evra bowed his head toward her in appreciation. He turned toward Lorcan. "I know I ask a lot of her. This is why I'd like her to go for a longer spell. A fortnight or more, whatever she feels is needed to spare her energy and help all the children. The wedding is, of course, postponed—"

"Why not move it up instead?" Finnegan asked. He shifted his weight and ignored Lorcan's glares. "We could do it today."

"No," Evra said. "That's not how we do things. We'll resume planning when you both return."

"Both?" Edriss laughed, open-mouthed. "No. No, Evra, I am *not* going away, for weeks, with this man."

Finnegan felt his cheeks redden. "Edriss, you're my betrothed—"

"Only because I haven't yet discovered a way out of his farcical marriage." Her vigor returned as she sprung to her feet. "I'm going alone, brother."

"You are not," Evra said quietly. "No matter what our relationship might be these days, I won't have you wading into a war zone without proper protection."

Her eyes fluttered in hard blinks. "When have I ever needed protection?"

Finnegan watched Lorcan's reaction and wasn't disappointed. "He's right, Edriss," Lorcan said slowly. "You can't go alone."

"You don't have a say in this," she snapped. "Unless you want me to send Finn's parts back to his father in a box, he's not coming, Evra. Period."

"Very well," Evra said. "Lorcan then."

"*What?*" Edriss and Finnegan said in perfect concert.

"There are only two men I trust to prioritize your safety as I would," Evra said slowly. "They're both in this room. You don't want to travel with Finnegan? I won't make you. But the alternative is Lorcan. Pick one."

Edriss shook her head, visibly incredulous. She thrust an arm in Lorcan's direction without looking at him. "Fine. Him."

Finnegan spun on her. "No." He looked to Evra for help, but Evra was watching his sister. "No, Evra. You cannot think this is a good idea. He's in *love* with her!"

"There is no one I know with more honor than Lorcan James," Evra said. He stood and crossed his arms. "If Edriss is more comfortable with her old protector, then so be it. This has nothing to do with rivalries or jealousy. The trip is about the children, nothing more or less."

"But—"

"It's done, Finn. It's decided."

Edriss lowered her gaze to the floor with a humorless laugh. Finnegan had to restrain himself with the table to keep from tossing her over his shoulder and showing her who was really in charge.

"Thank you, Evra," Lorcan said with a drawn, respectful nod. "I'll do everything in my power to keep her safe and will lend a hand wherever they need me."

"I'll just bet you will," Finnegan muttered. Raw, immutable rage festered in his chest. It swirled, tapping at his bones like a drum line. Nothing good ever came of letting his fury run, but nothing good had come of restraining it either.

Perhaps it was time to let his anger do as it wished.

If Evra didn't want him traveling to Greencastle, so be it.

But if Lorcan thought he'd won, he was in for a cruel surprise.

"I'll go after Rhosyn is safely delivered," Edriss said. She smoothed her dress and wiped the last of her tears.

"No." Evra pointed his glance out the window. "Alise is leading the birthing. You're needed in Greencastle." He glanced back. "Those children will survive these horrors because of you. Remember that when this all feels overwhelming, and it will. If it doesn't now, it will."

FIFTEEN
THE WHEEL OF YOUR INDECISION

Edriss kept a grueling pace. Lorcan had suggested they travel by carriage so they could pack more, but she had insisted Evra was sending others with supplies. A carriage would only slow them down. Every day the children spent with their grief and horrors was a day too long, she'd said, and he didn't disagree.

Lorcan loved Edriss's heart. He loved her passion, her intelligence, and her wit. He loved *everything* about her, including the stubbornness that had become the wedge between them.

In the hours between their meeting with Evra and their departure, he'd forced himself to endure the discomfort of honest reflection. He'd been so close to telling Edriss how he felt in the guard tower, but Finnegan's interruption had stopped his words cold, leaving him wondering if the Guardians were intentionally keeping him from speaking his truth.

But the only lingering emotion trailing him from that day was regret.

Regret that he'd forsaken happiness because he was terrified by the truth.

His truth.

Their truth.

He loved Edriss Blackwood to the depths of his soul, honor be damned. She deserved to know what he'd denied her out of fear—for her, for himself. He couldn't undo the hurt he'd caused her, and what she did with his confession would be her choice alone, but he could no longer convince himself that locking his feelings away from her was good for either of them.

Edriss spoke little on the journey. She wasn't rude, but spared no warmth, offering polite conversation when practical matters required discussion. When to eat. Where to water Nightshade and Frog.

Lorcan tried to start the conversation the first night, in the small, cozy inn they'd stopped at, just south of Pine Bluff. But as soon as she'd finished her soup and ale, she dropped coin on the table, mumbling a brief good night, and rushed off to her room.

He deserved her indifference. Her coldness. But it was all he could do not to crush her into his arms and tell her everything he couldn't before.

How he had he gone all those years denying his heart?

And for what?

He'd been so worried about causing a scandal for her when she'd been telling him all along she didn't care what others said or thought. Would he rather be known as the man who broke the heart of the only woman he'd ever loved…or the one who couldn't help falling in love with the most incredible human he knew?

Evra would hold his ground, but Lorcan had never asked him for anything. He'd never given his old friend reason to doubt the veracity of his loyalty. Loyalty had brought him and Edriss together in the first place, and weren't love and loyalty petals of the same flower?

She was suffering more than ever, and he was both the cause and, possibly, the cure. He might not have the authority to share Arwenna's secret, but he could see, in painful hindsight, that pretending to be her beau had been doomed from the start. Edriss had had the right idea all along, trying to infiltrate their ranks from within. He could expose his heart's truth without betraying Arwenna's trust.

He could stand at her side, arm in arm, and save both the Reach and themselves.

Lorcan finally knew what he wanted.

What he hadn't yet comprehended was whether, under all the deserved ire and detachment, Edriss still felt the same.

They arrived in Greencastle the next day, in the midday between noontide and dusk. Both of them were bone tired from the hard pace of the journey, and Edriss had been looking forward to a brief respite before rolling up her sleeves and heading to the reliquary to begin her work. She intended to work through the night and into the next morning, only stopping when exhaustion prevented continuing.

But waiting for her and Lorcan outside the Wayfarer's Inn was Rohan James.

The steward embraced his son and offered Edriss a light bow. She nodded, eyeing them both in puzzlement as she waited for an explanation.

"What are you doing here, Father?" Lorcan laughed and shook his head as he swept his gaze over Rohan. "Not that I'm not happy to see you after all these weeks."

Rohan ushered them both inside with a wary look. He guided them past the main tavern floor, full of boisterous patrons, past the bar, and into a dark nook not visible from the door. Edriss glanced back over her shoulder, sensing they'd been followed, but no one looked their way.

There were ales and stew already waiting for them. Edriss was too hungry to worry about decorum, and she dug in with enthusiasm, spooning the stew so fast, her mouth was stuffed between swallows. She caught both men staring, and she set down her spoon before taking a big swill of ale.

233

"No, go on, Lady Edriss. Eat." Rohan nodded at her bowl. Lines ringed his eyes, cradling deep crescents underneath. His cheeks practically hung off the bone, with gaunt hollows near his jaw that belied a lack of sleep, nutrition, or both.

Edriss sat back against the bench. She turned her head, regarding both father and son, before she spoke. "What is this, Steward?"

Rohan nodded at his hands, laced atop the table. He wore a grave, thoughtful look. "I don't know how to say what I need to say, so I'll speak the words and then we'll deal with them as we may."

Lorcan chuckled nervously. He cradled the ale between his hands, his knuckles white. "You're scaring me."

"You both may remember Lord Blackwood's recent sudden absence from the Rush."

"Still hasn't told any of us where he was," Edriss said with a quick upturn of her eyes.

"He was with me, in the Abbey." Rohan wrung his hands over the stained wood. "Because I summoned him."

Lorcan flopped back. "All right. Why?"

"Lorcan, when I asked you to take my place on the council, I had my reasons. Some of them I shared with you. Some I did not." Rohan lifted his head toward the ceiling and sighed before looking at them again. "Most pressing among them was that I had a network of spies in the field, all along the River Rush. Some in the Halls. Others in town or in places like Rivermarch."

Edriss tensed and straightened against the hard bench.

"Why would you keep that from me?" Lorcan asked.

"Because one of the people they were watching closely was believed to be able to read thoughts. And if you knew what I'd been doing, then so might she." Rohan turned toward Edriss with an apologetic glance. "Arwenna Ravenwood."

Lorcan frowned. "Why were you watching Arwenna?"

"Steward, you're not seriously implying Arwenna is involved in what's been going on?" Edriss asked.

234

"I would not have thought so, my lady," Rohan answered, "if Renardy Tyndall had not told me he'd seen her conversing with both Osman Derry and Leonarde Bristol, on several occasions. Renardy's extended stay in the Rush was on my request, but neither of us ever fathomed he'd link someone like Arwenna to any of it."

Lorcan's eyes were on the table. "Renardy was spying for you?"

Rohan nodded. "And I deeply regret asking him to, after what happened. They discovered what he was doing. It's why he was killed, Lorcan. I'm sorry." He looked at Edriss with a solemn nod. "My lady. I know he was your friend too."

Edriss shook her head in disbelief. What the steward was saying didn't add up. Arwenna was not among her favorite people at the moment, but Arwenna *loved* her sister. Evra. Alastrynia. She would never put their lives at risk. "Just because…because Arwenna was speaking with these men does not mean…" But she wasn't only speaking with them.

Rohan hooked a thumb around the handle of his mug. He hesitated and then lifted it to his mouth. He ran his sleeve along his beard to clear the foam. "Renardy…He was not only spying on Arwenna. He was enjoying the pleasure of her company."

Edriss almost leaped up but remembered they were in public, no matter how private their booth was. "Arwenna deserves better than fishwife tales being spun about her when she's not here to defend herself."

"It's no rumor," Lorcan muttered. "Arwenna told me herself about Renardy."

"What?" Edriss turned sideways in her chair.

Lorcan lowered his gaze to his lap without responding.

"Rafferty was also monitoring the Defenders, as was Cressida Wakesell, but I've since asked them to ease off," Rohan said. "I won't have the blood of more good men and women on my conscience. As it is, I'm weighing the prudence of recalling all those in the field who've been reporting back."

"You had the Tyndalls and Cressida spying for you, but you couldn't tell *me*?" Lorcan demanded.

"I couldn't tell you because…" Rohan turned the same apologetic look on Edriss. It burned her up inside. Did everyone think she was a lovesick fool for Lorcan James? "At first, I was protecting you, so if things came to a head, you could claim plausible deniability. But then word reached me about your dalliance with the raven, and we couldn't risk her finding out about the network of spies watching the Defenders."

Edriss shook her head. "What does this have to do with my brother coming to the Abbey?"

Rohan drank more of his ale. He raked his teeth along his cracked lower lip. "Seems Renardy was not the only man Arwenna has been spending time with. Cressida sent me a message encrypted in three layers of code. It took several of us to decipher it, but once we did…I knew I had to get Evrathedyn alone, in private, away from his other councilors and the prying eyes of the Rush." He inhaled through his nose. "Osman Derry and Leonarde Bristol."

Lorcan choked out a laugh. "No. That's not…Your intel is wrong."

Edriss stared at her congealing stew as her thoughts twisted around a truth she'd held close for the wrong reasons. She'd been protecting Lorcan when she should have been protecting her brother's family. If she'd only dug deeper, tried to understand *why* Arwenna was consorting with such terrible men…but she'd had so many other distractions…

It occurred to her Arwenna's relationship with Lorcan might be more nefarious than it had initially seemed.

Rohan looked at Edriss. "You don't seem surprised, my lady."

She shook her head, unable to meet Lorcan's demanding gaze from the side.

"Edriss?" Lorcan leaned in.

She winced and scooted away from him. "I…" Edriss reached for her ale without looking up. She wet her throat and started again. "I saw her coming out of Steward Derry's apartments one day. I thought…Well, I thought he'd coerced her but Finn

236

was there, standing guard, and he said..." She grimaced. "That Arwenna had been coming to his father's bedchamber for some time and that he was there to ensure no one found out."

"And you said *nothing*?" Lorcan demanded.

"You dare confront *me* about disclosure?" Edriss fired back.

"This has nothing...nothing to do with us. This is significant, Edriss. This is...How could you not say anything?"

"I said *nothing* because it was clear to me you were in love with her, and I didn't want your heart to get broken as mine had been!"

Lorcan fell back in his seat like she'd struck him.

"All right," Rohan said. He patted the air with his hands, urging them to speak more quietly. "I didn't mean to stir up difficult feelings, my lady. Forgive me."

"Nothing to forgive, Steward." Edriss screwed her jaw, pointing her glare into the distance.

"Are you sure there's not some other explanation for this?" Lorcan asked.

"I had hoped there might be," Rohan replied. "But one of my spies, a double agent with proximity to Ashenhurst, revealed Arwenna has been feeding the Defenders information about the whereabouts of other council members known to be loyal to Lord Blackwood. She's the one who..." Rohan shook his head with a sad sigh. "The one who, although perhaps not intentionally, helped enable Renardy's murder."

"How can that be?" Lorcan asked. His voice was cracked, strained. "And why...*Why*?"

"Only Arwenna can say for certain," Rohan said slowly, "but if I had to venture a guess, I'd say she's struck some sort of bargain with them, to save her sister."

Edriss crossed her arms and turned her thoughts inward. It felt...wrong, what the steward was saying, but the logical part of her mind couldn't shake the way it made all the pieces fit, finally. Why else would Arwenna be sneaking in and out of the beds of terrible men? Why else would she be so interested in Lorcan when she'd hardly given him a second glance before? Her behavior had shifted so dramatically, Edriss hadn't been able to ascribe it to anything rational.

Except this.

"I don't believe it. I...I can't believe it," Lorcan was saying. He hadn't stopped shaking his head.

"The truth doesn't require belief," Rohan said. "But a wise man does not refute a truth when placed at his feet. For all the shock Lord Blackwood wore when I told him what I've just told you, in the end, he accepted it. I'm sorry, son. Truly. I'm sorry for us all, and even for Arwenna, who must have felt like she had no other choice."

"But she did. She..."

Edriss looked at the steward, cutting off Lorcan's babbling. "Is that all?"

He nodded. "And now I must away. Good luck to you in your healing of those poor young minds. And be safe. Both of you. You can be certain the men behind this atrocious attack will be lingering to feast upon the suffering they've wrought."

Rohan dropped a stack of coin onto the table, swept to his feet, and left without another word.

Edriss started to do the same, but Lorcan clamped a hand atop her arm.

"I didn't know, Edriss. I'm sorry. I'm *so* sorry."

She tore away but stayed. "How could you know? I don't suppose conversation plays a significant part of your relationship."

"I'm not actually her..." He stretched his mouth into a wince. "I'm sorry my spending time with her caused you such pain—"

Edriss slid off the bench and jumped to her feet. "You think I'm upset with you because you chose another woman over me?" She rolled her eyes. "I won't deny it hurt, but I have no claim to your heart, Lorcan. I never have."

He watched her in devastated confusion.

"You really don't know?"

Lorcan seemed frozen.

238

Edriss turned her eyes upward with a bitter laugh. "It's *you*. You and your...your mixed messages, your heat one day and ice the next. You're...One moment you're *kissing* me and then blustering about honor in the same breath. You don't know what you want, Lorcan. That's the truth of it. And I lack the patience or heart to continue being stretched across the wheel of your indecision. I don't...I don't *care* what you do or who you do it with. Not anymore. Not ever again." She swept her hair off her face. "I'm going to go change into something practical and then I'm going to the encampment to sit with those poor children before we lose the day's light. I don't need you to chaperone me, so you're free to find usefulness wherever you please."

Edriss ground another batch of mind salve with her mortar and pestle. She measured the saffronia, valerian, lavender, poppy, and stramonium in the perfect amounts, in the optimal order. She pulled the oil of bergamot from her recipe box and emulsified the mixture, turning it into a paste-like consistency.

My Princess of Poison. She caught the words as the box closed on its own. Even still, they sent an ache between her shoulder blades, a skip in the otherwise-steady rhythm of her heart.

She turned away and pulled the delicate bundle from her satchel. Kava grown beyond the Rush was too small for any salve, but the broad leaves lovingly tended by the poison mistresses were large enough to wrap around a neck. It was precisely the use she intended for the children, to bring the healing as close to both head and heart as she could.

The salve would only go so far. When no one was looking, Edriss would mouth the words she'd spent her entire life learning and honing. They weren't words anyone would recognize but were constructs of herself made into magic. They were the difference between the salve offering temporary relief—or permanent.

Edriss hadn't learned this gift from Alise or Meldred. She'd conceived it on her own, spending years practicing it on herself before she'd found the courage to try it on another. It was Lorcan who'd first let her. After the first time, he'd come to see her after every tending trip, and she'd eased the terrible burden he carried on his heart of everyone he couldn't save.

But he'd never let her use it after Cesarina's death. For that one, he preferred his suffering.

Edriss waved down one of the handmaidens tending the children at the far end of the tent. The woman brightened and grabbed hold of a little girl, guiding her over.

"What's your name?" Edriss asked softly. She offered her best smile to the timid blonde with the red-rimmed eyes.

"Chelsea," the girl murmured. She stared at her feet.

"Chelsea. That's a beautiful name." Edriss reached up and smoothed the girl's hair back off her face. "You've been through something terrible. I'm so sorry, sweet girl. I know it hurts."

Chelsea nodded at the ground and sniffled.

"You carry a terrible burden, more than any child should have to. If I could turn back time, I would. But what if I could make it hurt less?"

Chelsea looked up. Suspicion curled the edges of her mouth.

Edriss pulled the doused kava leaf out of the bowl and unrolled it. She held it up for Chelsea to smell first. The girl scrunched her nose but didn't recoil.

"It smells like our garden."

"It does," Edriss agreed, still smiling. She glanced up at the handmaiden, who wore the horrors of the past days in her harrowed gaze. "I don't know about you, Chelsea, but I love my garden."

Chelsea nodded. "I like the lavender. Mama, she…She grew it right outside my window, where I could smell it always."

Edriss held up the pasty leaf. "There's lavender in this."

"There is?"

"Mhm. And other things that will remind you of happier times." Edriss lifted to her knees. "I, too, had to grow up very fast, Chelsea. Some children just do, and there's nothing we can do about it. I wish it weren't so. But as a child who had to think like an adult far too young, I know better than to lie to you. What you saw and what you've lost, it's real, sweet girl. It will be with you for all of your days. Grief is the way we hold onto love."

Chelsea sniffled.

"I would never take the memory of your parents from you. That would not be a gift but a terrible, terrible curse." Edriss held the kava leaf higher. "But I can help ease the pain of what you saw the other night, protect the memories of your mother and father you *want* to hold fast to. Do I have your permission to do so?"

Chelsea looked at the handmaiden, who flicked a gentle nod downward.

"This is your decision to make, Chelsea. It's as Lady Edriss said. You are now the one who must make these choices for yourself."

Chelsea tentatively watched both women. All she didn't— couldn't—say, lived in her dark, haunted eyes. Edriss would do anything to see them light up again. "Okay."

Edriss exhaled in relief. Her smile returned as she reached up to layer the kava around the girl's neck. Chelsea looked down, startled, and Edriss said, "You weren't expecting it to be warm."

Chelsea shook her head.

"It will get warmer as it dries. Not so terrible on a wintry day." Edriss smoothed out the leaf, wrapping it around the girl's neck until it connected in the back. Then she nodded at the hand-maiden and said, "Can you get the next child ready?"

The woman nodded back, leaving Edriss to perform the next part without the prying eyes of those who might be as inclined to burn her as thank her.

She whispered the words, learning them as they were said. They were always different—always unique, imbued with the magic of the moment and the need at hand. Chelsea closed her eyes, and a soft peace stole over her face. Her lids fluttered but didn't open.

When Edriss was done, she removed her hands and sat back on her heels. "All done, Chelsea. How do you feel?"

"I don't know," Chelsea said. She gingerly tapped the kava wrapped at her neck. "Tired. But not...not like before."

"The sadness is there. It's just not clawing to get out anymore, is it?"

Chelsea shook her head.

"Good." Edriss reached forward and clasped both of the girl's hands in hers. "Leave that on until the morrow. You can remove it when the sun rises. Where are you staying?"

"With my sister and her husband."

"Are they here?"

Chelsea pointed into a thick crowd of adults conversing with serious expressions.

Edriss pulled out a small vial and handed it over. "Inside of this are directions for how to reach me, should you ever need me again, Chelsea. You send a raven to this location, it will find its way to me."

Chelsea folded the vial into her hands, nodded in thanks, and scampered off.

Edriss hardly had time to take a breath before the next child was brought over, a boy named Stephen.

After Stephen, there was Hillary and Carval. Twins Nina and Noah were next, then a trio of siblings who had lost not only their parents but their grandparents, aunts, uncles, and cousins.

Edriss's heart had never been so crushed and helpless.

She'd evaded exhaustion, but it was coming. It always did.

The camp darkened. Beyond, dusk had faded to night. She'd stay until they made her leave.

She had just finished mixing another batch when an attendant she didn't recognize rushed over and dropped to a crouch at her side. The woman looked around before whispering, "Your friend is outside."

"What?" Edriss set the mortar and pestle aside, only half listening. She'd need to stop soon, but she still had the energy for another child, perhaps two.

242

"The man you came here with." The woman cleared her throat. "He's…Well, it's best you just come and see for yourself."

Edriss glanced at the huddle of children still awaiting her healing. Her focus lingered there, but the woman hadn't moved. Edriss started to leave her things behind, but something told her to bring them, so she carefully nudged the bowl into a sleeve that would keep the salve from spilling and lifted her satchel onto one shoulder.

When she exited the camp, a gust of air knocked her sideways. The cool night greeted her, bringing her back to the world she'd ignored for so many hours. Her eyes narrowed, adjusting to the darkness as she followed the woman beyond the charred ruins of the reliquary, down a small embankment, and into the town square.

Edriss stopped dead. At the center of the road was a pyre. It had been decommissioned, but the remnants of wood and brick at the bottom belied the frequency of its use. It was a jarring sight to behold in one of the Great Cities. Most had dismantled theirs and had long disposed of the remnants.

The woman turned to see if Edriss was still coming, but she waved at her to return to the children. She already knew what she'd find, and she preferred to approach alone.

Edriss ventured the rest of the way down the hill until the rest of the square came into view. On the far side of the pyre was where she finally spotted him—prostrate, his face inches above the dirt.

She spurred into action and rushed to Lorcan's side. He made no sounds, rocking forward and back with a blank stare. Her bag tumbled onto the stones as she dropped to her knees, scooping him into her arms.

Lorcan sobbed silently as he gazed up at the pyre. There was nothing she'd said or could say that would ease his sense of failure, but she *could* help, if he would let her.

"You've suffered enough," she said gently, arranging her materials. "There is nothing more to be gained in punishing yourself."

243

"There isn't…Isn't suffering enough, Edriss."

"I need your consent, Lorcan. This won't work without it."

"I don't want to feel better. Not about this. I don't want the pain to go away." He rolled his head back in her lap for a better view of the old bonfire. "I don't want to forget."

"I can't make you forget, even if I wanted to." She rolled the kava in the mixture, coating it. "But you will not wear the burden of this poor woman's death for the rest of your life. You didn't burn her. They did."

"I promised her…I promised her all she had to do was sign…"

"Her fate was decided long before you arrived in Deramore."

"All they had to do was write to the king!"

"But they didn't, because if they were wrong, they'd have all been stuck on pikes for laying hands on her. The king didn't help matters either, if she really was his daughter. He could have sent out a call to find her, and none of it would have happened. There is plenty of fault to go around, but none of it belongs with you. You may have been her only bright light in her final days." Edriss finished coating the kava. "The men responsible *will* suffer. I swear to you, they will. But your suffering does nothing for her. It only gives more pain to the men who draw their very power from it."

"I didn't—" He closed his eyes but didn't move from her lap. "I'm sorry they troubled you. It wasn't my intention for you to see me like this."

"I've seen you in worse conditions," Edriss said, smoothing the leaves in her hands. "And it's me, Lorry. Not some pretty girl you fancy, who makes your heart all nervous and fluttery. We're kin, remember?"

"Hemlock." His face drew tight in pain. "You're…"

"Going to ease some of this senseless pain of yours, finally." She held up the leaves. "Do I have your consent or not?"

She expected more fight from him, and it seemed to be coming, but then he squeezed his eyes shut and nodded.

Edriss went to work, stretching the leaves across his bare neck and smoothing them with her hands until they were adhered.

244

Closing her eyes, she bowed over him and conjured the magic of her whispers, offering the last of her stamina.

Lorcan's lips parted. Fresh tears ran down his cheeks. He mouthed the words *thank you.*

"There," she said softly. "It's late. You should go back to the inn. Get a warm meal in you, rest. In case you've forgotten, the salve will spend most of whatever energy remains to you. Unlike the children, an hour should be enough for you. You'll feel even better when you wake tomorrow."

He pushed himself up and out of her lap. "And you?"

Edriss glanced toward the encampment with a sigh. "There's still so many of them. How can I..." She looked at her hands, swollen from the day's work. She could hardly fold them into fists.

Lorcan swathed her inflamed hands in his. "Come back with me. You're no good to anyone if you're not looking after yourself as well."

"Lor—"

"Let *me* look after *you*, Hemlock." He squeezed, flooding her with warmth. "Please."

"I don't need..." Edriss rolled her neck into a stiff stretch. She was exhausted, but sleep was still hours away with her mind racing as it was. If she went to bed, she'd only lie in misery. "I'm not tired."

"Then...Then let's walk."

"I have another idea." She didn't know where the thought had come from.

"Oh?" He spread his palms against his face, clearing it.

"Do you remember what Greencastle is famous for?"

Lorcan shrugged. "Ale?"

Edriss scoffed. "Other than ale."

"I...no. I don't know."

"Ever heard of Confessional pubs?"

He laughed. "Fishwife tales. Not real."

"You mean to tell me that in all your travels, you've never come across one?"

He shook his head.

"Then you weren't paying attention. There's an entire row of them in the trade quarter, if you know where to look." Edriss pushed to her feet and gathered her materials, scooping them back into her bag. "Ever played?"

"Of course not. I've heard it's…"

"Scandalous? Immoral?"

Lorcan's mouth twisted into a devious grin. "When you put it *that* way."

Edriss lifted her shoulders into a shrugging stretch. "I could use a scandalous, immoral distraction after the day I've had. Unless you're too tired…"

He laughed and shrugged. Only in his eyes could she see the leftover fragments of his terrible episode. "Never too tired for one of your misadventures. Lead the way, Princess."

SIXTEEN
CONFESSIONAL

E driss walked a pace ahead of him, eyeing the shingles on both sides of the narrow alley with almost comical scrutiny. They all had ridiculous, nonsensical names, like the One-Toed Parrot or the Bloviating Kitten, squashed together via shared walls. The two things every establishment had in common were the soot-blackened windows and an air of having been long abandoned to time and neglect. But the red-cheeked patrons endlessly streaming out from side doors—giggling, whispering, eyes lowered—dispelled that notion.

"This one, I think," Edriss said, though it seemed mostly to herself, and jaunted up the double steps of an unremarkable gray building. The name on the shingle read The Smelly Ann, and when Lorcan asked what it meant, she mumbled something about it probably being named after someone's daughter.

Lorcan shook his head and followed her in.

It wasn't like any tavern he'd ever patronized. There was a bar, of course, and a fair number of tables, but most were empty. The bulk of the patrons congregated in dense pockets along the

247

sides of the room. Raucous laughter and thick smoke hit him in a wave, and he recognized the distinct tang of whiskey almost immediately, as though someone had shaken a barrel of it over everyone and everything.

A young man in a perfectly pressed ensemble stepped forward to greet them. "Good evening, travelers, and welcome to the Smelly Ann. We have two group rounds beginning soon if you'd like to join, or I have two rooms available for private sessions."

Lorcan shook his head, mystified, and glanced at Edriss. She turned her eyes upward, deliberating, and then she said, "We've had a long day. A private room would be lovely."

"A most excellent choice." The man flashed a gleaming grin. He had better teeth than most highborns. "Shall I add a pitcher or two of veracity ale to your tab?"

"Veracity ale?" Lorcan asked.

"Truth potion," Edriss said from the side of her mouth. "To ensure all confessions made are genuine. Ups the stakes."

He furrowed his brows. "How do you *know* all of this?"

"Cressida," she explained. To the host, she said, "We'd love some of the ale. Unless you're afraid of the truth, Lorry?"

Lorcan quickly shook his head. His heart was already beating out of step, no doubt only the beginning. He squinted, trying to make sense of what the other players were doing, but he was too far away to discern anything useful. "Of course not. But I still don't understand the rules."

"Shall I send a gamekeeper up with you?" the man asked.

"That won't be necessary," Edriss said and dropped a generous sack of coin into his hand. "I believe this covers the room, two pitchers of ale, and a little extra for yourself."

The man bowed low. "Much obliged, my lady."

Edriss's eyes flew wide at the honorific.

"As you know, *all* secrets are safe in a Confessional tavern, not least of all who we are in the world beyond our walls."

"Your discretion is much appreciated," she muttered and accepted the key. Dangling from it was a metal tab with the number seven engraved on it. She marched ahead with such confidence, Lorcan wondered if she *had* played before.

He followed her into the room, which, like the tavern itself, was unexpected. In the center was a broad table, a smaller version of Evra's council table. There were two drink carts and a catering table along the edges, but the furnishing that caught his eye the most was a plush bed at the far end of the room, its full glory obscured by crimson velvet curtains on all sides.

A healthy fire roared in the hearth, plenty of logs and kindling stacked nearby to keep it going all night.

A young woman entered and plopped two pitchers of ale on the table. Edriss tipped her in coin and locked the door behind her.

"What do you know about the game?" she asked. She still wore her cloak, despite the heat permeating the room from the fireplace.

Lorcan removed his and hung it on one of the wall hooks. He pointed at the kava leaf dried on his neck, and Edriss nodded, affirming he was safe to remove it. "Not much. Until tonight, I didn't think it was something people *actually* played." He rubbed the spot on his neck where the leaf had been. He already felt far better than he had when she'd found him.

"Hmm." Edriss lifted one leg and dropped it over the bench, then pulled the other over. "I've never played in a Confessional tavern, but I *have* played with Cressida and Finnegan."

Lorcan frowned as he took the seat across from her. "And where was I?"

"Tending," she said. "We didn't have veracity ale, so we spent the evening lying to each other, half-naked."

"I'm sorry, did you say *half-naked*?"

Edriss reached for the die in the center of the table. She dropped it into her palm and rolled it around with a finger. "Seven sides, all numbered. We take turns rolling. If you roll a one, two, or three, you have to surrender something you're wearing. Can be anything, but you must do it, or you forfeit the game and lose."

Lorcan suddenly understood why she'd kept her cloak on. "I see."

"If you roll a four, five, or six, you've rolled a confession. That means the other player gets to ask you a question, *any* question, and you must answer truthfully." She poured them both a mug of ale. As she took a deep sip, she pushed his toward him. "I won't make you drink it. But if you don't, I'll know your only interest is deception."

Lorcan lifted his mug in challenge to her words. He swallowed as much as he could before some came sputtering back up. "I'm not afraid of the truth, Hemlock."

"Good." She grinned. "And if you roll a seven? Well, then you must complete whatever challenge the other player puts before you."

"Anything?"

"Anything. Failure to follow through—"

"Forfeits the game. Yeah, yeah."

"It's no simple forfeit. The word will be branded to your forehead with ink that lasts several long weeks," she said. "And then not only will everyone know you visited a Confessional tavern... They'll know you couldn't honor your obligation."

"Right." Lorcan was already thinking of all the ways the night could go sideways. But there was opportunity as well. She wouldn't have brought him to such a place if she wasn't ready to hear his truth. "How does one...win? Or lose?"

"Assuming there's no shameful forfeit, a winner is declared when the loser no longer has anything to surrender. The winner earns the right to ask anything of the loser they wish, and the loser must follow through."

"If they don't?"

Edriss lifted her brows and looked to the side. "Well, it's a matter of honor. Something you of all people understand."

Lorcan's attention went to the drink cart, then to the bed. He choked out a nervous chuckle. "Why are we here, Edriss?"

"I don't know," she said after a pause. "Why are we here... Why am I here, with *you*...I've been asking myself this for the past hour. Today is the hardest I've had in a long while, and when

I saw you having your own awful day in the town square, this… popped into my mind, I guess. We both need an escape, as I see it. It's a ridiculous idea, I know, and there's still time to—"

"No," Lorcan said. He flattened his palms on the table. "I'm not forfeiting."

She watched him with a serious look. "It's not a forfeit if you back out before the game begins."

He shrugged. "Not backing out either."

"And what will Arwenna think of her beau engaging in a game of Confessional, privately, with me?"

Lorcan, emboldened by the surrealness of their setting, said, "You'll get the answer if I roll a confessional."

Edriss laughed. She cradled her ale in her hands, gazing at it with a dreamy, thoughtful expression. "You've always been very guarded with your truths, Lorry. I'll confess…This was probably in the back of my mind when I made the suggestion." She looked up. "But that's unfair, isn't it? I'm not entitled to know your truth. I'm not entitled to your time. Your concern. And I realize that, on this very day, I told you I didn't care anymore. That I was done. I only wish it were true."

A numbness began in Lorcan's chest. "Edriss…I'm sorry I've made you feel like we need to play a game for you to know what I'm thinking. We don't have to do this. We can simply…talk." He tapped his mug. "I've already drunk the ale. Whatever you want to know, you can be confident in my answer."

Edriss licked her lips and stared off at the corner of the room. "No. We came here to play. Let's play."

Edriss went first. She rolled a two.

Lorcan made a whistling sound and teasingly mimed pulling his shirt off.

It was fine. It was why she'd left her cloak on. She removed it with an impish grin and hung it next to his on the wall. "Your turn."

Lorcan rolled a seven.

Edriss eyed the dice in bemusement. "Already defying the odds. This doesn't bode well for you at all."

He cocked his head. "How so?"

"Most people with sense dread rolling a seven." Edriss drummed her fingers on the table, thinking. "Hmm. What humiliation can I dream up for you today?"

"You could try not to look so excited."

"Could I?" Edriss laughed. It felt good, a small release of the sorrow she'd been holding onto all day. "I think I'd like to watch you dance."

Lorcan's palms flattened atop the table. "I'm sorry, did you say *dance?*"

"Mhm. I did. Which is challenging, seeing as we have no music, but I'm sure you'll manage without it."

"Dance." He closed his eyes and tossed his head in disbelief. "You aren't serious?"

Edriss crossed her arms and waited.

"You are. Of course you are." He paled. "How...How would you like me to..."

"You're stalling for time."

"*No*, I'm only trying to understand—"

Edriss clapped her hands in time to a song they both knew, "The Ballad of Rhosyn and Thedyn," which had been sung all over the Reach when Evra had brought his new love home. She moved in time to the beat, widening her eyes and nodding toward the open floor.

"For the love of the Guardians," Lorcan muttered and made a dramatic show of peeling himself off the bench. With a glower, he hopped from one foot to the other, criminally out of time with her singing.

"What, exactly, are you dancing to, Lorry? Certainly not this song."

He swayed with a glare and spun around before resuming his chaotic hops. "How long do I have to do this?"

"Until I'm satisfied you've taken the challenge seriously," she replied, trying not to grin.

Lorcan bent over and whipped back up, then spun again and hopped in an even more frenetic rhythm, wearing an *are you kidding me* look she enjoyed far more than she'd expected.

"The challenge is *dancing*, not emulating the death throes of a deer after a hunt," she remarked drily, gathering even more joy from the disgusted look he shot her in response. "All right. I think this is enough. For my sake, not yours."

Lorcan groaned and slid back onto the bench. "You know you've just ensured your first challenge will be utterly humiliating?"

"You're assuming I'm foolish enough to roll a seven at all," Edriss muttered with a mischievous grin, reaching for the dice with a wink. She tossed it and it landed on a two. Sighing, she swung her feet around the bench and removed her boots.

"How's your smugness now, Hemlock? At this rate, I'll win before the fire needs tending." Lorcan snatched the dice and rolled. "A four. That's—"

Edriss rubbed her hands together. "Confessional! I can ask you anything I want now. And you—"

"Have no choice but to answer correctly. I know." He tapped both of his hands on his chest. "Do your worst."

Edriss inhaled a deep breath. There was only one thing she wanted to know—and she was sure he expected her to ask it—but her courage wasn't ready. *Always start with something easy,* she remembered Cressida telling her, when she'd imbued Edriss with her strategy for winning. *Lead up to what you most want to know. Let them think you're not going to ask what they expect you to.* "I want you to confess how you knew about Rivermarch," she said after she released a breath.

Lorcan looked at his ale and took another sip. "That's your question?"

"Yep."

"Okay." He sighed. "Finn. He's been following you for some time. Weeks. He's been subtle about it, so you wouldn't find out."

Edriss was aghast—more with herself than Finnegan, for how had she been so careless that the man had followed her for weeks and she'd never noticed? "Why didn't you tell me sooner?"

"Because I..." Lorcan's face twisted. He wanted to lie or at least soften the truth; she could see it, but the ale wouldn't allow it. "I decided to follow you as well. If you knew you were being followed, you'd have found more clever ways to give us the slip and then I wouldn't be there if you ran into trouble." He cleared his throat. "Also, you and I weren't exactly speaking."

She leveled a disgusted look at him, ignoring his paltry attempt to deflect. "As though you or Finnegan had anything more to offer said 'trouble' than I could?"

"I told you the truth, Hemlock. I never said it made any sense."

"Well it's good you didn't, for it *doesn't* make any sense. None at all." She snatched the dice and rolled before her anger could rise too high. Groaning, she said, "Six. Wonderful."

Roguish delight spread over Lorcan's face. He rubbed his hands together. "My turn to ask you a question."

Edriss held out her palms. "Ask away."

He sat back with a thoughtful look. "All right. I want to know how you really feel about Finn."

She snorted and swatted the air. "You already know, I..." Her face contorted, and panic spread through her. "Wait. No, that's not—"

"I can see you trying to lie!"

"I'm not *trying* to do..." Her breath caught. "I honestly thought I hated him. But I...suppose that although I'd...I'd like to hate him, he's grown on me. Lately he reminds me more of the way he was than the way he is."

Lorcan smiled with his mouth, but his eyes had darkened. "Go on."

"He's awful," Edriss said quickly. "But he's...kind to me. Most of the time. He looks after me, despite how I wish he wouldn't. He's never hurt me, and there are times..." She raked her teeth against the inside of her mouth. "Sometimes I believe he might actually love me and that he might not…not be as bad as his father. That if in the end I cannot get out of this marriage, he wouldn't be the worst husband."

The smile disappeared from Lorcan's face. "Do you love—"

"That's two questions. You only get one." Edriss shook her head at the table and answered anyway. "No. I don't love him."

Lorcan slumped in relief. "My turn." He hastily grabbed the dice and rolled. "Guardians deliver me."

Edriss brightened. "It's almost like you're *trying* to roll a seven." She tapped her chin and looked around the room for an idea. Her gaze landed on the drink cart, on top of which was a half-eaten loaf of bread the maids had forgotten to discard when they'd turned the room. "That. I want you to take a bite of it."

His nose curled up in revulsion. "No. Absolutely not."

"Are you forfeiting, Lorcan?"

"*No*, but you can't honestly expect me to eat something left by a stranger! What if I get sick?"

"Because if you're forfeiting…"

"Damn you, woman." Lorcan flipped his legs over the bench and stormed to the drink cart. With a glare, he ripped a crusty chunk off, shoved it in his mouth, and chewed it like a grazing cow, his jaw turning in overstated circles.

Edriss brought her hands to her mouth. "Oh my Guardians, spit it out, before it makes you sick." She bowed over the table, shaking with laughter.

Lorcan gagged into his hand and hurled the remnants into the waste bin. "Go on then, Hemlock. Roll a seven. You know you want to."

Edriss giggled and rolled. Three. "Ugh."

He waggled his brows and swallowed some ale. "You know what to do."

She lifted her feet onto the bench, removing first one sock, then another. She could have kept one—Lorcan didn't know the finer rules of the game, one of which was "socks count as one"—but she refused to cheat. "Don't get excited. Women love their layers."

"At the rate you keep rolling confiscations, those layers won't last too long." Lorcan was still laughing when he rolled a one. "I deserved that." He unlatched his sword belt and laid it over a nearby table. "But I, too, have layers."

Edriss rolled another three. She cursed under her breath and considered the least offensive attire left to remove. On a normal day, she'd have more options, but she'd dressed for practicality. With a groan, she unbuttoned her top dress layer and shimmied out of it, conscious of how thin the remaining layer was. Lorcan's eyes widened, but he kept his comments to himself.

That left only her shift and undergarments. The game would be over quicker than she realized if she kept rolling confiscations.

Lorcan rolled a four. "Another confession, it seems."

Edriss crossed her arms over the thin dress and asked the question he was expecting, before her nerves stayed her words. "You asked about Finnegan. I want to know about Arwenna."

His throat jumped with a swallow. "All right."

Edriss met his eyes despite everything screaming inside of her to look away. "Do you love her?"

Lorcan's answer came fast. "No."

"You sure?"

He locked gazes with her, took another sip of ale, and set it down, all without averting his eyes. "I'm sure, Edriss. I know how it looks, to you and everyone else, but things aren't as they seem. I want to say more, but I can't. It's not my truth to tell. But you want to know what I feel for Arwenna? Sympathy."

His answer didn't make sense. "That doesn't explain all the kissing, and…I mean, the entire Rush thinks you're readying for a proposal, Lorry."

"She could never have my heart, Hemlock," Lorcan said, seeming to select each word carefully. "It's not mine to give her."

Edriss twitched. "What does that mean?"

"You asked your question." He nodded at the dice. "Your turn."

She buried her frustration and rolled again. Two. "Dammit," she hissed, glancing down at what few articles remained.

"Not much left to remove, is there?" he remarked, smirking. "My victory is all but a foregone conclusion."

Edriss weighed her options. Her shift, her brassiere, or her undergarments. If she removed her shift, she'd be exposed for whatever was left of the game. Taking off anything underneath was a calculated risk, but it bought her time.

"Turn around," she ordered. He did, still smirking, and she reached under her dress to unhook her brassiere. "All right," she said, and waved the garment in the air when he was looking again. She tossed it to the corner. He followed it with a whistling sound.

Lorcan rolled a one and removed his vest. "Still fairly comfortable over here."

Edriss, eyes narrowed, rolled a four.

"What do I want to know about Lady Edriss Blackwood that I do not already?" Lorcan theatrically tapped his cheek. "Why did you *really* bring me here, after you told me you wanted nothing to do with me anymore?"

Edriss's mouth flapped in a useless attempt to find a round-about way to skirt the truth. *I don't know,* she wanted to say, but the words wouldn't come.

Lorcan held out his hands, waiting.

"To clear both of our minds of a terrible day, for one," she said. "But also…"

"Also…"

"I suppose…" Her breathing arrested. "I suppose I wanted closure."

"Closure?"

Edriss wrung her hands under the table. "I had hoped I might find the courage to ask…not how you feel about Arwenna but how you feel about me, even though I already have my answer."

His cheeky grin dissolved. "Hemlock."

She wiped a tear before it fell and shoved the dice his way. "Your turn."

Lorcan kept his eyes on her as he rolled. Three. He removed his shirt and dropped it to the floor. When he ran his hands down his bare chest, she noted a scar she'd never seen before, near his heart.

Edriss rolled a three. She shook her head and slid her under-garments off from under the slip. One more and she was done. One more and she'd never get to ask the question that would finally put her past in the past, so she could move on without wondering what might have been.

Lorcan had no witty comment for her. He lifted the dice and rolled a six. "Well." He swallowed. "Here's your chance, Hemlock. Ask me."

With the moment at last upon her, Edriss discovered herself tongue-tied. Maybe she didn't want to know. Maybe it was easier to finish the game and go their separate ways, never knowing.

"I…" She inhaled a shuddering breath. "Tell me about that scar."

"Hemlock." He watched her with a sad, urgent look.

"You've already told me how you feel about me, Lorcan. I was a fool for thinking I might trick you into telling me the truth, when you already have. Hearing it again…" She nibbled the edge of her bottom lip. "So tell me about the scar."

He didn't answer right away. She felt his eyes plying her in soft demand. "I earned it in the north, fighting the Ravenwoods. It's nothing. Was just a scratch, but you know how stubborn scars can be."

"I could have healed it for you."

"I didn't want to worry you."

Edriss scoffed. "I never asked you to protect me from everything."

"Nonetheless," he said, his voice low. "I always will."

"Time to end this." She snaked a hand forward and rolled. Seven. She sat back in surprise. "I guess I should be thankful it wasn't another confiscation."

"Come here."

"What?"

"I challenge you to come here." Lorcan pulled one of his legs to the outside of the bench. "And feel my scar."

"You want me to…feel your scar? That's your challenge?"

258

"Come here, Edriss."

It was easy. Too easy. She slid off the bench and warily came to his side. He guided her to sit, wrapped her hand in his, and pressed it to his heart. She felt the wild thumps under his warm flesh and lifted her eyes to meet his in surprise.

"You want to know how I feel, Hemlock, just ask my heart."

Edriss shook her head. Response eluded her. She was rooted in place by something resembling fear but was far, far worse. It was a road she could never turn back from if she went any further.

"Ask my heart how it beats whenever we're alone. Whenever you're too close. How it betrays me at every step no matter how hard I fight it."

"Roll." Her voice cracked. She said it again. "Roll."

He slowly reached beyond her and cradled the dice. It landed on a seven. "What are the odds of that?" He chuckled. "Do your worst."

Edriss froze. Every clever idea she had flew from her mind, replaced by a terrifying and exhilarating one, which had the potential to utterly destroy her if she were wrong.

But she didn't think she was wrong.

Not anymore.

"I challenge you to *show* me your true feelings. Not with words."

Lorcan wasted no time in reaching forward and grasping her hair in his hands. He pulled her in for a kiss that sent her heart palpitating wildly, his lips no longer soft like before but hard and full of command. He twirled his tongue against hers, his desperate moans vibrating the inside of her mouth.

When her arms reached around his neck, Lorcan slid his hands down to her waist and lifted her onto his lap, leaving them both gasping in strange delight. He ran his fingers down her back, sliding them under her ass with a light boost and a groan. She felt him try to speak, but he honored her request, instead cradling her against himself and kissing her with enough fearful desperation to bring tears springing back into her eyes.

Edriss slapped the table, searching for the dice. She gave it a sloppy roll, and Lorcan turned just enough to say, "One. That's game."

"Help me," she started to say, but Lorcan was already bunching her shift dress up around her thighs, his mouth still locked to hers. He pulled it up and over her head, letting it fall to the ground in a soft whoosh.

He broke the kiss and looked at her. His chest rose and fell, his lips parting slightly before he sighed. "You're so cursed beautiful, Edriss."

For all their closeness, he'd never seen her nude before. She tried to cover herself, but he peeled her arms back.

Lorcan dipped down and took her nipple in his mouth, sending a bolt of pleasure straight to her head. His warm breath was almost too much.

Nothing felt real.

Nothing had ever felt *more* real.

His mouth traced a path up her neck and lingered on the underside of her chin. "I love you. I *love* you. I have loved you for so long, I no longer know how to pretend there's anything innocent or simple about it. Honor be damned, Edris. I want *you*. I've always wanted you. If the Guardians see fit to punish me, I'll accept whatever sentence they deem fit, but if they try to steal you from my arms—"

Edriss twisted away. "Don't you dare say things to me in here you wouldn't say in the light of day."

Lorcan gripped her face between his hands and forced their eyes to meet. "I wanted to tell you that day in the guard tower, and every moment since, I've tried to find the courage. I'm sorry it took me so long. I'm *sorry* for all the hurt I've caused you in my twisted sense of right and wrong. If you don't feel the same, if you don't…want me anymore, if my hesitation has destroyed your love for me, then I'll respect your choice. I deserve it. But I won't run from us. Not anymore."

Edriss sucked in her bottom lip when he tried to kiss her again. "I want this too, but…not if you're still with Arwenna… however confusing your relationship may be."

"No. There isn't a relationship between Arwenna and me. But this arrangement she and I have, it's done. I'll talk to her as soon as we're back." Lorcan shook his head. He pressed his forehead to hers. "She knows I love you. She knows I could only ever love you."

Edriss nodded against him. She reached a hand out and searched for the dice again.

"I won, Hemlock," he said with a soft laugh.

"I know," she whispered, turning her eyes toward the table when she found the dice. She turned it until the number one was upright, and she set it down. "Oh, look. Your turn to remove something."

Lorcan's throat jumped. When he shifted beneath her, she felt his desire pulsing through the trousers she wanted to rip off of him. Everything cautious in her melted away when he started to unbuckle himself. "Are you—"

Edriss crushed her mouth to his. "Yes," she muttered against him. "I'm sure."

His hand stalled. "Marry me, Edriss."

She broke away. "What?"

"Marry me." He slid one hand away from his belt and gripped her thigh. His thumb traced her flesh. "Become my wife."

She shook her head, her thoughts and heart both struggling to catch up. "What about—"

"I'll talk to your brother. I'll tell him how I feel, how I've always felt. I'll fall on my sword, pay whatever penance he asks of me, but I'll stand firm. I'll…" He tilted his face down when tears filled his eyes. "I won't fail you again. I won't fail us."

Edriss finished removing his belt for him. She pulled it free and heaved it across the room, where it landed with a light clang near the hearth. "Don't you dare break my heart again. If you do, Lorry, it will be for the last time."

Lorcan carried Edriss to the bed. He'd carried her many times over the years, but there was nothing familiar about the way he held her as he brushed the curtains aside with the back of his hand…as he lowered her onto the plush blanket, allowing his gaze to linger long enough to drink her in. Every light, every shadow. Every peak and valley. He committed it all to memory, in case the morning brought painful clarity and regret for her.

It would not be so for him.

The moment she'd asked him to play the game, he'd known how it would end for him: with the truth. With a courageous embrace of what he wanted—finally.

He'd spent too many years denying her, and denying himself. The moment she'd looked into his eyes and told him she was sure, there was no going back.

Lorcan stepped out of his trousers and climbed onto the bed. Edriss lay with her head tilted, her eyes glistening and full of all the complicated emotions he felt weighing on his own heart.

But the heaviness cleared the moment he crawled over her and locked eyes with her once more.

"I love you too, Lorry," she said, soft and breathy. "Only you."

Lorcan trailed kisses around the edges of her mouth, up her cheeks, and around the corners of her eyes. She writhed under him with soft desperate sounds that nearly sent him crawling out of his own skin. "Only you," he whispered against her temple, sliding his hands down between them. Her body responded by rising toward his touch, an invitation more powerful than words.

He traced his thumb along the place he knew would set her aflame, and it did. Edriss bucked with a shocked gasp at the moment of connection, the shift pushing his palm downward, confirming she was more than ready.

Lorcan removed his hand and reached between his legs to guide himself. She tensed when he pressed in, but nodded to reassure him.

His head fell back when he entered her. Edriss made a gurgling, gasping sound, but then she was dragging her nails down his back, urging him on. He slid his hands under her back and tugged her up and into him. She nipped at his mouth until she had a firm command of her kisses.

He stole a moment to catch his breath, planting his lips on the soft down of her bare arm. The perfection of her was like a thousand cuts reminding him of all he'd almost given up. Every shared story, moment stolen…each test of trust and understanding.

"Yes," Edriss moaned. She jumped her hips and bit down on her lip so hard, he expected blood to bead up. "I'll marry you."

"Really?" Lorcan slowed his pace. "It's what you want?"

"It's the only thing I've ever wanted." Edriss's eyes rolled back briefly. "This. You."

Lorcan slipped his thumb back between her legs, growing harder at her little whimper when he found his way again. He moved in gentle circles, bringing her with him, because the only thing he desired more than making love to her was watching her come undone.

Edriss's mouth froze open, suspended in a thrall of pure pleasure. She arched upward, and in seconds she was writhing and shuddering, screaming her release. The force of it shattered his resistance, inadvertently finishing inside of her before he could pull out. He was spinning himself into a true panic when he remembered she'd been drinking a special tea ever since her betrothal had been announced. *Can't risk carrying Derry's demon spawn,* he'd overheard her say to Cressida.

Panting through the final throes, Edriss pitched forward and wrapped her arms around his neck, burying her face in the hollow of his collarbone. "You and me, Lorry. It's all I need. I can weather any other storm."

"Until the world ends, Hemlock," Lorcan promised and stirred to life for another round.

SEVENTEEN

UNDER THE SUN
AND SKY AND STARS

Edriss moved through the following days, trudging through nightmares and twirling through dreams.

As long as there was light remaining to the day, she was in the encampment, working with as many children as she could before dusk settled and the little ones were taken away for the night. Lorcan was there for every moment, guiding the children over and helping to calm them with his unique playfulness as she prepared the salve that would ease the terror encircling their poor little hearts. He was so good with them, so patient and kind, and in his gentle handling, Edriss saw a glimpse of the future that could be theirs, if they could only win the fight against everything keeping them apart.

"You'll make a wonderful father one day," she said to him as they cleaned her bowls and instruments in a nearby stream.

Lorcan's response was buried when he nuzzled her neck. She giggled and he pulled back, planting a victorious kiss on her jaw. "How many will we have, do you think?"

Her heart skipped several beats at how naturally he'd said *we*. "Does it work that way? Do we get to choose?"

"Well," he said with a mischievous twinkle in his eyes. "We get to *try* as often as we want. Only the Guardians can decide how to reward our...efforts."

"Wouldn't want them to think we weren't hard workers," she'd said, wearing her challenge in her grin.

They'd made love creek-side, an interlude that had ended with them having to scramble for their clothes amid stifled giggles when some washing women had come too close.

They had no secrets anymore. Edriss told him everything about her days in Rivermarch, filling in the details he hadn't had. Lorcan hadn't hidden his relief that the Greencastle trip would keep her from meeting with the man, John. She hadn't hidden her disappointment either.

And they spoke of Arwenna as well. More and more, Edriss understood the raven had gotten herself into trouble, serious enough she didn't want anyone to know. Lorcan was too honorable to betray a friend's trust, and *that* man was who Edriss had fallen in love with all those years ago, so she didn't ask him to.

Edriss knew what she needed to know. Whatever the arrangement between Lorcan and Arwenna, neither lust nor love had any part.

When they were with the children, they rarely spoke to each other. Edriss had never felt such a strong sense of purpose as she did when meeting with each little boy and girl, listening to their woes separately and relieving them of the worst parts. Within each little heart was so much pain, but she saw the futures they would have, *could* have, thanks to the healing magic she could give them.

But she couldn't have done any of it without Lorcan.

When her bones grew tired, he was there with warm cider and a bowl of stew. When her hands shook, he held them in his until they stopped. She taught him how to mix the salve so she could focus on whispering the words that would make it adhere to their pain and soften it.

"This is the most harrowing thing I've ever done," he said one night, after the handmaidens had ushered away the children they hadn't been able to get to. Edriss always prioritized them the following morning. "Harder than tending. But also…also easier, because I know we won't leave here until every child has some peace."

Edriss nodded, eyeing the scattered mess of materials. "I think it will happen sooner than we realized. Tomorrow, perhaps."

"Because of you." Lorcan studied her in soft admiration. "Because you're here from the time the sun rises to the time it sets. You have a relentless heart. I've never known anyone with one bigger or better."

"If I could've seen them all in a day, I would have. Every day they suffer, when I can't help them, feels like a failure," she said, beginning her cleanup. Lorcan leaned in to help. "But the thought of going back to the Rush…after…"

Lorcan reached a hand up and cupped her face. She closed her eyes for a moment, falling into his comforting touch. "No one has to know we finished early."

She looked up.

"I know what you're thinking, Hemlock. You're worried about the Defenders. What they might do."

Edriss lowered her gaze. She'd once said he couldn't read her the way he thought he could, but it had been a lie. He'd always seen through her words, straight to her intentions.

"But you deserve a reprieve. To *breathe*." Lorcan kissed her. He tasted like the awful cider. "We have another week before they expect us back in the Rush." He kissed her again. "Let's stay, Edriss. You and me. We can make ourselves useful in the village while there's daylight to guide us. They'll be rebuilding Greencastle for years. But the nights…The nights are ours."

"The nights are ours," she said, stifling a yawn. She crashed into his arms. Her raw exhaustion exposed her fears, and she couldn't help but voice them. "What if we go home, and Evra won't support us?"

Lorcan didn't answer, but she felt his thoughts churning. He held her in a hard silence that made her almost glad she couldn't read him this time.

They finished with the last child around noon the following day. Lorcan's heart had never been so full, watching Edriss handle the children with such tender care. If he didn't know better, he'd think she absorbed the pain she took from them. It had to go somewhere, he thought. But while her eyes grew heavier with each little one she helped, theirs lightened. Their pain would never be entirely gone, but it wouldn't haunt their lives either.

Lorcan's thoughts were divided between the children and a plan that he'd been cooking up for several days.

He'd tried to tell Edriss, but there never seemed to be the right time for it. Either they were focused on their aid or focused on their pleasure, but there was no space in between the two for anything other than healing, restorative silences.

At the end of each night, wrapped in each other's arms, the worries of the day dissolved, and he couldn't find the words.

Fear brought doubts hurling back. Not about her or him or how they felt. He was still uncertain about many things, but not the most important; he would never again deny his love for Edriss Blackwood. The entire world could burn down around them, and he'd still never go backward.

But her question about Evra was bigger than words. Lorcan had practiced the conversation he'd have with his old friend so many times, he no longer needed to practice it at all, but it all came back to the same real possibility that Evra would refuse their request to be together. Lorcan would die before watching Edriss be forced into marriage with another man, especially one so dangerous.

It was with this in mind that Lorcan's plan took on life.

He found small pockets of time, in between clearing debris and carting in wood and stone, to slip away. As each little detail came together, Lorcan fought against the lingering dread that Edriss would think him a reckless fool. That she had designs on something far more extravagant than what he could put together in secrecy and shadows, and she would believe he'd lost his mind.

But then he'd watch her sleeping against his chest as he listened to the soft, easy sounds of her peaceful breathing, dreaming through harmony that had eluded her most of her life, and he knew there were no fears strong enough to ever come between them again. The only thing left to do was love her. Always.

Lorcan would never forgive himself for living mired in denial for so long, but he eagerly awaited the opportunity to make it up to her every day for the rest of their lives.

Tomorrow, he'd show her everything he'd been planning.

Tomorrow, he'd promise her forever.

Edriss awoke thinking she'd slept late. The room was aglow—too much for early morning. She pulled herself up, shaking off the remnants of sleep, and tried to make sense of why there were hundreds of candles that hadn't been there the night before.

She searched around for Lorcan, but he didn't seem to be in the room. He might have been downstairs in the tavern, grabbing food for both of them—it would be entirely like him to let her rest—but instinct told her something else was afoot.

Edriss's warm toes hit the cold floor, waking her all the way up. She wrapped a quilt around herself and shimmied to the table, where a note was propped against a vase of freshly picked wildflowers.

She was already smiling before she even finished the words. *You'll remember the abbey we passed, along the forest's edge. Meet me there. L.*

A knock on the door made her jump. She called out to ask who it was, and one of the barmaids entered. She glanced around,

269

wide-eyed, and said, "Your beau pays well. Not to worry about the candles burning down the inn. I'll see to them after you leave." She turned around and made a beckoning gesture. A small girl trundled in, hoisting a dress over her head. The fabric covered her almost entirely. Only her elbows were visible. "I'm here to deliver this."

Edriss accepted the dress from the little girl, who sighed in dramatic relief, sanding her hands. The fabric was a light cream, embroidered with delicate floral patterns she immediately recognized as all her favorite plants for making salves. "What is this?"

"He offered no explanation with his payment," the barmaid said. She tsk-tsked the little girl, who scampered off, disappearing in a patter of footfalls. "But I'm supposed to ask you if you know the way to the abbey."

Edriss nodded, swallowing the lump forming in her throat. Tears stung her eyes, but it was too soon. She had a faint idea of what Lorcan had planned, and if she was right, there would be more than enough crying for the rest of the day. "Thank you. I…" She held the dress up and hung it on a wall hook. "Thank you."

The woman bowed and left.

Edriss fought a tremble in her hands as she carefully dressed herself. A peek beyond the windows showed a dusting of snow, so she fastened her cloak tight, checked herself in the mirror, and left.

Frog had already been checked out of the stables. Nightshade made a series of affronted snorts, as though she'd been expected hours ago. Edriss kissed her snout and whispered sweet words into her ears, and she calmed, allowing her to be saddled and mounted.

Edriss reached the forest's edge just after sunrise. She searched for the abbey and, with a sharp stab of panic, wondered if she'd misunderstood. But then she spotted it, right at the bend in the road, at the end of a short path that would be easy to miss if she weren't looking for it.

With her heart a fluttery mess, she dismounted and tethered Nightshade next to Frog. The hitching post had fallen into disuse, matching the abbey beyond. The realm was littered with such relics, victims of the Rhiagain crown and their mission to redefine faith.

She forgot how to walk. Breathing came just as hard, but she sucked on the cool air and tried to hold it. Snow was ripe upon the wind as heavy flakes came swirling around her in soft tufts, which took their time on their way to the ground.

Is this happening? she thought as she took the first step. The second was easier, but the third grounded her with doubts. What if she were wrong? What if all that awaited her was a romantic picnic or some other sweet surprise? What if she couldn't hide the disappointment in her face?

But what if I'm right?

Until that moment, Edriss hadn't contemplated the particulars of what lay ahead. Her heart's response had been a resounding yes, blocking out all semblance of reason. Every reckless thing she'd ever done had been in pursuit of doing what was right, and though she didn't think there was anything reckless about marrying the man she loved, impulsiveness only scratched the surface of what it would mean to elope with him in secret.

What it would mean for the only sister of the lord of the Westerlands to choose with her heart and go against the plan he'd already shared far and wide across the Reach.

But when Edriss saw Lorcan emerge from the abbey with a roguish grin, his hands folded in front of him and his dark hair falling over one eye, her doubts were carried away with the budding squall. She matched his grin, lifted her skirts, and raced down the path to leap into his arms with enough force to send him sprawling to the door.

"I'm guessing you figured it out," he said between kisses. "You're not mad?"

"No, you scoundrel, I'm not *mad*," she said, giggling, as he hoisted her higher. "Others will be, of course, but—"

271

"We're not thinking about others today."

"No," she agreed, sealing the word with a long, hard kiss. "Just us, Lorry."

"Just us, Hemlock." He gently set her back down. A flush appeared in his cheeks when he thumbed toward the door. "Aaaand the old, half-blind minister, who would perhaps prefer we wait until *after* the vows are read to consummate the union."

"No need to scandalize the poor man with the truth." Edriss winked. "I won't tell him if you don't."

"Guardians, I love you so much," he murmured and kissed her once more before taking her by the hand and leading her inside.

The minister knew who they were. Any union sealed under false pretense risked annulment, and Lorcan was taking no chances. Evra would still have to bless it, but that was another battle, for another day. Once Evra saw how happy his little sister was, his own heart would soften. It had to.

And she really was happy. She'd smiled more in the past week than the past year. The glow in her cheeks turned Lorcan's anguish to bliss. More than once he'd prostrated himself before the Guardians in penitence for all he'd put her through to get there.

His nightmares had ceased as well. He no longer saw Edriss's face on Cesarina's poor, singed body, nor did he see Cesarina herself. He hadn't wanted to be absolved of his guilt and had only agreed to relief because of the worry in Edriss's eyes, but the lighter burden left him free to love her even more.

The first three ministers had refused him right away. They were sworn to silence because of their sacred oath, so they'd never tell a soul about the conversations, but they couldn't help him. Their rejections only made him more determined to find someone who would take pity on two young lovers whose only desires were each other.

The third one referred him to Minister Warrenhap, who was a season away from permanent retirement. *He's more amenable these days and might take pity on you.*

And he had. *Young love is the only pure thing left in this realm. If you tell me this is what you both want, I will happily oblige.*

A generous donation to the minister's local reliquary was all it had taken.

"Lady Blackwood." The minister held out his palms, wiggling his fingers to request she come closer. When she did, he clasped her hands in his and squeezed. "Am I to understand you wish to marry this man, even at the displeasure of your brother, Lord Blackwood?"

"Yes, Minister," Edriss said. Her dark curls were brushed into buoyant waves, which Lorcan was desperate to run his hands through. "Among my wishes that affect my personal well-being, it is by far the greatest."

Lorcan's heart skipped so hard, he lost the cadence of his breathing.

"Very well." He released her and leaned over the pulpit to lift the heavy codex. It made a creaky groan when he flipped it open. Dust flooded the air. "You may be familiar with the old ways. Very few still follow them, but I believe all good marriages begin with good traditions. And you'll need all the blessings you can when you make your way back to Longwood Rush."

"We're happy to follow whatever tradition you feel is best," Lorcan said. He could hardly stand still. His hands wanted to touch her; his mouth warmed in anticipation of the kisses he'd steal when they were alone.

"Aye." The minister licked his thumb and turned one heavy page after another until he found the one he was looking for. "Ah. You'd think I'd know this by heart. I did, once. But the memory is the first to slip."

"Take your time, Minister." The kindness in Edriss's voice melted Lorcan to the stones.

"Shall I read the seventeen pages outlining all the ways marriage is sacred, or would you children prefer I skip to the vows?"

Lorcan and Edriss exchanged giddy grins. "Vows," they said together.

"Very well." The minister cleared his throat and adjusted his collar. "We begin by paying homage to the Guardian of Anguish and Tribulation. My favorite." His mouth ticked into a semblance of a smile. "Lorcan, turn toward Edriss and read the following."

Lorcan breathed deep and read the words. He had to refocus his gaze to hold onto them, his thoughts were racing so fast. "Although you come to me now in good health, there will be a day or perhaps many days when this will not be so. The Guardian of Anguish and Tribulation teaches us that the trials of our life hold more value than the whimsies. That our reward for enduring such trials are the times of peace that follow. I swear to you, Edriss, I will cherish the trials as deeply as I treasure the peace."

"And I, you, Lorcan," Edriss said, following the minister's instruction. He gave her the next vow to read. "As we have fought the odds to stand here now, together, so will there be more ahead of us yet to conquer." She squeezed tears from her eyes. "The Guardian of the Warrior's Aim teaches us the only path forward is through the fire, together. I swear to you, Lorcan, I will stand at your side through any fire, no matter how hot it burns."

"And I, you, Edriss." Lorcan shifted nervously, fighting his own tears. She'd never looked more beautiful than she did standing before him, her eyes wide with love and trust, wearing the dress he'd commissioned to remind her he loved her just as she was. "We bring not only ourselves but our pasts to this union. The Guardian of the Treasured Past teaches us that all memories are treasured, good or ill. They are a part of us as much as the breath we draw and the blood coursing through our veins. Edriss, I swear to you I'll accept your past and future equally, love them equally, and will endeavor for our pasts to become one, just as our future will now become."

"And I, you, Lorcan," she said, her voice cracking into a whisper. She looked down at the book and took a moment to gather herself. She blew out a breath, laughed nervously under her breath, and continued. "We join now as two, but it is our duty to turn two into three, three into four. The Guardian of Rebirth and Renewal teaches us that our love can only be strengthened by the creation of life. That we begin this new life today and carry our love forward, into the hearts of our children. I swear to you, Lorcan, I will teach our children how to love by never failing to show them my love for their father."

"And I, you, Edriss," Lorcan said with a trembling exhale. His vision was blurred by tears, and he almost couldn't read the page.

"Just one more," the minister said gently.

Lorcan wiped his eyes and continued. "While we treasure the present and revere the past, the future is but a mystery to us. Our happiness, our health, and our prosperity are not assured. The only certainty in life is death." Lorcan inhaled a deep breath. Edriss's violet eyes sparkled as she watched him. "The Guardian of the Unpromised Future, who has long looked after the Westerlands, teaches us we must live for the day, for the hour. I swear to you, Edriss…my love." He paused, overcome, when he imagined Finn saying these vows to Edriss—how close they'd come to it happening. "That I will cherish every *second*, every hour, every day with you. I will not dread the unknown, unpromised future, and will exist in the moments as they are given—with love, with fealty, and with a remembrance of these vows when my heart feels weak with worry, so that I remember not the fear but the love binding us together, through eternity."

"And I, you, Lorcan." Edriss could barely say the words through her tears.

The minister closed the book and looked at them both. He urged them to hold out their hands and clasp them together. Then he bound them with a thick white rope.

"I now bless this union, in the name of the Five. What has been bound cannot be unbound, save by death. You are now united under the sun and sky and stars, and you may proceed, without fear, without reprisal, into a future full of love and prosperity." The minister withdrew a dagger and sliced through the rope, handing the severed knot to Lorcan. "Let this rest upon your hearth for the remainder of your days as a symbol of your bond."

With the rope still clenched in his fist, Lorcan cradled Edriss's face in his hands and kissed his wife for the first time.

"Are you happy?" he whispered against her mouth.

"The happiest," she said back, trailing a sigh along his lips before kissing him once more.

"Good luck and fortune to you both," the minister said. He clapped them both on the shoulders before hobbling down the aisle. "You'll soon need all the Guardians can spare."

Edriss's sweaty palms slid down the wall as she clambered to grab hold of anything to harness the pleasure climbing beyond her control. She stretched to the tops of her toes as Lorcan slammed into her from behind, twisting his fingers between her legs with each powerful thrust.

I never knew this side of you existed, she wanted to say, *tried* to say, but she could hardly breathe, let alone speak. He was both generous and demanding, gentle and forceful. She didn't know how much more she could take, sore as she was. All she knew was she never wanted him to stop.

My husband, she thought and stretched taller upon her toes as she crested. Lorcan's groans turned savage, his pace quickening as he reached his own climax. He bit down on her bare shoulder just as the warmth spread through her. A feeling she was already addicted to.

Lorcan released her right as a note slid under their door. He pressed one hand to her forearm protectively and went to retrieve it. Her desire stirred back to life as she studied the cut of hard muscles scoring his back and the arc of his perfect ass, which she loved to claw and grab at. She'd decided to sneak up behind him and nudge him into another sweaty, strenuous round when she saw the look on his face.

He held up the note but said nothing. He seemed unable to.

Edriss slumped against the wall.

Whatever it said, one thing was all but certain.

Their respite was over.

EIGHTEEN
NO TIME FOR GOOD-BYES

Rhosyn's message was brief. It betrayed nothing but urgency. *Return with haste. Spare no time for good-byes.*

The fear in Edriss's eyes ripped Lorcan's heart down the middle. Rhosyn had offered no explanation, but it was the lack of one that sent the terror rising unabated within them both. There were the things that could be said, and those that could not even be written. Whatever had stayed Rhosyn's hand was no minor trouble.

Was it the baby? They'd received word that Rhosyn's labor had been a false one, but perhaps it had started again…perhaps…

No, Lorcan decided. If Rhosyn was in trouble, Evra would have sent the note, not her.

The silence upon them on the ride home was not uncomfortable. He'd never done well in the quiet unless he was alone, but with Edriss, words had never been a requirement. She had become his wife, and their language had evolved beyond conversation. The hand he stretched toward her every so often, across the small space between their horses, was always accepted. Their lovemaking was a passionate demonstration of all they couldn't say—and didn't need to.

Only one thing mattered now.

Whatever awaited them in Longwood Rush, they'd face it united.

Edriss glanced down the tree-lined approach with a shiver. The Halls of Longwood was her home, even if it had not always felt welcoming. Today she saw it through a blanket of trepidation that grew heavier the closer they drew to the Rush. The tiered gardens no longer looked magical but menacing, blobs of harsh color ringing the keep like a noose. Her family's colors, waving from the ramparts, were usually a comfort but were now dire warnings snapping against the chilled breeze.

Finnegan met them at the spot where the road veered from town and turned into the final approach to the Halls of Longwood. He stared from his mount in stoic resolve. His cheeks were ablaze, from either the cold, the trouble, or both.

"You finish your work in Greencastle?" he asked, clenching tight to his reins as he eyed them both.

Edriss and Lorcan looked at each other before answering. The desperation in his eyes, at returning to how things were, must have been reflecting in hers also. The only remedy for it was to break gazes before it was obvious to Finnegan too. "We made it through all the children but were hoping to help more with the rebuilding efforts."

"You made fair enough time." Accusation brimmed in Finnegan's expression. "But we have none left to spare. Come, quickly."

Edriss spurred her horse into a gallop to match his unexpected pace, Lorcan falling in behind.

"Are you going to tell us what's going on?" She had to yell to be heard over the crash of hooves splashing in mud.

"Are you going to tell *me* what's going on with you and Lorcan?" He shouted even louder.

"Nothing. Nothing, other than we're speaking again."

He'd obviously seen something, despite her attempt to hide it, and he'd find out eventually. But no one else could know about her elopement before Evra did, and until she knew why they'd been summoned home with such hushed urgency, she couldn't even think about how or when to tell him.

"Bollocks it's nothing." Finnegan turned a hard left when they neared the stairs leading up to the Halls, headed toward the stables. "It's never been bloody nothing, Edriss. I'm not a fool." He tossed a glare over his shoulder. "Nor will others be when they see how you are with each other."

It was unfortunate he'd noted the shift between them, but she supposed it must be more than just their lingering look. Love like theirs couldn't be brushed away, and she wasn't ashamed. She would march down the Halls with the same pride and confidence as she always had, and if people knew she was in love with Lorcan James and that he was in love with her, there was nothing she could do about it.

Soon enough, they'd all know.

But first, she had to find out what was going on.

"Finn," Edriss pleaded as they handed the horses over to the grooms. "Tell us. Please."

"It's the fucking raven," he muttered. He kicked the hay-covered floor and sent some unseen thing flinging to the wall. "Always fucking ravens, isn't it?"

Lorcan drew up behind Edriss. His warm strength felt like a protective shield. "What do you mean, it was the raven?"

"Your girlfriend." Finnegan spat at their feet, and Edriss stumbled into Lorcan to dodge it. It was then she saw the red spidering from his flared pupils, lining the lids of his eyes.

Instinct made her reach for him. "Finn...Are you all right?"

"No, I'm not fucking all right. That bitch tried to kill my father!" He tore away from her. His nose flared in rage. "And she...She *succeeded* in taking out both Bristol and Ashenhurst in the doing."

281

Edriss brought her hands to her mouth. She felt the air leave Lorcan behind her. "Oh, no."

"Bristol and Ashenhurst are *dead?*" Lorcan asked with a sharp breath.

"Dead as dead can be," Finnegan stated with a scornful laugh. "Promises not just spent but ripped away by a vengeful bitch with something to prove."

"Where is she?" Lorcan demanded. He planted his hands on Edriss's shoulders, easing her wave of jealousy that had rolled forward. She chided herself for reacting at all. "Where's Arwenna now?"

"Not in prison, where she belongs." Finnegan started toward the keep, but instead of heading to the main entrance, he guided them around the broad lower gardens, toward the back. "Evra's protecting her. *Protecting* a lying, murdering, scheming—"

"That's enough," Edriss stated. She flexed her hands at her sides, desperate for something other than the numb fear tingling through her limbs. Lorcan stayed close, one hand on her back. "She's still here, in the Halls?"

"With your mad aunt." Finnegan shook his head in fast passes and laughed again. "And your equally mad grandmother."

"Powerful women only terrify weak men," Edriss shot back. "Since you're taking us around to the back entrance, I can only assume they're in the servants' quarters?"

Finnegan darted down the steps without answering.

"And my brother? Rhosyn?" Edriss struggled to keep up. "Where are they?"

"Pretending like nothing happened." Finnegan rounded the corner and slipped down another set of stairs leading to the dungeon level.

"Why are Arwenna, Alise, and Meldred in the *dungeon*, Finn?" Lorcan asked.

"Because," Finnegan said, slowing when he approached the last handful of steps. He reached into the basket of blackened torches, removed one, and lit it on the nearby flame. "Bristol managed to stab the slippery bitch on his way to the Guardians. The women are mixing their herbs, whispering their strange words over her, when they *should* be helping my poor father, who is *still* unable to speak after she poisoned him."

Edriss stopped walking. "How bad is she…"

"Don't know," Finnegan said, shrugging. "And to tell you the truth, Edriss, I don't rightly care either. What you need to ask yourself is where do your loyalties lie? To a raven who has done nothing but take from you? Or to the man who will soon be your father?"

She decided it wasn't the time to bring up the terrible things his father and the other men had been involved in. "My loyalty is to the Westerlands, as always. But as you said, we are short on time, and I—"

"You're as politic as your brother, aren't you? Will you never answer me directly, Edriss? Ever?"

Lorcan grunted. "Look, Finn—"

Edriss stayed Lorcan's words with a hand on his. Finnegan didn't miss the subtle movement, rolling his eyes with a cold sneer. "How is your father now? And *where* is he?"

"In the infirmary." Finnegan's nose flared in anger, but he saw something on her face that calmed him. "I need you to heal the raven so she can be held to account for her crimes. My father is stable, but he'll need…more than the physicians could offer. But if the raven dies before justice is served, I'll…" He couldn't finish.

"I'll help your father, Finn, as soon as I'm done with Arwenna. I promise. I assume the other two are beyond…beyond my aid?"

Finnegan snorted. "Unless you've learned to raise the dead, I'd say so."

She shook her head, exhaling her bewilderment. He was too angry to offer answers, so she'd have to find them for herself. "Which room?"

He tilted his head and led them farther down the dark hall before rounding a corner that abruptly stopped when a massive arched door loomed, flanked by a handful of stone-faced guards.

Finnegan shifted his torch to one hand and rapped on the door, tweaked his mouth into a glower, and waited with radiating impatience.

The door cracked open. One of Alise's eyes appeared, darting left and right in examination, before the door swung wide and they were ushered in.

Edriss stifled a scream at the sight of Arwenna. The raven was lying on a pile of furs, stacked atop a broad table, shivering under clean blankets. A nearby heap of bloodied rags and clothing required no words.

"What took you so long?" Meldred asked from the other side of the room. Edriss hadn't seen her at all until the old woman stood, appearing behind Arwenna. "Was the fact she's dying unclear?"

"Nothing was clear," Edriss said, breathless, taking in the scene. There was blood on the stones, seeping into the mortar. The wall sconces had burned near to the wicks, their flames flickering with dying energy, the slightest shift in air threatening to snub them out entirely. "Rhosyn just said...said to come."

Lorcan stepped around Edriss and went to Arwenna's side. His hands fluttered above her in helpless twitches. "How long has she been like this?"

"Two days," Alise said. She brushed her face along the inside of her filthy sleeve and sighed. "She's in shock. She hasn't been conscious since we closed her wounds."

Finnegan made a disgusted noise from where he hovered in the doorway.

"No one is forcing you to be here, Finnegan Derry," Alise said. "Your father will live. Arwenna may not."

Edriss gathered herself and turned toward Finnegan. "Let me do what I can here and then I'll come to your father's side. I promise I'll do everything I can for him."

Finnegan's face twisted with rage. "I'd have killed the bitch myself, with my bare hands, if I didn't want to see her hang for her crimes."

284

Lorcan stood straighter at the threat, but Alise appeared next to him and shook her head. "He's angry. His father may be a traitor, but even traitors can be fathers."

Edriss felt an invisible weight lift from her heart. Alise knew. What she knew, how much, for how long—none of it mattered. What mattered was she did, which meant one more person Evra respected would join the chorus of voices trying to save the Westerlands.

Though, with Ashenhurst and Bristol dead and Derry convalescing, she didn't know what it might mean for the Defenders. Certainly there were plenty more zealots, ready to step forward and fill the need for leaders.

At least they'd *known* who the three men were.

Just as fast as the relief had come, it was replaced by the sinking revelation they would effectively be starting over. She'd have no choice *but* to meet with John, no matter what Lorcan said or thought about it. The alternative was more than her conscience and heart could bear.

With a start, she realized the meeting in Rivermarch was supposed to be *tomorrow*.

She had no time to waste.

Finnegan's rage filled the room with fresh tension, but he made no move to leave. Edriss knew he wasn't there from any illusion of support. As soon as she healed Arwenna, he intended to take her into custody.

Edriss approached the table. The dim light hid the worst of it, but Arwenna's face had never been so pale. Thin blue lines meandered across her face, crisscrossing a stern but still expression on their way down her neck, before they disappeared under the thick layer of blankets.

"Two days she was like this," Edriss mused aloud, thinking of how much time had been wasted. "Where's Enchanter Grimoult? Or the other healers?"

"Arwenna is now a fugitive," Alise said with an aggravated sigh. "Evra's truce with the Sepulchre is still tenuous. If we ask their healers to use their abilities on a murderer, it will only fuel the cause of the Defenders."

"And my father?" Finnegan demanded. "What of him?"

"You can understand why a magus would not wish to heal a Defender of the Righteous Dawn," Alise said coolly.

He had nothing to say to that.

"Where's Evra? And Rhosyn?" she asked Alise, as she peeled back the blankets to review the wounds. She forced herself not to look away. Arwenna's breastbone was peppered with stab wounds of various depths, and when Edriss pulled the blankets lower, she could see those weren't all of them.

"Waiting for you upstairs, dear," Meldred said. "I expect they intended to see you as soon as you arrived, but the traitor's son brought you here first."

"You dare speak of my father after what this raven did to him!"

"Finn," Edriss said softly. "Accountability will come later."

Lorcan moved to her side. Low enough only she could hear, he whispered, "Would you like me to stay or go speak with your brother? Whatever you need, Hemlock. Just tell me."

Relief took hold. She hadn't realized how much a part of her still feared he would choose Arwenna until that moment. Though the exact nature of their relationship was unclear, she'd believed him when he'd said it wasn't what it seemed. "Go," she whispered. "Tell him I'll come see him as soon as Arwenna and Steward Derry have been healed. And then I'll...I'll tell him. All right?"

Lorcan lingered, and she feared he might kiss her in front of everyone, but he squeezed her hand, mouthed *I love you,* at an angle only she could see, and left.

Alise flashed her a knowing look when he was gone, but she said nothing.

"I'll be outside the door," Finnegan said with a stern look of warning. "Waiting."

"All right," Edriss said with a long breath after he left. She removed her cloak and draped it over an empty chair. As she approached the table, she unbuttoned and rolled her sleeves to her elbows, tucking them snugly into the crooks. "Do we have anything to drink?"

Meldred lifted her cane and pointed it at the corner, where a half-drunk wine carafe sat, coated in layers of dust.

"Never mind." She peeled the blankets all the way back, warmed her hands together, and went to work.

Lorcan found Evra and Rhosyn in their private chambers. With Alastrynia asleep on her lap, Rhosyn rocked in a chair; she was still full with child, but he wondered if the stress of recent events might soon change that.

"*Lorcan.*" The word left Evra with a whoosh of relief. He stormed across the room to greet him with a brief, tight hug. "Where's Edriss?"

"With Arwenna," Lorcan said as he pulled back, though he was looking at Rhosyn. Her drawn, tired face regarded him with heavy gratitude. "If anyone can help her, Lady Rhosyn, it's Edriss."

"Just Rhosyn," she replied with a tired smile, then closed her eyes and resumed her rocking. "And thank you, Lorcan, for bringing Edriss back so swiftly. You've always been so good to her. To us."

Evra nodded toward the door to the next room. He planted a soft kiss on his wife's forehead before he led Lorcan away. He closed the door behind them and gently clicked the lock. His body shuddered with an exhale that seemed long held. "Lor. Thank Guardians you're both back."

"Rhosyn? Is she…"

"She's fine, other than all the false starts with her labor. Days now, the physicians say. Meldred, however, insists they're all wrong, and we have weeks left. I reckon the truth is somewhere in the middle." Evra gestured for them to sit.

Lorcan moved toward the table, and Evra joined him. "What happened? Finn, he…I don't know how much of what he says that I can trust."

"On this, he unfortunately speaks the truth," Evra said. "I know you think me a great fool, Lorcan."

"Ev—"

"I've known all along. I knew it when you and Edriss first came to me, and I knew it when I made the alliance with Derry."

"You…What?" Lorcan tilted his head in confusion, still wrapping his thoughts around Evra's confession. "Then, why—"

"Comfortable men make mistakes." His fingers traced circles around the corners of his red-rimmed, sunken eyes. Though barely one and twenty, Evra wore his troubles like an old man who had been through wars. "It served us better for Derry and the others to think I was an idiot than to think I was on to them."

"But—" Lorcan struggled to formulate the right question through his rising anger. "Why keep it to yourself? Why not tell *me*—and *especially* Edriss, who has been truly suffering these past months?"

Evra's mouth curved into the start of a smile. "You and I both know Edriss leaves no illusions about her feelings. She wouldn't have been able to convince Finn of her loathing if she knew it was all for show."

"I disagree." Lorcan gripped the edge of the table. "I disagree, Evra. Respectfully. She would do anything for the Westerlands. Anything for *you*. She, of all of us, knows what's at stake if we fail."

"Well, I rather think we have, don't you?" Evra slumped back in his chair and gestured around. "Bristol and Ashenhurst are *dead*. Derry…He may recover. He may not."

"Edriss will fix this."

"The question is should she? Is it even worth keeping up the act now that the chief conspirators are dead?" Evra lowered his hands. "Of course, more men will rise in their place. Only if I was the fool my sister believed me to be would I think this is over."

"Edriss doesn't think you're a fool," Lorcan said. "But she does think her brother has abandoned her to politics. And *this* you can fix, Evra. You can fix it today, before more hurt comes between you two."

"Ahh," Evra said. He reached for the wine decanter in the center of the table, poured a mug, drank it down, and laughed. "But I can't, Lor, because Derry is now our only sure connection to the Defenders, isn't he?"

Lorcan thought about the man, John, and the looming meeting that Edriss had become, unfortunately, free to attend. It might lead somewhere promising, but it was all but certain to lead somewhere dangerous. "What does that mean for Edriss?"

"I'm still considering what it means for each of us. But for now, I ask you—no, I *command* you to keep what I've told you to yourself." He tried to pour Lorcan a mug, but he shook his head, needing a clear mind. "Do you understand what I'm asking you?"

"You want me to keep yet another secret from Edriss?"

Evra balked. "What secret have you kept from her?"

"You already know, according to my father. Part of it, anyway." Lorcan eyed his hands, wringing in his lap. "Derry, Bristol, Ashenhurst...They threatened Arwenna. Threatened the lives of Rhosyn, Alastrynia, you."

"I didn't know about Arwenna until I traveled to the Abbey. Honestly, I thought I had time to find a way out of this for her. I was searching for a way to pull her safely out of their web without making it worse," Evra said, head shaking at the table. "But I knew there had to be threats involved. She would never betray Rhosyn like that. I waited too long to intervene, and that's on me. It will always be on me."

"She only told me what she wanted me to know. Most of it, I see now, she kept to herself." Lorcan unraveled his hands but kept his head hung. "I was trying to help her. And as weak as her idea was, it was better than anything I could come up with."

"She left out the part about her working with them, I assume?"

"Evra, I thought I was *preventing* her from working with them by going along with her ridiculous idea to pretend we were in relationship. They were supposed to think she was working me

289

Sarah M. Cradit

for information and was going to feed them false intelligence to buy time. I had no idea…no idea at all she was giving them real information the whole time. No idea she inadvertently got Renardy killed because of it." He looked up in apology. "I really thought you'd abandoned us, or I would have convinced her to come straight to you. If I'd known all along you were on our side…"

"The rest of the picture is finally starting to come into focus." Evra glanced off at a dark corner of the room with a contemplative stare. "And her affairs with the three men? Were those part of your plan, or was it more of her conspiring on her own?"

"I didn't know until my father told me." Lorcan leaned in. "I thought it was just Derry and Bristol."

"And Ashenhurst. Renardy as well, though he was on our side. Perhaps others. We'll likely never know the full extent of all she was up to."

The revelation thrust him into silence. Finn had known. His father had known.

Edriss had known.

She'd known and, despite believing Lorcan was in love with Arwenna, had protected him from the same pain she was living with.

"We could spend years reliving the past, wishing we'd created a different future," Evra said, his head shaking. "But we can't. What's happened cannot be undone. Arwenna *poisoned* three men. The first two are dead, the last one…We'd be better off if he had died. But if we *save* him…If Edriss can spare his life…He'll believe we had nothing to do with Arwenna's violent act. We can distance ourselves from it and solidify Derry as an ally. Use him to finally take down the whole cursed thing."

More of the hazy picture started to form clarity. "You didn't bring Edriss back to save Arwenna—"

"Do not…" Evra held up hands. "Do not finish that thought, Lor. I *did* bring my sister back to save Arwenna. Rhosyn's heart would break irreparably if Arwenna died, and so would mine.

We all love Arwenna and want what's best for her. We want her to heal, to be whole again, even if she doesn't think she deserves it." He drew a deep breath. "But we need Osman to live too. We need to end the violence. He's our last confirmed connection to any of it."

"You would..." Lorcan's breath caught, realizing what Evra was implying. "You would still wed Edriss to Finn?"

"It kills me to even speak of it." Evra lowered his eyes. "But it's an act that can be undone once the Defenders are brought to heel."

"But not before she's been forced to share his bed!"

Evra leaned forward. "It won't come to that. I wouldn't let it."

"You think Finn will accept his wife doesn't want to come to his bed?" It took great restraint for Lorcan not to tell him Edriss was already married. It would put a stop to the wedding on the spot. But she wasn't there to speak for herself, and he would not speak for her. It wasn't fair, and it wasn't what she wanted. She'd been clear the news should come from her.

For all he knew, she'd *want* to go through with the sham wedding, if it meant bringing them closer to taking the Defenders down.

"I know. I *know*." Then Evra did something unexpected. He buried his face in his hands and cried. "I'm no good at this, Lorcan. I've tried to be, and I'm just not."

"Hey..." Lorcan reached across the table and laid a hand atop his. "That's not true, Evra. We'll figure this out."

"Will we? I thought I was doing right by Edriss, by all of us, and now look what's happened. Arwenna has committed *murder* twice over because she didn't feel safe coming to me, and now I'll be forced to try her for these crimes. It will kill Rhosyn, Lorcan. She'll never recover from it. And Edriss..."

Lorcan's thoughts spun wildly out of control. Edriss, sold to a traitor...Arwenna, imprisoned...There had to be a way out of both conundrums. He didn't even want to think about what might happen with Rhosyn and the baby.

"What day is today?" he asked, his mind working around an idea—albeit a terrible one.

Evra answered with an odd look.

One day until Edriss's supposed meeting with the Defender. Lorcan had been so relieved their trip to Greencastle had prevented her from putting herself in such danger, but now there was nothing to stop her. The healing only slowed her. "And the..." He blanched. "Wedding?"

"Two days hence. Derry insisted on moving it up. If I refuse, we lose an ally."

Two days. It wasn't enough time. Not nearly enough time.

But what else did they have?

Evra was staring at him with a helpless, eager look that clearly said, *I hope there's a good reason you're asking me.*

Maybe there was. Maybe there wasn't. Edriss couldn't go anywhere near the traitor, but *he* could...Lorcan could go in her stead, wedge his way into whatever the man had planned for her.

The rest of his fool-hearted plan came together in seconds. Seconds that were each so valuable when racing time.

"Evra, do you trust me?"

Evra shook his head in confusion but said, "Of course, Lorcan."

"I need to go away. Today. *Now.* I may be able to fix all of this...It's a longshot, but—" Lorcan exhaled and locked his gaze to Evra's. "Please don't wed her off to Finn until I get back."

"I don't know if I can—"

"Evra. *Please.*" Lorcan closed his eyes to slow his speeding heart. He wouldn't betray Edriss, but he could share his own truth. "I love your sister. I have always loved her. Even thinking about her with a man who doesn't love her, doesn't understand her, doesn't cherish her...is enough to make me want to burn the world to the ground."

"Ahh." Evra folded his hands together and directed his gaze down and to the side. "I always suspected. Why wait until now to tell me?"

"Because I thought honor was more important than love, than happiness. I didn't want you to think I had acted untoward with her while I was looking after her. You made it clear to me, as her guardian, that there were certain responsibilities and expectations, and I took them seriously. It wasn't until...until recently when I saw what my life would look like without Edriss. It would not be a life worth living."

"And Edriss?" Evra still hadn't looked up. Dried tears stained his face. "How does she feel?"

"I won't speak for her," Lorcan answered. "But if you go to her, Evra, and you tell her you're ready to hear her truth, she may feel safe offering it to you. She loves her brother so much. She's only ever wanted your approval."

Evra looked away when he wiped his eyes. "Let's take this all one day at a time. You said 'until I get back.' Where are you going?"

"I can't tell you," Lorcan said, his jaw wincing. "I'm sorry. If I'm wrong, I might not come back—"

"Lorcan!"

"If I'm right...Maybe I can fix this. All of it."

Evra reached into his vest and pulled out a crumple of vellum. He smashed it onto the table. "It wouldn't have something to do with *this*, would it?"

Lorcan tentatively leaned forward. He read. *You should know your sister has been consorting with rebels. The meeting will happen at dawn, in Rivermarch, unless you stop her.* His jaw slackened as he looked up. "Who sent this to you?"

"It was sent anonymously, but I know the handwriting, and if you look closer, so do you."

He studied the vellum. He recognized the handwriting, but it made little sense. "Finn?"

"If he knows, then *they* know."

Lorcan's mind was turning...turning. What *was* Finn's motivation? To protect Edriss? To give Evra a chance to protect her before the Defenders came for "Henry"?

293

"Are you going to tell me why you're surprised about the letter but not the meeting?"

Lorcan let the note flutter on the table. Edriss wouldn't have wanted Evra to find out like this, but there was nothing he could do. "Finn and I followed her to Rivermarch. Finn had been trailing her for a while—I don't know how long. The day he took me with him, we saw her consorting with someone Finn said was affiliated with the Defenders. Possibly with access to people in the highest ranks. She was in disguise, and I don't think, at least at the time, they knew who she was."

"She didn't tell you?"

Lorcan shook his head. "I blame myself. I wasn't there for her when she needed me most."

"Because you were there for Arwenna."

"I did what I thought was best. I couldn't have known—"

"It's not an indictment, Lor. I know who you are." Evra nodded at the letter like it carried disease. "Should we be worried she'll attempt to go tomorrow?"

Lorcan thought about it for the briefest moment. He nodded.

Evra slapped his palms onto the table and looked away in frustration. "And what am I to do, lock her into her apartments?"

"No…" Lorcan again saw the flash of dangerous excitement in Edriss's eyes when she'd stepped out of the room after healing that man. The way she'd come alive. Nothing would stop her from taking the meeting, especially not after the only other men they could name were dead or incapacitated. "I'm going to meet with the man instead."

"*What?*"

Lorcan glanced toward the window and the darkening sky beyond. "I'll need to leave soon if I'm going to make the meeting. You need to find a way to keep her here. Prolong…the Osman situation. She won't leave with him still ill. Just like she wouldn't have left Greencastle with children still needing her aid."

"No." Evra shook his head in disbelief. "No. I'm no more amenable to you walking into such danger than I am sending my sister into it."

"Respectfully, Evra, I'm not asking. And I'm going alone. This man will smell a trap and then we'll have nothing." Lorcan's foot tapped the other in nervous rhythm. It was a terrible idea. Edriss would never forgive him if he got killed. But if he couldn't reach the man first, she would, and that wasn't going to happen. If Lorcan was lucky, he could sway the man to take him instead.

Maybe they could end this.

Finally.

"Before you try to stop me, remember that Finn is one of them. Finn, who sent you this note and *may* be trying to protect Edriss, may *also* have told them who she was." Lorcan didn't think Finn would go so far, but he'd never risk Edriss's life on unconfirmed intuition. "They might come for her."

Evra sighed and buried his face in his hands again. "You'll never engage this man, learn his secrets, and make it back in time for the wedding."

"Then you'll have to find another way to stop it."

"How?"

"You were always the smartest of us, growing up. You always had the answers. Probably all those books you loved so much." Lorcan almost grinned. "I know you. You'll find a way."

Evra shook his head. Lorcan imagined the events of the past few days had been enough to cause any man to forget his words.

He pushed to his feet before he lost his courage. "There isn't time for me to say good-bye to Edriss. I'll explain everything when I get back, but please, don't tell her I've gone to put things to rights. If she thinks my leaving has anything at all to do with the Defenders, she'll guess where I'm going and follow me. I can't assure her safety if that happens."

"What, exactly, should I tell her when she realizes you've disappeared?"

"Tell her..." Lorcan thought about it. "Tell her I said, 'Everything is going to be fine, Hemlock. Trust me.'"

Evra looked away again and back at him. He slowly nodded. "And if you're not back before the wedding?"

"I will be," Lorcan insisted, though he wasn't sure it was true.

"You better come back, Lorcan. She'll never speak to me again if something happens to you."

Lorcan grinned from the side of his mouth. "Knowing she's here waiting for me is all the motivation I need to keep that from happening."

NINETEEN
I LEARNED IT FROM YOU

Edriss had begun to doze. She was far enough along that her breathing had slowed. Her arms and legs felt weighted, unneeded. The tingle in her chest, the tickle of relaxation that greeted her right before her dreams would visit, started and abruptly stopped.

Arwenna awoke, gasping. The suddenness of it sent Edriss shooting to her feet in a bewildered daze.

Edriss squeezed her eyes to clear her disorientation. While most of the sconces had burned out altogether, a few lingered, though wouldn't for much longer. Alise and Meldred were gone— where, she didn't know, as they'd slipped out some time after Edriss had succumbed to her exhaustion.

It couldn't have been long.

She approached the table with thin hope. Arwenna's wounds should have been fatal; only Alise's tinctures and salves had kept her holding on long enough for Edriss to arrive. It was the gash nearest her heart that had given Edriss the most trouble. She'd never fought harder to save someone, not even the traitor John, with his missing arm and decimated body.

Bristol must have put up quite the struggle on his way to the unpromised future of the afterlife.

Arwenna looked up at her with wide, scared eyes. Her mouth trembled as though readying words. Tears came instead, big fat drops that coursed down cheeks still stained with cracked, dried blood. Without adding her voice, she mouthed, *I'm sorry.*

Edriss's heart softened, though it had never truly hardened toward Arwenna, not all the way. "Don't speak, if it troubles you," she said softly. She reached for the rag and bowl, to wipe some of the crumbling blood from Arwenna's brows, but the basin was ice cold. "We almost lost you. Your only job now is to focus on getting well."

Arwenna laughed, a gravelly sound that reminded Edriss of the dead. "Did they tell you what I did?"

Edriss went to grab her chair and dragged it to the table. The shrill, echoing screech made them both wince. "Bristol and Ashenhurst are gone. Derry survived."

"Pity." Arwenna turned her face back toward the ceiling. "No doubt he's making me out to be the villain."

"I…" Edriss faltered. She lowered her head, breathed, and began again. "I understand why you did it. I was…was also trying to take these men down."

"Rivermarch, you mean?"

Edriss looked up. "Did Lorcan tell you?"

"That man isn't capable of betraying you." Arwenna shook her head. "Osman did."

"Osman?" Edriss paled. "How did he…"

"They have spies everywhere. But it could have just as easily been Finnegan who told him."

Edriss sat back, numb. She hadn't realized she'd still been holding on to the thin hope that Finnegan wasn't one of *them.* But what were the odds a son wouldn't follow in the footsteps of a father? Childhood affinity wasn't stronger than nature itself. "I know you were…visiting the steward."

"Fucking him," Arwenna stated. "Don't mince words to soften your disgust. Not just Osman but Leonarde and Roland. Only a fool would have thought it would accomplish anything, but..." She turned her palms upward as if to say *alas, here we are.* "Don't look at me like that, Edriss. No one forced me to do anything. No one turns their noses up at men when they use sex to get what they want. I only used the power the gods gave me."

Edriss shook her head through a befuddled exhale. "I don't understand why you didn't come to me. I meant it when I offered to help you. We would have been so much stronger together."

Arwenna turned her head all the way to the side. Edriss had once thought she and Arwenna had matching eyes, both a rare violet, but nothing about her eyes felt familiar anymore. "Because I had to choose between saving my sister and her family or selling you to the Derrys. Forgive me, Edriss, or don't, but I'd make the same choice again."

"I don't under—"

"That was the deal. Save my family in exchange for keeping Lorcan 'occupied' so he didn't chase after you. It's not what I told him, of course, because he never, ever would have agreed to help."

"So it's true. You were...*actually helping* the Defenders? The same ones you just murdered?" Despite Rohan's pronouncements, the revelation still shocked Edriss to her core.

"*I* was the one who proposed Lorcan and I pretend to be in love, to keep them mollified. He never liked the idea, and even less did he like keeping it from you."

Edriss was still processing the former revelations and couldn't wrap her head around the newest. "You mean, all the kissing and—"

"Meant nothing. And kissing was all it was. Even that was a burden for him," Arwenna said. "He insisted on telling you. I invented a reason he couldn't, made him swear not to. Because the truth, that I needed him distracted so you would turn away from him, so the Derrys could isolate you and ready you for marriage, would have ruined everything."

Edriss steeled herself. There was little to be gained in asking Arwenna to explain her motives when the damage was already done, the losses already tallied. She couldn't even allow herself to feel relief about Arwenna and Lorcan's 'relationship,' with all the horror surrounding them. "Why tell me now?"

"Because…" Arwenna closed her eyes. Her tongue flitted out and wet her cracked lips. "Though I don't expect you to believe me, after all this, I do love you, Edriss. I once cherished our friendship, and of all the things I am losing…That is among the hardest. And I cannot leave here with those betrayals unsaid." Her eyes opened. "He loves you. Desperately loves you."

"I know he loves me," Edriss said with a defiant rise of her shoulders. "And I no longer require others to reassure me of what he himself has made blissfully clear."

Arwenna's smile was slow but genuine. "He finally told you."

Edriss didn't answer. She couldn't say which was the stronger call to reticence: her stubbornness or the desire to keep her experiences with Lorcan private. Most of all, she didn't like the way Arwenna was looking at her, as though she'd had something to do with Lorcan's revelations.

Edriss had never felt more conflicted between wanting to help someone and wanting never to see them again.

Her thoughts caught up. "You said you were leaving…What did you mean?"

"Well I cannot stay here, can I?" Arwenna laughed, the same awful sound from earlier. "I've made a terrible mess for Rhosyn and Evra and forced them into an impossible choice. They pardon me, they lose the respect and loyalty of their people. They don't, Rhosyn has to watch her only sister thrown into prison for the rest of her days. Or worse, executed—for real, this time."

"But where would you *go?*"

"North. Back to my people."

"The same people who threw you off the side of a mountain?"

"Yes," Arwenna said. "And no. The ones responsible are gone. My mother, the one who saved my life, may welcome me back.

300

Without Rhosyn, there is no female to carry on our line." Her hand went to her belly in an almost instinctual way. "And now I know I *can* grow life, that it wasn't me after all."

Edriss's mouth dropped open. "You're with child?" How had she not sensed it when she had been healing her? Had she really been so distracted?

Arwenna nodded. "Don't ask me who it belongs to. I couldn't say." She half laughed. "I only know it's not Lorcan's, Edriss. It was never me he wanted, and even I have boundaries I won't cross."

Edriss leaned forward, fear rising in her throat, to feel Arwenna's belly. *Please let there still be life.* She felt it and gasped, looking up at her once friend in wonder.

"I could've told you she's still there." Arwenna smiled sadly. "I don't know if my mother and others will accept a half blood, especially once they know the father is a monster—whoever he is. But even if she isn't my heir, I can't let anyone take her from me. And prison is no place for a child, is it?"

Despite everything—or perhaps because of it—Edriss still wanted to solve Arwenna's conundrum. She considered the possibilities, but they each had flaws. They each traded one problem for another.

"Have you told Rhosyn you're leaving?" Edriss asked.

"No," Arwenna said. "Nor will I. She would do everything she could to stop me. Though I have no right to ask anything of you, Edriss, I'm asking you to tell Evra for me. Wait until I'm gone and then tell him. He's the only one who will know the right words to deliver the message."

"You want me to enable your cowardice." Heat flooded Edriss's face. "You'd really slink out of here without so much as a good-bye to the people who love you?"

"Yes," Arwenna said smoothly. "For if I can spare Rhosyn the pain of a prolonged sendoff, it is one last kindness I can give her. I've failed my little sister, not just here in the Rush but our whole lives. She has a good heart, and so does Evra. Mine is half-rotten.

Not all the way so." She laughed, as though sharing an inside joke with herself. "But enough that I don't regret killing those men. I don't regret doing what was necessary to save Rhosyn and her family. All I do regret is that I wasn't strong enough to stop evil from spreading. It was arrogance that made me believe I could."

Edriss wanted to argue Arwenna's point, insist she had a good heart as well, but Edriss was no longer so sure. She didn't even know the woman lying on the pile of blankets. "You'll break her heart, Arwenna. You must know it."

"I'll break it more if I stay. And if I'm seen walking free here, everyone will think Evra and Rhosyn allowed me to leave." Arwenna grimaced when she pulled herself to a seated position. Some of the blankets fell away, while others clung to her. "I'll send a raven when I get where I'm going, so they know I made it safely." She chuckled again. "What a strange concept it is to me, sending ravens. You ever asked a Ravenwood to carry a message for you, they'd shit on your head as they flew away laughing."

Edriss could have done without the visual. "So this is it? You're just…leaving?"

"That's it," Arwenna agreed. She swung her legs over the side of the table, and the rest of the blankets shrugged away. She rolled her neck and jumped off. "Thank you for saving my daughter's life, Edriss."

"I—"

"Didn't know. I know." Arwenna towered over her with a strange smile. "*You* are true of heart. Not just kind, but true. You would put your sacred duty as a healer ahead of crimes, ahead of wrongs. Even if you'd known everything I just told you, you'd still have helped me, wouldn't you? And why, when you leave here, you'll go straight to Osman and save him too."

Edriss choked up. She nodded. "How will you leave without them taking notice?" She sniffled through her nose and looked around. The only window was a small rectangular opening not even a child could fit through. "You can still shift?"

Arwenna nodded.

"In *here?*"

"Go on. I'll be fine. I'll be gone before you reach the stairs."

"What about the guards? And Finn?"

"*Go.* Embrace the happiness you've earned, Edriss. Few truly deserve it in the way you do." Arwenna touched her shoulder, gave it a light pat, and pointed her toward the door. "Perhaps we'll meet again in the next life."

Edriss reluctantly left the small room. The door closed behind her.

Finnegan wasn't outside, but he'd left behind two of his guards. She tried to move past, but they stepped into her path to block it.

Edriss scrunched her face in exhausted annoyance. "She's inside. She's conscious. Alise and Meldred will be back soon."

"We were commanded to keep you from leaving, my lady."

Edriss rolled her shoulders back. "By *whom?*"

"Junior Steward Derry, my lady," the other one said.

"He has no jurisdiction here and you both know it, or you wouldn't be looking at each other with such fear in your eyes." Edriss stepped closer, and they stepped back. She almost laughed. "Here's what's going to happen. I'm going to return to my own chambers to change my clothing, drink *something,* and hopefully swallow a couple of bites of bread. After, I'm going to see my brother, so I can give him a report of Arwenna's condition. When I'm done, I'm going to heal your boss's father as best I can." She lifted to the tips of her toes. Both men recoiled their heads to the side. "And you can come with me or not, but you won't stop me unless you want Lord Blackwood to hear about the men who laid hands on his only sister."

Edriss dropped back down, crossed her arms, and waited.

The guards exchanged nervous, fidgety looks. She tapped her feet to hurry them along.

"I…" The one speaking slowly shook his head at the one simply staring back. "I guess I'll follow Lady Blackwood then. You wait for the junior steward."

The other one nodded, a furious series of bobs that made Edriss dizzy. She pushed through them and started down the hall. Stopping at her room before seeing her brother hadn't been part of the plan until she'd said it, but she prayed it gave Arwenna the time she needed to flee.

It was the last thing Edriss would ever do for her, even if she did come back, and she wanted to make it count.

"Watch that door! The raven doesn't leave," the one following her called back as he jogged to catch up.

Evra sat next to the bed, massaging his wife's swollen belly. Rhosyn could barely stand anymore. She seemed to diminish more and more each day, until all he could think about was how hard it had been on her, bringing Alastrynia. Their second child seemed intent on coming into the world with the same challenges.

A son, they'd said. *An heir,* whispered the people, but Alastrynia was his heir. He knew what others would think, but on this matter, he didn't care. They would raise all their children to be brave and bold, capable of greatness.

At present, it seemed almost too tall of an order. Two years ago, when he'd taken the helm as lord of the Westerlands, he'd been drowning in indecision, but he'd made a choice about the leader he wanted to be. He'd never wavered. But it wasn't the same as never failing.

Looking back at his choices, they seemed as foolish as they were. He had more regrets than he should, and little time to make them right before it was too late for his people. His land. His family.

A small knock stirred him from his self-recrimination. He started forward but the door opened, even though he'd been explicit about no visitors, but it was Edriss who walked into the room, her dark hair mussed and her face drawn and pale.

He put a finger to his mouth, pointed at Rhosyn, and tipped his head toward the other room, where only hours before, he'd heard Lorcan's confession. Was she there to make one of her own? Was he ready to hear it?

But if you go to her, Evra, and you tell her you're ready to hear her truth, she may feel safe offering it to you. She loves her brother so much. She's only ever wanted your approval.

Evra hadn't even closed the door before Edriss said, "Arwenna is gone. Fled back to the north. No, she is not coming to say goodbye, and there was nothing I could say to change her mind. She wanted you to hear it from me."

He dropped onto the nearest chair. "Fuck."

"Yes," she agreed. Instead of sitting, she paced, her breaths irregular. "Yes, Evra, among all the terrible things happening in the Westerlands, we can now add this. Though I have trouble blaming her. Would you not do the same if you were carrying the child of a terrible man and facing the potential of death or life imprisonment?"

Evra nearly laughed, if only because he could think of no other response. "Arwenna is *pregnant?*"

"Yes, and with no inkling which of the Defenders is the father. I suppose when the child is born, Arwenna may look upon him or her and see the truth for herself, but I rather think she doesn't care. She knows she cannot raise the little one if she stays, and she's not wrong."

"I would've found a way to pardon her," Evra said, hating the way his voice sounded, weak and grasping. He heard his late father's words for the first time in a long time, coming back to remind him he was no lion like the men who had come before. *Are you a man who does, or a boy who thinks?*

"Maybe," Edriss said, clearly only to appease him. "But put yourself in her place. She felt she had no choice."

"Did she at least…leave a note? For Rhosyn?"

Edriss shook her head. "She left nothing but heartache, brother. And though I know it will be your inclination to rush after her, I advise you not to. She's never been happy here. She's made her choice. It's not our place to understand it, only to respect it."

She was right, but how could he explain it to Rhosyn?

He prayed their son came before he had to tell her.

"But that isn't..." Edriss resumed her pacing. "Isn't why I've come to see you."

"Why don't you sit? You're making me nervous."

"If I do, I may lose the courage, Evra, and I've done something you need to know about. As my lord, but also as my brother."

Evra patted his vest, where the vellum he'd shown to Lorcan was stuffed. He'd show it to her, after, but he wanted to hear, in her own words, what she'd been doing in Rivermarch.

"I'm just going to say it," she said, her hands twisting in the air. "Lorcan and I were married in Greencastle several days ago."

Evra was almost certain the stone floors had disappeared, and he was falling through what remained. He was still falling when he tried to grasp hold of *something* to say, to ease his utter disbelief, but there was nothing. Nothing except "You...eloped?"

Edriss nodded, pacing away from him. "Lorry and I...In Greencastle, we...Once you really accept you love someone, you'd do anything to fight for them." She turned to look at him, her mouth curling like it had when they were little and she'd been about to cry. "And I love him, Evra. I *love* him. I'm sorry for not telling you first, but you were going to wed me off to a man who is involved in burning women...burning women *like me*." She shook her head at the floor. "But did it never occur to you that you abandoned me to the same sort of fate you risked your life to save Rhosyn from?"

Her words stole the air from Evra's lungs. How had he let it get so far? How had he let his beloved sister suffer so much? All it would take to ease her were a few simple words, words he'd denied her for far too long and would never do so again. "I believe you, Edriss. About Finn. About all of them. I thought I was protecting you by not bringing you into my plans. I know

306

telling you this isn't good enough. It's not *nearly* good enough, and I'll spend however long is needed making it up to you." He stood and went toward her, though he left some distance, sensing she wanted it. Respecting her boundaries was the least he could do. "And though I wish…I wish I could have been there, to stand with you, I cannot blame you for what you did. For any of it. Lorcan. Rivermarch."

She twisted around. "Rivermarch?"

"Lorcan told me."

"Lorry…Where is he?"

"He…" He knew he was going to fumble. "He left. He said to tell you, 'Everything will be all right, Hemlock. Trust me.'"

Edriss recoiled. Her face went blank. "He's gone? He left the Rush?"

Evra nodded.

"When?"

"Not long ago."

She puzzled with her thoughts for a moment and then said, "Where?"

He didn't answer. He didn't want to lie.

Edriss's face darkened. "You know, and you won't tell me."

"I know he'll be back soon."

"That's not an answer, Evra!" She thrust her hands out to her sides, where they became fists. "Where is my husband?"

"You can ask him when he returns," Evra said, bracing for more of her ire. But all she did was turn away with one arm wrapped around her torso, her head shaking.

Evra reached for her shoulder. He absorbed the twitch when he touched her and pulled her closer anyway. "I'm *sorry*, Edriss. I'm so sorry. I'm sorry I didn't tell you. I'm sorry I made you feel like I didn't believe you. I love you, and I only want you to be happy. I'll give Osman some excuse to delay the wedding until I can figure things out." He gently spun her and pulled her into his arms. "You have my blessing. You and Lorcan both."

Tension rippled through her stiff posture, but then she melted, falling against him with shaking sobs.

"He told me how much he loves you. I saw in his eyes how far he'd go to protect you." Evra held his next words a moment longer before saying them. "He's the only one here who always has, and it shouldn't be a punishment. For either of you."

Edriss shook her head against his chest. He cupped the back of her head and tried not to cry. "You think I'm upset you ran away to university." She tilted her head back to look up at him.

"You have every right—"

"I'm not upset you left, Evra." Edriss wiped her eyes and unwound herself from him. "You did what you had to do, and knowing you were safe from Aeldred's loathing gave me comfort. As bad as I had it, he treated you so much worse."

Evra didn't know what to say, so he waited for her to finish.

"What *hurt* so much was how you treated me when you came back."

His face pulled together in a frown. "Edriss, you're the reason I went north to find magic. To save you."

Edriss laughed at the floor. "I'm one reason, but you went to save our people, which was the *right* reason. If it had just been for me, I'd never have let you go." She looked up. "All I wanted was my brother back, but what I got was a man I hardly recognized, who no longer seemed to recognize me either."

"Edriss, I'm so sorry." His chest felt raw and tight. "That was never my intent. This has all…all of it…It's all gone so opposite of what I wanted."

She lifted her shoulders. "Can we not all say as much?"

"I should never—" Evra's voice cracked. "Never have put distance between us. And I should never, *ever* have stood in the way of your happiness."

Edriss craned her teary face upward. "All I ever wanted was your approval. Your respect."

A lump rose in his throat as he remembered Lorcan's words. "There's no one else in the world I trust more than my sister. No one I respect more. I'm desperately sorry I ever caused you to believe otherwise."

She wiped her eyes. "The past is past. But right now, in the *present*, what are we going to do about these treasonous bastards?"

"I have some ideas," he said, "but first, go help Osman. Guardians know if we don't, we'll have his cohorts descending on the Rush before dawn."

Lorcan couldn't move. It wasn't only the wood splintering into his wrists, lifted above his head, though that would have been enough. Pain had greeted him the moment he'd found consciousness, sweeping in like a reminder with no clarity. He couldn't pinpoint what hurt the most because *everything* hurt. A lot. Opening his eyes hurt too, but he did, and that was when he saw the moon, partially obstructed by thick clouds.

Laughter filtered in from his left. It only took seconds to realize they weren't laughing at him, but they would, when they realized he was awake. He didn't know how he could be sure, but he was.

It was one of the few things he was sure of, in the middle of his dark, stabbing confusion.

The other was that he was in the worst trouble of his life.

Annoying mirth died to snorts and whispers. He didn't recognize any of the voices, but he hadn't expected to. More of the story came together in his mind, stitching together like a poorly woven blanket.

He'd gone to Rivermarch. The meeting with Edriss's contact wasn't scheduled for several more hours, but they didn't have hours. They hardly had *minutes* to spare. So he'd done a foolish thing and asked around about the man.

Lorcan tried to adjust himself, to stretch out the burning ache in his shoulders, but it proved to be a terrible mistake. Fresh pain shot straight to his head, stabbing the backs of his eyes, the tension made worse.

A memory of falling came back to him. Not falling, *crashing*. Down, down to the earth.

He realized he was on his knees, on something wet. More wood. A platform. A careful tug on his hands revealed the source of his bondage without needing to look up: stocks. He swallowed his pain and wiggled his hands anyway, and that was when he heard the rough metal of the locks.

Rain pattered down around him, sliding down his cheeks and dripping from the ends of his hair. Squinting, he examined the soaked boards and thought he spotted blood mixed with the rain, but it was too dark to tell, and his head was still swimming.

Had he even spoken to the man? That was still beyond his recollecting. He didn't think he had, and in retrospect, he supposed that made more sense than a high-level Defender popping out from the back room of a tavern with nothing but smiles and information.

But a whisper of light lined the crests of the Seven Sisters, which meant dawn was coming.

He'd finally get his meeting.

Finnegan answered the door to his father's apartments. He held a cup of tea in his hands and wore a hangdog grin. Muttering an apology, he ushered Edriss in.

"It's not your fault," he said as she accepted the tea. "What happened. I'm sorry for how I spoke to you earlier."

Edriss nodded and held up the tea in a truce. She was far too tired for a conversation, let alone an argument, and she was more than aware of how fast dawn was approaching. Lorcan would no doubt already be in Rivermarch—Evra had refused to confirm, but she knew—which meant she had to work quickly if she was going to catch up to him before the meeting.

"How is she?"

Edriss gripped her midsection to hold herself up. It wasn't just bringing Arwenna back from the brink that had weakened her but the culmination of all the healing she'd done lately. All those poor children. A part of her wondered if she was even capable of what Osman needed, but she silenced that voice, because she didn't have a choice.

"Edriss?"

"She'll live," she answered, which was part of the truth but not all of it. How much did Finn know? Had his remaining guard gone inside to check on the raven and discovered her missing? If so, how far had she made it?

Right here. Right now. Focus on what must be done and then you can address the rest.

"That's all? 'She'll live'?"

Edriss's eyes fluttered as she blinked away the powerful threat of sleep. She looked down at the tea, warm and inviting, and took a sip. "Where's your father?"

Finnegan lifted his arm and pointed with it. "Bedchamber. The physicians left just before you arrived."

"What have they said?" she took another sip, nearly emptying the cup, and set it on a nearby table.

Finnegan stepped next to her. He eyed the door with an intense look. "That his heart is failing. Other organs will soon, if they aren't already. He's been having convulsions and hallucinations he might never be rid of—if you can't heal him, that is."

"I guess Arwenna was paying attention in our lessons after all," Edriss muttered as she reached for the door. She rolled her shoulders to bring life into them again. "Would you mind bringing in more of the tea?"

He smiled from the side. "Of course."

When he left to fetch the tea, Edriss entered the room. Hundreds of candles were lit. Some were strongly scented, but none matched the stench of impending death. She'd encountered it enough to know it in every stage—little deaths, like illnesses, and big ones that were beyond her help. Osman's was somewhere in the middle. He was far enough along to the Guardians that she

311

could let him die and no one would blame her. She could end his reign of terror, simply by doing nothing at all.

But that wasn't entirely true. More men would rise in his stead, and there was an advantage in knowing her enemy. If she saved him, he would be indebted to Evra—would, she hoped, lead him to a way to finally end the whole mess.

Edriss dropped onto the chair at Osman's bedside and went to work. She started at his ankles, blue from dysfunctional circulation caused by poison. They came to life again under her hands, his heartbeat pulsing against her palm, showing her he was responding even better than she'd expected.

She worked up his legs, which were disturbingly scrawny when compared to his otherwise-portly frame. His sharp, bony knees felt like weapons, and she imagined him digging them into the bed as he took advantage of Arwenna's vulnerability.

It wasn't until she was almost done when Finnegan returned. By then, she was losing the fight with sleep. There was nothing gradual about the sway working over her. It came on so fast, she caught herself dozing in mid-thought.

Finnegan set the tea on the table beside her and drew a chair close. "He responding?"

"Mhm." Edriss squinted and then widened her eyes, fighting the call even harder. She only had his head left, and she thought perhaps it wouldn't be the worst thing if the monster had seizures the rest of his life.

"Almost done?"

Edriss nodded, sleepiness becoming so pervasive that even words felt like a significant burden. She worked her hands around Osman's temples, channeling her hatred for the man into one last burst of energy. She had no time for rest, but she had no choice but to find some. Otherwise, she'd never make it to Rivermarch.

"Good. Then there's something you need to know."

Edriss sluggishly looked his way, still working her hands along his father's face.

"The raven is gone. The man you foolishly gave your heart to? He's left the Rush to be with her. Ah, no, no, no...Don't say anything, Edriss. Your energy is depleting by the second and will be lost altogether soon. Before it happens, you'll hear what I have to say."

Edriss opened her mouth, but her jaw felt so heavy, she couldn't even close it again. Instead, it hung, useless.

Something was wrong.

It wasn't just exhaustion from too much healing.

"He doesn't *love* you, Edriss. He never has. He loved the way you made him feel, like the hero in the stories you read as a girl. But Lorcan cherishes, above all else, his pride. And when you needed him the most, he left to chase a raven who doesn't even want him."

His eyes flashed toward the teapot, and Edriss's breath choked in her throat.

"You..." Her hands flew to her neck.

"All those hours I spent watching you in the herbarium. You didn't think I was paying attention?"

Edriss tried to stand, but she fell. Finnegan caught her in his arms and lifted her back onto the chair like a ragdoll.

"Tell me, is it true what they say about the poison mistresses? That they feed upon their own concoctions until they're immune?" Finnegan laughed. He scratched his head. "Guessing *not*, since you're about to pass out, aren't you?"

Edriss clawed her hands through the air like she was falling. She *was* falling. Away. Away.

She only realized she'd hit the floor when she looked up and saw Finnegan's shadow looming over her. "I learned it from you, Hemlock," he said, and the darkness swallowed her.

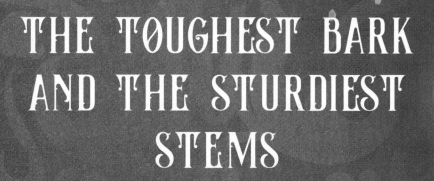

THE TOUGHEST BARK
AND THE STURDIEST
STEMS

TWENTY

TO THE ENDS OF THE EARTH

Lorcan awoke shivering but warm. Opening his eyes revealed the blinding glare of early morning sun, burning the tops of his hands and head. A chill wind ripped through Jademarch's Apostles Square, where he'd been on display for almost three days. He'd been too delirious to keep time himself, but the crier of hours appeared on the steps of the town jail every hour to remind him. At dawn, the crier turned the large wooden numbers housed in the shortest spire of the jail, swapping the old date with the new.

He remembered nothing about being moved from Rivermarch to Jademarch, but he was keenly aware his transfer meant no one would know where to find him. Evra would assume he was still in Rivermarch. Or dead.

His chapped lips cried for moisture, but he had none to spare. They'd first sent young boys to offer food and water at irregular intervals, but that had only been on the first day. By the second, any "kindness" they'd extended had been replaced by brutal interrogation.

Painful, tortuous interrogation.

317

Strange faces came at first and then "John" himself had paid Lorcan a personal visit, greeting him with a hard punch from his regrown arm. He'd said nothing, only stood watch for almost a full tick of the sun, before he disappeared again.

Lorcan had been beaten, half-drowned, and more. He lost track of it all, because at some point, pain was pain, and there was no delineating old from new. At times, he stopped feeling it at all, and he didn't know if it meant he was evolving or dying.

Maybe both.

He *would* die before he ever told them what they wanted to know, which was where to find his wife and how to lure her away from safety. In the beginning, he'd thought they really didn't know "Henry" was Edriss, but over the long hours of whips and kicks—set to the unforgettable tune of heckling from Defender sympathizers passing in the square—he realized they'd known for a while. Maybe "John" had even known it had been Edriss who'd worked so hard to save his life. All that mattered was the fact they knew.

But then they'd stopped asking about Edriss.

They'd stopped feeding him.

Watering him.

That could only mean one thing. It was too terrible a notion to consider, but he had to, if he was going to draw upon the resolve needed to survive and find her.

If they no longer needed his help to find Edriss, then they already had her.

Rhosyn went into labor again three days after Edriss had disappeared.

Disappeared was the word others used.

Kidnapped was the harsh reality of the situation, and Rhosyn was relieved to hear Evra no longer trying to soften their trials with pretty language. She'd watched him do that ever since she'd followed him to the Rush to be his wife and equal. If she hadn't known the goodness of his heart—how hard he was trying to do the right thing, no matter how imprudent—those errors would have driven an irreparable wedge into the seams of their marriage.

But she *did* know her husband. Knew his heart. Above all, she knew he would eventually find his footing and be the leader their people needed and deserved.

Rhosyn had never foreseen the catalyst would be something so personal.

They knew who had taken Edriss, but not to where. There'd been no ransom note, no demands. It could only mean they already had everything they needed.

Rhosyn pushed all thoughts of Arwenna out of her head and heart. Her sister's downfall was a trouble for later—one, she'd learned, had never been hers to solve. When everything was over, she'd consider what, if anything, could be done, but the answer at present was nothing.

Nothing could be done about Arwenna, but Edriss still needed their help.

She'd never seen Evra so animated, so determined. When Edriss had missed breakfast, he'd sprung into action, a blunt contrast to the idle caution he was known for. By noontide, he'd had hundreds of scouts, led by Thennwyr Blackfen, spread all over the Reach in search of her.

Before night fell, they'd realized Lorcan was in trouble as well.

There were many things Rhosyn could say to her husband. He'd acted too late. He'd miscalculated. He'd kept secrets—which hurt the most, for he'd kept them even from her. But of all the people in his life, she knew him the best, and what he needed was something only she could offer.

"My love," she said. He held her hand at the bedside, but his thoughts were tugged elsewhere.

He should be in the place his thoughts had traveled, but he'd never leave her. Not unless she made him. He would let the world burn down around them before he let harm come to her or their children.

Evra blinked and looked over. "Everything all right, love?"

"It's still early," she whispered, already hoarse, and the screaming hadn't yet begun. "My contractions are hours apart yet. Might
be days."

Evra wrapped her hand in both of his and brought it to his
mouth for a soft but intense kiss. "I'll be here for every second,
Rhosyn. I won't let you endure it alone."

She unwound their hands and reached hers up to cup his
cheek. "No, love. You won't be." He started to argue, but she shook
her head. "I have Alise and Meldred. A hundred capable physicians within the Rush, should I need them. More midwives than
I know what to do with."

"*Rhosyn*, I have over a thousand men out there—"

"Evra. Listen to me." Desperate, she squeezed his face. She
could leave no room for rebuttal, no matter how her heart ached
to think of him leaving. The dangers he faced were real, and thus
was the possibility it was the last time she'd ever see her husband
alive. "You could have a hundred thousand men out there searching for Edriss, but what those men need is their leader. Their lord.
They would ride to the ends of the earth to serve you. They believe
in the peace you've tried so hard to bring to the Westerlands—
and still will, when this is over and the men responsible for the
atrocities are held to account."

Evra's head shook. Tears slid down his cheeks. "I can't leave
you," he said, but in his voice she heard the truth; he was afraid to
leave her but already knew it was what he needed to do.

"Am I a lady of the Westerlands?"

"What?"

"Your sister recently said to me, 'You're a lady of the
Westerlands now, Rhosyn. We're made of the toughest bark and
the sturdiest stems.'" Rhosyn smiled. "And I'm also a Ravenwood,
who has endured and survived trials that would destroy a weaker
person. Much like Meldred, Alise, Edriss…There's little in this
world that could take me down. Your absence will not break me."

Evra shook his head in place of words. He reached up to wipe his tears away with his thumb. "I have erred, Rhosyn. I've hesitated and hedged and let down those who love me and depend on me."

"You have not always solved things the right way," she said, gentle but firm. "I seem to recall our relationship began with you holding me hostage in a barn."

He shook his head. "Every day I wonder why you agreed to marry me."

"Because you led with your heart, an imperfect heart I love dearly for its purity and purpose. But now you must lead with your head, husband. You must compose your bravery, as you did when you scaled Icebolt Mountain against all advice to reach me. Bring your people together in action. There is nothing wrong with believing men can change, but some never will, because they don't *want* to. They are already who they were meant to be. Men like that would dance on the grave of your kindness until there was nothing left but dust."

Evra hung his head. "If something happens to Edriss, because of my inaction—"

"Go," Rhosyn said before she lost her own courage. "Go and lead your people, Evrathedyn. There is no greater cause than land and love, and the Westerlands is ready to fight to the death to protect both." She reached for his knee and squeezed. "And when you come home to me...and you *will*...Your reward will be meeting your son."

"We haven't even discussed a name, Rhosyn."

"We have time for that." She tilted her head up and waited for him to kiss her. "Go, love. Bring Edriss home. Bring Lorcan home. And while I know your method will be far gentler than mine, I'd be absolutely delighted if you brought me the heads of every Defender on a pike."

Edriss had never understood the word bliss, but ah, she understood it now.

She and Lorcan were swimming in the warmest water, among fish too colorful to be real. Every few strokes, he swept her into his arms for a kiss—or sometimes more. His hand kept moving to her belly, where their child grew. It was still early, but she had enough of a soft bump for him to cradle in his palms.

My cup is full. I could never ask for more, he said, twining his legs through hers and locking his hands into her soaked hair. *Can we just stay like this forever?*

Oh, please, Guardians, yes, she had started to say when Lorcan disappeared. The water was no more. She whipped a hand down to rub it across her midsection, but it abruptly stopped with a jarring burn at her wrists.

"You're awake." Not Lorcan.

Edriss ripped at what she was understanding to be rope binding her wrists, but all it accomplished was more searing pain. Then she remembered. "Finn."

"I'm sorry this was necessary. I really am." His voice thinned as he moved across the room. It wasn't a cell but a lavish bedchamber, full of expensive furnishings and smelling faintly of lavender. She didn't recognize where she was, though it would have been more surprising if she had. Even the Derrys weren't dumb enough to kidnap her and take her somewhere she knew. "If that raven bitch hadn't poisoned my father and his friends, we could have quietly married in the Rush, with your brother's blessing."

"I would never have married you, under any condition," Edriss said and spat as hard and far as she could. It landed only a foot away on the bed she was tied to, inches from her gown. "As for Arwenna, the only thing she did wrong was not finishing the job."

"Guardians," Finnegan said, whistling through his teeth. "Do you always wake up this feisty?" He laughed to himself. "Don't want to answer? No matter. I'll find out soon enough for myself."

"Any body part you bring anywhere near me gets bitten off."

He turned toward her with a grin. "Promise?"

"Disgusting," she snapped. Instinct had her tugging on the ropes again, an act she instantly regretted when fresh pain rocked her. "I knew all along who you were. *What* you were. You spent so long trying to convince me otherwise that I almost believed it." She snarled into a laugh. "Thank you, Finnegan, for removing all doubt."

He moved closer, no longer smiling. "Everything is so simple for you, isn't it, Edriss? So black and white. Everyone is either good or bad. You leave no room in your life for nuance."

"That's simply not true," Edriss replied. "No one in my life is wholly good or bad. Not even me."

"Except Lorcan, right?" He dropped over the edge of the bed, landing on his palms. "No matter how much he ignores you, neglects you, chooses others over you…He can still do no wrong."

What he said stung, but she no longer harbored fear or doubt where her husband was concerned. "Lorcan has his share of things to atone for. What he doesn't have is blood on his hands."

Finn turned the corner of his mouth upward. "How could you ever be so certain when the two of you were so good at keeping secrets from each other?"

Edriss shifted to dull the ache between her shoulders. If she asked Finn to loosen her bindings…a reprieve…he might. But it would give him more power than he already had. "If you mean Rivermarch, I already know the two of you were spying on me."

"Did he tell you the name of the man you healed?"

Edriss stilled. She forced her face to clear. "I assume you know him."

"Aye." Finnegan shifted his arms and sat on the edge of the bed. "Malcom Fox. Wasn't top of the chain until Bristol and Ashenhurst were murdered, but he is now. I don't have to clarify what chain though, do I?"

"Not unless you want to add insulting me to your many crimes," Edriss spat. But her heart raced at the confirmation. At the name. Malcom *was* important to the Defenders. Lorcan wouldn't know it until it was too late.

"Your meeting was an ambush," he said, reading her silence. "I didn't know it then, but I dug around. Malcom didn't know who you really were that day, but he knew damn well you weren't who you said."

Edriss scoffed and angled her face away, protecting the privacy of her fears. Lorcan had gone to confront no mere foot soldier but the *general* of the movement. Had he walked into the ambush they'd laid for her?

Tears pooled in her eyes. Finnegan would think they were from the pain searing her shoulders, traveling up into her trembling biceps and raw wrists. If he knew Lorcan had gone in her stead, he'd have said something. But his silence could mean anything.

"Of course, now he knows." Finnegan looked down at the quilt folded beside him. He batted it to the ground.

"Wonder how," Edriss murmured, cursing herself to stop responding and feeding his sick game of control. Every word was a point to him, stolen from her. Nothing he'd said was useful. She needed him to say something that was. "And so you, what, have tied me up in Rivermarch so I can have the meeting after all?"

"We're not in Rivermarch, princess." Finnegan traced a finger along the bedspread, looking down at his phantom work.

That's something at least. "I know you're not stupid enough to bring me to East Derry."

"Is that a compliment?"

"Nicest one you'll ever get from me." Edriss shifted again, careful not to disturb her tender, raw wrists. "What do you think you'll accomplish with this, Finn?" She cringed to use his nickname, doubly so when he grinned, but a softer touch might be the only thing that would work. "I won't pretend I haven't been displeased with Evra's lack of action, but I would be very surprised if kidnapping his sister didn't stir him to raise his banners."

"I think that's precisely what my father is hoping for." He looked up with a long sigh. "I know you think I'm just like him."

Edriss stifled the cackle burning her throat. She opted for silence.

"He's my *father*, Edriss. What else am I supposed to do?"

She couldn't keep her words inside. "Not be a traitor to your lord and country, for starters. Our father was a traitor to his people, and we managed to avoid becoming monsters."

Finnegan pulled up to his knees and crawled toward her. He hovered nearby, like a wulf sizing up prey. "It doesn't have to be like this, Hemlock."

Edriss reared back, mouth wide in outrage. "Don't you *ever* call me that."

He dropped onto the heels of his feet. "Where's your guardian now? Oh, yes. He followed the cursed raven back to her cage in the mountains."

"We both know he didn't follow Arwenna." She knew where he'd gone. What she didn't know was how he'd fared in Rivermarch.

"Wherever he is, once again he's neglected to choose *you*."

She swallowed the dryness in her throat. Water sounded amazing, wine even better. But asking would give Finnegan another point. "Why am I here, Finn?"

"My sisters are handling all the planning, so I can't answer any specific questions, but..." He tapped his cheek. "By this time tomorrow, you and I will be married. *I* wanted to do it sooner, but Father insisted we had to wait for our highest-ranked guests, and the rest will be here by dawn. By then it won't matter when your brother raises his banners. He'll be too late and will have no choice but to respect the laws he holds so dear."

"The law? It's not *legal* to coerce a woman into marriage."

"Coercion is hard to prove."

Edriss's entire body shuddered with rage. If he were foolish enough to unbind her, he would regret everything he'd ever said or done against her and the Westerlands.

She tilted her chin upward with a hard, proud look and said, "You're too late anyway. I'm already married."

"Oh, I know you are, Edriss," he said, close enough she could smell the tang of liquor on his breath. His laugh brushed her chin. "And I don't care."

TWENTY-ONE
NOTHING SAYS TRUE LOVE
LIKE ROPE BURNS

John" was not how Lorcan remembered him. It might have been his swollen eyes or perhaps even the hazy glare from the sunlight beating onto the square, but where the man had been yellowed and gaunt in the abbey, he now seemed as menacing as a giant. It was Lorcan's first good look at the man since being taken captive.

"My name is Malcom Fox. I already know you, however. You're Lorcan James, son of Rohan, of the late Tatiana. Born in Greystone Abbey. Spent most of your youth in Longwood Rush raised alongside Lord Blackwood, his siblings, and his friends. You've been serving on the lord's council in your father's stead, though as I hear it, you haven't been doing much of anything in that regard. Am I for—" The man comically slapped his palm to his forehead, but there wasn't anything funny about the gesture, about the peril in his dark, beady eyes, too small for his generous face. "Of course, of *course* I'm forgetting something. I've forgotten the most interesting, most salient point of them all! You've risen quite high in recent days, haven't you? Even if no one yet knows."

Malcom lowered into a squat. A thin smile slowly spread across his pocked face. "Refresh my memory, if you don't mind. When a junior steward marries a lady, does it make him a lord? Or does she take your pathetic title?"

Lorcan's heart plummeted. He glared his response, forcing a calm upon himself that he wasn't sure was convincing. He bared his bloody teeth to distract from the tremor in his mangled hands, hanging limp from where they dangled from the stocks. At least one of them was broken, but he couldn't discern which because his sense of left and right had been beaten out of him. *Add it to the list,* he thought.

"Man of few words. Unless you're unable to speak?" He looked behind him. "Sometimes my men go too far. Not entertained enough at home, I suppose."

Lorcan spat a wad of blood. There was still some lingering in his mouth, so he swallowed it, focusing on the viscous trail it made down his throat and not his fear that they knew about far more than a secret wedding.

"Hmm. You must have known her meeting with me was a trap. So why did you come alone?"

Lorcan wet his lips and asked, "How's your arm?"

Malcom chuckled and looked at it. He flexed his hand. "She's gifted, your wife. A heathen, but unlike others, she won't die for it. Fortunately for her, she has something more valuable to us. Unfortunately for you, you'll have to die in order for her to give it to us."

"Then do it already." Lorcan spat again, but this time it ran clean.

Malcom regarded the spittle with a creased brow. "Right about now, they'll be prepping Edriss for her wedding. Her *real* wedding. I told Derry to wait until she was widowed, but it isn't as if anyone will question what date or time we put on your death notice."

Lorcan wanted—needed—to know what the man was talking about, but withholding his words were the last bit of command he still wielded. The promise of death wasn't unexpected. Sometime between dusk and dawn, he'd realized no cleverness, no bargaining, and no miraculous feat of strength was going to set him free. He would die there, and the worst part was knowing his wife was in the hands of monsters. The sinking, gnawing feeling he had, thinking of her in their grasp and the horrible things they'd do to her for fighting back, was enough to make him vomit onto the stones, inches from where Malcom was kneeling.

It can't end like this. I can't let them have her.

"Not much food in that, is there?" Malcom remarked. "Won't matter soon."

"Why are you here, traitor?" Lorcan squinted upward. In his nerves, he struggled to find a clear stream of thought, his mind filtering through dozens of experiences and never landing on one. But they all had one thing in common; they were memories of his time as a tender of death—of the interrogation techniques his father had taught him, to assess which women could be saved and which would be beyond their powers of persuasion. "You have what you want. You have Edriss." He clenched after releasing the words.

"We do," Malcom stated. Though Lorcan already knew it was true, it cut deep to hear it confirmed. "And by noontide tomorrow, she'll be one of us."

"Do you always play with your food before you kill it?"

Malcom looked surprised and then laughed. "Do you always jest when you're in mortal peril?"

"Can't say," Lorcan said. "First time." He'd stopped trying to find a better position for his aching shoulders hours ago, but he shifted anyway, more alert. "You're counting on Lord Blackwood to be as passive as he's always been. But you took his sister, man." *You won't get more than a chance. Two at most. Get it right.* "If you don't think he'll have an army in Rivermarch by tonight, you're deluding yourself."

Malcom whistled through his teeth. He bounced on his heels. "I rather hope he does. Then there's no chance of him stopping the wedding."

Not in Rivermarch. Malcom is here, in Jademarch, but Derry and the others are somewhere else. Think. Think. "What makes you so sure he won't know where to find her?"

"Our little upstart lord wouldn't debase himself by showing up in a place where he doesn't have men who love him to protect him."

All right. All right. We're getting somewhere. It's probably safe to assume that when he says Evra wouldn't show up at the place, Evra hasn't been there before, which rules out most of the Westerlands.

But not all.

Think.

"Why am I here?" Malcom repeated the question Lorcan had asked earlier. "I guess I wanted to lay eyes on the man bold enough to defy a lord he's sworn fealty to. It's unfortunate you're such a do-gooder, Lorcan. We could have used a crafty man like you on our side."

"Don't you have a wedding to make?"

"So I do," Malcom said. He pushed to his feet with a stretch. "If I leave now, I can make it by dawn."

Lorcan silently cheered the man's unintentional revelation. Dawn. That meant almost a full day's ride into a Defender-friendly town. It ruled out everything but the south, and though Evra had spent some time in the south, it wasn't much. But most of the peninsula was loyal to him. He could draw a circle around Greystone Abbey and find nary a sympathizer. Except…

Deramore.

They took her to the belly of the beast.

"Farewell, Lorcan James. When next we meet, it will be at the whims and mercies of our fickle Guardians."

"Not gonna kill me first?" Lorcan peeled his lips back in a snarl. "A smart man wouldn't leave it to chance. You'll find out why when I break these bonds and come for you."

"I could. Maybe I should." Malcom laughed. "But then it would spoil my wedding gift." He sucked in through his teeth.

"Who am I kidding? The gift is for me. Oh, how I'll enjoy watching Lady Edriss watch you beg for your life right before I take it from you."

Edriss refused to look in the mirror. The women had come to prepare her early, and once they finished their work, Edriss would be again tied to the bed—in all her lace and frills and rouge, her curls pinned in a hundred places—to wait. She'd sleep that way, if she slept at all. And when dawn turned to day, they'd parade her in front of her enemies and bind her to one.

What a disgusting farce it all was. Surreal was the only word she could come up with to describe how it felt to be primped and fussed over on the eve of what would become the worst day of her life.

No. Nightmare was more accurate.

"Lady Edriss, you are a vision," one of them said, and the other murmured her enthusiastic approval. "Forgive me for saying so, but—"

"I'm not angry with you. None of this is your doing," Edriss said, spreading her words as evenly as she could. They were not the object of her angst. "But I hope you'll understand I have no desire to speak."

Edriss caught her reflection long enough to see the women exchange nervous glances.

"Ma'am, if we've upset you, we apologize." The woman who spoke—her name was Senyse, Edriss suddenly remembered from the haze of tulle and whispers of the past few hours—set the rouge pot she was holding aside, looked again at the other woman, and sighed. "If we could help you, we would."

"Don't let your masters hear you speak to a loyalist this way." Edriss kept her eyes on her hands, wrung over a dense patch of lace in her lap. Her wrists were ringed in raw red spots. Nothing the women had done to cover the angry flesh had worked, and it had only made it look worse. *Nothing says true love like rope burns.*

"I won't have your blood on my heart in addition to everything else."

"Not everyone is here because they want to be. Some of us left families behind," the other woman—Nora—said quickly, leaning in to add in a hushed voice: "They'll kill you, my lady. Once you've delivered them heirs for their twisted cause, they'll have no need of you."

"Nora!" Senyse exclaimed in a whisper, but she, too, leaned in.

"Oh, I know," Edriss said, laughing. Laughter was all she had left. Reality was too dizzying to face without humor. While she might not be bound at the moment, there were a half dozen guards outside the room, waiting for her to do something foolish.

"My lady?" Senyse asked, clearly wondering if Edriss had lost her mind.

Probably she had. But there was still plenty of fight in her to go down kicking, screaming, and spitting.

"Don't mind me." Edriss traced the raw flesh of one wrist with her finger. "Nothing like a wedding to bring out my morose side." If only she didn't have the recent memory of joining with Lorcan to refute that. Could she have faced the day ahead? She couldn't know. But the vows she and Lorcan had spoken, heart to heart and hand in hand, were still so freshly embossed on her soul that there was no way she *couldn't* think of them, when in hours she would be forced to say them again, through gritted teeth and with a heart full of rage.

"What will you do?" Nora leaned against the vanity table. Senyse joined her. Any interest in wedding preparations was over.

Edriss picked at the skin already scabbing over. A bead of blood appeared on the surface. She spread it around, a fresh reminder she was still alive. Still, in some ways, free. There were choices to be made and not much time left to make them. "The only thing I can do." *Keep fighting.*

Senyse leaned in, biting down on her lip with a conspiratorial look. "We hear things sometimes, my lady, things we aren't meant to hear."

"Is it true, what they say? That you're already married to another?" Nora asked, finishing for her.

Edriss's eyes glossed instantly. It was one thing to disappear into her memories of Lorcan alone, where it was just her and him and all the precious moments making up the story of them. But the women speaking about it tightened the knot choking her heart.

Lorry, where are you?

She almost lied. Though they seemed sincere, it was impossible to know if Nora and Senyse were working both sides and reporting back on everything she said. But did it matter anymore? Finnegan knew, so they all knew. Her secret elopement was no longer a secret at all. "Yes. I am."

They both gasped, half-delighted, half-horrified. "Then there's still a way out!" Senyse exclaimed in a hushed whisper.

"Not even a Defender would go against such a sacred law as that," Nora said, nodding her agreement.

"You don't understand," Edriss said. She closed her eyes. Was she really going to say it aloud? To make her fear real, whole? *Speak your fears to conquer them*, Alise had once said. "By the time they force me to marry Finnegan Derry, my husband will already be dead."

Her eyes opened in a flash. Something inside of her had come alive, shifted, and *roared* at the sound of her worst fear spoken into life. She flung herself out of the chair, which went toppling back. Senyse caught it before it hit the floor.

"My lady?" Nora asked in a rush of excitement.

"Is there a way..." *If you ask this, there's no going back. No pretending your intentions are anything but death.* "If I asked you to bring me something, could you? Only if it's safe for you to do it."

"What?" the women asked in unison.

Edriss told them.

Lorcan had heard horror stories of men, manacled and starving, pulling the flesh from their hands to free themselves. It seemed so farfetched as to be unbelievable, but faced with a choice between de-gloving himself and leaving his wife at the mercy of the Defenders, he was ready to feel whatever pain the desperate act offered.

Even if he had a knife, he wasn't in a position to use one. That, at least, would have been a cleaner cut, maybe even something he could recover from. Scraping his flesh along the splintered wood would mangle his hands beyond use. He'd be unable to ride, hold a sword, or do much of anything. But he could do *nothing* freezing and starving to death in the middle of the square.

All of it was a problem for when he was free.

Until then, there was only one thing he needed to focus on.

He braced himself with a deep breath and held it tight in his chest. He beseeched not the Guardian of the Unpromised Future but the Guardian of the Warrior's Aim, for he would have one chance to get it right. One chance to be quick enough and precise enough not to render himself unconscious from the pain or bleed to death before he could wrap the damage.

Lorcan breathed out and sawed his left hand across the splintered wood.

Screams put his further efforts to a sudden halt. He had no idea where they were coming from. The vise holding his neck was so tight, he could barely turn his head. Then he heard the clashing of steel.

Dozens of boots stormed the square. Their wearers' shadows blocked the setting sun, giving him a welcome pardon from the unforgiving glare. But then the shadows drew larger, closer. *If this is the end, protect my wife. That is my last wish. My only wish. Protect Edriss. Keep her safe from those terrible men. Keep her—*

"Is this him?" A voice Lorcan recognized was so close, he was able to look up and see the source.

Baron Lawrence.

"*Yowch.*" Rafferty Tyndall joined him, making a wincing sound as they took in the state of him. "Yeah. It's him."

"Lorcan James?" The baron knelt into his view, just as Malcom had done. The eternal grief he'd come to know the baron by was missing from his face. In its place was firm, stoic purpose. Lorcan couldn't decide if he was dreaming or still wishing. Perhaps he'd freed himself and succumbed to the hallucinations some men experienced when pain overtook them.

"Lor." Rafferty clapped his hands. "Mate. You're safe. We cleared the place out. There's several dozen Riders guarding the perimeter, and beyond that, another hundred spread throughout the village. How are you alive, after all this?"

"They wanted me to suffer. To bring Edriss here to watch me suffer and then die. The Defenders' entire mission has always been about suffering." Lorcan choked on his shock, his gratitude. Tears started but he cut them off. He accepted he *wasn't* imagining his allies or the boots or the taste of freedom. The Guardian of the Warrior's Aim *had* heard him after all, and had answered him in the most beautiful, unexpected way. "How did you know I was here?"

"Lady Alise," Lawrence answered. "She's had you followed for weeks. You didn't notice a tail, all this time?"

"What?" Lorcan's sandpaper tongue licked his split lip to no avail. "No. Why would she do that?"

"For Edriss," he said and pushed back to his feet.

"Please...*Please* tell me you have her."

"Evra is searching for her right now," Rafferty said. "He has men all over the Reach—"

"There's no time," Lorcan bellowed. His arm flopped roughly to his side, and he realized the baron had cut the lock and freed him. Scorching pain shot straight to his head, and he had to take several breaths to speak again. "There's not fucking *time*, Raff. They're marrying her to Finn at dawn in Deramore."

"That fast?" Rafferty shuffled in place with a dark look at the sky. "We'll never reach her in time."

The baron finished freeing Lorcan and helped him to his feet. Lorcan couldn't stand but was too relieved to be embarrassed about needing assistance. *The Guardians have heard my prayers. This isn't over. This isn't over.* "We will if we leave now." He released the baron and stumbled, only for both men to come catch him again. "If we ride hard and don't stop, we'll make it just in time."

Rafferty blew out and shook his head. "We need to send word to Lord Blackwood. His men are spread all over the Reach right now, looking for her."

"We'll get a raven to Longwood on the way to Deramore," the baron said and then they were dragging a laughing, sobbing Lorcan across the square.

It wasn't the first time Evrathedyn Blackwood had led an army in his short tenure as lord of the Westerlands, but it was the first time he'd done it in his homeland.

Somehow, charging up to the far north with banners and men had been a far simpler matter than waging war against his own people.

He told himself it was why he'd chosen to believe diplomacy and compromise would be the key to winning. Men like his father and his father's cronies had already taken far too much life and passion from the Reach. Taking more was a cost too high.

Standing at the top of a small hill, fighting the chill breeze knocking him and his officers sideways, and looking out into the field of thousands of his bannermen and their forces ready to fight, Evra realized he'd missed the point all along. The *only* thing worth dying for was love of family and land.

There were six battalions spread across the field, each made up of hundreds of soldiers, led by men and women he trusted. Rohan James headed the southern peninsula, Cressida Wakesell the forestlands. Ridge Tyndall led the northern foothills, while Feldred Blakewell—younger brother of the disgraced Tedric—led the southern. Marckus Carlisle had the southeastern borderlands, and finally, Thennwyr Blackfen had rallied every Rider of the Rush.

Evra hadn't even needed to call him. Blackfen loved Edriss and had only stayed away on Evra's command, a decision as misguided as his call for peace. He'd been so concerned with his sister's reputation, he'd not considered she might be happier to give it up in order to have a real father.

There were so many things he'd do differently if the Guardians gave him the chance.

Starting with the way he'd kept his darkest thoughts from his wife, who knew him best. Thinking of her alone in her birthing chamber sent a pit of despair into his belly, but she wasn't alone. She had two of the people he trusted most helping her bring their second child into the world.

A guttural howling wave from the sea of soldiers stirred everyone alert. Cressida rode forward and responded in kind, slamming her fists against her gleaming plate armor. Her men banged on theirs, their cries escalating until the other units joined in. Soon it was all he could hear, the deafening roar of a Reach ready to ride, fight, and if needed, die.

"It won't come to that," Blackfen said at his side. "I don't need to read your mind, my lord, to know what plagues it."

"I'll never forgive myself if we're too late, Thennwyr."

"She's alive," the Rider said. "I feel it here." He tapped his chest. "And here." His head.

"There are some fates worse than death."

"Aye," he agreed. Evra could barely hear him over the cacophony of battle cries. "But for the rest of them, death is the only fate."

"I would prefer no men die today," Evra said, scanning the hungered faces awaiting the command to ride.

"And yet some will, Lord Blackwood. We win when we take more of theirs than they do of ours."

338

TWENTY-TWO

THE SIXTH TENET

I'm already married, she'd said, and Finnegan had known. He'd *known* and was still determined to push forward, confirming her worst fear.

Lorcan was dead.

Those three words were the worst that had ever raced across her mind, and once she'd given them life, there was no taking them back. Pretending was for children, and Edriss Blackwood had never been a child, not even when she was playing by the river with her friends or daydreaming under the stars of the Guardians. Osman Derry would risk no one questioning the gainful marriage he'd made for his only son. He'd never give up the power the union brought himself and the people of East Derry.

So Lorcan *had* to be dead.

As she waited in her fluffy gown Senyse and Nora had reluctantly dressed her in, her hair curled and pinned, and with enough rouge on her cheeks to make her want to drag her palms down her face and melt it all away, the words had a transportive effect. She was dreaming. Floating. Drowning. Somewhere other than walking down the echoing hall of a cold, dank keep she'd never seen before in her life. Reality blurred, splintering into vague observations: the flurry of guards surrounding her ensuring she didn't bolt, the hammering in her heart as she grasped how quickly and violently her life had changed in mere hours, the bitter aroma of boar simmering nearby...

None of it was real.

It couldn't be.

Edriss held the illusion until she emerged into a magnificent banquet hall. Centering the deep room was a long table, adorned with candelabras all the way down, platters of all kinds of foods, and gleaming, colorful decanters, all of it stretching farther back than her vision could carry. Every chair was occupied, and her anxious eyes couldn't settle long enough to make out any of the faces. But then she did. The Bristols. All of the remaining Ashenhursts, save Meira. The man from Rivermarch—who she'd learned was named Malcom Fox—was there too. There were Glenlannans and Richlands and others she knew, their allegiances, at last, confirmed.

Here they all are. In one cursed place. And instead of taking them down, I'm their prisoner.

"My son is a lucky man. Maybe he'll show his gratitude by allowing me to share in the spoils." The words, hot and disgusting against her neck, made her jump back into the speaker, Osman.

Edriss gathered herself and pivoted. "I could have let you die in that room, Steward."

His nose wrinkled, beading with sweat. "You should have. If you were half as clever as you suppose yourself to be, you would have."

"Traitor or no, I swore a vow to myself to save lives, not take them."

Osman grinned as he leaned down to whisper, "And that's why your brother and all who still preach his foul heathenry will lose. Before the year ends, I'll have everyone boasting the usurper's name dead and strung up along the approach to the

340

Halls of Longwood. Those unnatural women you call your aunt and grandmother. Your brother's demon issue. All except you, of course." He straightened with a leer. "At least until you've borne my son enough heirs to secure our legacy. *Many* women perish in childbed, you know."

Heart racing, Edriss stretched to the tips of her toes and said, "Yes, but *all* men are susceptible to poison."

Osman reached into his pocket and brought out her necklace, which he dangled out of reach. "The first thing I'll do when my son is lord of the Westerlands is burn that disgusting garden to dust and ash."

Edriss almost reached for her necklace by instinct. It had been her mother's, and it was Edriss's dearest possession, a gift from a woman she'd been denied the opportunity to meet. If she had no other wins left to her, she'd persuade Finnegan to get it back for her. "I can find something in *any* garden, however ordinary, Steward. And you have to sleep sometime."

"Father, leave Edriss alone." Finnegan stepped up behind Osman, wearing his dressing armor. But instead of the ocher and gold of East Derry, he wore the colors of the Rush: emerald and silver. Her breath stilled at the bold message it sent.

"You look stunning," he said in a breathless rush, and she almost forgot he was no longer the sweet boy of her childhood who'd always been all too eager to play her husband. "Truly beautiful, Edriss."

Edriss glanced out into the sea of faces and snorted. "How little words mean when spoken by one who is so comfortable with lies."

Finnegan glared at his father, who lingered a moment before reminding him they were starting soon. When Osman was gone, he looked back at Edriss and said, "I don't know what he said to you—"

"You do. Of course you do. Filth, lies. It's all *any* of you know." She swept her frilled arm toward the massive table holding every

Defender of the Righteous Dawn who mattered. "You had a choice, and you chose this."

"I didn't choose this." He tucked his chin with a defiant head shake. "It was chosen for me."

"You're not a victim!" She stepped closer and dropped her voice low. "You could have joined us, Finn. Lorcan and I, my brother... We could have protected you. And you know this is true, even as you shake your head and claim I know so little about the world." Her heart raced as fast as her words. "Well, know this: I *will* avenge my husband. Laugh and sneer all you like, but I *will* take down every last man in this room before you've disposed of me, and all of the Westerlands—nay, the *kingdom*—will know what weak and cowardly men do when they don't get what they want."

Finnegan watched her through a long, uncomfortable silence. Edriss searched for signs of remorse, of any sign he might, finally, understand he could still choose the right side, but he was already too far gone. For all the small moments she'd spent instilling her own peaceful values in Finnegan, Osman had a thousand more, drilling fear and hatred into him.

"Thank you all for coming with so little notice. Our noble cause has suffered a blow with the losses of stewards Bristol and Ashenhurst, but we are wounded, not beaten. Never beaten. A righteous cause always rises, again and again and again."

They both turned toward the abrupt shift in energy. Malcom Fox was standing in front of the nobles' table, waiting for everyone to cease drinking and chatting. His smile was thin and cold, and when he shifted it toward Osman, it chilled further.

Malcom nodded around at everyone. "Still, let us take a moment of silence to honor our fallen brethren, who perished for our great cause."

The room fell silent. Osman bowed his head with a snicker, but Finnegan didn't move at all.

The pause lasted less than five seconds.

"All right then. Most of you know me, but for those who do not, my name is Malcom Fox, and it is my great pleasure to invite you to a day that will become known, for many years hence, as the one that turned the tide squarely in our favor. I'm sure some of you have unraveled the surprise, and for the rest of you, I'll not leave you in suspense."

He spoke the words with the authority of a leader.

She'd have her meeting after all, it seemed, but in a far, far different way than she'd planned.

Edriss fought back queasiness and forced herself to pay attention.

"Tonight our vision at last takes a turn toward a brighter future!"

Applause greeted his announcement.

"We have all toiled, prayed, sacrificed..." He nodded along with everyone else. "Yes, *sacrificed*, so that our glorious, taxing labors to cleanse our land of heathenry would not be undone by the boy lord who sucks on the foul teat of change!"

Edriss was trying to grasp how many men were actually inspired by such asinine words when she was shoved by someone and faltered forward into motion. She moved on her own afterward, holding fast to a bravery that would be continuously challenged until there was nothing left of it. The rest of Malcom's words slipped into the din of the frenzied fervor of men and women she'd known all of her life. Most of the people in attendance didn't surprise her, but some did. Some cut deeper than she had been ready for.

Lorry, wherever you are, I have loved you to the depths of my soul. We are one, in this life and the next, and I will find you when this is over and they have nothing left of my physical body to take. I will find you, and we will discover a new place, together, among the stars.

"Who are you talking to?" Finnegan asked quietly, pulling up beside her.

Edriss clamped her mouth closed. She didn't know she'd said it aloud.

"You look anxious."

Edriss shot him an incredulous glare from the side. "You don't say so?"

"Don't listen to him. When this is done, we can make our own way, Edriss. It doesn't have to be…the way they want. Once we're wed, they'll have no say in it. They chose me, and soon, they'll answer to me. Whether or not they've realized it is another matter, and not my concern."

Edriss was too stunned to put order to her words. "You… Guardians, Finn, you speak of murdering my family like it's some mere quibble you and I can move on from. Have you not realized if they can depose one lord who doesn't do their bidding, they can depose another?"

"They're still alive. Your family," he said quietly as he guided her up the brief steps, drawing her closer to the end of her life as she'd known it. "The others wouldn't want you to know this, but your brother has raised his banners, and we don't have a third of the force he does. Once we're married—"

"I'm already married!" Edriss hissed.

"Once we're married," he said again, slowly, as though speaking to a child, "we can put a stop to the rest. We can ask your brother to step aside peacefully—"

"There is no peace in violence, and you know this. You know this, and you'll find any way to justify your madness."

It seemed as though he were about to smile, but he only fixed his gaze ahead and quirked his mouth. "You're the smartest person I know, Edriss. You've known this day was coming since Lord Aeldred died. You just weren't ready to see it."

Edriss purposely averted her eyes from the hundreds watching her in the wretched dress she'd forever think of as her funeral shroud. None spoke up in her favor. Her loss would be a gain for them all. "You speak of power shifts but neglect to delve into the root of the power. Where it comes from. Yes, power can be seized, Finnegan, but when your cause is death, how can you stand in complacent acceptance as though there's nothing you could have done?"

344

"No one else has to die," he said through clenched teeth. "Don't you understand? You're not listening to me."

"I'm listening," she answered coolly. "It's you who hasn't heard what awaits us both."

"As we have already been through the ancient honors of the Five Tenets of Betrothal, we can move into the simplicity of the vow exchange," Malcom said to the crowd. He turned a toothy grin on Edriss and Finnegan. His eyes narrowed in hatred, and Edriss took an instinctual step backward. "Come, and let us show all those who stand for righteousness what our joyous future looks like."

"What about the sixth tenet?" someone cried out.

Edriss and Finnegan both briefly stopped and searched for the source, but before they found it, two other people had shouted the same thing. More calls for the sixth tenet followed.

Malcom's tight smile cut through the bouncing requests. "We do not honor the Betrayer—"

"It's tradition!"

"If we do not, then the Betrayer may curse this union!"

"Let no one say we did not honor all of our Guardians, good and ill!"

"It doesn't matter," Finnegan muttered. "None here would ever object anyway."

He was right. And yet, Edriss's heart raced with hope as she imagined someone, *anyone*, standing up against the madness about to unfold. All it would take was one.

Malcom, brimming with annoyance he didn't bother to hide, rolled his palms against the back of a chair. His back arched like a cat awaiting the right moment to pounce. But then he straightened, raising his hands to show he wanted silence.

"Very well. You're right. We will honor the Betrayer by sending our pleas into those among us." He turned toward her and Finnegan. "Finnegan Derry, are you prepared to fight to the death anyone who challenges this union?"

Finnegan shifted, his mouth moving in discomfort. "Aye... Aye, I am."

Malcom nodded and rolled his eyes. "And who here would dare stand against this blessed union, for—"

Thunder clapped across the room. Startled gasps rippled through the banquet hall as everyone turned, some standing, to watch the massive rear doors flung wide. Leather and steel cut through commotion that Edriss couldn't see from her place on the floor.

But Finnegan could. She knew it from the way his eyes slowly stretched to full width. The way his mouth parted and then opened altogether, wordless, scoring across his paling face.

"LADY BLACKWOOD'S REAL HUSBAND STANDS AGAINST THIS UNION, TRAITOR!"

Edriss stumbled back. A row of guards kept her from tumbling altogether.

She knew that voice.

She knew that man.

And if her heart had not already known what her eyes could not confirm, the stunned anger rolling through the Defenders was more than enough.

Finnegan's hands went to his sword. He started forward, but something stopped him.

Edriss did the only thing she could.

She bolted toward her husband. Her real husband. Her *only* husband.

Osman looked like he might levitate and start breathing fire from his nose. She heard his fist slam into something and then him scream to take Lorcan into custody.

"I'm afraid we cannot do that." Malcom Fox's voice overpowered the pandemonium. "For Lorcan James has issued a challenge in the name of our Betrayer, and to dishonor it would be to dishonor this union. James and his cohorts are to be treated with the honor of invited guests, as tradition demands. Guards, stand down, but stay vigilant."

Edriss was pulled from all sides, parts of her dress tearing off as she fought her way to the back of the room. She felt

Finnegan's shadow pulsing behind her, his heavy boots hammering echoes inside her head, but he wasn't the only one trying to hold her back.

"Let the lady pass. Let her pass." Malcom's order, full of resigned annoyance, carried across the melee. "Just keep the madman from trying anything foolish."

The guards blocking her stepped away, and she raced freely the rest of the way.

When she emerged from the crowd, her strength failed her and she fell to her knees. She looked up into eyes she would know in any lifetime and within her broke the dam that had been holding her together through the hardest hours of her life.

Edriss buried her face in her hands and sobbed at her husband's feet.

"My love." His voice was strained with pain. "Hemlock."

She looked up and stifled a garbled cry at the sight of him. His face was bruised and bloated, lash marks trailing down his neck before disappearing under his cloth armor. He was restrained by five guards, hardly necessary in his condition. His sword hand trembled so hard, the tip of his steel skittered across the stones, and his other hand…It was…It was…

What did they do to you? she mouthed. Her voice squeaked in pain of her own. Hard, shining rage burst forth and shoved her to her feet and then she had his mangled face in her shaking hands. She refused to look away. "Lorry?"

His bruised throat moved in a swallow, which made his whole face wince. He offered her a smile that nearly sent her back to her knees, but then he looked past her.

No, above her.

"I challenge you, Finn, to stand and fight," he said, so calmly it filled Edriss with a fresh terror. She understood then that though he was standing before her, he *had* died—and come back to her a new man, ready to die again. "I challenge you to face me and stand for the crime of kidnapping my wife." Lorcan's tongue swiped across his cracked lips. He twisted against the guards' restraint. "Among other crimes."

Edriss looked at his beaten hands and back at him. She dropped her voice to a low, urgent whisper. "Lorry, no. *No*, you will not do this. You can scarcely hold your sword."

She leaned up to say the words again, but Lorcan caught her lips in his and said, into her mouth, "I have to, my love."

"Let me at least...at least heal you first..." The alarm in Lorcan's eyes, at her revealing the truth of her magic to others, was misplaced. The Defenders already knew, and if she could help him, she didn't care if the entire realm knew.

"You'll do no such thing," Osman said. "He issued this challenge as he is now. He'll fight as he is now."

Edriss shook her head wildly. "There is no rule that says I cannot help him!"

"Lady Edriss, keep your faith." It was another voice she knew. Baron Lawrence. She was too stunned to wonder why he was there at all. That revelation led to another, as she realized there were others too, like Rafferty, and she wondered how many they'd brought with them. Not enough to stop this, or every Defender present would already be in custody.

Finnegan pulled Edriss away from her allies and nudged her toward a guard. The guard tugged on Edriss's arms and started dragging her away.

Edriss's feet left the ground and kicked at the air as she screamed, "He's not fit to fight! You did this to him! Finn, *look at me*, you *coward*, you cannot go through with this!"

But Finnegan wouldn't look at her, and neither would Lorcan.

"I have to, Edriss," Finnegan said, so low she almost didn't hear him. "And so does Lorcan."

"Lorcan James!" she cried out, wriggling so hard, she felt something snap in her shoulder. Sharp pain rocked through her, but her fear was louder. "Lorcan, I forbid you from doing this! I forbid it, do you hear me? Do you hear me? *I* will fight! I will defend my own honor! LORCAN!"

She was too far away to hear what was said between Finnegan and Lorcan, who stood face-to-face, locked in intense conversation. They both nodded and shook hands.

It was done.

Finnegan turned away, and so did Lorcan, but as he did, he caught her eyes and nodded once. His mouth moved in the shape of words she didn't need to hear to know.

I love you.

Followed by *RUN*.

TWENTY-THREE
A TRUE MAN HANDLES
HIS OWN BUSINESS

It was still midday but the sky had darkened, bloated with clouds and violent foreboding. Fitting, Lorcan thought, for his last time laying eyes on the sky. On anything. He'd tried to drink up every detail of Edriss's face before she was ushered away, but all he could conjure was her fear and panic, and it hurt so much more than it helped. She knew he was sacrificing himself to save her, but what she didn't know was that he had far more fight left than it might appear.

Lorcan could swing and scream for hours if it bought his wife enough time to escape.

It was a longshot either way. His arrival was a distraction, but it was unlikely they'd take their eyes off of Edriss long enough for her to make a move of any kind.

He had to try anyway.

"I hope you have a better plan than letting Derry kill you," Rafferty muttered as he fumbled through wrapping Lorcan's sword hand. It was unusable before the swaddling, and it was hardly serviceable after, but he didn't have to win the fight. He only had to last long enough to buy time.

"Where's Lawrence?" Lorcan asked. He barely registered the pain of Rafferty manhandling his mangled fingers. He was disconnected from his body, floating free of the injuries that should prevent him from standing against Finn.

"Exactly where he said he'd be." Rafferty gripped a swath of fabric in his mouth and tore another strip. He kept looking up and past Lorcan every few seconds, but they were still alone. The Defender guards were close enough to stop them from doing anything foolish but not close enough to hear what was said. "You have more important things to worry about, such as how you plan to survive this mess."

"Tell me anyway." Lorcan closed his eyes and inhaled hard through his nose. "I need to hear you say it."

"He's up on the ridge. He sent two men to survey the keep, dressed as kitchen staff." Rafferty tied off a bandage and ripped another. "You really think you can hold Finn off?"

Lorcan let out a raspy exhale. On the journey to Deramore, he'd figured out one of his lungs was punctured, but he had hoped it was just the strain. With a moment to steady himself, he could feel the tiny holes as air passed through the wrong way. "Keep wrapping."

Rafferty paused and sat back in his chair. "You don't have a plan at all, do you? You mean to let him kill you?"

Lorcan swallowed down a swollen knot. He could no longer tell injury from inflammation, but without a healer, he'd die soon either way. "As long as we learn the lay of this keep so you can find my wife and get her away from here, nothing else matters."

Rafferty hung his head with a short, amused shake. "You really did it then? You eloped with Evrathedyn's sister?"

"I married the only woman I've ever loved." Lorcan flexed his bandaged hand. It was almost too stiff, but all he needed was enough strength to hold the sword. Enough energy to dance around until he had nothing left. "Ever *will* love. No matter what happens here today, there'll never be another, Raff. Not for me."

"You always did fancy her. Even when we were little."

"We were friends then. All of us." He glanced across the courtyard, looking for Finn, but it was only the guards.

Rafferty sniggered to himself, reminiscing. "Oblivious to the horrors our fathers engaged in. There we were, playing pretend, while the world burned."

"We were just children," Lorcan said. "But we're not children now. We've all chosen our sides, and fate will decide whether we suffer for it."

"What about the raven?" Rafferty shoveled the sheets and ointment back into the box. He stayed his movements a moment and slid his jaw in a bitter circle. "You know...It still hasn't hit me that my brother is gone. It will, one day, when this is over and I can afford the distraction of grief, but...but she's the reason Renardy is dead, Lorcan. And she just gets to...to *fly away?*"

"I'm sorry about Renardy. I really, truly am." Lorcan bowed his head. "I won't defend what she did. I can't. But we've all been backed into impossible corners. We've all lost. Every one of us. This all has to end soon, or there won't be any more blood left to spill."

"Aye," Rafferty agreed. He stood and helped Lorcan to his feet. "I suspect it *will* end soon. I'm less confident on who will emerge the victor." They both turned their attention to the guards approaching. "You know Edriss will kill me if we leave here without you. Or you, if you're not already dead. Knowing her, she might kill you a second time for sport."

"Just get her out of here, Raff." Lorcan gripped his sword as tight as his bandage and wounds allowed. He fought the burn ripping through every tendon and hoisted his steel higher. "Let me worry about the rest."

Finnegan begged his father to leave Edriss in the keep. She was already a red-faced mess, and the duel would traumatize her. Of all his regrets, causing her pain was among the worst.

Delusion had played a part in his belief he could put back together what others had broken in her. There had been a time when he hadn't been a perpetrator in the destruction and could claim neutrality. Until his father had nearly been assassinated by the traitorous raven, there'd still been a chance he might abandon the Defenders and join with Evra, going against his own blood.

It was too late to change course. His father was alive but would never fully recover. Whether Edriss could have done more or not—whether he'd drugged her too soon, keeping her from her best healing—was a problem belonging to the future. Kidnapping Edriss had been an open declaration of war on the Blackwoods. If Lorcan had come, the rest of the banners would arrive soon enough.

The first of the day's light was spilling over the horizon, enough glow to see his way to victory.

Finnegan pulled his gloves taut. His breath furled in the cold air and he shivered, exposed on the hill for all gathered to watch from below. Underneath the soil he stood upon was the Deramore jail, a place many said the Guardians had cursed. Finnegan had been inside enough to believe they'd forsaken it altogether.

Osman was his second, though he didn't need a second in a fight that would be over as soon as it was announced. Lorcan did, but he was too foolishly proud to let Rafferty take his place or even to negotiate a different conclusion.

"End it fast," Osman snapped. He blew into his hands with a violent shiver. "It won't do to have Edriss making a damned scene."

"Then we shouldn't have brought her." Finnegan glared at his father from the side. He could hardly stand to look at him. They'd never been close, but the loathing had begun after Finnegan's mother had died and there'd been no one left to smooth the ogre's edges. Osman was a weak man, whom fortune had placed in the right situation at the right time. No cleverness could be ascribed to his unexpected rise. "There's still time to hold her back."

"And leave any doubt her husband is dead?" Osman grunted. "If Fox had handled matters the way he was supposed to, instead of playing with his kill, this would already be over." He kicked at the icy grass in defiance. "No, she'll witness it so we can put this matter to bed, for once and all. Anyone who learned the unfortunate truth about her first marriage will know it ended here, today, on this hill."

Finnegan closed his eyes and adjusted his stance. Osman's heartless approach was unsurprising, but it further underscored why his children had never seen him as a father. Lorcan had been Finnegan's closest friend until Aeldred had died. The rise of the Defenders had created the wedge that came between them, which had quickly widened to a chasm, impossible to close.

No matter what animosity had festered the past two years, the idea of taking Lorcan's life left him feeling nothing but hollow misery. If only they'd had that ale, cleared the air...

It was too late for regrets.

A retinue of guards appeared from the other side of the witch's pyre, marching toward a raised platform with a view of the hill. Finnegan heard Edriss's indignant curses before he saw her, a speck of wild fury in the middle of a sea of armor. Her face was blocked from view, and perhaps it was a mercy. For him anyway. There would be no mercy for Edriss Blackwood.

"Where are the rest of Lorcan's men?" Finnegan asked. He only saw Defenders in the crowd.

"Dining like kings, most like, thanks to that upstart, Fox," Osman murmured. He spat a wad of disgust at his feet. "Thinks he's in charge now, just wait."

"How many were there?"

"A dozen or two at most. Not enough to matter."

Finnegan turned slightly toward his father. "Are you not concerned there might be ten times as many waiting for us beyond the ridge?"

"We'd already know." Osman nodded toward the dense tree line. "We have patrols all over the forest."

355

"Evra has already called his banners. It's not a matter of *if* but *when*."

"Let him come." Osman cackled. "I hope he does."

"And when they arrive? And we're outnumbered?"

"It'll be too late. There will be a new lord of the Westerlands." He grinned and elbowed his son. "You."

Finnegan shifted toward the commotion rising from the keep. Lorcan was draped between Rafferty and another man, who both were dragging him up the hill.

"Guardians' sake, the boy has a death wish," Osman said, shaking his head. "Fox's fault anyhow. No reason for him not to have ended this in Jademarch beyond his love for sadism."

"Where's Lawrence?"

"Who?"

"The baron, Father? He was standing with Lorcan when they broke into the banquet hall. He's not with them now."

"How should I know?" Osman shrugged. "Now look. If it were *me*, I'd make Lorcan suffer. I harbor no soft spots for my enemies. But I know he was your friend, so I'm going to give you a piece of advice, a way to offer him some mercy so you can live with this." He mimed drawing his sword and angled the phantom steel upward, underneath Finnegan's breastbone. "Right here. One thrust. Right through the heart. It will be over fast."

Finnegan gulped and nodded. Fresh sweat beaded along his temples, despite the brisk chill. He rolled his hand over his sword hilt and drew a hard, deep breath, blinking away the dark spots threatening his focus.

Edriss's screams carried at a volume higher than the crowd's. Or maybe he was just listening for her. She spat her words like a curse, and though he could understand nothing, they were an indictment, of *him*. *You have a choice*, she'd said, and he'd thought her so naïve, a princess whose life had never been as complicated as his. But that wasn't fair, because Edriss had known suffering her entire life and had come out of it stronger and more resolved to do better than those who had made her.

356

Lorcan stumbled out of Rafferty's and the other man's arms when he reached the top of the hill. He fell to a crouch, almost toppling, swaying, but then steadied himself with a shaky rise to his feet, which nearly ended with another fall. With the shock of the initial moment passed, Finnegan appreciated the extent of his old friend's injuries. His face was so mangled, he was hardly recognizable. The blood caked around his mouth had come from internal wounds, judging by the fresh blood on his tongue. Though his hands were wrapped, only his ring finger and thumb seemed capable of holding onto the sword he drew agonizingly slow.

Rafferty glowered behind Lorcan. Finnegan shoved his gaze downward, like the coward Edriss said he was. He hadn't known at the time that Renardy's death had been ordered by his father, but he'd since learned.

You have a choice, Finn.

Get out of my head, Princess.

"You…" Lorcan gurgled and spat a wad of blood on the grass. He wiped his mouth on his arm and started over. "Will not lay another hand on my wife."

"And who cares about a dead man's words?" Osman grunted, but Finnegan held out a hand to quiet him.

"She wasn't yours to marry, Lorcan." Finnegan stepped closer, so his words were just for Lorcan. "If you loved her as much as you claim to now, you would never have let a betrothal come to pass between her and me. You would never have let another man call her his."

"The only one owed that explanation is Edriss, and she has it." Lorcan's eyes closed. His jaw pulled at the corners when he groaned. "You can still do the right thing."

Finnegan ran the back of his hand across his mouth and laughed. "That's your problem, Lor. You've always believed yourself to be the arbiter of what's right, what's wrong. But here's what you don't understand: none of it matters." He lifted his shoulders. "None of it. What *matters* is what the people want, and if the people of the Westerlands wanted peace, they'd have run the Defenders out of the Reach two years ago."

357

"Fear!" Lorcan's scream was raspy. "*Fear* has kept them from rising. And Evrathedyn's restraint hasn't helped. But he won't sit idly by after what you've done to Edriss. This *will* end soon." He squinted his swollen eyes in a fluttering blink. "My deepest regret is I won't be here to watch him take you down."

"Enough talking." Malcom Fox appeared. He made a sniffling sound and pointed at both men. "You fellows know the rules?"

"There are none," Lorcan said with a bloody grin. "Right?"

"I was regretting letting you live, but not anymore. This is going to be even better than I imagined. Lady Edriss will enjoy quite the show this morning, and so will all these witnesses." Fox laughed. "Once the fight starts, there's only one way to end it. Before we begin, I must ask you both, Do you still consent to this challenge?"

"Aye," Finnegan said. He scowled to cover the doubts rising.

"Very much *aye*," Lorcan said, glowing with fury. His sword dangled from his fingertips.

"Last chance to appoint your second to take your place," Fox said. "There are no switches mid-fight."

Finnegan and Lorcan both shook their heads.

"Very well. Each of you, back up ten paces. I'll count down to one and then the duel begins. It takes as long as it takes. As I said, it ends only one way, so choose your moves carefully." He raised both of his hands in the air and gestured for the men to take their steps. Once they were in place, he started the countdown. "Three. Two. One. Begin."

Finnegan waited for Lorcan to make the first move. He didn't have to wait long. Within seconds, Lorcan ambled forward, his sword held bravely out to his side. He swung it and Finnegan blocked it with ease. Lorcan swung again, and Finnegan lifted his sword for another effortless parry. That went on for a few more blows, before Lorcan dropped to his knees and held up a hand, indicating a desire to rest.

When Finnegan honored it by backing away, Osman called out for him to finish it. Screams from the crowd mimicked his request, but it was Edriss's cries he pulled from the crazed din and took to heart.

"This isn't a fight!" Rafferty exclaimed, reaching for his own sword before Fox's guards drew theirs. He reluctantly retreated. "It's an assassination."

"Get up," Finnegan said, coaxing him. He shook his head. "Lorcan. Get *up*."

Lorcan had one foot planted before he swayed again, falling backward. Finnegan leaned in and offered a hand, blocking out his father's noises of disgust. Lorcan eyed it with suspicion but took it and hopped back to his feet.

Before breaking his hold, Finnegan hastily leaned in and whispered in Lorcan's ear. The message was short and fast, to keep his father and Fox from studying them too closely, but his words were far from simple. They would change the course of his own life forever, something he had known before he'd spoken them.

Lorcan's only response was a wheezy gasp, but it was all the acknowledgment Finnegan needed.

They took their places again this time, set to more fevered hollers from the crowd, but Lorcan raised his trembling arms out to his sides and dropped his sword to the grass. His flank was fully exposed, giving Finnegan more than enough space to work with.

Edriss howled Lorcan's name. Finnegan's name. Her shrill cry pierced through the last of his hesitation, and he thrust his sword through Lorcan's lower abdomen with a roar of triumph.

He pulled his sword back to a spray of fresh blood. Lorcan met his eyes on his way to the grass before he fell, face first.

Finnegan quickly dropped to his side, his heart beating so hard, it drowned out the crowd's bloodlusted excitement. He reached for Lorcan's neck, impatiently counted down the seconds, and looked up at his father with a solemn nod.

Osman and Malcom whipped the crowd into a victorious frenzy. Everyone seemed to feed off each other until the energy built up so high, the ground felt like it had been struck by thunder.

But all Finnegan heard was Edriss. Her screams of horror. The frantic howl she made, which was more beast than woman. "LOOOOOOORCAAAAAN!"

He watched the guards carry her away, kicking and screaming. She almost floated above them with all her twisting and squirming, but not even her rage was enough to overpower a dozen men.

"The victor is declared! The usurper is defeated!" Malcom cried out, his arms raised. "We shall all take a break after this dramatic interlude, and later this afternoon, Finnegan will claim his rightful place at the side of Lady Edriss."

"It's done. Take a rest." Osman clapped Finnegan on the back so hard, he pitched forward and dropped back to the grass beside Lorcan.

Lorcan, his oldest friend. His dearest friend.

"Leave him," Malcom snapped. "We'll collect him later."

"No," Finnegan said. He squeezed the tears collecting in his eyes, letting them fall before wiping them on his sleeve. "A true man handles his own business. I'll see him to the dungeon myself."

Malcom chuckled to Osman, mumbling something contemptuous and utterly unimportant to Finnegan, who had little time left to carry out the rest of his plan and absolutely no idea whether he even could. Whether his sword had struck too far or too close to where he'd been aiming.

He waited until he and Lorcan were alone and scooped him up with a heavy grunt. The dying man was unconscious and bleeding out—but breathing. "Guardians, Lor. Not as dainty as you look, are you?"

Finnegan dug deep for strength and raced them down the hill toward the keep.

Edriss lost all sense of time. She knew she was screaming because her throat was hoarse and her mouth was hinged so wide, it had locked that way, but she couldn't *hear* anything. She couldn't feel her bloodied nails splintering as she clawed the door they'd locked from the outside. All she could see were scorching dots of rage spreading across her vision like a violent brush stroke.

Lorcanlorcanlorcanlorcanlorcanlorcanlorcanlorcanlorcan—

Long after she lost her voice, she whispered his name, a sound carried on the soft wind of hope that she'd never let die, not even after years of neglect and abuse as the bastard daughter of a malevolent man. She'd watched Finnegan deal the death blow, the subtle nod he'd flicked, confirming it was done. It wasn't like before, when she hadn't known where Lorcan was and she could imagine some brave escape. She'd seen him fall to the grass and die.

He said to tell you, "Everything will be all right, Hemlock. Trust me."

But it wasn't all right. It would never be all right. Those words had become fluid and without meaning, empty promises floating on a sea of nothing. *Just us. Until the world ends.* Ah, but the world *had* ended. For her, it had ended when Finnegan speared a sword through her husband.

Her rage turned to an exhaustion so total, she couldn't recall the moment she'd slipped from consciousness at all. The next moment of awareness she had was the door swinging open, shoving her out of the way, sending her tumbling.

It slammed closed, from a force she couldn't see.

She scrambled to her knees but was knocked back again by a rush of legs and grunts. She couldn't rouse herself fast enough to make sense of what was happening, but then powerful arms lifted her to her feet, and she found herself looking up at Finnegan.

He grasped her face in his and held it tight. "Listen to me, Edriss, and listen carefully. He's alive, but not for long. If you can save him...then save him. But I have to come back for him soon, or they'll kill him—*really* kill him." He shook her. "Are you listening?"

Edriss nodded, dazed, her lethargic gaze shifting between Finnegan and the bed, where Lorcan lay bloodied and crumpled. He was angled away from her, so she couldn't see his face. There

361

was no movement, no telltale rise and fall from breathing, but Finnegan had said he was still alive. Why had he said it?

"Edriss!" Finnegan slapped her cheek. She recoiled, but it was enough to turn her attention to him. "*Listen* to me. As far as they know, Lorcan James is a dead man, and if they find out I intentionally fumbled a mortal strike, I will be too. So you have *one chance* to save him. The guards out there now are mine, but in two hours, they change. He *has* to be gone by then. Do you understand?"

"I…" Edriss's shallow breaths quickened. "I don't understand what's happening."

"I couldn't kill my friend." Finnegan released her and looked down at his feet. "I couldn't kill someone you love. But it doesn't mean he can't die from his wounds." He grabbed her by the shoulders and spun her hard, toward the bed. "I'll give you *one* hour. One hour and then I have to come back for him, no matter how bad it is."

Edriss nodded, unable to speak…unable to think with the revelations competing for placement. Lorcan was alive. Maybe. Finnegan had saved him. Maybe.

Maybe. Maybe. Maybe.

"Okay." Her voice cracked. She cleared her throat and tried again. "All right."

Finnegan seemed to wait for her to say something else, but when she didn't, he shook his head and went to the door. "One hour, Edriss. It's all I can give you." Then he left.

She was alone with the huddled figure on the bed. Dead. Alive. He could be either, as long as she stayed standing—as long as she didn't go to him to confirm Finnegan's audacious claim. *I couldn't kill someone you love. But it doesn't mean he can't die from his wounds.*

Edriss closed her eyes and tilted her head back. She whispered without sound, a beseeching prayer to the fickle Guardian of the Unpromised Future.

She sucked in a long, shaky breath and released it slowly.

One hour.

Edriss rolled up her sleeves and crawled onto the bed. "My love," she whispered. "Lorry."

He didn't stir. Her heart crept into her throat. She couldn't even swallow. "Lorcan." She leaned over him and pressed her shaking fingers to his neck. The seconds were the longest of her life, but she'd never, ever forget the faint thrum of his still-beating heart.

Drawing on the lore of a tale she'd heard a hundred times—of how Rhosyn had breathed life back into a dying Evrathedyn on Icebolt Mountain after his brave last stand against evil—Edriss surrounded Lorcan with her love and turned it into life.

TWENTY-FOUR
I DON'T CARE WHO HEARS US

Lorcan was floating. On nothing, into nothing, away from nothing. As his weightlessness spread from limb to limb, he soared higher, and the sudden rise drew his eyes to his hands, once more whole. He brought them to his face, no longer bloated beyond what his fingers recognized but slim and strong, defined in all the right places.

His pain was mostly gone, though his flesh and bone wouldn't soon forget. And something…Something still burned. The sensation followed him as he floated on, through nothing, into nothing, and away from nothing, until it was all he could think about. He swatted at the back of his head, unable to shake the sensation his scalp was on fire.

Lorry.

Edriss. He wasn't hearing her voice so much as experiencing it. *Knowing* it was there—it was everywhere. She couldn't follow wherever he'd gone, but he'd known as much when he'd said good-bye to her in the banquet hall. It wasn't the parting he'd take with him though. The precious moment he held fast

365

to was the feeling of her sleeping against him in the inn as the world had moved on without them. The way her slightly open mouth had left a soft trail of drool on his chest from her peaceful exhaustion. How when she woke, all she offered was a sheepish grin of apology, wiping it away before returning to the important business of cuddling.

Lorry.

I'm here, Hemlock. I'm always here. For you, always. The words lived exclusively in his mind, but he had a feeling she'd hear them anyway. At least that was his hope, for the oppressive agony of never being able to communicate with Edriss again was even worse than he'd imagined when he'd opened his arms wide and given Finn permission to strike.

I'm going to attempt to purposely miss anything vital, but you need to focus on slowing your heart, or you'll bleed out anyway. Finn had spoken so fast, Lorcan had to rerun the words to make sense of them. *I'll get you to Edriss, but it's up to you to keep yourself alive until then.*

Lorcan hadn't had time to ask why, to understand Finn's change of heart. The whole of Deramore and the Defenders had been watching Finn for signs of hesitation, and both of their lives depended on there being none.

Lorry.

The searing sensation became stronger, and even with both hands pressed to the back of his head, it did nothing but escalate it. Still floating, he opened his mouth to scream, but nothing emerged except air, then he was shifting, tumbling, feet over head, and rolling—

"Lorcan!" Edriss hissed. She straddled him from above, turning his face back and forth in her hands.

Lorcan's response was a hard puff of breath, then another when he tried to speak. He reached for his head, but the burning feeling had become something more recognizable: the warming calm of a crackling fire from a nearby hearth.

"Guardians, it's about time." Edriss folded herself atop him and buried her face in his neck with a stilted sob of relief. She slid her lips along his healed flesh. With a small whimper of hesitation, she moved the kiss to his mouth, a gentle touch full of fear. Before she could decide him too weak for affection, he shot a hand up and cradled her face to kiss her better.

Edriss was the first to break away. She rolled her lips inward, flitting her tongue across the space where his had been. "Is this real? Are you really here? With me?"

He noted she hadn't said, *You're safe.* "Are we..."

"Dead?" Her laugh was soft, full of relief. "No, love. Not yet."

"No, are we..." Lorcan coughed. He closed his eyes to focus his endless race of thoughts. His lips still buzzed from the kiss he'd never wanted to end. "Still in Deramore?"

Edriss's smile dissolved. "Afraid so." She climbed off and burrowed in beside him on the bed. "Finn brought you to me, but..." Her head shook. "You're alive. You're *alive*, Lorry, and you're here, with me, for whatever time is left to us."

"We're together, Edriss, after everything that's happened to us both. It means something. I refuse to believe the meaning is anything but a promise of the future we've earned." Lorcan groaned and tried to move again, but he had to stretch first, to clear the stiffness. "You healed me."

"You sound surprised."

"Not about you." He winced and angled downward, to kiss the top of her head. "He purposely missed, Hemlock. He saved my life."

Edriss hardened against him. "It's because of him we're locked away in this room."

"I know, but..." Lorcan wondered if the torture had clouded his judgment. But he'd had plenty of time to think over the long days in Deramore, and his thoughts kept bringing him back to the day Finn had brought him to Rivermarch. *I want you to agree to hear me out. I want you to listen and keep an open mind.* How different might things have been if Lorcan *had* listened? "He could have killed me.

367

He had the perfect opportunity, and he betrayed the Defenders instead." When Edriss started to rile, he kissed her forehead and sighed against her soft flesh. "I'll never forgive him, Edriss. Never. But that has nothing to do with me. It's what he's done to you that he'll answer for. Bringing me here, to you…All it's done is earn him a more merciful death than his comrades will get."

"Soon he'll come take you from me again. He'll force me back into the banquet hall, knife to my throat, and compel me to say vows I'll never mean. And after—"

Lorcan rolled with a grimace and faced her directly. "It's not going to happen."

"We can't *stop* it from happening. We're locked away in here. I already checked the windows. We'd die in the fall if we tried. The only way out is through a dozen guards and then hundreds more beyond them. We're surrounded by Defenders on all sides." She laughed bitterly. "There's no way out but the one they choose for us."

"Evra will come." Lorcan inched closer and rested his forehead against hers. He fought the urge to leap to his feet and check the doors and windows anyway, but he wanted her to know he trusted her. "He will."

Edriss tilted her head away. "Finn said he raised his banners, but he wouldn't have told me that if it were true. My brother won't risk war for me, nor would I want him to."

"We're already *at* war, Hemlock." Lorcan dipped his head down toward hers and kissed her, desperate for more of the connection he'd believed lost to him forever. "We've been at war for years, no matter what others might call it. And now it's going to end, one way or another. Evra knows. He's always known about the Defenders, but—"

"I know," Edriss stated, cutting in. "He and I spoke as well, before I was taken."

Lorcan coughed, clearing the thickness sitting in his lungs like a stone. "Does he know? About us?" If he didn't, he would soon, after Lorcan's outburst in the banquet hall.

Edriss nodded. "He knows. And not that it matters now, but he wasn't mad. He wants us to be happy."

Lorcan's tension lessened into relieved laughter. "You're serious? He was good with it?"

"Shocking, I know." She curled her legs up and nuzzled closer. "All this time, we might have saved ourselves so much frustration. Then again, he wasn't the only obstacle in our way."

"I was a fool," he said softly. "The greatest fool. And you've been too easy on me for it."

Edriss sniffled. Her eyes were full of the heaviness of exhaustion when she looked up at him. Dragging him back from the brink of death had taken so much from her, and it was time for him to take care of her. "Maybe I was just tired of fighting so hard for happiness."

"I'm sorry, Edriss. I really, truly am."

"I know, Lorry." She wrapped her arms around her drawn-up legs, and that was when he saw the rope burns around her wrists. A sudden rush of anger rendered him dizzy. He had to close his eyes to ground himself. "And though we're in the worst conundrum of our lives, I have no regrets. I would never choose differently. I would never choose anyone but you. But us."

"No," he said, choked with emotion. "I wouldn't either. Death can't be worse than never having chosen you, Hemlock."

"I suspect we'll get the chance to put that to the test," she said lightly.

Lorcan flexed a hand, marveling at the wonder of the transformation. He lowered it onto her bare arm and brushed it along the soft down coating her pale flesh, memorizing it in the same way he'd done the night they'd played Confessional as though it was the last time he'd have the chance. "I have something I need to tell you."

Edriss stilled.

"It's about Arwenna." His hand fell away from her arm. "You know that was…It was for show only. I couldn't tell you why, no matter how badly I wanted to, because it wasn't my secret to tell.

But Arwenna is gone now, and the men threatening her are…"
He sighed. "She came to me the night Renardy died—"

"I know." Edriss pressed a hand to the side of his face, cradling it. "I already know. Arwenna told me everything."

Lorcan's head tilted against the pillow. "She did? When?"

"Before she left to return to the north." Edriss turned her eyes toward the ceiling. "She said she came up with the idea to pretend you were in love, to keep Osman and the others satisfied she was keeping you distracted and away from me."

Lorcan held his breath while she spoke, but the last revelation had him nearly choking on his shock. "The last part…She said that?"

Edriss nodded. "You didn't know?"

"Of course I didn't know! She told me she was supposed to work me for information about the loyalists, that if we were seen together, they'd believe she was playing their sick game. She never said…I *never* would have…" Lorcan trailed off in disbelief. "When my father said she was playing both sides…"

"I think it may be more nuanced than that," Edriss said softly. "Arwenna was trying to protect her family. But all choices have consequences, and we're living the consequences of hers now."

Lorcan felt the air leave his lungs again. All that time he thought he'd been helping Arwenna, when he'd only been helping Osman and Finn keep him and Edriss apart. Knowing she'd done it to protect Rhosyn and the children only softened the betrayal. It amounted to a betrayal he could never get over: her willingness to sacrifice Edriss and to make him complicit in the act.

So much damage and hurt, and for what?

"Stop torturing yourself," Edriss said, reading his silence. "Others may love you in spite of your big heart, Lorcan, but I love you because of it. Savior complex and all. My paladin. My lightbringer." She laughed. "You're probably going positively mad in our current predicament. But this time, your damsel will have to remain in distress, I'm afraid."

"I'm *not* giving up." Lorcan's words cracked. He cleared his throat. "I'll never stop fighting for you. I'll fight for you until they tear the very last breath from my body and then I'll keep fighting as the Guardians take me home."

"I know, my love." Edriss kissed him. She left her lips pressed to his as she sighed. "Finn will be here soon to take you away from me again."

"No. *No*, I won't—"

"How will you stop him? With what sword? With what might?" Edriss brushed her lips against his again. "He's going to get you out of here, Lorry, and *that* is what gives me the courage to face tomorrow."

Lorcan clasped her face between his hands. "I won't *leave* you here, Edriss. I'm not going *anywhere* without you. Not this time. He'll have to kill me—"

"Can you not put me through the pain of watching my husband die a second time?"

Lorcan exhaled, scoffing, fighting her words and his. "You've never been one to surrender so easily. Why now?"

"Look around you!" Edriss tore away, gesturing around the room. "There *is* no way out of this. I even tried to get the servant girls to bring me my vial or some plants from the garden that I might combine to make *something* useful, but they haven't returned, so now I have to live with wondering if their blood is on my hands too." Her head shook, her hair falling over her eyes. "We can't count on anyone anymore. It's just us, until Finn comes for you, and then I *need* to know you're safe and far away from here, or I cannot do what he asks of me."

"For the love of the Guardians, Edriss," Lorcan cried. "He's not...He's not putting his hands on you ever again, for any reason."

"Oh, he won't touch me, Lorry. Not like that. It's one thing I'll never allow as long as I'm still breathing." Edriss slid her face along the pillow to wipe her tears. She kept her eyes averted from his, leading him to a sudden, terrible revelation.

"You're not...*No.*" Lorcan shoved forward in the bed and leaned over her. "Edriss Blackwood, you tell me I'm way off base with the fears spinning through my head right now. You swear to me I'm overreacting."

"It will be me or him," she answered slowly. "Him if I can find a way. Me if I cannot."

Lorcan was weightless again. Floating. Both there and nowhere. Tethered to the moment, to *her* and also far away, disconnected and reaching for something that wasn't there.

He could spend the next few minutes begging her not to do it, convincing her he would find another way, or he could *show* her why it was never, ever an option. He could *show* her how his fight had not died with him, despite his defeats.

Lorcan leaned down and gathered her into his arms with a burning kiss. Edriss stirred to life under his touch, but she pulled back and said, "They'll hear us."

He kissed her again, running his hands down the awful tulle until he found flesh again. He ripped at the fabric until he had full command of her thighs, tugging them up and around his hips. "I want to make love to my wife, Edriss. I don't care who hears us."

A fire of excitement flickered in her eyes, and she lunged upward to deepen the kiss, wedging her hand beneath his waistband. With her other hand, she ripped at the buttons and buckles, grunting through her frustration until she finally had him free. Before he could take another breath, she circled his cock with her hand and had him pressed against her opening, all the permission he needed.

There was no time for all the things he wanted to do to her. He stayed his desire long enough to look into her eyes, where everything lived that mattered to him. When he pushed inside with a loud, desperate moan that matched hers, one sure to be heard in the hall, his thoughts cleared and his heart took over.

Edriss clawed through the air until she had his face, half sobbing, half moaning through her ardent kisses. Her hips jumped in urgent demand, which he met with each yearning stroke, once more committing every sound and shape to a place no one but her could ever follow.

It had been Edriss in the beginning, and it would be Edriss in the end—to whatever end.

"You are mine," she said, her voice choked from the force of his thrusts. Her sweaty arm hooked behind his neck, holding herself aloft. "Let them hear. Let them all know who I chose."

"I've always been yours," Lorcan said, breathless, as he came.

Edriss fought sleep. She performed no accounting of time, so she had no way of knowing if they had minutes, seconds. She would waste neither. Hope was Lorcan's weapon of choice. Hers was realism.

The ache between her legs helped keep her awake. Lorcan had taken care of her, twice—once with his tongue, which had been a delightful surprise after he'd just spilled inside of her, and the other with his hand while she had still been recovering.

She wanted more. She wanted so much more than she could ever have. She wanted everything. All of it. All of him. She could ruminate on how unfair it was after fighting so hard to find one another, but life for Edriss had been one tumult after another. It was all she knew. Only those who had been treated fairly their whole lives ever cried over unfairness.

Lorcan's hand languorously traveled along the interior of her thigh. She protested, but her hips lifted, answering for her.

Clamor in the halls stopped him. He gripped her leg and pushed up, listening.

"He's back," she said. It couldn't be time. She wasn't ready.

"No." He squeezed her thigh and met her gaze. "No. Listen."

"What?"

"Swords." Lorcan swallowed. His eyes fluttered in fearful blinks, the rest of him as still as stone. "Something's happened."

Edriss tore away and bounced off of the bed before he could stop her, untangling her dress from her waist so it fell back into place. She ran to the door on her tiptoes and pressed her ear to the wood. She heard the swords. The clashing and grunts of opposing forces.

Lorcan joined her. He tried to nudge her behind him, but she stopped him with an indignant scowl.

"We need to find…something…" He conducted a frantic search of the room. "Something to defend ourselves with…"

"You don't think I've already done such a check? Unless you can rip apart the bed frame or chifforobe with your bare hands…"

Lorcan froze. His eyes dilated. He gestured for her to step away from the door, and this time, she didn't argue. She backed away, straight into his arms, where he held her and whispered, "It's stopped. They're outside the door."

Edriss nodded, inhaling a shaky breath. "We go down swinging. Kicking. Biting. We take as much of them with us as we can."

"Until the world ends, Hemlock," Lorcan said, folding her tighter with a squeeze before letting her go.

"Until the world ends, Lorry." Edriss squared up, waiting for precisely that.

They exchanged wild looks when the door handle shook. Edriss waited for the sound of a key entering a lock, but it didn't come. Instead a series of violent strikes followed and the door flung wide, bounced off the wall, and nearly closed again from the force of the swing.

Edriss released her trapped breath, stunned. "*Father?*"

Lorcan exhaled a choking sound. "Father?"

Thennwyr Blackfen and Rohan James stood in the doorway, faces drenched in the hard sweat of battle and swords bloodied at their sides.

But they were…smiling.

Thennwyr wiped his eyes on his sleeve and charged forward first.

"*Edriss.*" He sheathed his sword and dropped to his knees before her. He looked at her like he feared she might disappear forever. Like it would break him if she did. "Are you hurt?"

Edriss bit down on her lip to keep from crying. She shook her head.

"And you?" Thennwyr stood and approached Lorcan. He opened his arms, and Edriss walked into them. "You don't look half as terrible as I expected from Rafferty's description."

"Your daughter saw to that." Lorcan dropped to a crouch with the weight of his sudden sobs. "Is this really happening?"

Thennwyr lifted Lorcan and shoved his free arm underneath his. "We need to get out of here. We'll make for the courtyard, where Lord Blackwood has hopefully scored a victory. But if we spot trouble along the way, we have instructions to secret you both out of here through the servants' entrance and ride immediately for Greystone Abbey."

Rohan kept guard at the door, looking down the hall every few seconds. He glanced inside. "We'll have to be quick, but go slow. Son, you all right?"

Lorcan nodded. "Enough to get us the fuck out of here."

"Lady Edriss, you and Lorcan will stay between Blackfen and me." Rohan waited as Thennwyr unlatched two daggers and handed one to each of them. "Pray to the Guardians it does not come to this, but if we find trouble bigger than us, you go for our swords. If you cannot get our swords, you use these, and you fight your way down to the first floor. Look for the kitchens. Find them, and you'll see the servants' entrance. Our horses are tethered nearby." He quickly reviewed the path again and made them confirm they understood. "Are we ready?"

Edriss looked at Lorcan. He looked at her. They nodded together.

"Wait. In the unfortunate event we're separated, I don't want to forget to give this to you," Thennwyr said, reaching inside his shirt. In his hand dangled Edriss's necklace. "Rafferty recovered this. One of the guards bragged about having it in their possession, and he was more than happy to relieve him of it."

She gasped as she accepted it.

"Fyana loved you, Edriss. She loved you enough for a hundred lifetimes."

"Thank you," she whispered and slipped the necklace back over her head, settling it against her heart, where it belonged. "Thank you...Father."

Rohan tapped the door with a grim smile. "Let's go."

TWENTY-FIVE
ARMOR SHINED
AND WEAPONS SHARPENED

Lorcan clutched Edriss's hand as they rushed down the hall, sandwiched between Thennwyr in the front and his father in the back. He paid close attention to how fast she was fading. So was he, but his own exhaustion was irrelevant. She needed him. More, she needed him to be okay, so he would be.

The stones ran red with blood, discarded bodies littered every few feet. *Enemies*, he reminded himself, though it was hard to hold onto his contempt when they were no more than corpses. Men who had paid the ultimate price for a cause that had used them and left them to die.

In his mind, he'd imagined an empty hall, a soundless escape. But there were a dozen guards still clearing the path ahead, and just as many behind. Shrieks of desperation, of pain, rang all around, a battle still actively being waged.

They turned down one hall and then another, slowing when the guards had more obstacles to deal with. His heart lived in his throat, in anticipation of the turn that would lead them back to danger. Their fathers didn't speak on the tense passage,

377

communicating through hand gestures and solemn looks, deepening Lorcan's sense that they were headed away from safety.

Edriss had one hand wrapped around the vial resting against her chest. Her stoic stare was full of icy contemplations.

Onward they moved, practically tiptoeing, listening for trouble they'd hear long before they saw. Lorcan's mind had always had a tendency to wander, and in their isolation, without knowing exactly what was going on, he forced his thoughts to fall into a rhythm of sorts. The pattern had a calming effect, a sense of control in the space immediately around them. Shuffle forward. Pause. Listen. Screams. Shuffle forward some more. Pause. Listen. Screams. Begin again.

He was counting these steps in his head when a door flew wide to their left and two guards leaped out, aiming straight for Edriss. Lorcan, swordless, threw himself in front of her, bracing for the inevitable spearing, but Rohan was faster. His sword sliced across both the guards' necks in one clean cut. One slumped just inside the doorframe, the other against the stone wall.

Edriss pointed her wide eyes at Rohan, but he nodded for her to keep moving. Lorcan, stunned, watched him a moment longer. He'd heard tales about his father's soldiering, but he had never seen it with his own eyes before.

More death awaited them down the next hall. They stepped over bodies, the shock of which kept Lorcan from thinking of them as real, organic. *Men* who'd had lives before they had been taken. Men who may not even have believed in what they had been conscripted to defend but had died for it either way.

Thennwyr stopped when they approached a bridge connecting two halves of the keep. The guards waited in the middle, gazes pointed out and down. Thennwyr held up his hand for Lorcan and Edriss to hang back and stepped closer, peering down at whatever was below.

He nodded to himself with a hard sigh and turned. "Clear," he said. "It's done. It's over. Edriss. Lorcan. Come look."

Edriss glanced at Lorcan before rushing ahead onto the bridge. With her hands clamped to her mouth, she stumbled back. Lorcan ran to join her, and as the courtyard came into view, he saw what had startled her so.

Green and silver, as far as the eye could see. A sea of friendly colors. Hundreds. Thousands. There were other colors too; the men wore not only the banners of the Rush but of their own houses, coming from all corners of the Westerlands. How Evrathedyn had called so many together so fast was an astonishing feat Lorcan couldn't comprehend—evidence of how long they'd all been waiting, armor shined and weapons sharpened, for their lord to stand and say *enough*.

In the center were a hundred or more men and women on their knees, their hands bound behind their backs. They were still wearing their wedding finery, in elaborate gowns and formal armor, dressed for a far different event than the one the day had delivered. Lorcan recognized so many of them. Some families had kin on their knees *and* kin in armor. Houses forever divided.

"He came." Edriss leaned over the railing. Her gaze swept the incredible scene with a daunted look. He imagined the swift rise of her pulse, her racing heart, at the sight of so much emerald and silver. "Lorcan, he came."

"I knew he would," Lorcan said, though he was as much amazed as Edriss was. He'd watched Evrathedyn raise an army and march north to rescue Rhosynora, but what he was seeing before him was a rallying of an entire land of people. What he saw was a leader leading.

Evrathedyn looked up, squinting through the haze of midnight fog, and spotted them. His smile was slow but broad and welcoming. He reached up to brush away tears with his thick gloves, bowed, and nodded to his left, where Cressida stood, and his right, where Rafferty stood, before he stepped forward.

Silence settled over the gathered, friend and foe alike.

Thennwyr and Rohan joined Lorcan and Edriss at the balcony to watch.

379

"I'm not one for speeches." Evra's voice carried on the cold air, his breath swirling in a cloud in front of him. "I've never been good at them. I've never known the right words to stir people, and so, I've often relied on silence. Silence, I believed, was diplomacy. It was the antithesis of war or provocation. It stalled disaster rather than inciting it." He looked down with a quick chuckle. "How wrong I was. And it took my dear sister, who is a far more shrewd politician than I will ever hope to be, to help me see it."

One of the bound men started yelling. Lorcan couldn't understand him, but Cressida marched forward and silenced him with a cool look alone.

"I made a grave error, friends. In my idealism, I believed terrible men could change and become good men. That if given the opportunity to heal and take a new path, they would embrace the second chance most are never offered." Evra nodded at Cressida, who proudly trooped back into the circle of conquered Defenders. Her armor gleamed in the light of the full moon. "I've kept my words close to my heart for too long and will do so no longer. What you see before you are the last vestiges of a rebellion of hatred and death. These are the leaders of the Defenders of the Righteous Dawn, the perpetrators of the burnings and fear and terror that I ordered stopped two years ago when I became lord of the Westerlands. It's no secret I never wanted the job. But it's mine, and now I must act with the authority and responsibility the role demands."

Cressida waved her bannermen in from the sides. They swarmed around the circle of prisoners. "Defenders of the Righteous Dawn! Your rebellion ends here. Now. Lord Blackwood has decreed you will stand trial as is your right as a citizen, beholden to the laws of our Reach. *They* will decide your fate. But do not think you have escaped punishment, for no barrister, no jury has been exempt from your destruction. They have all lost sisters, daughters, wives, and mothers to your terrible misdeeds. The death I would gladly enjoy offering you would be too kind of an end for the damage you've wrought upon your own people."

Edriss leaned in for a closer look. Whatever she saw melted the joy from her face.

"What is it?" Lorcan asked.

"Finnegan is with them." She pointed. "Right there in the middle, next to Malcom Fox."

Lorcan had already spotted Finn in the huddle of criminals. He hadn't decided how to feel about it, in the middle of so many other shocks. Edriss was still at his side, and they were finally free to love one another. It was all the ruminating he had room for. "Remember what you said to me back in the room. He chose this, Edriss. He's there because he chose this."

"I know. But not all choices are so simple." She rolled her hands over the damp stone balcony. Whatever she had been considering saying next turned into a miserable nod.

Cressida's guards yanked the Defenders to their feet. She had grabbed one for herself too. Malcolm. She whispered something in his ear that made his face bloom with rage. She rolled her eyes with a laugh before turning back toward Evra.

"Malcom Fox, am I to understand you are the current leader of this faction of rebels?" Evra asked the bound man.

Cressida ripped the gag from Malcom's mouth, hard enough for him to turn an indignant glare her way.

"The Defenders have no leader. Only idealists who would see this Reach returned to righteousness and glory." His words were met with a wave of laughter, which deepened the red in his cheeks. "You forsake the name of the Great Aeldred! The Great Andarian! We do not accept your heathen leadership, Lord Black*rook*. We do not accept your heathen wife, your heathen offs—"

Cressida elbowed him in the belly and he bowed over. "Try again, coward."

Malcom opted for glowering silence.

"Leader. No leader. It's nothing to me," Evra said. "If you will not stand in defense of your cause, I'll not offer the opportunity again. You're at the mercy of the law now." He waved a hand, and Cressida ordered her men to usher the Defenders out of the courtyard. "There will be no more rebellions, no more burnings, no more persecution of magic, and no punishing women for having a voice and a message. Those of you in this crowd, unbound, I see you. Many of you were forced into service to the Defenders, and I will not punish you for the crimes of your controllers if you forsake their message of hate and destruction. Here. Now. You may resume the lives you left behind, and work to rebuild them." When he shifted, his hand lowered to his sword. "But know that if I discover there have been efforts to rekindle what we have today extinguished, the swift hand of justice awaits. It may be the last thing you ever know."

Evra held his arm aloft, pointed at the balcony. "But my vision for our people has always been peace and joy, so let us end with some of both. My dear sister was kidnapped by the Defenders of the Righteous Dawn and held captive for days. They conspired to have our dear friend and ally, Lorcan James, murdered, to keep him away from my sister. But as you can see, they are both alive and well, despite these sinister efforts. I blame myself, for if I had not agreed to entertain a union between my sister and Finnegan Derry, our enemies would not have been so emboldened in trying to force the act." He looked right at Edriss as he said his next words. "A union mired in secrecy and shadows, reliant upon the efficacy of lies. Because Edriss is already wed, good people of the Westerlands. To the man standing now at her side, Lorcan. A marriage I bless with my whole heart."

Edriss took a step back in surprise. Lorcan could only laugh as he took in a scenario he never could have imagined, even in his wildest dreams. Rohan clapped him on the back with a gleeful chuckle.

Surprise followed by joy was the exuberant reaction of the loyalists. Nothing came from the Defenders, but most were gagged.

"Lady Edriss and Steward James are as much the future of this Reach as my own children—as my Alastrynia and, I am pleased..." He choked up and had to pause. "Pleased to announce, a son has been born to us. One I am eager to return home to meet once our unfortunate business here in Deramore has concluded."

Lorcan reached for Edriss's hand. He twined their fingers, shared a quick look with his wife, and raised their joined hands together in the air. Edriss shook with happy tears as the roar of applause made the bridge under them tremble.

"Evrathedyn failed to mention this before we rode for Deramore," Thennwyr said with a slow, stern sigh. "But for whatever it's worth to you, Edriss, I'm happy for you."

Edriss, sniffling, turned and walked into her father's arms. "It's worth everything, Father."

Thennwyr held her in a stiff, awkward embrace and then his entire expression crumpled. He folded himself around her and sobbed.

"You're a fool for eloping," Rohan said. "But you chose well, son. You chose with your heart." He tugged Lorcan's arm and pinned him in a tight, quick hug.

Men and women filtered in from the sides and streamed into the courtyard. They lowered to their knees in fealty one by one, and Evra approached them one by one, offering his blessings of pardon.

"Is…Is that it?" Edriss asked. She turned toward Thennwyr and Rohan. "Can it really be over, after everything?"

"It's far from over," Rohan said solemnly. "The trials will last years and will create a new era of divisiveness. But we are more united today than we ever have been, and that will carry us through these new challenges."

"And if the juries find them innocent?" Lorcan asked.

"Then they will face the wrath of the public, a fate far worse."

"You're right," Edriss said. She studied the bound Defenders with a solemn look. "More will rise in their name, and we have to be ready for them. Evra has to be ready for them."

"He will be, my lady," Rohan said. "I think your brother at last understands the ruler he wants and needs to be."

"Please, call me Edriss," she said with a shy smile. "We're family now."

Rohan's cheeks bloomed with pink. He twisted a grin to the corner of his mouth and eyed the stones at his feet. "That we are."

"Shall we go down and join them?" Thennwyr asked. He tightened his longbow's holster and secured his sword.

Edriss watched the situation in the courtyard for several more moments and then nodded.

"We're safe, Hemlock. All of us. Finally." Lorcan brought her hands to his mouth and kissed them, then locked his mouth to hers. A ripple of excited cheers streamed up from the courtyard, and they laughed, their lips still pressed in a kiss. "We did it."

"We did it," she whispered. She bit down on her lip with a soft, contented sigh. "All right. I'm ready."

By the time Edriss and the others made it to the courtyard, the prisoners were already gone. Many of the bannermen had left as well, to fill their bellies. The heady smell of stew was ripe in the air, set to joyous laughter and conversation in the distance.

Edriss spotted Evra huddled together with Cressida, Rafferty, Ridge, and the baron. Rafferty perked up with a wave and an awkward smile. The others turned in kind and, one by one, lit up with smiles of their own.

Evra broke away and ran toward Edriss. Before she could say a word, he scooped her into his plated arms with such a tight crush, she had to wiggle to breathe.

"Edriss. Guardians. Are you all right? Did they hurt you?"

"I'm fine," she tried to say, but the words were buried in his breastplate.

"I'm so sorry, sister." His face rested against her scalp. "I've never been so wrong."

Edriss pulled away and rubbed her hands down the sleeves of his silver armor. "This suits you. Not so much I'd recommend another war."

Evra looked around at the empty courtyard. "I wanted to believe it was only a rebellion, but there's still so much healing to be done in the Westerlands."

"There is," she agreed. "But since you've finally embraced this truth, you can lead our people toward that very thing. And you must. You know that, don't you? This cannot be a moment. It must be an entire shift, Evra. Everything you've done here today will be for nothing if you return to your old ways."

"I know." He glanced away. "I know it now. I don't deserve the way they look at me."

"Not yet you don't." Edriss debated offering him such hard truths. But saying the words aloud would spare them all a lifetime of heartache later. "You don't deserve it, Evra, but no leader does until he's earned the respect. You inherited this role, but it doesn't mean you were qualified. But it is *yours,* brother. And now you must earn the right to serve the people who would—and have—died for the peace you promise."

Evra listened without interrupting. When she was done, he shook his head with a short laugh. "You're right. About all of it. You always have been. I'm going to restructure our council to be more effective, more useful, and I want your guidance on how to do it." He breathed deep and looked past her, at Lorcan. "You look better than I expected after hearing Tyndall's report."

Lorcan laughed and nudged Edriss with his shoulder. "I'm married to the best healer in the Westerlands."

Evra grinned. "So you are." He turned all the way around. "There's stew, bread, and ale for everyone, and though it feels dissonant to celebrate the downfall of our fellow Westerlanders, I'm beginning to understand that I should follow my people's lead where these things are concerned."

Edriss followed his focus. Though it was hard to make out details in the distance, the celebration was happening at the base of the hill leading down from the keep, in the town square. She'd not been to Deramore before her kidnapping, but Lorcan had, and she was realizing how traumatizing it must be for him. No amount of easing erased the terrible memory of what he perceived as his greatest failure.

She looked over at him. He'd always hidden his grief behind smiles, but Edriss smoothly read Lorcan's subtleties. She knew when he was hiding pain.

But she saw no pain in him then. Only joy and relief. He was laughing at something with Rafferty and Ridge, something Cressida had said no doubt, and there was no sign at all that he was covering anything darker.

"Where did the baron go?" Evra asked, looking around. "Maxim." He waved at the baron, who approached with a wary, reluctant look. "Edriss deserves to know what you did today. And you deserve her knowing."

Maxim's nose flared in a grimace. He squinted against the horizon. "You're making much out of nothing, my lord."

"Tell me," Edriss said. She stepped in front of him. "You're here, so it was something. I want to know."

"I had you followed. Lot of good it did." He turned his eyes upward.

"I see." Edriss glanced at Lorcan, who seemed to already know. "Why?"

"Why do you think? You're addicted to trouble, girl."

They all laughed, Lorcan the hardest.

"He's being modest, Edriss," Evra said. He stretched his hand up to clamp it atop the baron's shoulder. "It was because of him Thennwyr and Rohan knew where to go when the melee started. It allowed them to find you before the Defenders had time to react and move you beyond our reach—or worse. Even with our victory today, we were so close to losing you and Lorcan."

"And," Lorcan said. "He saved my life. I would have likely died in Deramore."

She let his words settle before responding. "This true, Baron?"

He shrugged and looked away. "We all had a part to play."

Emotion welled in her chest, and she threw her arms around him before she could talk herself out of it. He stiffened, his arms at his sides, but moments later was holding her as well, sighing. "Thank you, Maxim. Though I suspect it will be enough to make you regret your involvement, I want you to know you have true friends in my husband and me."

The baron mussed her hair with a playful shove. "You're right. I already regret it."

"Arwenna," she said after a comfortable pause. "Has there been word from her?"

Evra shook his head. "No word, no. No sign of her in the Westerlands either. Whether she's made it back to Midnight Crest...I can't say."

Edriss nodded slowly. Her gaze traveled the animated conversation between Lorcan and the others; it moved again to the pillars of smoke billowing into the air from the town below, then it moved to her father and Rohan, who stood off to the side, alone and waiting.

"You have every reason to be angry with her," Evra said with a curious tilt. "To never want to see or hear from her again."

"We are all damaged and hurt in our own ways," Edriss said. She watched her father fidget with one of his daggers, a distraction. "I'm not angry with Arwenna, Evra. I feel sad for her. After all that happened, she's still just as lost as before. The only thing I want for her is peace."

"It's all any of us want for Arwenna." He followed her gaze and made a clicking sound with his tongue. "I...I made a mistake, Edriss."

She laughed. "Another one?"

"About Thennwyr." He breathed deep again. His plate armor clanged when he shifted awkwardly. "I was the one who asked him to keep a respectful distance."

Edriss turned back toward him. "What are you saying?"

"He didn't want to stay away from you. He fought me so hard, and I nearly caved, but I thought—" Evra steeled his jaw. "I thought I was doing right by you. By keeping scandal away from your name so you could make a good marriage, a happy one. I know it's no great secret he's your real father, but I thought calling attention to it, by having him around publicly, would just bring more misery to you when you've already borne so much." He grimaced. "But that's exactly what I brought to your life. I denied you the man who loved you, and I denied you the father who loved you, and if I could go back in time and do it all over, I would. I would change everything."

Edriss wiped the burn away from her eyes. For the past two years, she'd blamed herself for Thennwyr's absence in her life, believing he'd lost interest or had grown ashamed of his dalliance with the late Lady Fyana. He'd gone so cold so fast that Edriss could summon no kinder explanation, and so she'd buried the pain alongside her others. "Thank you for telling me."

"I'll make it right," Evra said. "It changes now. I'll not stand in your way on anything ever again. You're more than capable of deciding for yourself what's best for you."

Thennwyr looked up as though realizing he was being watched. He flashed an uneven smile at Edriss and went back to playing with his dagger.

"When will you return to the Rush?" Edriss asked, still watching her father.

"In a couple of days," Evra answered. "There's still work to be done here. I'd stay longer, but..."

"Your *son*!" Edriss exclaimed with a broad smile. "Oh, I can't wait to meet him, Evra."

"My son," he said, shaking his head in wonder. "I'll leave Tyndall and Lawrence for another fortnight or so to clean up the remaining mess. Will you stay for long?"

Edriss looked at Lorcan, who was watching her. He grinned and blew her a kiss. "We'll return in the morning so I can check in on Rhosyn and the baby..." She trailed off. "There is one thing I've been wondering about."

"Oh?"

"I know how Lorcan found me," she said, "but what I don't know is how you found Lorcan."

388

Evra brightened with a knowing chuckle. "You have Aunt Alise to thank for that. You roused her suspicions pretty good, and she was going to have you followed, but she had Lorcan followed instead. Said her instincts told her he was the one to follow." He sighed. "She was right. Because Lorcan knew exactly where you were. If not for Alise's intuition and your husband's quick thinking, we might have been too late."

"I like hearing you say that. Husband." Edriss closed her eyes and breathed in the cool air, letting it refill her well of life, of hope. There was still so much yet to do, but tonight there was only one thing she needed. "I can't stay another moment in this cursed keep."

"I'll have a tent made up for the two of you while you eat."

"I'm not hungry," Edriss said. She reached a hand behind her, knowing Lorcan would see it, find it, and take it, and he did. There were things she'd needed to say—and hear—but nothing could keep her from her husband's arms. "And Lorcan and I need more than a tent tonight, after everything we've been through."

Evra's flush was immediate. "Ah, right. Sure. Uh…enjoy."

Lorcan held his laughter only until they reached the other side of the courtyard. "Did you just tell your brother the two of us were going to go find a proper inn, to fuck?"

"Say that word again," she said with a twinkle in her eye, knocking sideways into him as they walked underneath the trellis marking the courtyard's entrance. "But next time, wait until I'm sitting on top of you."

"You'll never have to ask me that twice." Lorcan spurred into motion and yanked her down the hill amid more whispers and giggles and hard-earned joy.

EPILOGUE

"Y ou know my gift of sight is highly unreliable. It's fickle, full of secrets and lies with the truth wedged somewhere in between." Alise bounced Edriss's soft, dark curls in her hands and let them fall neatly down her back. She'd spent the past two hours helping her get ready. Her gentle words and careful details were the soft touches of a mother-daughter relationship that had been denied Edriss, but though she'd missed out on having a mother, she realized how much she'd gained in having women like Alise and Meldred shaping her life. "But your mother, Edriss. She had *such* a talent. Everything good about you came from Fyana. She was rumored to be descended from one of the Seven Sisters herself. I don't suppose Aeldred ever told you that, did he?"

Edriss shook her head. The room was new to her, as were the rest of the apartments, a gift from Evra and Rhosyn to the newly wedded couple. Someone had spent great care arranging the furnishings and decor, and the result was a home accoutred for a man and a woman readying for a family. The soft pastels of her childhood were gone, replaced by the rich, dark tones of maturity.

391

She clutched her mother's necklace in her hands, against her chest. She'd never remove it again. "Lord Aeldred spared no words for me beyond the cruel ones. He blamed me for my mother's death...and for many years, I did as well."

"It was no one's fault. Childbirth is still the biggest peril to women. Fyana knew the risks and was willing to take them. All mothers are." Alise ceased playing with Edriss's curls. "He wasn't always like that, my brother." Alise spread her long, jeweled fingers atop Edriss's shoulders. "The Aeldred who met and loved Fyana of the Roses was only a whisper of the Aeldred who would one day choose to continue our father's terrible work. Everything good in him died with her, but he was already on the path when she passed."

Edriss felt the familiar flutter that took hold anytime she learned something about her mother. She'd always been too afraid of asking about her, worried she might be denied or, worse, would learn something that would destroy the image of beauty and goodness she'd created in her mind. "Why did they call her that? Fyana of the Roses?"

Alise chuckled quietly and released Edriss, settling onto the chair beside her. "You know your mother didn't come from one of the Great Families?"

Edriss shook her head again. "Assume I know nothing, Aunt Alise, and you'll be right."

"Ah, well..." Alise cast her eyes aside in recollection. "She was a vision, your mother. Straight out of the fantastical tales of princesses we all heard as children. She came from a small village in the Whitewood, in the foothills. I forget which, and it doesn't matter now. But there's a reason Deramore and Jademarch were the worst hit for burnings. It's from the mountains that *real* witches hail, Edriss. Cunning women with talents unlike anywhere else in the realm. Women and also men who commune with nature, who draw upon their sacred bonds with the trees, grass, flowers, streams, and sky to mend and build. Aeldred met her on a progress of his youth. Took one look at her, so he said, and was willing to forsake his entire legacy to be with her."

Edriss turned the corner of her mouth upward. "That doesn't sound like him at all."

"No, not the man you knew. Most certainly not." Alise cupped her hands in her lap and turned her focus there. "And fortunately for my brother, our father, Lord Andarian, had a soft spot in his heart for love. As hard as it is for you to imagine Aeldred in love, can you see your grandmother, Meldred, head over feet for a man?"

Edriss burst out laughing. The idea *was* preposterous, but it also filled her with glee and a strange longing for the future awaiting her. Her grandmother was as tough as a blacksmith's steel, but she'd had a life before that. Edriss would have her own life to live, and when it was time to become the wise crone for the next generation, she would. With gladness.

"They were still happy when I was a girl, until our dear oldest brother perished in a hunting accident and then there was no joy to be found in the Halls again. Not until Evra brought Rhosyn to the Rush and ushered in a new era for the Westerlands."

"Evra told me Aeldred was a second son. I didn't know about the accident. I'm sorry."

Alise hitched her mouth in a quick grin. "You'd have thought Aeldred would have had more empathy for Evra's plight, but he spent the years following Arathedyn's death wasting away in the shadow of our father's grief. And then when he met Fyana, it was as though a new light had been kindled in him, and I saw the brother I had loved and played with return. My father…Well, he must have seen something in Fyana that lighted something in him as well, for he went against the unanimous advice of his council and approved the marriage between Fyana and Aeldred." Alise shook her head with a nostalgic brow lift, clearing whatever thoughts lingered. "But you asked about Fyana of the Roses. You might have learned the poison trade from your grandmother and me, but there's a reason only you can apply mind salves. There's a reason they call you the princess of poison. There are many who remember where you came from—who remember the foreign bride who would simply pass her hands along a path, and roses would bloom by the thousands."

Edriss smiled as she imagined it. "That's impossible."

"I assure you, it is not." Alise jutted her head to the side. "The gardens were always here, but it was Fyana who made them flourish. She could speak to the flora, breathe life into them, and ease the inevitability of their eventual demise. And she told the most fantastical tales, Edriss. She actually claimed to have been born of the roses, without a mother and father, and some believed her."

Edriss clutched her necklace tighter. "Did you?"

Alise shrugged with a short laugh. "I fancy myself a practical, rational woman, but Fyana of the Roses challenged that, day after day." She brushed her hands down her gown with a sharp intake of breath. "Anyway, that was a very long way of telling you that while *I* never saw a clear sight of your future, your mother did. Your mother told me she saw you standing beside love. Sleeping and waking beside love. Choosing love."

"I..." Edriss feared any words would slow Alise's revelations. No one had ever spoken to Edriss at such length about her mother. Everything her aunt offered was a gift.

Alise snorted. "I never put much stock in it myself, as you know. My husbands were naught but disappointments—rather large, unwieldy ones. So I dismissed her words as the sentimental musings of a mother. But I see now they were more." She pushed to her feet and towered over Edriss. "You are one of her roses, Edriss. The greatest of them. She saw you seize this fate, and now she watches you, from the arms of our blessed Guardians, get to enjoy it."

Edriss lowered her eyes, full of tears. She didn't want to cry. But tears were not weakness, she knew. Tears were strength when she felt she had none. They were an outlet for her grief and fear but also the overflow of her joy. What a gift it was to have more joy than she had the capacity to harness. She swore to herself never to waste it.

Alise leaned down and embraced her from behind. "Whenever you want to know more about your mother, all you need to do is ask me. Ask Meldred. But there is one other who knew her best of all."

Edriss looked up and met her aunt's eyes in the tear-blurred reflection.

"Your *father*," Alise whispered. "And he'll be there today, standing at your side. No more secrecy. No more hiding. Be proud of the love that created you, for this same love flows through you and will flow through your marriage, which will carry you all the rest of your days, darling girl." She kissed her temple. "Now, go. Go show the Westerlands the love Edriss Blackwood chose for herself."

The last time Lorcan had seen so many people gathered at the Halls of Longwood was for Evra and Rhosyn's wedding. He couldn't be certain, but he thought there were more this time, the line of celebrants stretching down the long approach to the keep, waiting to enter through the floral-wrapped open doors and offer their blessings of joy and peace for the happy couple.

The pilgrimage had been Evra's idea. *The wedding you had, however small and secret, was real. I don't want to replace it. Only to show all of the Westerlands that I bless the union, so there can never again be anyone with designs on destroying it.*

Lorcan stood on the balcony above the double doors, watching the elaborately dressed men, women, and children make their approach. The stream of people was seemingly endless. Every time he thought he spotted the end of the line, more rounded the corner in the distance.

He nearly leaped into the crowd when two hands encircled him from behind. He laughed and wrapped them in his own, tugging her tighter. "Hemlock," he said and spun around. "There you are."

"Have you been waiting long?" she asked.

The answer was so simple, and yet even that was too much for him as he drank in the sight of her. She wore the gown he'd had made, but without the subterfuge of abandoned monasteries and secret vows, her joy was radiantly on display for all to see her as he did. The gold of her dress sparkled in the day's light, setting ablaze a dotting of sparkles someone had painted high on her cheekbones and along her temples. She was beauty and magic, a figment of his fantasies and the truth of his heart. She was everything he'd ever needed—everything he'd ever wanted or ever would want.

"Lorry?"

"Ah…" He gathered her hands and brought them to his mouth. "What was the question?"

Edriss stretched up onto the tips of her toes and kissed him. She nudged their hands down and deepened the kiss, sliding her tongue along his in teasing passes that made him grateful the balcony covered everything from the torso down. "You look so devilishly handsome."

"Do I?" Lorcan looked at his ceremonial armor. His father had it crafted for the event, and Lorcan had been so nervous, he hadn't paid any mind to the details.

Edriss kissed him again before turning toward the crowd and waving. Many waved back, calling out their well wishes as they pointed. "Where's Evra?"

"Not entirely sure," Lorcan said. He glanced behind him. "But he'll address the masses once they finish their procession."

"Hmm." Edriss tilted her head back and closed her eyes. Sunlight bathed her face. "I'm not in any hurry. I like it out here. The leaders of the Westerlands should be more visible, shouldn't they?"

Lorcan held her and looked at the clear, beautiful sky. It was a wintertide miracle, a day without frost. He couldn't have asked for anything better. "Earning your keep as the new senior councillor, eh?"

Her smile spread wider. "I could demur and pretend it's not what I wanted, not what I was meant to do…but you'd know I was lying."

396

"Never make yourself smaller for anyone, Hemlock." He brushed his lips along her scalp. "Especially not me."

"No," she said. "Never again."

The quiet that followed was familiar, comfortable. Lorcan enjoyed the shape of her, the soft floral scents that would always be home. They watched the celebrants make their way to the keep for the next hour, before Edriss spoke up again.

"Rhosyn heard from Arwenna," she said. Her voice trailed at the end, as though she hadn't settled on a feeling. "She made it to the north, but she didn't go home. She's staying with Steward Frost in Midwinter Rest."

"I'm glad to hear she's safe," Lorcan said cautiously. "And that she found refuge somewhere other than with the people who caused her such harm."

"Me too," Edriss said quietly. "You know, if she ever comes back...Perhaps we can set her up with Baron Lawrence. They've both lost. They're both...grumpy."

"I could see it," Lorcan agreed.

"Peace. It's all I want for either of them."

He almost didn't say it. He wasn't sure if he should—if keeping it to himself this time would be better. But there were no secrets between them anymore, and holding onto his question any longer would turn it into one. "I know you still have nightmares sometimes."

Edriss rolled the back of her head along his chest, watching the people below. Her hands caressed his arms, draped over her belly. "I suppose you would know, wouldn't you?"

He hesitated a moment. "You say her name."

She sighed. "Well, that's the thing about nightmares, isn't it? They draw on our fears, which are often not founded in anything but insecurity."

"Edriss—"

"It's not what you think," she said, speaking fast, then sucked in a quick breath before she continued. "I know how you feel. I have no worries anymore, not about us." She tilted her face back to look at his. "I know who you love." She returned her gaze to the road. "But in my nightmares, sometimes I see you kissing her again. I see her telling me she's leaving, except this time you do follow her."

"I hope Arwenna found what she was looking for," Lorcan said, "but I would not have followed her, for any reason."

"I never said my nightmares were rational," Edriss said with a dour laugh. "They'll eventually go away, as all awful things do. But I'll take these any night over the ones I had before the Defenders were brought to heel."

Lorcan didn't know what to say, so he held her tighter and rolled kisses along the top of her head. With time, even those nightmares would pass, just as his terrible ones of Cesarina had. Because of *her*.

Another hour passed, and the crowd thinned. They watched the last revelers enter the keep, and within minutes, everyone who had entered the Halls exited again in a thick, excited rush, returning to the outer courtyard and the broad road.

Evra, Rhosyn, Thennwyr, and Rohan stepped onto the balcony. Rhosyn had a bubbly, talkative Alastrynia by the hand, and Evra held their newborn son, Andren. While Alastrynia had been named for their fallen brothers, Astarian and Augustyn, Andren honored their treasured sisters.

Instead of passing his son off, Evra held him higher and stepped closer to the balcony. Applause roared from below.

"When can we expect news of your own?" Rhosyn asked, coming up between Edriss and Lorcan.

The couple exchanged flushed looks. "We're not in any hurry," Edriss said, her attention on Lorcan. "We've waited this long to enjoy each other. I'm not quite ready to share him."

"I'll never be ready to share you," Lorcan said. Fire rose in his cheeks when a welcome but inconvenient memory surfaced, of Edriss moaning under him. He cleared his throat and shifted his gaze downward to ground himself. "But one day I'll be willing to, if only to see what a wonderful mother you'll be."

"You're still young," Rhosyn said, smiling. "You're right. There's no rush."

Evra turned back. "Are we ready?" He nodded at the men standing in the back. "Blackfen. James. You'll join us at the front."

Rohan stepped forward, but Thennwyr stayed put.

"It's enough...enough to be here, sir," Thennwyr said, his voice choked.

Edriss broke away from Lorcan and approached her father. "But you don't belong back there, Father. You belong with me. At my side. And it's time everyone here knows it."

Tears rolled down the stoic Rider's face as he nodded. She took his hand and led him to the balcony.

Lorcan joined them, settling in between Edriss and his own father.

"I never thought I'd see this day," Rohan remarked, scanning the sea of gatherers. "But how glad I am to be wrong."

"The future of the Westerlands begins here and now," Evra said. He smiled to those at his left and then his right. "And we are all an integral link in this unbreakable chain. Let us share with the Reach all they have to look forward to in our era of peace."

Edriss reached back and crushed the pillow in her hands to stifle her scream. Her thighs clamped down on either side of Lorcan's head, the pleasure too intoxicating for her to harness. She moaned and bucked forward, nearly rocking them both off of the bed.

Lorcan climbed up and over her, wiping his mouth on the back of his arm with a sly look. "I'm sorry, was that too much for you, Lady Blackwood?"

Edriss leaped forward to push him onto his back. She flipped herself over the top of him and leered down at his surprised expression with a playful glare. "You're really asking for it, Steward James. I mean *really* pushing."

Lorcan bit down on his lower lip and reached between his legs. He angled his head against her opening. "Pushing like this?"

Edriss's eyes fluttered back. She wanted to tease him, bring him to the brink and make him cry for mercy, but desire weakened her, reduced her to a panting, smoldering mess. "Like that. Yes."

Lorcan slid all the way in, driving a guttural whimper from the back of her throat where she'd trapped it. The devious grin died on his face, and he was lost to the same yearning that had crumbled her resolve to bits. "How is this our life?" he asked between gasping breaths, as she moved seamlessly to a rhythm they both understood.

"It's not our place to question it." Edriss moaned as she reseated herself to drive him deeper. Another wave of pleasure gripped her, and she lost her bearings. "Only to appreciate it."

"I can't wait to appreciate you every single day, for the rest of my days." Lorcan panted. He leaned up to kiss her without breaking her stride. His hand slapped at the nightstand until he found their wedding rope. "Every. Single. Day."

"And night." Edriss wrapped her arms around him and flipped them so she was underneath again. With her eyes on the rope— her favorite—she used the last of her words to whisper along the edge of his jaw, "Harder."

He peeled back, his eyes dilating and then narrowing as a darker, more demanding side of him emerged—the side she worked so hard to summon night after night, to guide them over the edge and into the endless call of bliss.

Lorcan bound her arms with the rope and pinned them above her head with a wicked grin. "For you? Always."

The Book of All Things continues with a new story in
The Belle and the Blackbird.

ALSO BY SARAH M. CRADIT

KINGDOM OF THE WHITE SEA
KINGDOM OF THE WHITE SEA TRILOGY
The Kingless Crown
The Broken Realm
The Hidden Kingdom

THE BOOK OF ALL THINGS
The Raven and the Rush
The Sylvan and the Sand
The Altruist and the Assassin
The Melody and the Master
The Claw and the Crowned
The Poison and the Paladin
The Belle and the Blackbird

THE SAGA OF CRIMSON & CLOVER
THE HOUSE OF CRIMSON AND CLOVER SERIES
The Storm and the Darkness
Shattered
The Illusions of Eventide
Bound
Midnight Dynasty
Asunder
Empire of Shadows
Myths of Midwinter
The Hinterland Veil
The Secrets Amongst the Cypress
Within the Garden of Twilight
House of Dusk, House of Dawn

For more information, and exciting bonus material,
visit www.sarahmcradit.com

ABOUT SARAH

Sarah is the *USA Today* and International Bestselling Author of over forty contemporary and epic fantasy stories, and the creator of the Kingdom of the White Sea and Saga of Crimson & Clover universes.

Born a geek, Sarah spends her time crafting rich and multilayered worlds, obsessing over history, playing her retribution paladin (and sometimes destruction warlock), and settling provocative Tolkien debates, such as why the Great Eagles are not Gandalf's personal taxi service. Passionate about travel, she's been to over twenty countries collecting sparks of inspiration, and is always planning her next adventure.

Sarah and her husband live in a beautiful corner of SE Pennsylvania with their three tiny benevolent pug dictators.

www.sarahmcradit.com

SARAH M CRADIT

WEAVER *of* WORLDS

Made in the USA
Middletown, DE
26 November 2023

43545603R00253